Shakespeare Loves Bollywood

Shakespeare Loves Bollywood

by

Patrice Kyger

ISBN: 978-0-557-06854-8

To my children, always

Contents

Acknowledgements ix

Chapter 1 1

Chapter 2 15

Chapter 3 25

Chapter 4 33

Chapter 5 39

Chapter 6 49

Chapter 7 65

Chapter 8 73

Chapter 9 83

Chapter 10 99

Chapter 11 117

Chapter 12 125

Chapter 13 133

Chapter 14 147

Chapter 15 155

Chapter 16 165

Chapter 17 175

Chapter 18 181

Chapter 19 189

Chapter 20	197
Chapter 21	205
Chapter 22	217
Chapter 23	225
Chapter 24	233
Chapter 25	243
Chapter 26	251
Chapter 27	259
Chapter 28	275
Chapter 29	283
Chapter 30	297
Chapter 31	309
Chapter 32	319
Chapter 33	335
Chapter 34	341
Chapter 35	345
Chapter 36	351
Chapter 37	359

Acknowledgements

Writing, I've found, is magic.

That is, it seems like magic to those who want to know how it's done, how plots and characters come to mind, when writers hear dialogue, how those doves appear in our hands. Presto! Applying the seat of the pants to the seat of the chair, day after day -- likelier, night after night -- is a great deal closer to trudge than enchantment . . . so it's just as well that other people rarely watch.

Yet when it works -- the right phrase, the scene crystal clear, the character true to life -- yes, it *is* magic.

With much gratitude I'd like to thank those who have helped in ways large and small in the writing of *Shakespeare Loves Bollywood*, so profound thanks go to:

My extended family, friends, and neighbors. You would sometimes ask with varying degrees of caution, "So, how's the writing going?", and receive answers of enthusiasm or despair, depending on the day. I needed your reminders, though, and your casual assumption that writing fiction was in my bones.

My ex-husband, for being there for our children. I am so grateful for your continued presence and support in their lives.

Suketu Mehta, for permission to quote from your excellent *Maximum City: Bombay Lost and Found*, a book that brings Mumbai to life.

Julie Lynn, of Mockingbird Pictures. You encouraged me even after my silliest writing, and made me feel I would someday produce better work. I hope this book is a start at proving you right.

Martha Spano, for generously lending from your library of contemporary Hindi films. You have an eye for excellence, a massive store of knowledge about Indian filmmaking, and share both with warmth.

Elaine Kroner, for reading my numerous manuscripts over and over, noting errors and confused passages, making suggestions, and bringing a meticulous eye to the whole, while presenting all comments with your habitual kindness. Like everyone who knows you, I count myself lucky in your friendship.

And finally, to my three children, incredibly wonderful people, bright and warm and caring. You've been loving, supportive, and enthusiastic about this project, you've kept me grounded, and I feel immensely fortunate in you. Hugs and kisses!

CHAPTER 1

Rachel Hill swam in a warm and frothy sea of humanity. Large, small, walking, carried in arms or wheeled, they were a cresting wave breaking in the same direction, toward one goal: to propel themselves and their bundles past JFK's security. Their flight to New York from Heathrow had been packed and delayed. By now, released from the temporary imprisonment of lapbelts, vetted and passed for inspection by immigration and customs, the tired crowd surged for the doors that led to Manhattan in this cold December of 2007.

For many, the city was unknown. For Rachel, it was home, the welcome end of a day-long journey. Her wheeled cart was heaped high with luggage stuffed with clothes, shoes, books . . . and English biscuits and snacks harvested yesterday from Oxford shops, mementoes of her six-month sabbatical from NYU's Department of English. She'd had to pay extra luggage fees, of course, but it was worth it to import the taste of Britain, to savor her sabbatical a little longer.

Eager to reach a cab, she tossed the long lime-green scarf she wore firmly over her shoulder, and shoved at the cart.

A large family group strolled in front of her, too large to pass. The Western-dressed turbaned men, and the dark-haired women clothed in the traditional trousers-and-tunic *salwar kameez* of northern India towed several children with them, as well. Despite her itch to reach the nearest taxi stand and cross the river into the city, Rachel slowed and smiled.

The people ahead looked so wonderfully familiar!

In Oxford, she and her daughter Melina had lived for their sabbatical half-year in an area containing numerous Indian families, part of the flood from the sub-continent. This particular remnant hailed mainly from metropolitan Delhi and Mumbai. To them as to Rachel, Oxford, though wonderfully green and academic, was a small provincial town. The men habituated to it through their associations with the university and work in diverse firms. The women, however, often assimilated through their children, who immediately took on British customs: when they weren't in school uniforms, they wore jeans and T-shirts. Their Indian mums, though, sometimes preferred traditional *salwar kameez* and saris to an Englishwoman's trousers, skirts and sweater sets.

Rachel had grown close to the Patel family two doors down, whose daughter Nisha, the same age as Melina, observed their moving in through her front window. Ten minutes after their own entry into the house, Nisha was knocking on their door. Within twenty-four hours, the two girls were phoning, texting and arranging to meet.

The family ahead of Rachel now paused, their voices raised. She listened, reminiscing.

The Patels proved more than just friendly neighbors. Over months of shared dinners and conversation, they introduced Rachel to Indian cuisine, culture, jokes and a smattering of Hindi. The Hindi language had received a nudge from an unexpected source: movies. Like most Indians, the Patels were both enthusiastic and knowledgeable about their country's films.

"You've never seen –? My God! Nisha, *beta*, show Melina . . . you've a DVD player in that house? We'll lend!" said Pinky Patel, Nisha's mum, one evening.

Walking home, Melina's arms were piled with borrowed DVDs. All week she hurried through homework to watch them while Rachel typed at her laptop, her labors interrupted by rhapsodic cries from the next room. The actors! The exotic locations! The music, songs, dance – especially the dance!

"They've all got English captions, come see!"

"Melina, those don't compare to what you're used to at all," Rachel called back. "Steph's spoiled you with the classics. 'Casablanca', 'Philadelphia Story', 'The Way We Were' . . . Indian movies have nowhere near that quality."

"It doesn't matter!"

"Doesn't . . . oh, heresy! What would Steph say?" Rachel resolutely refused to bounce into the living room to see why Melina was so excited.

Her boycott ended eight days later. Nisha was over, and the two girls planned a movie night.

"But Aunty –" Nisha's cheeks grew pink. "That's what we call friends' mums, just a polite name . . .."

Rachel touched the girl's shoulder. "Aunty's fine."

"I really think you'll like Indian movies!" Nisha pleaded. "My mum does!"

"Forget it," Melina told her, "my mom can be so stubborn."

"I'm not stubborn," objected Rachel. "Not that stubborn."

"Prove it. Try one, just one, watch it with us! We'll make the popcorn!"

With a theatrical sigh, Rachel allowed herself to be dragged to the couch, aware that she could spend the next three hours in far more productive ways. There were researches to complete, books to read. Wedged between two girls, their eyes alight with anticipation, she gave herself points for flexibility, for at least trying to understand her daughter's odd quirks.

"This one's called 'Bunty aur Babli', those are the two characters' names. You'll laugh," Nisha promised as she pressed play.

"Right." Rachel loaded the word with irony.

Three hours later, after a madcap romp through India with a pair of con artists, Rachel sat up and wiped her eyes.

"Well?" Melina demanded.

"You win," she admitted. "Fine, bring on the Bollywood!"

After that, she and Melina would curl up together after a day of school and study, exploring what Indian films offered to a couple of intense movie buffs whose favorite neighborhood DVD rental store was an ocean away. They discovered an unforeseen trove of delights, from comedies to dramas to opulent epics. All, even the comedies, came accented with music and dance. Both were evidently essential to Indian viewers. Then there was the acting. Compared to American styles, some of it was a little broad, but most actors possessed skills that Rachel – working within the framework she'd learned from Steph – saw as perfectly synonymous with anything Hollywood . . . though Indian men expressed more emotion than, say, Brad Pitt. She knew the plots could be derivative ("stolen!" – that from Steph, in imagination), but, frankly, Rachel didn't care. Were they romantic, sentimental? Yes. So? Hindi-language films fed her, they were emotionally satisfying, and, like Hollywood, generally ended "up" in the W of American movies versus the downer, depressing M of, say, French films. Who cared if what she saw reminded her of "When Harry Met Sally" or "The Miracle Worker" or even "Othello"?

With borrowed movies in Hindi – and their English subtitles – Rachel and her daughter experienced an unexpected cultural growth spurt, as well as a tendency to say "*accha?*" instead of "is that so?".

To understand India, she mused now, pushing her luggage cart, one had to recognize the essential place its movies and their music held in popular culture. And to understand Indian people, well, you had to *watch* Bollywood.

Movies proved only the start. She and Melina were now unabashed fans of all things Indian. Who could have predicted that Rachel's English sabbatical would produce an insatiable hunger not for cream teas, but for syrup-soaked *gulab jamuns* and *jalebis*?

Then there were the clothes. Stowed in her luggage, folded between layers of tissue paper, were the unpredicted results of one foray in search of the sweet *laddoo*, orb-shaped morsels dense with cashews, raisins and cardamom. Emerging from the grocer's, she and Melina spotted an adjoining shop whose window gleamed with jewel-toned fabrics. The Punjabi seamstress took their measurements and designed for them two elegant *salwar kameez*, Melina's green, Rachel's a haze of bluish-purple. They had worn them to great approval at the engagement party of Nisha's older sister Parvati. To decorate her forehead, Melina even borrowed a sparkly stick-on *bindi*.

"Ah, you look beautiful!" said Pinky. "*Jaise ma vaise beti*, like mother like daughter. No, not like that!" She pulled the long scarf, the *dupatta*, from Rachel's shoulders. "Drape it more down on the chest, there, that's prettier, looser, it won't bother your neck."

The party outfit led Rachel back to the same shop in search of something more everyday, and the lime-green scarf she now wore over her very Western cableknit sweater was part of that second purchase.

Rachel slowed to avoid bumping into the woman in front. She nodded. "*Namaste*," she said.

Hearing the Hindi greeting from a stranger wearing a *dupatta* yet not the least bit Indian, the woman was startled.

"Watch the door." Rachel gestured ahead. The woman turned back to face another crowd, this time the pleading, eager faces of those meeting loved ones.

There would be no one to greet Rachel, however, no volunteer who'd ventured over the East River to Queens, so each face, grinning, anxious or sobbing with relief, was as anonymous as the next. Her progress was arrested by tearful embraces over the restraining cord. Cries of *"bhaiyya! bhabhi!"* filled the air.

The printed signs, though, those names raised by numerous dark-suited drivers, had always fascinated her. Behind each was a story, a tale of business status or a newcomer welcomed. Her progress arrested, Rachel had time to scan the block letters propped up by waiting chauffeurs.

MR. CHOPRA. One of the men ahead, perhaps, who'd hired a limo to handle numerous people and bags.

S. A. BOOTEN. Good ol' Sex Appeal Booten, known for making board meetings highly diverting.

CHO FAMILY, CHO FAMILY. The Chos were evidently being met by two limos.

HI, RACHEL!

What?!

Spotting an opening, she shoved her heavy cart to the restraining rope.

"Steph! What are you doing here?" A hug over the cord, the fervent embrace of a woman whose ultra-short dark hair carried auburn highlights. Rachel's vision blurred. She brushed at her eyes. She hadn't expected to be met, yet it was so like Stephanie Zimmer to turn up unannounced. "I thought you'd have clients!"

"Nope, c'mon, let's haul your bags. I borrowed a car, tons of trunk, and your place is still fine, I checked before coming over," Steph assured her.

Rolling back into the tide of returning travelers, Rachel was caught by the current and finally spit out at the ropes' end. "I can't believe you're here," she marveled.

"I wanted Rubén to come with, but he claims to be scared of my driving," Steph replied over her shoulder. "Really, he just wanted to spend quality time with his, get this, girlfriend."

"Get out! Your son has a girlfriend? As of when, and how come I haven't heard?"

"I found out just yesterday! He's kept it quiet, when did that kid not confide in me? She lives in Jersey, came into the city this morning. Ironic, isn't it? He goes off to college on the West Coast, manages to snag a girl whose parents live twenty miles west of our place."

At the curb, Rachel caught her breath. "You look really good, Steph, for a potential mother-in-law."

"Stop! And for God's sake don't tease him, either. He's very earnest about the whole thing. Speaking of serious, how's Ian?" Steph glanced up. "You need some color, Rachel, you look like Hamlet's uncle."

"His dad, and no wonder, I haven't seen decent sun for three weeks."

"Ian took you to the airport?"

"No," said Rachel, light, "it's miles from Oxford to Heathrow."

Frowning, Steph examined her. "Something's wrong. No airport fight, so what happened?"

"Nothing. We broke up, that's all." Rachel gave a small laugh. "Where's this fantastic car?"

"The owner needs it back to drive up to Stratford, he's got a friend in 'Lear'. Can you get them all?"

Keys in hand, Rachel nodded and hefted the biggest suitcase, the monster, up the first of five steps to her feng shui-red front door.

"Sure?"

"No worries," said Rachel. "If I have trouble, I'll bother one of the neighbors." She gestured toward the four brick houses ringing the cul-de-sac of Hansen Place, an asphalt hiccup off East 88th Street. "Someone may be home, even if it's only Mrs. Burke."

"Ah, the infamous Mrs. Burke! Who for some reason seems to still hate my guts, after all these years . . .."

"She probably had some horrible experience with her own therapist." Rachel unlocked the heavy door. "Tell the car guy thanks, will you? Oh!" She unzipped a suitcase and rummaged through it, coming up with a red and yellow foil bag. "Would he like prawn-flavored potato chips?"

Reflected in a heavy antique mirror, her wrinkled black coat lay atop Rachel's luggage. There would be time enough for unpacking. For now, she wanted to reacquaint herself with her home, the brick house she had known forever as Gran's.

In childhood, the house was a magical place, full of secretive corners and the smell of baking, governed by a thrice-divorced woman who welcomed her only granddaughter as a companion at her beloved theaters, seventh row center. It was from this house that Rachel apprenticed herself to the city, growing to love its noise and bustle, so vibrant, so different from relaxed, oak-lined Connecticut. It was here, investigating her grandmother's volumes of Shakespeare, that she first discovered the playwright's words. It was here she first sensed the urge to teach.

She wandered and sniffed, breathing in the old-house smell. The scent was full of character and memories, quite distinct from her recently-built Oxford flat.

She ran her hands lightly over furniture, pictures, books, things she hadn't seen since last June, all the accoutrements of her New York life.

She and Melina had certainly reveled in their sabbatical. Melina had celebrated a birthday in Oxford, thirteen candles on a marzipan-decorated cake, and learned to wear her school uniform's tie without wincing. She absorbed Indian-ness from Nisha's family, yet other schoolfriends possessed quintessential Brit names like Lucy and Zoe and Imogen, with accents to match. By the time she flew off for a post-Christmas week with her dad and stepmother, Melina sounded like a junior version of Kate Winslet.

As for Rachel, she loved the changes of scene and accent Oxford brought, the mild English air filled with the scents of trees and grass. Her students were largely witty, attentive, motivated, and often astoundingly bawdy, a truly Shakespearean trait. She also adored the appalling amount of research she accomplished at the Bodleian Library, research she intended to utilize in a book, notes for which lay inside that huge piece of luggage. For the rest –

A knock at the door was immediately followed by an insistent ring. She ran down the stairs. Already? She peeked out. Yes, there was her white-haired neighbor, bearing what looked like the usual gift plate of cookies.

"Mrs. Burke, you're amazing, I just got home!"

"I know, I know!" Surrounded by the scent of Elizabeth Arden, the woman entered without invitation. "I saw the car and driver and you with your bags, so I knew you could use these. Snickerdoodles, sweetheart, real butter. Melina here?" Mrs. Burke's curls practically vibrated.

"She's with her dad."

"Oh, that's a shame! With snow on the way, too! Well, these, you can freeze for her. So," the woman settled herself on the sofa, "how was England? You know," she reminisced, "your grandmother once had a boyfriend from London. Very handsome man!"

"It wasn't Gran, Mrs. Burke, it was the other neighbor, Mrs. Lovell." Rachel perched on a chair arm. She glanced at her watch. "My friend Steph will be back any minute, you remember Steph?"

Alarm gripped Mrs. Burke. "Yes, of course, sweetheart. Listen, I'm running late for my painting class, we have a new teacher, so calm, he should be teaching yoga. Another good-looking one, what a doll!" She reached the door. "Oh, did you meet a man while you were in England?"

Rachel's forehead wrinkled. "Yes, I did."

"And?" The woman's curiosity was voracious.

"He wasn't . . . calm enough."

"Oh, what a shame! You wait, though, there'll be another, pretty girl like you. They should be so lucky!"

"To be totally candid, Mrs. Burke," Rachel led the way to the door, "it doesn't matter. I'm going to be much too busy." The open door revealed Steph, her hand poised to ring. Rachel's eyebrows rose. "You remember Mrs. Burke, Steph."

"Give Melina my love!" The older woman shoved past and scurried across to her own home, where her Nikes disappeared behind a dark-green door.

"Steph, you have incredible powers. Snickerdoodle? Real butter!" In the kitchen, Rachel rinsed out the electric kettle and put it under the tap to fill. She searched cupboards. "I know I left teabags."

Lilting music played, and a man's voice crooned in Hindi, a seductive accompaniment to the fabric-strewn living room.

"It's a *dupatta*. From northern India, where it's cooler. You wear them like this." Rachel pulled one of the colorful long rectangles to her, looping it, allowing the ends to trail behind Steph's shoulders and tugging the center down to drape on Steph's thin chest, as Pinky Patel had taught her. "Or you can hang it straight across your neck, or carry it over a single shoulder, that's very businesslike. Melina and I picked out a baker's dozen for you."

"Like so?" Steph experimented with a red *dupatta*. "Thanks! Much prettier than a mug labeled 'Greetings from The Globe Theatre'."

"I considered a mug," Rachel said, grinning.

"Man, you guys have really gotten into all things great-and-Indian, haven't you? I could tell from the e-mails, but this," she held up the *dupatta*, "you don't bump into this at Marks & Sparks, you've got to know where to search. What's with that?" she asked, her forehead wrinkled.

"Well, between the Patels and the *balti* restaurant a few blocks away, one thing led to another," Rachel admitted, "and now there's a thousand-recipe Indian cookbook I'm working my way through, I own a *salwar kameez*, Melina downloaded ten CDs' worth of songs from iTunes – that's one playing now – and we've amassed a collection of Hindi-language movies. Amassing, I should say. Amazon loves me, I ordered a bunch last week to be delivered to my office."

"You ordered Bollywood? You're not just watching that stuff, you're bringing it into the house?" Steph's voice rose with distress.

"Come on, Steph, even you, the movie purist –"

"Seriously, Rachel!" She looked genuinely appalled. "With all the effort I've taken to introduce Melina to great American films?"

"Don't blame me, she'd bring them over from the Patels! This one was Nisha's favorite, that one was good but the songs were better, etcetera, etcetera. You might enjoy them, honest! We do. They've got humor, passion, emotion . . . we've become sort of," Rachel hesitated, "actually, pretty knowledgeable, really. I can tell you all about Shah Rukh Khan's latest."

"Who?"

"SRK? Indian megastar? King of Bollywood? And then there's Hrithik Roshan . . .."

Steph appealed to the ceiling. "Cary Grant, save me!"

"So . . . Ian." Steph's spoon circled her tea. "You said there was more, so spill."

"It's boring."

"Bore me."

"No," Rachel insisted, "you don't want to hear something so stupid."

"Rachel, I listen to stupid all day."

"This ridiculous? Secretive forays out to Woodstock, a few miles west? Lies, more lies, excuses for researching topics he wasn't even interested in? Long dark hairs in his sheets? So stupid."

Steph sat up. "When?"

"A few weeks ago."

"During Hanukkah?"

"I didn't want to ruin it for you," Rachel replied, cookie in hand. She bit into it.

"But it's the holidays!" Steph shoved at the table, jiggling the two cups. "The most stressful part of the year, everyone's wound triple-tight, and he plays 'hide Mr. Yummy'? What an ass!"

"Yup." Rachel sipped hot tea. "Totally. So after an initial boo-hoo, I ran through several languages' worth of profanities. Then one of my colleagues found out. Owen gave me a crash course in ancient Welsh. Which can be colorful," she mused, "and terribly throaty."

"God, I'm sorry. What a jerk. What do they say over there? Sod him?"

"Absolutely." Rachel raised her cup and clinked it against Steph's. "Sod him! And break out the champagne!"

"How's Melina with it?"

"Fine, she barely knew him. Didn't much want to, come to that. At the time it seemed silly, but –"

"Genius."

They drank, gazing out the square kitchen window at gray, snow-heavy clouds. The same sort of clouds had covered the southern half of England for weeks, in sympathy with Rachel's own mood. She had stared out from her second floor at English skies heavy enough for rain but too light for snow, wondering at her own gullibility.

Steph set down her cup. "Post-It?"

"By the phone."

Steph chose a pen from the daisy-decorated can on the counter. "Name other than Ian," she intoned, and scribbled onto the bright pink paper.

Rachel shook her head. "Don't, Steph. I'm not buying any more tickets to the single persons' lottery. And I'm *definitely* not doing internet dating again."

"Rachel, listen. Listen! What happened after Jason left? You withdrew. Then for a few years you worked your ass off, then you went to Oxford, and poof! Ian." Steph's voice grew high. "C'mon, Rachel, just go out with regular guys until a kindred spirit shows up! You need the practice."

"Practice? I could care less," Rachel replied, draining her cup and setting it firmly on the table. "I've got to get back to classes, start Melina back in *her* school, there's a brand-new department chairman, God knows what he's like, and then there's this book I'm planning –"

"Rachel!"

"I'm too busy," Rachel said firmly. "Way too busy to even think about sharing my life."

CHAPTER 2

The evening air smelled of snow. Overnight it might dust the streets. Traffic would then clog them with dirty slush, and frozen clods shoveled from sidewalks would add to the mess. Nevertheless, there was something festive about water falling in six-pointed innocence from dim skies onto concrete and potted shrubs, turning a child's hair into a field of stars.

Rachel had emptied her suitcases, stowed clothing and shoes and food, and carried to her desk far upstairs, on the narrow house's third floor, the computer memory sticks and scraps of paper with notes and data for the new book. She was eager to talk about it with someone her age. For a thirteen-year-old, Melina listened to Rachel's theories with considerable grace, but getting another adult's opinion would help. For now, though, it was time to build a cheerful fire in the enameled woodstove installed within the living room's hearth . . . except that when she left New York in June, Rachel had given no thought to winter firewood.

So she plumped down on the sofa, dragged a fuzzy plaid throw over her legs, and began a list of things to do. Too many things to do, and mainly non-delegable things like *Get firewood*.

Run by office – that was tomorrow morning, to reacquaint herself with her desk, grab her notes from last year, catch up with colleagues who'd drifted in for a post-Christmas look-see. Her own spring semester began with her graduate student advisees and three sections of undergraduate English 232: Shakespeare's Comedies. Rachel adored teaching the comedies, witty and warm and ever-fresh. Students loved them, the course was painless literature for even future chemists or economists, and if they had trouble understanding Shakespeare's language, there was always the *No Fear* series. William Shakespeare had certainly known human nature . . . and what he didn't know, he unabashedly cribbed from other writers, as they did to him. "As You Like It", for instance, was an obvious rewrite of a novel called *Rosalynde*. Even in his own time, the man was infamous for borrowing other people's plots and characters and, well, dressing them up. What other writers felt about such theft . . ..

Yet something had happened to the Shakespeare histories seminar her former department chair, Bates, had approved a month before a stroke felled him and hastened his retirement. The last time she'd checked the schedule, the course was conspicuously absent. By then, though, she was far too busy arranging her removal back to the States to fire off queries. Where was her seminar? What had happened to it?

Histories ??, she dashed off.

School supplies came next. Not for her, for Melina, due in eighth grade at St. Anne's School the day after New Year's. The school's last-summer list was somewhere in the pile of papers (*Important stuff!* read the pile's Post-It) sitting on the kitchen counter.

Rachel transferred the stack to her lap and riffled through an abbreviated history of the past six months' travel. Here were the well-used UK maps, both Michelin roadmaps and the ultra-detailed ramblers' maps – marking every stone and stile – that had guided them on walking paths through farms as well as towns. There were brochures and guidebooks from sites she and Melina had been part of: their favorite London movie theater, the one that ran several Indian movies each week . . . the Museum of Childhood, where they cooed over antique dolls . . . the London Eye on a brilliant, cloudless day . . . a Sheffield festival for which they spent six hours in tight traffic, passing the time singing Beatles songs and passionately arguing over last night's film . . . Oxford Story, with its rail-traveling desks . . . Blenheim Palace . . . .

Blenheim, a favorite of Ian's. Rachel hurled it at the wastebasket, gave herself two points, and dove back into the stack. Aha! St. Anne's list. Eighth grade, she noted, increased the emphasis on science. She glanced at fifth grade's requirements. Oh, days of innocence. Damn, would Melina's uniform even fit from last June?

Uniform? she wrote, making the question mark big and bold.

Tiny shadows at the double-hung window drew her attention. Outside, the streetlamp illuminated small tumbling softnesses. Rachel launched herself from the sofa to peer up into the leaden sky.

Snow, real snow! She hadn't seen genuine snow for a year. In England it had rained, sleeted, drizzled. But authentic snow south of the Pennines was rare, and leaving just after the Christmas rush of parties and dinners meant Rachel forfeited her chance to catch a midwinter storm engulfing Oxford's golden spires. Urged to stay "just one more day!", she'd bowed out of further revelry, pleading work back in New York as an excuse.

"'Course it's an excuse," her colleague Owen Griffith told her, setting down his pint of lager fifteen hours before her departure. "You could stay with our lot another week without shirking, it's just a bloody sense of responsibility tugging your skirts. Screw responsibility, Rachel, Ian's left you for some slag, and that's cause enough to rejoice! Wanker Ian . . . stuck in his beloved Press, running the publishing show for all of us who actually write the damn books! Twat! I'd like to see him on the rugby pitch, show him a good time, we would." He took another pull at his beer. "And if he did his Zulu warrior, got his first put –

that's his first goal, love – I'd strip his pants down myself! Gently gently, of course." He leered, his massive hands outstretched as though to yank down a pair of shorts.

The doorbell rang. The pub in memory faded, and Owen with it. Oh . . . New York, she was home after all, wasn't she? No more angst. She opened the door.

"It's snowing!" Steph crowed.

Pizza, red wine, and the friend who brought them made the world a much more inviting place.

"Humor me, name one thing you want in a man," said Steph, stifling a small burp.

"Honesty."

"I'm talking more than basics here, Rachel. Honesty's got to be a given."

"A good sense of humor, then, the wry kind. The kind kind." Rachel yawned. "I should call Melina, she loves snow."

"How's California?"

"Stylish. Her stepmama made another shopping run."

"I'm agog," said Steph, grimacing. "How does Ellie get all that work done and still have time to shop?"

"Professional shopper plus assistant," Rachel explained. "The store has Melina's sizes on file, shopper picks three jeans or dresses or jackets, Ellie's assistant fetches them so that Ellie herself presents them to Melina . . . who naturally looks ravishingly pretty, and even if she didn't, wouldn't hurt anyone's feelings by declining. Ellie accepts her gratitude, ecstatic at once more proving herself the world's best stepmother."

"With minimal contact with the real-life, very human stepdaughter. That's some act."

"Elementary, Watson. The last mushroom?"

Steph plunked down on the floor cross-legged. "Yours. And Jason?"

"He sounds ecstatic. Re-designed his life, right coast to left, oral surgeon to producer husband of young producer wife . . . I'm reading between the lines." She poured wine into Steph's upraised glass. "Maybe it's in their water. So, what with parenting at a distance, and Ellie doesn't want children, Jason's set." She met Steph's eyes. "Lucky him."

"Yuck."

Rachel tsk-tsked. "Enough. *Bas,* as they say in Hindi. Did I tell you about my book?"

"No, and don't."

Rachel tipped up the bottle. The last drop slid into her glass. It was odd yet predictable, Steph's refusal. Normally, she'd discuss any subject at nearly any free time – except for Rachel's work. Oh, the department's personalities and minor battles were fair game, Steph reveled in the emotional tit-for-tat of academia, which could be just as vicious and no-holds-barred as that of any Fortune 500 corporation or political campaign. The details of classes, students, research, and writing, however, were of no interest to her.

"But it's –"

Steph held up a hand. "Nope! It's about the Bard, that's more than enough for me."

"The Bard and film. Movies, Steph," Rachel wheedled, "your cup of tea!"

Steph stretched, wiggling her toes. "Shakespeare as a filmmaker? Since when?"

"Forget it, you don't want to know," Rachel teased.

Steph sighed. "What's your working title?"

"'West Meets East: Shakespearean Themes in Indian Cinema'."

"Ohmigod! Rachel! How over-the-top can you get? You're carrying this Bollywood thing into the next galaxy!" Steph struggled back up to the sofa. "It's one thing for Melina to get all starry-eyed over –"

"Would you rent even one of their movies, if I suggest it? Just one?" asked Rachel.

"Of course not, I'd have to read the dialogue."

"And you didn't for 'After The Wedding'? Don't be so prejudiced, there's a whole sub-continent of devoted film lovers in India, millions of people just like you, Steph! Do you realize their theaters start screening hit movies at six in the morning? You can't get more fanatic than that!"

"All that brings to mind is how depressing it would be to roll out of bed to watch three hours' worth of melodrama."

Rachel hooted. "Oh, you are so lucky Melina didn't hear you! Here she can see first-run Indian films right in midtown. They open the same day they open in Mumbai, we won't need to take the train into London. Frankly, I'm looking forward to it, too."

"But why? They're supposed to be so derivative, all they do is steal plots from our movies, Brit movies," Steph said, dismissive.

"Okay, okay . . . some of their plots are borrowed from ours, I'll give you that much. But even Shakespeare was influenced by other writers, the Italians, the French. Not to mention his own London lads, the guys he competed against. Besides, inspiration is just the first step in Indian movies. They spin stories in entirely new directions. And they add songs. And dance! Plus, with Melina just thirteen," Rachel gestured with her glass, "it's reassuring to be able to watch a movie without worrying about inappropriate scenes or dialogue. Or cynicism. The ones we watch, Steph, U-rated ones, they're . . . good. Dramatic, yes, sometimes happy, sometimes sad, but entertaining and positive and hopeful."

Steph yelped. "Fairy tales, you're watching fairy tales?"

"C'mon, you said yourself, American movies have lost a lot of innocence."

"After 9/11, yeah."

"That's not the whole story, and you know it. It's the suits making decisions and coming up with males between twelve and twenty-five being the crowd to cater to! You feed that group, you end up with immature – oh, don't get me started. In India, whole families go to movies together, an entirely different audience."

"But what does all that have to do with Shakespeare?"

Rachel grinned. "I thought you'd never ask."

An hour later, Steph tipped up her glass. "God, I love wine! Aside from what sounds like a ridiculously silly book, then, you're set?"

"Except for my seminar. Bates approved it before his illness, we agreed to Thursday afternoons, but I don't see it on my plate."

Steph straightened. "Could it be that new chairman?"

"Harris? No, it was set, what's there to screw up?"

"What's he like?"

Rachel shrugged. "Whiz-kid, Yale, Rhodes scholar, NYU. Teaching at Virginia ever since his doctorate, became an assistant department chair a few years ago."

"So he was here for grad school years ago. Hmm, interesting. The prodigal son returns?"

"His search and interview process must have been instantaneous. By the time Bates reached the ER, I was in England, so the department gave me a pro forma vote online, but . . .."

"Wait a minute!" Steph coughed and cleared her throat. "Wait a minute, Harris hops in as head, that means he was unofficially anointed even before Bates's stroke, doesn't it?"

For a long moment there was silence.

"He bears watching, this man Harris," Steph pronounced. "First name?"

"Marc, M-A-R-C." Abruptly, Rachel laughed. "Like the Medieval and Renaissance Center. Sorry, that's a department joke."

"Marc, related to Mars, martial. Warlike, aggressive. Watch your back, Rachel."

"He can't be that bad." Rachel went to the kitchen and returned with two bottles of water and her phone. "What's in a name? Here, let's call California." She punched in the number. "I packed sunblock, but will she use it? . . . hey, Melina, it's Mom! And Steph's here," she added. "It's snowing, honey, enormous wet flakes, and if you were here you'd dash outside and stick out your tongue!"

Rachel folded the pizza box and stuffed it into her small trash can, where it stood upright. She stuck the wine glasses in the dishwasher, and crumpled and tossed two Klondike Bar wrappers. They bounced off the cardboard box. She scooped them from the floor and pressed them down.

Flicking off the kitchen light, she climbed the narrow runnered steps to the second floor. At the landing, she turned right to her bedroom and stopped in the doorway. Her walls glowed soft yellow, a welcoming golden patina. On them, framed close-ups of flowers gleamed red and pink and coral. A plump down comforter spread over a bed larger than the one she'd slept in in England.

She faced a queen bed in a large room that until recently she'd looked forward to sharing with Ian.

It would have been cozy, wouldn't it? It was supposed to be cozy. She had spoken of the house so he could picture it, imagine the two of them lying in bed of a Saturday afternoon, hands intertwined, heads together on one pillow as in Ian's house on those weekends when Melina spent a sleepover night at a friend's.

"How many bedrooms?" he asked one evening.

"Three. Melina's is on the third floor, and there's a tiny study up there, too, with a pull-out sofa. I could finish the basement, I suppose. Nothing's been done to it for years, it's still stuck in the nineteenth-century."

Ian's laughter rang out. "I love it, as though the eighteen-hundreds were a very long time ago, indeed! A sense of history, love!"

"Hey, my sense of history extends all the way back to 1564!"

"So where is this marvelous house located?"

"Right in the city. Hansen Place. It's a bump that runs off the street, maybe fifty yards?"

"Hip, trendy, morphing?"

"Well, no," Rachel admitted, stroking the wheat-turning-silver hair behind Ian's ears. "More established than hip."

"Ah, an isle of tranquility in the American metropolis!"

"Well, it is," she insisted.

"Rachel, darling, I grew up in a rambling dinosaur of a house in Hampshire, built with the expectation of eight children and at least three servants." He tapped her nose. "But I look forward to the change. It's one thing to visit New York, another to live there."

Luckily, she could hear his voice, the tones which she now recognized as condescending, without feeling more than a brief *frisson*. How close she had come to complicating her life in painful ways! And – something she hadn't fully identified before – whenever she mentioned Indian movies, Ian had tossed her glances of silent disapproval. He just wasn't into Bollywood, he insisted. But it was more than that, she saw that now. It was a cold fish denigration of color and light and whatever it was in Hindi movies that made Rachel feel life was a worthwhile mix, a *masala*, of hope.

"*Aankhon meh teri*," she sang softly, sleepily tugging her white down comforter around her. The Hindi film song was accompanied by an image of dark velvety eyes. "*Ajab si ajab si aadayein hai . . . .*"

In your eyes . . . .

Early next morning, she opened her front door to snow two inches deep. Delighted, she glanced about. Each stoop was white. Clearly none of the neighbors had swept or shoveled their own yet, either. Theirs, however, held plastic-wrapped tube shapes. Rachel grabbed her to-do list and added *Re-subscribe newspaper.*

A quick cuppa, an insertion into warm coat and boots, and she was off with a bulky purse, slim satchel, and a loaded MetroCard left by the phone last summer.

Her bus slushed its way south along Fifth. The air was heavy with the inky scents of Times and Post and Wall Street Journal, and crowded with readers . . . and listeners, telltale cords dangling from their ears. Clad in jeans and blazer, surrounded by suits and impressively tailored overcoats, Rachel felt underdressed. She'd forgotten this sense of a massive book within which academia was a tiny, and not terribly respected, paragraph. In Oxford, university was all. In New York, it was piddling, except where it served the interests of commerce. Not that she totally approved of the Oxford approach, in which the university, an ever-expanding entity, loomed over the town. Its own members could take themselves far too seriously. Ian at the Press, for example, when his paper delivery was delayed.

"Just a day, though," she'd commented, turning from the computer where she read the New York Times online, "it's not like you're publishing time-sensitive material."

"We have a printing schedule, Rachel!" he stormed. "Off by a day, the work . . . look, it's like drains, all right? I need it to flow!"

"Flow, yes, right. Flow."

Really, how lucky she'd been on that day of discovery, long dark hairs in his bed! Extraordinarily, dodged-the-bullet lucky. It hadn't felt like it at the time, of course. At the time, it felt like a sucker punch. In a way, it still did. Yet chance . . . kismet . . . something had led Rachel to discovery of what Owen called "the wanker".

She leaned a bit to her left. The charcoal chalk-stripe ahead – he must be South Asian, who else could own such a head of thick, wavy, black hair? – had replaced his Journal with a Post, and she could just read it over his shoulder. The Post was refreshingly agitated: schoolchildren lectured by unqualified teachers, real estate moguls reneging on deals, cops receiving in-kind services from prostitutes.

She was definitely back in the Big Apple. But what surprises did it hold for her?

CHAPTER 3

S he spent a contented half-hour re-familiarizing herself with her office desk, shelves, even the light that filtered in through the smudged window behind her. On the ledge lay reminders of Melina's little-girl years, first-grade crafts and small hands. Someday Rachel would take those home. Meanwhile, she hung her new calendar. January's photo – Mumbai's palm trees, their fronds tossed by Arabian Sea breezes – gave a salt-skimmed sensuality to the room's dry eight-by-eight.

Despite carpeting, the hallway echoed. These weeks between semesters might be harried elsewhere, but rarely at the emptied university itself. Most students traveled over the holidays, and faculty showed their faces with reluctance.

Rachel entered the English departmental office. "Hi, Jenny."

The young woman behind the flat screen looked up. "You're back!"

"I'm back, and you're tan."

"Florida, two days on the Gulf, Nick's residency's exhausting. God, how are you? We've missed you! Oh, and," she reached behind her and dragged forward a heavy brown bag, "your DVDs, they've been arriving all week. How's Melina, is she here?"

"Just me, she's good, thanks." Rachel drew closer and leaned forward, dropping her voice even further. Her head bobbed toward a connecting door. "Is *he* in?"

"Marc? He's wandering, I can call him for –"

"No! Not yet. What's he like?"

"Forty-ish, Yale, then here, D. H. Lawrence, Virginia," Jenny recited.

"I got that. What's he *like*?"

Jenny brightened. "Nice! Funny. Excellent writer, says 'please', puts in demon hours."

"And the general reaction, post-Bates?"

The younger woman hesitated. "Well, you know . . .."

Rachel dug in her purse and pulled out a dozen Bounty Dark chocolate bars wrapped with string. She slid them over the desk.

"Ooh, my weakness!" Jenny took a breath. "Okay: effective new broom. A thousand percent more energy than Bates on his best days. Multiple shake-ups anticipated. Woolsey's sweating for his own sabbatical."

"You're kidding," said Rachel, fascinated.

"In his defense," Jenny's eyes darted to Harris's door, which bore no nameplate, "he's totally passionate about the department, about getting it more money and respect, in that order. He might do it, too. He's a good talker, and administration adores him. No joke, Rachel, he's their blue-eyed boy . . . literally. Plus good-looking, in an athletic kind of way."

"Arrogant?"

Again Jenny hesitated.

"That would be yes?"

"Let me put it this way," said Jenny, "maybe he's got a lot to be arrogant about."

Rachel leaned back. "Really! His poor wife!"

"Single. No kids. Briefly married a long time ago in a galaxy far, far away. I'm quoting." Jenny's phone rang. She glanced at the displayed number and let the call go to voicemail. "Not gay."

"He came on to you?"

"No, no, totally appropriate. But he walks these hallowed halls, the guy sheds pheromones like dandruff. It's seriously palpable." Jenny grinned. "He should be bottled."

"Anyone bite?"

"Helen –"

"No!"

Jenny smirked. "But unrequited."

"A man of taste, then," Rachel observed, "or allergic to Botox."

"Careful, her claws are bared. Hell hath no fury, etcetera. That's Shakespeare, isn't it?"

"Congreve, actually, a play called 'The Mourning Bride'. But often miscredited."

"Anything else I can catch you up on?"

"My histories seminar?"

Jenny popped chocolate into her mouth and shrugged. "Sorry, Rachel, I haven't heard a thing. Want to leave a message for Marc? No? You sure?"

"If I left one now," said Rachel, "I'd have to call you this afternoon to tone it down." She grabbed her purse. "Not to worry, love. I heard that expression often enough, these past six months. Listen, enjoy the chocolate, hug Nick for me, and do me a favor? Don't let Harris know I was in. In case he thinks I should have paid court."

Outside, the streets were just as slushy as before, despite a pale sun. Rachel checked her watch for the third time in two minutes. She felt confused and irritated. What had happened to her seminar?

Never mind. For now, there was the to-do list. She could walk off her emotions and also accomplish a few things. She strode north against a chill wind that made her nose run.

Was there any logical reason to cancel her seminar? Time . . . money . . . been there, done that? Bates hadn't named any. Nor had any colleagues sniped before Rachel's departure for green Oxford pastures. Marc Harris didn't know her from Eve, so what machinations were in his brain? Or . . . was Harris perhaps a reverse Shakespeare snob? He wouldn't be the first. Shakespeare was generally so revered, so iconic, that faculty who specialized in other writers were often rebelliously dismissive. And Harris focused on D. H. Lawrence, a writer of questionable sexual politics and misogynistic characters.

Rachel found herself on a street corner, simmering. That must be it. Despite Jenny's description, Harris was likely an anti-woman bully, and though he might wield charm, he had cancelled Rachel's seminar without even notifying her.

"Bastard!"

A woman wheeling a strollerful of twins shot her a resentful glare.

"Sorry!" Rachel called.

Reaching East 17th Street, she stopped. Across the street gleamed Sephora.

Truthfully, Rachel always felt out of place in Sephora, that palace of feminine pleasure, where women soothed themselves through color and scent. She felt like a stranger in an aromatically strange land. When Melina first asked to visit – her sixth grade had been heavy with girls whose older sisters worshipped at the store's altar – Rachel had gladly escorted her through the glass doors, ready to be amused. A large bright room filled with perfume and makeup was not Melina's thing at all. Now, a used bookstore . . ..

But Melina was enthralled.

"Look at this!" Her dark braids fell forward as she examined pot after tube after box of subtly-scented, colorful goo. "Try it!"

"Try it, you'll like it," Rachel teased. "Light hand with the samples, sweetheart, you don't want to scare people, take years off their lives."

"Lookit! *You* should use this stuff!"

Now, despite her churning emotions with regard to the cancelled seminar, Rachel would spend time at the altar herself. In her blazer pocket was a daughter-created list and a Sephora gift card Melina had saved for months, another present from Ellie. "In case you happen to pass by," Melina had said, airy, handing the card to Rachel.

"Did you pack both swimsuits? The school one and the pretty one?"

"In case you *want* to go."

"Me? Sephora? Want? When aliens suck out my brain and replace it with a Barbie doll's."

"Brilliant, could we get her dream house?"

"We *have* a dream house."

"Please? While I'm away?"

"Sweetie, there are at least a dozen Sephoras in LA."

"I don't want to go there," Melina said, twining her arms around Rachel. "Sephora is our place. It'll help you remember me!"

"Oh, like I'd forget." She stroked the long brown hair.

"You might even find something for you . . . perfume, eyeliner, blush. Hey, when I get home, I'll draw on your wrist with the henna Nisha gave me! Remember those scenes, before Indian weddings, the henna parties? Like the 'Monsoon Wedding' one?" Melina began to sing, shaking her shoulders in time. "*Madhorama pencha . . . .*"

Humming the tune, Rachel crossed with the green light. Though cosmetics were low on her list of must-haves, even Steph had compared her to a ghost. Maybe she *was* wan.

The trouble with Sephora was that it didn't resolve problems, it created them.

Melina's list was check, check, checked, following her very explicit instructions and the helpful diagrams she'd drawn to indicate which shelf. The gift card would be used up – thank goodness, thought Rachel. Yet blush for herself . . . she glanced in a nearby mirror. Her paleness had not magically brightened. If only Melina had accompanied her! Compact versus tube, powder versus liquid versus gel, and then there were pots that looked so antique they might have belonged to Great-Aunt Agatha.

She was swamped with indecision. Say she stayed with powder. Restricted herself to a healthy English rose. Eschewed the fanatically expensive brands. That reduced her choices to, oh, thirty or . . ..

A shadow fell over the Tawny Pink.

"Excuse me?"

Beside her stood a man with the confused yet determined air of someone wandering in an unfamiliar setting scattered with pitfalls. "I was wondering if you could help . . .." He sketched a vague gesture toward the fragrance wall.

"Oh, no," Rachel assured him, "I'm the last woman you want. I'm lost here, myself."

"Well, it's not expertise so much as it's my mom's birthday, she has every electronic gadget in Brookstone, most of them purchased by me, so the word 'frivolous' came to mind, and that led to perfume, and people from work suggested this place," he said. Once more he gestured toward the mirrored shelves stacked with colorful boxes and bottles. "If you wouldn't mind, I could use a woman's nose."

"A woman's nose?" Rachel took a step forward.

"Exactly. I don't trust mine, it might pick Eau de Sanitation-Department-on-strike. Not something even for my mom, who's pretty forgiving. Please?"

Biting her lip, Rachel followed him to the brightly-stocked wall. "What's she like?"

"She's . . ." and the hands spread wide. They were beautiful hands, she noticed, the fingers long and well-kept.

"Victorian furniture or IKEA? Red roses or daisies? Steak or turkey?"

"Ah! Scandinavian . . . daisies . . . and she prefers fish."

"Does she smoke?"

"My mom? No way."

Mentally blessing Steph's taste in perfume, Rachel selected a sampler bottle. "Try this, it's not too sweet."

He stretched out his wrist, then withdrew it, shaking his head. "No, my chemistry won't work. Would you mind?"

If this was a line he employed in all ten Manhattan Sephoras, Rachel thought, he had definitely honed it. He looked irremediably sincere. "Every woman is different," she pointed out, "and what smells fine on me might be vinegar on someone else."

"Then we'll add olive oil, drizzle it on romaine," he joked. "Please."

Relenting, Rachel misted her own left wrist. The droplets instantly evaporated, leaving behind a scent light with citrus.

"May I?" Again, the blue eyes were guileless, their small rays revealing a warm sense of the ridiculous.

With a raised eyebrow, she offered up her wrist. The man bent over it, but instead of giving a polite, shallow sniff, he inhaled through both nose and open mouth. A second later, Rachel found him gazing down at her, his face etched with concern.

"You okay?"

"Yeah, sure, of course, no problem," Rachel babbled, vaguely off-balance. Her arm shot to her side. She clung to her basket of cosmetics and took a deep breath. "Fine! I'm fine," she assured him. Yet her vision swam, and she was thankful to be wearing flats rather than heels. "I'm fine," she repeated, and turned away, feeling hot. It must be her hormones, had the flight from England affected her cycle?

"Okay," he replied. His arms remained in mid-air as though to catch her. "But could we try another bottle? This one's terrific, but —"

"I don't think so." Rachel glanced about for a cash register. "Wish your mother happy birthday for me." As though she'd drunk too much shiraz, Rachel moved unsteadily and fast toward what she hoped was an employee who would take plastic.

"Wait!" The man caught up with her. His bulk – more muscular than slender Ian's – loomed as he matched her step.

Rachel stopped. "I need to get back to work."

"So do I. I just wanted to say thanks, and, you know, get your number, invite you for a drink sometime, glass of wine, Perrier?"

"No, I don't think so."

"Cup of coffee?"

"Really, I –"

"Five-minute meet at mascara?" he persisted. "Next aisle?"

"Thanks," she said, "but I'm really intensely busy. Really."

His hands surrendered, but he smiled. "Hey, it's just making a new friend. I'm sure you've got friends."

Rachel blinked. "Look, you're clearly an intelligent man, and you have a nice sense of humor, and an interesting-sounding mother, and good luck with the perfume, but really, no." She thrust out her right hand.

He took it in his own warm one and gave it a small squeeze before letting go.

A few moments later, Rachel slid Melina's gift card through the machine. She glanced back. The man was again at the fragrance wall, in his well-kept hand a boxed bottle of the light scent she now wore.

He turned and caught her eye. His fingers reached toward Rachel as though to touch, and abruptly closed.

CHAPTER 4

Hell, Rachel," said Steph, carrying salad to the alcove of her Greenwich Village flat, "that's a meet-cute any other woman would adore! Straight out of Romantic Comedies 101."

"Okay, what you do is, you rip off part of the hot *paratha,* dip it into the plain yogurt, then pop it in your mouth. They're also good warmed up for breakfast. And watch out for the lime pickle, it's spicy," Rachel warned. "A meet-cute? Any other woman can have it, I don't care."

"I thought you were too busy."

"That, too. Where's Rubén tonight?"

"Meeting Franny's parents, he'll be in later, and if you think you can distract me from this –!" Steph clinked her glass against Rachel's. "Allow me to point out that you sound less like a woman who's too busy and more like one who thinks she can't handle the pitch."

Rachel dug her fork into the chicken *dopiaza* she'd picked up from an Indian restaurant staffed with slender men from Goa. "He was weird."

"How is *he* weird? You're the one who bolted like Bambi."

"What kind of guy asks a strange woman to try on cologne? For his mother, no less?"

"The kind who maxed out on Brookstone. An attentive son. An inventive son." Steph gestured with her own fork. "Maybe he was lying, maybe he's really an orphan. Or he was buying for his wife. Ring?"

"No, but plenty of marrieds don't wear them."

"Call him single." She gave Rachel an ironic poke. "What were the odds of his lucking out in Sephora, of all places, when he'd feel twice as comfortable somewhere earthy?"

Rachel's nose wrinkled. "What, a strip club?"

Steph snorted. "I mean the Yankees' dugout! Instead, he faces a battalion of enemy perfume bottles, he spots you, the two of you share some chemistry, poof!" She speared a bite of chicken and waved a grandiose hand. "Poof, you're out the door. He didn't say he wanted to nail you, he offered a cup of joe. You could get off your high horse and drink some."

"I'm too busy," Rachel murmured.

"Yeah, I heard that one." Steph leaned back in her chair, a French bistro number, one of a matched pair she and Rachel had discovered on the sidewalk a block away, abandoned by their owner. They had lugged them back to Steph's building, where Rubén, then only twelve but large for his age, hefted them up three flights of stairs. "Tell me something new, Miss Stubborn."

"Why?" Rachel set down her fork and took up a *paratha*.

Steph wadded her paper napkin and hurled it across the table. "When a therapist scribbles away, she's listing what you're silent about! Screw the 'too busy', lose the 'I don't care', give me some meat. I get frustrated with the same old same old from you. Until you drink that coffee or tea or Yorkshire Brown Ale with the guy, you'll be stuck on the outside. And he inhaled your wrist! Forget his mom, he wanted to know what *you* smelled like." Her chair landed with a bump. "Proof of the pudding, babe."

"Next, Aretha, you'll say it's in his kiss," said Rachel.

"Okay, make fun! Perfume Man's disappeared, but you still need practice shots. How long has it been since you played the field?" A door squeaked. "Rubén?" she called.

A young man walked in, suit jacket slung over one shoulder, his deep brown eyes bright with suppressed laughter. "Hey, Mom, hey, Rachel."

Steph hugged her son and dragged a folding chair to the small table. "Sit, sit! Are you hungry?"

"God, no, they fed me tons. It was like being at Grandma's." Rubén settled his large frame into the chair, rolled up his shirtsleeves and loosened his tie. "Welcome back to the land of the free, Rachel."

"Thanks. You look great," she said. "The parents must have loved you. Did they love you?"

"You remembered to thank them?" queried Steph.

"Mom, c'mon!" Rubén fondly gripped his mother's wrist.

"We forget you're twenty, we still see you on the floor surrounded by Legos," Rachel said. "So, tell, who is this incredible girlfriend, what's she like?"

"Franny Rogers, grew up in Jersey, but thinks she'll stay on the West Coast."

"Is she into money, too?"

"Investment banking, please," he reminded her.

"Rubén will have a foot in two financial camps," Steph noted proudly. "His Latino roots plus my Hadassah connections? Very cool."

"Franny's into developmental psych," Rubén explained. "She's the eldest of five, did the whole mini-mom thing."

"Pretty?" asked Rachel.

Rubén's cheeks grew pink. "Listen, if this is the third-degree, at least offer me a beer," he protested, and went to the kitchen. He returned with a longneck bottle. "Red hair, freckles, blue eyes, five-nine, great legs."

"Do I get to meet her?"

"Of course, Rachel, you've known me as long as Mom has!"

"True, true," said Steph reflectively. "Read-aloud at PS-whatever-number. Can't believe it's been ten years since I sat down with you and *The Hobbit* and thought, 'I've got to adopt this great boy'." She stroked her son's hair back from his forehead.

"And here we are," added Rachel, "'When A Man Loves A Woman'. How did you two meet? Was it cute?" she added. Her ankle was kicked. "Ouch!"

"I guess," said Rubén, "if billiards is cute. She sank my three. Incredible aim."

Rachel arranged her comforter and tussled her pillows into shape, reflecting. It was easy enough for Steph to airily play matchmaker. With Rubén's adoption, Steph had abandoned dating and men seemingly forever and without regret. Devotion to the son who'd had a hard start in life became Steph's *raison d'être*. A scene from years ago swept across Rachel's memory: Rubén attending his first high school dance, and a panicked maternal call.

"You'll be fine," Rachel said soothingly, handing over the M&Ms and Coke she'd stopped to purchase. "*He'll* be fine. It's all rubber-banding, Steph."

"How would you know?" Steph wailed. "Melina's only eight, she's not a teenager with hormones and social envy and –"

"He's socially envious?"

"He could be." Steph sniffled.

Rachel led her to the sofa, ripped open the M&Ms, and located the remote. Surfing, she found a movie channel airing a screwball comedy, one of Steph's favorites. They watched the first scenes unfold.

"Drink your Coke. It's all rubber-banding," Rachel repeated. "Rubén moves off, he moves back. He moves farther, he still comes back. He learns how to draw animé, goes off to summer camp, takes fencing lessons . . . and comes back. Different, maybe larger and smellier, but here."

Steph's next words came mumbled. "I can't have a man in my life, you know. The adoption, all the changes. But . . . I don't want to make room for a man, adjust for one," she said softly. "I like my life, I like my magazines just so, I like always finding my scissors. Rubén understands that."

"You're so lucky he's just as anal as you," Rachel said with a straight face.

"I never wanted the whole package, you know? I thought I did. But a husband . . ." Steph shook her head, "not for me. But you, you're different."

"I am?" Rachel asked, surprised.

"Oh, yeah." Steph gave her an appraising stare. "Oh, yeah, you have a lot of love to share with a man, still. Jason didn't take it all."

Still, the burnt cat shuns the fire. And this little pussycat, thought Rachel, wants nothing to do with flames.

Hours had passed since she'd remembered her missing seminar. What she'd fretted over this morning had faded before the events of the day: Rubén's girlfriend, Steph's analysis, and, of course, the man in Sephora. Idly, she wondered if he'd already presented the birthday bottle to his mother . . . if there actually was a mother. What was her reaction? Did she appreciate the effort?

Yet Rachel's seminar was still AWOL, and she had yet to come up with a reason.

She picked up the phone. Pressing seven digits, she waited for the recorded voice to finish. "Hey, Jenny, it's Rachel Hill," she told the emptiness. "Listen, set up a meeting for me, any morning this week, with Marc Harris, okay? Thanks."

There. Booked. With a clear conscience, she could dial into Pacific Standard Time. Humming, she pressed buttons.

CHAPTER 5

Despite the morning's overcast skies, the street surface was smooth, and after hours of organizational work on her book Rachel wanted to slip on trainers – oops, sneakers! – and set out on a long, vigorous walk. It would do her good to get out and stretch, even under the gray.

She missed Oxford. Beyond ridiculous Ian – who was worth no thought at all, she chided herself – she missed the town itself with its lovely warm buildings and quads, trees and flowertubs, its black-clad academics. There, six months seemed to have passed in an instant. Her last days' memories were still a blur of packing and goodbyes, dinners and gifts, a rapid trek to Heathrow to package Melina over the North Pole to her dad, then back to the furnished flat to empty it of their few possessions and say a final goodbye to Pinky Patel.

Yet the bulk of the past six months was vivid with amusing students in a variety of British accents, river picnics, Melina's new friends, and weekend trips across the country, guidebooks in hand. After ten days of terror-driving on the left, Rachel adjusted, and Melina developed into a brilliant navigator.

"If you follow the A435 and hook around Evesham, you can catch the A439 northeast, then it's just ten miles. Watch the reservation!"

Rachel swerved left. "Who are you, Geronimo?"

Melina gave an exaggerated sigh. "The median. The part that's – hello! – reserved from the road?"

"Oh, reserved. Like restaurant dinners."

"Dinners are booked, Mummy."

"Mummy? Two countries separated by a common language, sweetheart."

Then there was the increasing acquaintance with the Patel family – Pinky and Sanjay, their daughters Parvati and Nisha. They'd begun casually, Rachel knocking on their door to retrieve Melina for dinner or homework. As she and Pinky warmed to each other, there were reciprocated invitations for tea and dinner, quick conversations and borrowing of eggs, notebook paper, and, of course, DVDs. Parvati's engagement party was a highlight, not least because Rachel and Melina found themselves the only non-Indians in attendance. "Our American *bhabhi*," Sanjay referred to her, an embracing compliment from any NRI – that is, a non-resident Indian – whether they lived in Britain, America or the Mideast.

From outside came a pair of voices nurtured in the heart of the Confederacy. Rachel pulled on a warm jacket and grabbed her keys.

"Hey!" she called, locking up. Several yards away stood a couple in their late twenties, Bitsy and Dan Tolliver, looking so pulled together, so polished, it was as though a page of Vogue had landed in Hansen Place. Rachel met them between parked cars.

"We didn't see you back!" exclaimed Bitsy, with a rapid hug and air kiss. "You just sneaked in! How are you?"

"Fine, and that means you're still clocking insane hours?"

"You know it!" said Dan. "But we're rakin' it in, Rachel. Check out these earrings!" He lifted Bitsy's hair to reveal impressive diamond studs.

"Wow, gorgeous, what's the occasion?"

"Three years, married three years, our last year of law school," he said proudly.

"Next month," Bitsy added. "Oh, and save the date, we're throwin' a party on February twentieth, that's the first Saturday we could find. You have to come to this one, Rachel!"

"With a man, or without," Dan supplied. "What's wrong with the men in this city, anyway, that a woman like you is still single?"

"And guess what? My uncles are comin' up from Richmond to roast a pig for us right here, right in the Place! Over in that corner!" Bitsy pointed.

"No kidding," said Rachel, fascinated.

"If you'll agree? We need everyone's consent, you're the last neighbor. Please, please, say yes, Rachel?"

"Sure, I haven't been to a pig roast in years."

"Great! My uncles really know their stuff," Bitsy said, her arm through Dan's. "They bring all their own equipment, start the night before, they'll be drinkin' and swappin' stories –"

Dan grinned. "Come over and see us that Friday night, Rachel, the party before the party. Bitsy's uncles are single. Well, Uncle Bob is."

"By that time, Tom's divorce might be final," Bitsy confided.

"Honey, Rachel doesn't want a man who's just gotten free, she needs one who's tired of canned tuna and take-out."

"Well, the minute you clone yourself, Dan, let me know, okay? I could use some diamonds," Rachel joked. "See you guys later."

"The twentieth of February, Rachel, mark your calendar!"

Walking the city was good for legs and heart. It was also excellent for perception. From the Upper East Side southward down the stretch of Lexington Avenue, Rachel strode at a rapid clip. Within her backpack was a collapsible zippered bag useful for tourist finds in England. At least that was what she'd intended. Not that postcards and mementoes didn't find their way into its scarlet confines . . . but the bag had carried much more than memories of a day here, a weekend there. It had become as practical as another arm when she and Melina ventured into the uncharted territory of Indian grocery stores. Spices and herbs, sauces and snacks and sugary desserts – and the occasional rented DVD – had left hints of themselves.

Tucking the red pouch into her backpack this morning, Rachel sniffed it. The aromas of turmeric and coriander carried her back to the days of experimenting with dinner, often an hour delayed while she followed a new recipe from Punjab or Bengal. Melina would nibble peanuts to stave off hunger pangs, her homework spread out on the table before her.

With the scents rose memories: Rachel's first *aloo gobi*, inspired by "Bend It Like Beckham" . . . the time she'd overcooked *paneer saag* . . . and a panicked call to the Patels when oil-heated, explosive mustard seeds whizzed through the kitchen. Even the ceiling was speckled with dozens of brown dots that over the next month fell one by one onto their hair, tiny reminders.

Now, she headed down to a Manhattan mecca of Indian foodstuffs, Sinha Trading. Checking online for its opening time, she'd noted the photo, the sunny, can't-miss-it yellow of the store's awning, and the giant slogan that reassured: "We Stock Everything Indian You Can Think Of". In her pocket was another list. More mustard seeds – she knew enough now to slam the pot's lid as they heated – cumin seeds, ground coriander and raw ginger, the combined spices of *garam masala*, more dried pomegranate seeds for the *paratha* Melina loved . . . oh, her mouth was watering! Perhaps the store would have a refrigerated case of desserts. A few bites of *laddoo* or *jalebi* would bring back memories. Maybe she'd buy a few to save for Melina.

Wait a minute. Wasn't that –?

Rachel stared at the door beside her. A Moroccan restaurant, its shuttered windows boasting red curtains. Had it been four years? Five? Same name, same posted menu, probably the same low table where she and her dark-bearded date sat cross-legged and tried to find common ground. He owned a store. Something to do with Latin American art. Masks? Something like that. He'd grown up on the East Side, found himself a place off Lexington Avenue, a man memorable for a comment Rachel had shrieked to Steph later.

"To me," he pronounced, scooping up *mrouzia*, "Central Park is the Rockies."

"Can you believe it?" Rachel later demanded over the phone. "A few blocks west and he's in the Donner Party!"

"Rachel, the internet is not a good venue for you. You're meeting guys who're surprised you look like your photo."

Steph was absolutely right, the internet was barren for Rachel, despite glowing stories related by others whose sisters, colleagues, doormen, found "the one" through Match or eHarmony or some other FindLove.com. Scratch speed-dating, too. Ditto to activities she tried at others' insistence: ultimate Frisbee . . . swing-dancing, sweat-soaked and loud . . . and contra dances, where Rachel grew dizzy being spun too fast by partners who ignored her protests, including one whose elephantine T-shirt read: *I'm not fat, I'm Fluffy.*

Sinha Trading's windows contained movie posters and phone card ads. Inside, women with dangling earrings double-checked their own shopping lists.

Rachel paused and inhaled. The air was filled with spices. Shelves overflowed with boxes and bags printed in English and Hindi. The store held spices both ground and whole, flours and lentils, sandwich cookies with Shah Rukh Khan's photo on the packaging, pastries and fantastic deals. But would she really use that many black cardamom pods?

Many items were still wholly foreign to her. This large bag of snow-like flattened rice, for example, which she gathered was an easy filler, rather like oatmeal. At least if she'd understood Pinky Patel correctly.

"Oh, it's not very nutritious," the woman answered her question, one sunny afternoon in Oxford. Behind Rachel, the girls waited, impatient for her to finish chatting and drive them southeast toward a mall and what Nisha's sister Parvati described as "fantastic shopping, yeh?". "My mother came from Punjab, I don't cook with that." Pinky dismissed rice flakes with a flick of her fingers.

Rachel examined the bag. Even accounting for India's regional differences, she couldn't think of a good use for it. Not yet, at any rate.

"*Suniye?*" Excuse me?

Rachel edged closer to the shelf to allow the speaker, a woman in an emerald green sari and yellow *choli* blouse, to pass. A small girl wearing pink Oshkoshes clutched her hand, her eyes round with a curiosity mirroring Rachel's.

Her Indian cookbook could explain crushed rice, she was sure.

It felt cozy here in the store, even if half the products were unfamiliar and labeled in Nagari script, a total mystery to Rachel. While she could say "*accha*", she had no idea how it might look on page or packet. She glanced sideways. The little girl was gazing solemnly at her. How pretty she was, with deep brown eyes and dark curls, and skin the lovely color of raw sugar. Rachel waved at her. The eyes widened. Perhaps a strange woman whose own skin was unusually pale looked too odd to smile to.

Rachel could empathize. There were times when – watching movies with Melina – she caught sight of her own pallid ankles and gave a start of surprise. Immersed in Indian films, where everyone but dancing European extras was dark-haired and many were also darker-skinned, it was a shock to recognize herself. Had color leached out? Could it be replaced?

Metaphors, she mused, were unpredictable.

She leaned over the cold steel fence rail, scanning the East River. One pleasure boat had passed, those on board well-wrapped against wind and spray as they sped south. How different that mad dash full of motor noise from Rachel's last riparian adventure! She'd been punted on the Isis back in Oxford's early autumn, a lazy day complete with bread and French cheeses, pears and chocolate on a grass-spread cloth when they tied the punt to leafy branches leaning out over the river. The distant crack of a cricket bat reached them from white-clad men, and wine flowed until it was time to weave their way back with the current, their laughter drifting with it.

There really was nothing like messing about on the water.

Back and forth, back and forth, commercial traffic trolled upriver and down, and across the way loomed Queens, where perhaps someone else viewed the same gray river and imagined Rachel's presence on the opposite bank.

What a thoroughly silly notion! Her cheeks flushed with more than cold.

Her backpack had grown heavy in Sinha Trading, so weighted with bulk spices, jars and bottles that she'd taken the bus north. Now, at Schurz Park just a few steps from home, she spilled a handful of *sev* into her palm and nibbled the crispy snack, sharp with green chilies, debating which direction to take with her book.

West meets East, the Bard encounters Indian movies. It was initially a random thought from months ago, an idea that fluttered into her mind as she, Melina and Nisha – settled into the sofa and well-supplied with Britain's M&M-like Smarties – watched "Krrish", one of Nisha's favorites. On the screen, a field of flowers, a man and woman dancing and singing, and what did that have to do with Shakespeare, anyway? She shook her head to focus.

" . . . *koi tumsa nahin, oh, koi tumsa nahin* . . .." Oh, there's no one like you . . ..

Still, Shakespeare himself dealt with love and passion and their conflict with order and . . . Rachel watched the colorful images without seeing them. The idea had settled in for a stay, and the more she considered the theory – not that Shakespeare knew Indian literature, but he would have appreciated it, and what were films but a popular literature turned visual? – the more sense it made. That was the point when she knew she was hooked on Bollywood.

"I told you you'd like them, Aunty!"

If Shakespeare could examine Hindi movies, what would he admire about them? In her mind she'd created a simple table of contents. Introduction. Chapter 1, History of Indian Film. No, too pretentious. Overview of Indian Film. There, that was manageable. Chapter 2 . . . Duty and Familial Obligations, perhaps. Everything else flowed from that, both in Shakespeare's world – with the primacy of duty to king and lord, as well – and in classic Indian thought.

Yet it was true that modern life hammered on that door so severely, it had splintered. The number of arranged marriages in India, for example – now, there was something Shakespeare was familiar with, marriage arranged to keep property in the family! – was falling, though websites devoted to bringing together interested parties were still heavily subscribed, especially as Indian families moved out into the world. Then there were the sites that matched divorced singles, a population virtually unimaginable in the India of twenty years ago. Yet even they – especially they? – searched for love.

That would be her third chapter. Love. In Hindi, *pyaar*, the kind of love more devoted than romance – *mohabbat* – and a great deal more contained than *ishq*, passion. Rachel had learned how nearly impossible it was to watch a U-rated Indian movie in which the word *pyaar* failed to appear, and often used in conjunction with *shaadi*, marriage. Love and marriage, the connection, the conflict. The Western desire to experience the first before entering into the second, versus the fast-falling Eastern tradition that advocated love developed within the safe surrounds of marriage and extended family. The clash between the two beliefs, and the rising Indian middle class's assumption of Western values, haphazardly mixing them with homegrown ones. And William Shakespeare? He'd certainly seen his share of marriages in which love played a very minor role. Yet throughout his comedies ran the theme of lovers meeting each other, recognizing each other, and what would the fathers say?

The whole problem of Romeo and Juliet, mused Rachel, was that they were too young, too impetuous and taken with each other, and lacked the kind of joint family structure that supported the young Mohandas Gandhi and his wife when they married at the fragile age of thirteen.

Thirteen! With a start, she glanced at her watch. No, still too early to call Melina.

Rachel placed the top on the salad spinner and handed it to Steph.

Steph raised her voice above the noise of the rotating basket. "Ask yourself this: do you feel like you're missing something? Is there a part of life that if you died without getting it, you'd have regrets? Here you go."

"You mean more than a Jag?" Rachel joked.

Steph sighed. "Long day. Two couples, a bunch of singletons making strides, one newbie presenting with . . . oh, right, we're talking about *you*. Maybe you're fine. Maybe coincidence will show you."

"Stop, no more Jean Cocteau's 'coincidence is God's way of working undercover', if you actually met him you'd run screaming," said Rachel. "Hand me the plates."

"And yet, even the cowardly Freud occasionally came up a winner," Steph reminded her. She sloshed wine into an empty glass. "So if an 'aha!' moment hits you, well, listen up, hon."

"If coincidence is going to show me what I'm missing, I wish it would hurry the hell up."

"Your problem, Rachel, is you don't like surprises," Steph pointed out cheerfully. "But even bad surprises push you forward."

"My own private guru! *Rotis*, please, and can you reach the *aloo gobi*?"

They carried dinner into the living room.

"Cheers! Tonight's feature, to offset your incredibly bizarre Bollywood trend, is a classic," Steph announced.

"'Casablanca'?"

"I mean classic scary."

"Nazis are scary."

"This is not Nazis," retorted Steph, "this is water and fish and my beloved Steven."

"Oh, right, just when you thought it was safe. And you've still got a huge crush on that poor man? God, Steph, get a grip," Rachel said, amused. "Move on!"

"To what? Steven Spielberg's respected . . . talented . . . funny . . . sexy, even."

"Stop!" Rachel grabbed the remote and pressed play until the screen glowed with the first moments of "Jaws".

CHAPTER 6

It was too bad Melina slept three times zones away, Rachel would have appreciated her "you go, Mom!" encouragement, as encouraging as a teenager awakened at six o'clock could be. Yet she could hardly do that to the LA household. Though, trundling down Fifth Avenue, it occurred to her that a pre-dawn phone call might not be at all unusual, given Ellie's workload.

Rachel's ex-husband Jason and his wife Ellie seemed oddly right for each other, despite the difference in their age and experience. Somehow they worked well together, had done so for the past few years. *Beshert*, Steph had supplied her with that great Yiddish word. Meant to be, just made for each other. Whether at birth, by the stars, or through the give-and-take of life, Jason and Ellie had reached melding point at the same time, and the fact that his new wife resembled Jason's mother was simply coincidence.

"Rah-rah for them," Rachel murmured. She glanced about. Bus behavior tended to be measured, this much newspaper spread and no more, allowing for less deviation than, say, the subway, where a muttering rider might be practicing Russian or running through his lines or, of course, in need of meds.

"Here," Jenny welcomed her, pouring hot water into a dark blue mug with a tea bag. "Earl Grey, plain?"

"Thanks." Rachel accepted the mug with a lifted eyebrow.

"Marc's idea, let people be comfortable while waiting."

"How charming."

"Isn't it? He's ready anytime, he said." She gestured toward the door.

"Big of him," said Rachel lightly. "Any chocolate left?"

"Just one, I should have stuck them in the freezer, Nick would never have looked there. Good luck!"

Grabbing her satchel, Rachel opened the department head's door – still sans nameplate – and entered. She had forgotten how much light this corner room received, with windows to east and south. Her pupils contracted in the strong morning sun.

"Marc? I'm Rachel Hill," she said. Temporarily blinded, she offered her hand, and felt it embraced by two larger, warmer ones.

"Rachel! I was hoping to meet you . . . again."

The deep voice came at her from a few inches above. Rachel squinted. Broad shoulders, smiling mouth. Blue eyes. Brown hair.

"Thanks again for your help with the perfume, I got points from my mom for 'instinctive good taste'."

"Oh, my God."

"This from the woman who thought my third-grade peanut butter, jelly, and American cheese sandwiches were tacky."

"Oh, God."

"Would you like your hand back?"

It flew to her chest. "You knew it was me?" she asked, stunned.

"Please, sit." He moved the comfortable chair an inch forward. "At Sephora? No, not at all." Instead of retreating behind his desk, the department head pulled forth a second chair to face hers. "I had no idea. I'm very pleased."

"I ... I . . .." Words had traitorously abandoned Rachel. She fumbled her mug onto the desk.

"You, however, look less than delighted. Shall we do some business? The initial shock over, you're wondering about your invisible histories seminar, you're mad as hell, and you're not going to take it anymore," said Marc, leaning forward.

Rachel found her voice. "Exactly. Bates approved that course, it was go."

"I know. I'm sorry. A couple of students even signed up."

"What?"

"Only two. You were expecting more? Because the computer lists just those, and two aren't enough to keep it on, if you recall."

"Two?" she croaked.

"Don't take it personally, another semester you'd have to beat them off with sticks, I'm sure, but this particular spring we're apparently low on histories buffs." He grinned. "'Once more into the breach' has its fans, I imagine, in other years. Don't take it as a criticism, Rachel."

"I'm not," she mumbled.

"Fine," he said, clearly not that credulous. He shuffled through paper files. "But I do need another class covered, since Melissa Horn's unexpectedly requested family leave to adopt a daughter," said Marc, drawing a forest green folder from the colorful stack. "Critical theory," he said, handing her the folder, "which I understand you taught four years ago."

"Gaaah!" Rachel gaped. "Tell me you're kidding!"

"You'll be fine, Rachel, same sources, same text," he assured her.

"Sources? Text? My God, I despised that class, I burned the handouts, I promised myself never, *jamais, nunca, jamás, kabhi nahin* –"

"Whoa, whoa, whoa!" Marc held up a hand. "You lost me after *jamais*, but I get it. You hate critical theory, it's a Saddam of a course, you'd do anything rather than teach it."

"Close to anything," Rachel amended.

"Even though I need you . . . that is, the department needs it covered, since quite a few more than two students have signed up. I have no idea why they consider critical theory essential to their well-being, but there you go. And then, of course, there's the money," he added, smiling.

"The money . . . yes, I heard you talked people round your little finger," she said bitterly.

"Yup." He nodded. "Known for it."

Rachel weighed her options. Agree to Perfume Man's request, and besides her lovely comedies, she'd have to slog through an entire semester of that wretched theory course, the only one that in all her teaching years felt like torture. Say no, on the other hand, and Marc Harris seemed pleasant and understanding today, but tomorrow might reveal him as a vindictive bastard. And she needed his support for her book. Involving film was not exactly a common choice for English academics, especially film from a land completely foreign to Shakespeare. Depending on the season, and her outlined proposal, it could take quite a long time to find a publisher. During a wait-and-see period, she'd need her department chair's goodwill.

"Fine, I'll take it," she said, her voice tight.

"Thank you, Rachel. Truly. I appreciate your willingness to help me out of a bind. Now, this past semester," he leaned forward, "how did you like Oxford?"

"Loved it." Abandoning her mug – let him clean it up! – she gathered purse and satchel. "And I'm gone."

"Wait!" His hand motioned her to sit. "I'm not finished."

She gave a heavy sigh. "How much more damage can you inflict?"

"Just pro forma stuff, learn more about my faculty," and he pulled out another folder, this one red. "What are you writing?" His fingers sketched in the air. "Writing. What are you working on?"

"It's a . . . well, it's still in the planning stages."

"Got a working title?"

"Yes, it has a title," Rachel said, annoyed. "It's about Shakespearean themes in contemporary Indian film."

"Really? Fascinating. Book, or article?"

"Book."

"Got a publisher?"

"Not yet. I know someone at the Oxford University Press, but . . .." She was horrified to feel her cheeks grow hot. "They may still be interested," she said, defensive.

"Good. Let me know if you need more connections. I have –"

"Thanks." The word was cool. She got to her feet.

Marc rose, as well, meeting her at the closed door. "Wait, can we do lunch?"

"It's ten-thirty."

"Late breakfast?"

"I had my bagel. Besides, there are places to go, things to do." She shook the green folder at him. "Sources and text, remember?"

"Rachel, really, I'm sorry." He leaned against the door, preventing her from flinging it wide. "I wouldn't have asked for the change if it weren't in the department's best interests. I didn't know it was you, I mean you the woman I met the other day. Your name, of course, but . . . and then when you strolled in, I thought, well, thank God, here's a chance to get to know her."

"Oh, you'll know me," Rachel assured him. "You'll recognize me as the faculty member who despises every Wednesday evening. Door?"

It opened and Rachel was out, passing Jenny with a grimace and a silent vow to never again enter Marc Harris's too-sunny corner office.

Hansen Place smelled of cinnamon and lamb, so the Nassirs across the way must have returned from their lengthy stay in the Middle East, visiting their huge extended family. It would give Rachel an opportunity to deliver the British gifts Melina had selected for the two studious, overscheduled teenage daughters,

Neg and Nema, girls she saw irregularly but enjoyed giggling with.

If their mother, Noor, was home, Rachel would also have the chance to talk with someone rational – for a change.

She let herself into her own house and ran up the stairs. There was the pile of red-wrapped presents. She found the two, crossed to the Nassirs', and pressed the bell. The door was opened by a striking woman in a cream silk sweater and pearls.

"Hi, Noor, welcome back! How are you? Are the girls home?"

"Come in! No, they not home yet, out shopping with my mother." The woman led her into a living room of pale-blue moiré. "Melina is here, too?"

"Still in LA, I pick her up in two days. She chose these, though, for your girls." Rachel handed over the brightly-wrapped packages.

"Very kind! My daughters have gifts, too, I send them to you when Melina home."

Damn. Rachel should have waited to have her own daughter convey the gifts. In matters of manners, Noor tended toward formal. Rachel felt more breezily American than usual.

"Did they do well there? Have a good time?" she asked.

"Of course. See family, visit cousins, improve language. Here, they speak only with us. There, surrounded," said Noor, relaxing into her chair. "But happy to be back."

"Mmm-hmm." Rachel could well imagine the relief of adolescent girls released from a land where to be female meant enduring intense supervision.

"How are you?" Noor queried with a keen look. "Happy to leave England?"

"Oh, England! Yes. Mostly yes," Rachel said. "Sorry, today's been confusing. I mean my feelings are topsy-turvy, it's a long story." She gestured. "Mixed-up."

"Aha." Noor's eyes gleamed. "A man."

"No, no man," Rachel replied, recalling her frustrating meeting with Marc Harris. "Thank God."

"You want fix up?"

"Sorry?"

"You want date, husband and I fix you up?" Noor pressed. "Husband knows lot of men!"

Rachel descended the five treads from Noor's, aware that the woman watched from her window. With a final wave, she let herself in and leaned back against her own front door with a feeling that she had of her own volition swept up long skirts and climbed into a tumbrel leading to the Place de la Révolution.

Why on earth had she told Noor yes?

Of course the woman had pressured her, that was to be expected. Her description of the male-rich atmosphere of her husband's engineering workplace ("All educated men, too!") was also predictable. And Noor's practiced eye estimated Rachel perfectly. "You five-foot-seven?" Well, yes, she was.

But politely agreeing that Noor might enlist her husband to find Rachel a date? She must be crazy. Or more thrown by her meeting with Marc Harris than she'd thought.

"Won't be Muslim man. But plenty of others," Noor continued, cheerful. "Like fish! We find one for you."

Rachel stared into the long mirror beside the door. Something odd was happening to her. She had scoffed at Steph's insistence that she needed dating practice, and here she was, falling in with Noor's offer. Perhaps she'd caught some sort of bug?

She put a hand to her forehead. It felt positively cool.

Rachel climbed the stairs to her bathroom, flung aside the shower curtain, and turned on the tap. Water gushed into the tub. A good soak, that's what she needed. She glanced at the small mirror. Turning from side to side, she frowned. Her fingers rose to her cheeks. Lightly, she pinched.

Four years ago she had recycled the books used for her critical theory class, never dreaming she might have to teach the despised course again. Several phone calls and a bookstore foray resulted in the basic texts, including a volume badly-organized and phrased in a style reminiscent of Dickens. Rachel plunged into reading.

By afternoon, she'd found a workable rhythm: read two hours, toss the pages aside and vent her irritation in frenzied housecleaning. The small bedrooms had never looked so neat. Dust bunnies hopped into the Hoover, woodwork was smudge-free, and even the light switches lost their fingerprints. Two more reading hours, and the living room's cushions were pounded outside for dust and stray buttons, accompanied by a colorful array of invective against critical theory, the books' authors, and, naturally, Marc Harris. Damn the man! – in as many languages as Rachel could summon. Refreshed by the cold, she shook out lambswool dusters. Bits of fluff floated eastward through the clear air, toward the river.

She re-entered the house to a ringing phone. "Hi, Steph!"

"Still reading?"

Rachel groaned. "Still breathing?"

"My last two clients cancelled, ditch your deadly boring books, meet me in Bloomies?"

"Steph –"

"Half an hour!"

Thirty minutes later, Rachel entered Bloomingdale's. Her arm was snatched.

"What is it today? Shoes? Bags? Cruisewear?" asked Rachel, amused.

"Better."

"Better than shoes? No way!"

"Cut it out! There's a humongous sale on jewelry."

"Oh, jewelry."

"Don't say it like that."

"Like what?"

"Like you're saying 'comic books'."

"It's pretty comical how much jewelry you already have," Rachel pointed out.

"All you have to do is sit with me and say, 'oh, how pretty!'."

"Oh, how fun!"

Coral, turquoise and pearls surrounded them, and the Bloomies associate bringing new items up from the glass case was in cahoots with Steph, oohing and aahing in unison. Like a wind-up doll, Rachel had dutifully repeated her three-word line, giving it various shadings each time. Now, before Steph could object, she slipped off the stool.

"Back in a minute."

The case ahead of her held watches, intensely expensive watches, the sort advertised in architectural design magazines. She glanced down at her left wrist. Though its black leather strap needed replacing, her own watch was perfectly serviceable if a bit severe. Yet she lingered by the case to prolong her absence. Steph was more than supplied with "oh, how pretty!".

Her mind ran again to her book. Chapter 3, Love. That would be a long chapter, with sections on . . . hmmm. Love approved by parents, by friends . . . by society . . . and then, the cream: disapproved love, forbidden love, and love between people already committed to another. She could expand that. In fact, it made sense to expand it to include the diverse passions masquerading as love. Shakespeare, a product of his time, had a great deal to say about passion, which Elizabethans had largely regarded with jaundiced eyes. Regulated passion was acceptable, if odd. But passion run amok . . ..

A sparkly sound, a jingling, interrupted her train of thought. Rachel found herself staring at a man's Dolce & Gabbana. The sound . . . Christmas bells? Still? Leftover Christmas bells on sale? Confused, she looked around for the source. There it was, ahead on the left, a woman behind a semicircular table. On the table rested wooden tree shapes, a foot high, with upflung branches holding – oh!

Rachel walked forward.

Both table and wooden trees held bangle bracelets in a rainbow of colors. The smiling woman in a yellow sari jingled a handful together. "Hello!" she greeted Rachel. Her own arms shone with bracelets. They jangled with her welcoming gestures. "Come see!"

"Oh, how pretty!" This time Rachel meant it. The circles *were* lovely, bright with glass, the metals scrolled and carved.

The woman held out her hands. "Give me your arm!"

"Oh, I don't know, they're not really –"

"Just to try. Red? Silver?"

Shaking her head at her own whimsy, Rachel unbuckled her watch, tucked it into her jeans pocket, shrugged off her purse and coat, and pulled up her sleeves. She felt the woman's warm hand, then the bracelets cool and tight around her fingers, her wrist, her arm. They shone like moonlight. She shook them and was rewarded with the same pleasant ringing.

"Other arm." In a moment her right arm, too, supported a series of circlets. Rachel let it drop. The bracelets jangled to her wrist.

"There! They're lovely on you!" Her accent carried notes of England.

"I don't know, I feel all . . ." Rachel's reserved smile grew wide, "as though a *dhol* drum ought to beat. *Bole churiyan, bole kangana*," she sang under her breath.

"*Haay main ho gayi teri saajna*," the next line was sung back to her. "You actually know that song, that movie?" the woman asked, her face alive with curiosity.

"'Kabhi Khushi Kabhie Gham'? Yes, of course, a modern classic. Incredible actors, immense sets, wonderful songs . . . and the dance scenes!"

"At the Pyramids?" The woman laughed. "Nothing succeeds like excess! As a director, Karan Johar pulls out the stop, his movies are like opera. It was an incredibly popular film, but not many of you know it, non-Indian Americans, I mean."

"I do." Rachel placed her arms one above the other, tapping the bracelets together. They jangled, a happy musical tone. "*Bole churiyan, bole kangana,*" she sang again. "I suppose I really should be twirling, dressed in a sequined *lehnga.*"

"*Jao!* Go ahead!"

"Here?" Rachel looked around. Oddly, there was no one nearby. "Without the long skirt?"

"Even without the long skirt," the woman encouraged her, "or lights, or Amitabh Bachchan!"

Rachel laughed. Shyly, she made a hesitant turn, her arms raised and crossed. The bracelets sang. "How's that?"

"Again! More!"

"More? Here? With your bracelets?"

"Why not? Get in the spirit! I buy these in Delhi, bring them once a season, *kyon nahin*, why not?"

"Why not? Oh, I could think of . . .." Rachel left off. Giving in to the moment, she turned again, and then again, clapping her arms together to hear the bangles sing, round and round and round, the sweet sound of bells.

"Turquoise? Or coral?" asked Rachel.

"Where have you been?" Steph demanded. "And why are you out of breath? Oh my God, you have a brown Bloomies bag! You actually bought something? Tell me it's for you, not Melina!" She snatched the paper bag from Rachel's grasp. "What's in here, sleigh bells?"

"Bangles."

Steph pulled them out and held them in front of her, gazing mournfully at Rachel through the bracelets. "These are Indian," she accused.

"Yes, they are."

"We'll certainly hear you coming. You're not planning on wearing them to work?"

Rachel grabbed the shiny circlets and dropped them back into the brown bag.

Steph kicked aside a pair of the red leather pumps. "Too big, too small, too Dallas. Shakespeare say anything about shoes?"

"Um . . . 'these clothes are good enough to drink in'?"

"Not bad. So, how's your attitude toward the guy who offed your seminar?"

Rachel shrugged. "He is what he is. It is what it is."

Steph grinned. "You have three great classes and only one crap one, could be worse."

"It's his 'oh, let's have breakfast!' that gets to me, what does he think, I'm going to cave just because he once sniffed my wrist? Please. And upping the ante? First it was coffee or chardonnay, now it's breakfast, what next, dinner at Le Cirque? I'm not interested, okay?"

"I thought you were too busy."

"That, too."

Ten minutes later they emerged onto the sidewalk. Rachel clutched Steph's arm. "At the corner, those two guys? Marc Harris."

Steph glanced sideways. "Gray coat?"

"Black."

"Wait here."

Facing Bloomies' large window filled with bright post-Christmas sale signs, Rachel watched from the corner of her eye as Steph walked up to the two men, by her gestures miming being lost. Moments later, she was crossing the street in animated conversation with Marc Harris. Reaching the opposite curb, Steph thanked him with gracious gestures. Marc nodded, rejoined his friend in gray, and headed downtown.

Her cheeks flushed with cold and high spirits, Steph returned with the next light.

"Well, he's clearly bright and helpful and probably an Eagle Scout, but now he's both colleague and boss, and you're too busy and not interested, and he screwed your schedule, and what clse? Oh, that's it. So forget about it."

"No joke," Rachel said darkly.

Steph's brown eyes examined her. She looped the handle of Rachel's bag over her little finger, and shook it. From inside came the bracelets' shimmering, jingly music.

"On the other hand," said Steph, "he's *dishy*."

"I'm going to an India Association meeting tonight," Rachel said. She propped the phone between chin and shoulder as she tugged on a pair of tights.

"What's that?" came Melina's voice.

"They get together, apparently for a program, talk, *laddoos*. It's at the Rubin Museum down in Chelsea. Himalayan art and a six-story spiral staircase. Think of climbing that in a sari and heels!"

"You gonna drag Steph with?" Rachel heard a grin.

A cold drizzle sprinkled Rachel as she walked the last block. Ahead was the Rubin Museum. In front stood a group of dark-haired men out for a smoke. They nodded as she passed and approached the heavy door.

One of them threw his cigarette down and ground it with a leather-booted foot. "Allow me." He pulled the door wide.

"Thanks."

"You've lived in India?" he asked politely.

"No . . . not yet. I've just come back from Britain, which is where –" Rachel gestured to her *salwar kameez*.

"Welcome, then!" He held out a be-ringed hand. "Purandar Dutta."

"Rachel Hill."

"I'm coming upstairs, I'll introduce you to the Punjabis. You don't want to hang around with the others," this for the benefit of the watching men, "all those people from Bengal!" Laughter followed them up. "They can't help it, they're just stuck in 'better than you' mode."

Rachel followed Purandar up the spiral staircase. All about were women gorgeously dressed, escorted by men whose clothing varied from Western-cut business suits to *kurta* and designer jeans. The conversational level was high, and music echoed from the walls.

"Are you on our mailing list? I only ask because you can be," Purandar gestured toward a table with forms and pens, and bent toward her to be heard above the noise, "and become a member, too. Or check us out first, drink some wine, eat *laddoos*."

Rachel laughed. "Those are non-negotiable, aren't they?"

"And multi-purpose." Grinning, he handed her a glass of white wine. "Every kind of celebration, from weddings to aceing a test. Plus, where else but Hinduism would you find such a pragmatic use of sugar? Offer *laddoos* to the god, the prayers go to him, the snack stays behind to be eaten. What do you do, Rachel?"

"I teach English at NYU."

"I'm in publishing, the Pollack Group. I don't suppose you're writing anything commercial?"

She shook her head and gave him a thumbnail sketch of her book.

"*Accha?* Really? That's great! I love it! Man, you can always get Indians with movies! The national pastimes, cricket and films. Name me some of the ones you've seen."

Scouring her memory, Rachel embarked on a list, widely interrupted by Purandar's enthusiasm ("Yeah, that one's great!"), memory ("I remember seeing that in India") and informed comment ("Not his best . . ..").

"Amazon is my new best friend," she said wryly.

"You can order direct from the producer, you know. Yeah, yeah, Yash Raj, Eros Entertainment, Red Chillies, they'll be glad to take your money. Mention my name . . . I'm kidding! Listen, if you ever write non-academic," Purandar handed her a business card, "call me first. Okay, see over there, beyond that huge group of Gujaratis? Those are Punjabis, my people. I'll take you over, they'll pass you around."

Purandar was as good as his word. Rachel was immediately taken under the wing of Purandar's aunt Gurpreet, whose garnet-colored sari carried an elegant gold-and-silver border six inches wide. All evening Rachel was circulated among friendly Punjabis like a valuable package, one with an inquiring mind and a *dupatta* that kept slipping from her shoulders.

CHAPTER 7

It was Rachel's turn to wait behind airport security ropes, scanning faces. She hoped her daughter's appearance had not altered. What if Melina had done something to her hair, dyed it pink or green or henna red? Or gotten her nose pierced? Or was now tattooed? Or . . . there she was.

"Sweetheart!" Rachel hugged her tight. "Thank God, no visible changes!"

"Ooh, that's right, I forgot to tell you about the butt implants. I'm kidding, Mom, kidding!" Melina grinned. "Ellie offered, but . . . Mommy, it's a joke."

"God, Bini, stop it, my nerves are frayed with critical-freakin'-theory, I have no humor-judgment at all. How was the flight? Crying babies?"

"Two. I've got an extra bag," Melina said, apologetic.

"Aha, Ellie strikes again!"

How fabulous it was to have Melina beside her in the cab, to listen and watch her expressive face as she related stories of warm weather and huge houses! Los Angeles had smoothed the unconsciously acquired English accent, as well, Melina no longer sounded quite so Keira Knightley.

"Daddy says hi," said Melina, accepting an M&M from Rachel's purse.

"Did you see him much?"

"Oh, yeah, he scheduled time every day. Sometimes we'd watch DVDs together. He's gotten into old movies."

"How old?"

"Steph-old, he's into classics, too, now, isn't that funny? Since he and Steph hate each other. All he talks about is angles and cuts, production values, deals, locations . . . it sounds weird. He used to talk teeth."

"Oh, well," said Rachel, looping her arm through Melina's, "it's just new. I imagine he's picked up a lot just from hanging with Ellie. It's as if I started talking RBIs and bunts. Baseball, hon, your uncle could explain better than me."

"Oh, how are they, Steve and Mette and the boys?"

"She e-mailed yesterday. Rain, rain, and more rain. In Denmark, this is a wet, dark time."

"Candles at Christmas, lots and lots of candles, remember?" Melina said dreamily. "Oh, hold on." She dug in her pocket and came up with a cell phone. "It's Nisha!" She clicked and began to talk.

"You might as well have that thing surgically implanted into your wrist." Rachel nudged her daughter to keep it short. "Give new meaning to the phrase 'talk to the hand'."

"What did you do to my room?" came the anguished cry.

Puzzled, Rachel ran up the steps two at a time. From the doorway, she surveyed the bedroom. "Cleaned it?"

"You moved my ribbons, they were here!" Melina pointed to her dresser.

Grasping her daughter's finger, Rachel re-directed it toward the wall, where ribbons hung in colorful stripes from a decorative hook. "It's their new place, you know, all loose and dangly. Harder to get entangled, easier to grab. And your earrings, I figured you'd bring new ones, so I moved them, see? –

this empty space for the newbies, so they're surrounded by all your really old favorites, 'cause *they* know the ropes."

Melina shook her head. "No, but it's a good thing I'm home."

"Too true, Bini. Any more crises of location?"

"I can deal."

Rachel cleared her throat. "Aside from earrings, my dear, how many new clothes?"

"Not too many, honest." Melina's cheeks grew pink. "Honest!"

". . . and Molly, her assistant, took me twice to an eat-in In-N-Out, we dove into the fries, plus, Mom, they make killer chocolate shakes, you'd love them!" Melina stopped talking long enough to swallow a bite of red lentil *dal*. "And she drove me to Santa Monica one afternoon, I got to ride the merry-go-round and walk out on the pier."

Rachel sat back. Melina's enthusiasm was infectious, and so unlike the general run of articles about adolescents, the ones with ominous warnings of anorexia and drugs and depression. "You sound a little less Brit, honey."

"Do I? Are you quite sure?" – in the Imogen-ish tones acquired in Oxford.

"Oh, hey, I take it back! So, Ellie was good to you?"

"Yes, Mom, she was perfectly nice to me," Melina said, patting Rachel's hand. "Don't worry."

"Good. Good."

Melina's tone grew confiding. "You know what I missed most when I was in California?"

"Crowded sidewalks?"

"I missed India . . . I mean, what we had of it in England. Nisha, the Patels. Watching movies with her, with you," she said, mournful. "No one knew what I meant if I said 'accha', and with all their huge movie collection, Daddy and Ellie have no Bollywood. I mean, none. Gurinder Chadha movies, yes, but she's British. Can you believe that?" She sighed. "They're missing so much!"

"Oddly enough, I know just what you mean," said Rachel. "That's why I made this dinner. You and I, we lived in Oxford, but we sort of ended up in Delhi. More apple *raita*?"

They ate in thoughtful silence.

"So Rubén has a girlfriend?" Melina ventured.

"Rubén has a girlfriend! Amazing. Haven't met her yet, but it sounds serious." Rachel transferred their plates to the small sink. "He's seeing her every day over the break."

"Are they going to get married?"

"Give them time, honey, they're only twenty."

Melina's fingers fidgeted with each other. "And . . . is there something you want to tell me?"

"Tell you what?"

"You know, married . . . engaged . . .."

"Lost, sweetie. What are you talking about?" said Rachel, puzzled.

Melina opened a cupboard and dragged down a packet of English biscuits imported in Rachel's luggage. She perched on the counter and ripped it open. "Something Ellie said." She took a careful nibble. Rachel held her hand out. Melina dropped a cookie into her palm. "She says you'll be getting engaged soon."

"What?" Rachel was bewildered. "To whom? There's no man, not even one on the horizon, my God, you were with me just last week. Believe me, since then, fate has not presented me with my Mr. Knightley, or Krishna, or any other hero you can think of. How did Ellie come up with that?"

"Tarot cards."

Rachel choked, coughed, and was pounded on the back. "Get out of town!" she sputtered. "Tarot cards, are you kidding me?"

"It was one night, I was in the family room watching 'Bride & Prejudice'. Ellie plops down next to me on their nine-foot sofa, and the next thing I know, she's offering to do them. The cards. She took some sort of course a long time ago."

"Eerie music plays, torches flicker, sweet maiden's mom wonders how to thwart stepmother's dark schemes." Rachel hummed in a minor key. "At least it's not tongue-piercing. So the cards showed me in white? Maybe they meant 'Swan Lake', which would be disastrous, since I was last *en pointe* at twelve, I'd probably land flat on my face."

Melina chose another cookie. "Ellie said the cards showed a man. And she was positive it wasn't one of my teachers or someone like that, it would be your man."

"*My* man."

"The cards were definite, Mom." Melina dusted sugar from her lips. "He's coming."

Putting her head down, Rachel laughed so hard the table shook. Crumbs spattered the floor.

"You okay?"

Rachel wiped her eyes. "Melina, that is one . . . incredible . . . story. Oh, God! Listen, hon, as I've said repeatedly to Steph, I'm way too busy for a man, but I promise to let you know if my own personal Tommy Lee shows up."

"Who?"

"Obscure reference, never mind. Time for bed."

Rachel rose early the next morning, a cold and clear Saturday with skies so blue they looked Crayola-ed. The day was booked: Melina would meet schoolfriends before classes began on Tuesday, two bags of outgrown clothes waited to be shlepped to the resale shop on Second Avenue, and Rachel still had too much reading left. Thank goodness college classes began in mid-January. On the other hand, every room in the house gleamed.

"Sweep through my place next," suggested Steph when she called. "I'll even create a dark and grimy corner especially for you. Wait, no, it all sparkles, since as of this morning the official meet-the-girlfriend is tomorrow night. You come, too, Rachel, you and Melina! Please? It would take some of the pressure off. We'll eat here, Rubén and Franny will leave after dinner to hike over to Times Square."

"What show are they seeing?"

Silence.

"Steph? Which show?"

"Rachel, Times Square? Zillions of people, descending ball, confetti?"

Hanging up, Rachel nearly tripped over the stack of books lying in wait. She must be really out of it, to completely forget about New Year's Eve. Perhaps it was the anxiety of preparing for a course she hated. If so, dinner at Steph's would be a good way to sashay into the next twelve months.

Two hours later, Rachel re-entered her home to an overload of Indian voices.

"Melina!" she yelled up the steps. A dark-haired figure still in pajamas bounced onto the landing. Rachel turned down her thumb. Exasperated, Melina disappeared, and the music weakened a notch. "More!" Rachel shouted. A moment later, and she could barely hear the male singer.

"Satisfied?" asked Melina. She pored through Rachel's bags. "What'd you get?"

"Movies, French cheese and bread, artisan chocolates, all for tomorrow night, so don't even think about opening them."

"Indian movies?" Melina looked as eager as a puppy. "No? *Kyon nahin?*"

"Because we haven't yet indoctrinated Steph, and you know how rigid she is about her films. Classics only. If you only knew her pride when you began to recite lines from 'It Happened One Night' at the tender age of four! We have to get her in the proper mood before introducing her to movies with emotion and dance. She's already biased against them."

Melina stroked the box of candy. "Chocolate, please, pretty please? Oh, you had a call." She ducked into the kitchen, returning with a scrap torn from a sheet of lined notebook paper. "Someone named Quentin Lake."

"Blake?"

"Lake, bigger than pond, smaller than ocean."

"Who is?"

Melina shrugged. "I should know?"

"I must say, it's refreshing to hear such a very N'Yawk expression rendered à la Judi Dench." Rachel laughed and picked up the phone. "I hope he's not one of those guys who sells real estate with a capital R. So incredibly compensatory. Hello, I'm returning a call from Quentin Lake?"

"Speaking," said a pleasant tenor voice.

"This is Rachel Hill, you called this morning?"

"Yes, Rachel, of course," the voice replied. "I called at the suggestion of Hussain."

"Hussain –?" Rachel riffled through her memory.

"Hussain Nassir. I believe he's your neighbor?"

"Oh, Noor's husband! Sorry, yes," Rachel replied, fending off Melina's attempts to listen in. "He asked you to call?"

"That's right." For some reason, Mr. Lake sounded perturbed. "He suggested you might be available to go out?"

Tailed by Melina, Rachel dashed up to her room.

" . . . I apologize for the lateness of the invitation, but tomorrow night there's a party, dozens of New York's finest – finest writers, I mean – will be there, so if you don't already have plans . . .."

New York's best writers, partying? Did she have pressing plans that would prevent her from chatting up some of the city's most famous residents? It was the kind of choice that would seem obvious to a random passerby, but wasn't she too busy? On the other hand, who could be too busy for this kind of invitation, even if it did involve a blind date?

"I'll keep Steph company," Melina whispered. "Go!" She gave a thumbs-up and scooted off Rachel's bed.

"Um, yes," Rachel told him, grimacing, "that sounds good, I can meet you there . . .."

A few moments later, she stepped out to the landing. Apparently Melina had lost interest. Excellent, it prevented her from having to explain a decision which, now that Rachel examined it, seemed less about the written word and more about distraction.

Plop! Something wet brushed her cheek. With a shriek, she jumped, grabbed the damp washcloth from the floor, and hurled it back up at Melina leaning over the third-floor banister. "Take that!"

"Yuggh!" Melina ran down, tailing Rachel to the living room. "You've got a New Year's Eve date?"

Rachel frowned. "Maybe I should call him back."

"Why? I heard him say writers, you like writers."

"Okay, okay! While you and Steph munch chocolate, I'll be swanning about with New York authors, famous and infamous, deep in conversation. Listening in, anyway."

Melina settled onto the next-to-last tread of the stairs and eyed Rachel through the posts. "It'll be like that party scene in 'You've Got Mail'. Hey, maybe Quentin Lake's the one Ellie saw in the tarot cards!"

"Oh, right. Where's that cold washcloth?" Rachel mimed tossing it.

Wielding an imaginary bat, Melina swung, missed, and fell backwards on the steps.

CHAPTER 8

Steph lived in the Village. The party was sited in the East 60s. Rachel had figured it would be nearly impossible on New Year's Eve to even find a taxi to convey her uptown, so she was taken aback when the cabbie, having magically appeared just as she flung up her hand, and maneuvered his way north while regaling Rachel with gossip of a previous fare, a rock star whose name she failed to recognize ("C'mon, you know him!"), deposited her a full twenty minutes early.

What was she supposed to do with twenty unexpected minutes in a thoroughly residential area? At night? In heels?

She examined the address she'd scribbled on the slip of bright yellow paper. Yes, there it was, a brownstone very like its neighbors. The rooms were already brightly lit. As she watched from the sidewalk, a uniformed maid set down an hors d'oeuvres-filled round platter below the window. A moment later, the maid was joined by a woman in taupe lace.

Taupe lace meant very well-heeled, indeed. Perhaps the party-givers had something to do with publishing, rather than writing. At least Rachel had the right kind of clothes, a silk top and an unimpeachable black taffeta skirt she bought two years ago for a now-forgotten university event. Dressing for social occasions was always so tricky. The word "casual", for example, could mean jeans. Or, come July, a sundress. Or it could be a codeword signifying "cashmere sweater and pearls".

Twenty minutes, she needed to keep herself entertained and safe for just twenty more minutes. In sensible shoes, she would simply circle the block. But black satin heels? She could likely make it across a room full of authors. Roaming irregular concrete sidewalks, however, presented challenges.

What would the heroine of an Indian movie do at this point? Rachel pondered, scanning the surrounding houses. Well, she'd have to keep on the move or seek a safe shop, to avoid Indian men accosting her in the hope of conversation or much greater intimacy. And then – Rachel smiled ruefully – circumstances would present the hero an opportunity to approach and rescue the woman from unwanted attention. Naturally . . . according to the conventions of Bollywood.

Not just Bollywood, though. How many American films also placed the hero in a white knight position? Plenty! Here, for example, was a situation ripe for coincidence and swelling violins, the heroine settling down to wait, and the hero – ta-daa! – ambling down the sidewalk toward her. Rachel shook her head. Thinking in *filmi* terms was too, too colorful . . . and unrealistic.

Crossing the street, she carefully lowered herself onto the steps of the brownstone directly opposite the party house, making sure her coat was tucked underneath to protect her legs from cold granite.

A large platter of hors d'oeuvres and a maid, she reflected, meant money. If this Mr. Lake was, like Noor's husband, an engineer of some sort, he clearly had connections to wealthy wordsmiths or people who dealt with them. Editors? Agents? Whatever. Writers presumably enjoyed expensive food and drink like everyone else. More, maybe.

Quentin Lake had described himself telegraphically. Tall and rangy, redhead, handlebar moustache. Rachel recalled a boy she'd dated in college, with a similar moustache. He had waxed his, so he looked like a beau from the 1890s, as though at any moment he might clap on a boater and fling one leg over a velocipede. She'd be bound to recognize Quentin in such a moustache, unless the room was filled with refugees from barbershop quartets.

She had departed Steph's a few moments after Rubén and his Franny. In the doorway she gave Steph a kiss and a thumbs-up. "Franny's great! Lively and cute and totally into him."

"You think?" Steph fidgeted with the doorknob. "This is his first real girlfriend."

"She's a catch and so is he. They're sweet together, and I loved her stories, Rubén needs that kind of humor in his life." Rachel took hold of her friend's shoulders and gave them a light shake. "You did good. How do I look?" she asked to distract.

Adjusting a wrinkle, Steph nodded. "Just don't lose any glass slippers, m'dear."

"Abfab, Mummy darling!" Melina called from a plushy deep chair.

"Abfab, indeed," Rachel murmured now. A door opened behind her, spilling light onto the steps.

"Well, hey!" came a male voice.

Rachel turned.

"Don't get up," the man continued. His bulky silhouette lurched, in its left hand a champagne bottle. "Henry. I'm Henry. Up on third floor," he waved to it, "and was just gettin' started cebrelate . . . celebrate, came out for air, and look who I found!" He lowered himself to the step beside her.

"I'm just going." Rachel got to her feet. A pincer at her wrist, however, kept her from dashing across the street.

"Where? Party's just gettin' started!"

"Are you invited, too?" she asked, light.

"Too?"

"Your neighbor's event," she pointed, "right there. No?" She pirouetted and twisted her wrist from his sharp grip. "*Adiós!*"

"Wait!"

Rachel swiftly crossed the macadam and took the taupe-lace's steps at a run. Behind, she heard a car stop. She glanced back. The cab blocked her from the celebratory Henry.

"Hey, come back!" came his voice.

Hurriedly, she rang the bell. The door opened, revealing the maid from the window. Behind her, the cab's sole passenger, by his height and breath male, bounded up the steps.

A cry came from across the street. "Hey! In the black coat, what's your name?"

Rachel surrendered the coat in a rose-fragrant hall.

"Sounds like he wants you," the man behind her said. "I'm meeting my date here," he told the maid, "medium height, light brown hair?"

"Total stranger," murmured Rachel, flustered. She glanced up. The tall man's handlebar moustache was, though snowy white, admirably thick. "Quentin?"

He glanced down, his eyes severe. "Are you Rachel Hill?"

Rachel felt icily disapproved of. Across-the-street Henry was still calling, she could hear him through the closed door. Perhaps Quentin thought the stranger was a clumsily discarded lover.

"How do you do?" said Quentin. "Let's go in, shall we?"

Twenty minutes later, the house was crammed with people discussing books and writing and tussles with editors in a struggle entertainingly different from the one academics faced. Nobody expected a college professor to write bestsellers. Yet Rachel fervently wished herself elsewhere. Across the street with Henry, even. If only she'd asked Steph to fake an emergency call! The party swirled with talk and arguments by people whose names she recalled from book sections – or was it gossip columns? – yet rather than eavesdrop on an account of the depredations of New York Times reviewers, or a comparison of recent advances, Quentin kept maneuvering her to one side, drenching her with a shower of anecdotes about himself.

He drew her to a ceramic bowl of pistachios, shelling nut after nut and popping each in his mouth with a moist sucking sound. "You're too young to even know where Vietnam is, I bet," he said.

"East Asia. I took geography," Rachel replied disarmingly. "Did you have a low draft number?"

"Five." Two more pistachios. "They wanted my ass. I was living in Virginia with my dad, he got me out."

"Out of the draft?" she asked, puzzled.

"Out of society. I went underground, vanished. Didn't use my social security number for anything. Traveled for five years, worked construction, waited table, anything that paid cash." Five more pistachios met their fate. "But that's behind me. These days I have it made, I work on projects I like, the rest of the year I wake up late. I live alone, I prefer it."

"'I Am A Rock', then?"

Quentin nodded, sloshing his scotch. "You get that! That's very good, I'm impressed." He shelled another pistachio. "So, Rachel, what would it take to make your life less boring?"

"He didn't say that!"

"Oh, he did."

"What did you say? I'd have left heel marks on his instep," Steph confided to Melina.

"I considered tossing my wine at his bristly and very white moustache, but it was a burgundy. Dry-cleaning bills," Rachel amplified. "So I ended up admitting that my life may be frantic or frustrating or full of minor challenges, but it's never boring. And exit, stage left, out the door."

"Arrogant ass! From a purely professional standpoint, Rachel, it's total projection, the guy's own life is a yawn, so he tells you yours is."

"Exactly. I found my coat, and hailed a cabbie who once drove Sting. I should have left sooner." Rachel licked chocolate from her fingers. "But it was a lot like reading one of those gruesome stories in the Post. You know you should turn the page, but somehow you can't. Then the final comment, the coup de grâce –" She drew her thumb across her throat.

"It's so true," Steph mused, "give a loser enough conversational rope, and he'll do you the favor of hanging himself."

"'Many a good hanging prevents a bad marriage'," Rachel quoted.

Steph handed her another square of bittersweet chocolate. "That Will Shakespeare, always one for the *bon mot*."

"No Bollywood hero would ask you a question like that," Melina said, decisive. "Can you imagine? They wouldn't, they just wouldn't! Even when they argue, they're better than that."

"That's an interesting yardstick. What would a Hindi movie protagonist do?" Rachel mused, interested.

"He'd be a hell of a lot more polite."

"Melina!"

"He would," her daughter answered, and popped another chocolate into her mouth.

"Wait, wait, what's this hero business? What hero? Joseph Campbell-type?" asked Steph.

"It's the classic male role in Indian film," Rachel explained. "Based on the *Ramayana*. The guy who's good-looking, generally fair-skinned, also kind and virtuous, like Lord Ram."

"Dances well," supplied Melina. "And he's not violent, except when he tackles the bad guys. Those, he eliminates."

"A sense of humor, and he doesn't try to seduce the heroine. An all-around Boy Scout, generally. There are exceptions, where he becomes the hero in the last ten minutes. You know, steered down the wrong path, he wakes up – poof!"

"Ethics, then? Got it. So how many of those do you think are out there, I mean in real life?" Steph's nose wrinkled with doubt. "I'll give you five bucks for every one you find between now and June."

"It just wasn't meant to be, Noor. Another one? Um . . . thanks, but it's not the right time for me . . ." Rachel glanced at her kitchen clock, "okay, sure, I'll send them back at five." She hung up.

From upstairs came high-pitched laughter and a Bollywood soundtrack, the Indian *dhol* drums in a rapid beat. They were painting nails, Melina and the two Nassir girls. Nema and Neg had appeared at the door at ten o'clock sharp this Monday morning, the day after New Year's, clutching gifts of Bedouin textiles which Melina enthusiastically draped over the living room furniture. The girls then escaped upstairs to revel in nail polish, an item Noor Nassir wore herself but considered inappropriate for her daughters unless they acquired it while with Melina, to whom she had taken an immediate liking.

Sixty nails would take some time to dry, re-paint, and dry again. They'd need extra sustenance. Rachel threw popcorn into the microwave and hunted for cookies.

Noor's daughters were apparently well-acquainted with Indian movies. When Melina brought out a DVD, they grabbed it ("We just saw this at home!") and raced up the stairs, leaving Rachel to reflect on the long arm of Bollywood. So the Middle East, too, was frantic for Hindi-language product. That meant an audience of millions more.

Rachel dumped the popcorn in a bowl and carried it in one hand, cookies in the other, up to Melina's door. "Food!" she called.

The door opened a notch, releasing a distinct bittersweet smell. Melina's hand appeared.

"Open wide, here comes the airplane!"

"*Mom.*"

Rachel caught a glimpse of Nema and Neg, whose nails shone in various shades of crimson. They had also experimented heavily with eyeshadow . . . which Noor would never see, as her daughters routinely scrubbed their faces before leaving Melina.

She descended to her own room. Critical theory, she found, mixed well with New Year's Day parades. She gave the

TV screen a quick glance. On it drifted a Rose Parade float covered in the ubiquitous "vegetable matter". Flowers, grasses, seeds, pods, anything was fair use as long as it had once grown from the soil. There was an embracingness about that rule that appealed to Rachel. It was rather like Bollywood movies, which typically included romance for the love-inclined, drama for angst aficionados, colorful costumes and attractive contemporary clothes for the fashion-aware, and humor, music and dance for everyone. Which was, now that she thought about it, very Shakespearean of them. The Bard had broken with classic drama's rules, pleasing himself as well as his audience.

Where Bollywood went further was in marketing reach and ingenuity. Shakespeare would be green with envy. In a stunningly effective practice, Indian movies' songs were released weeks ahead of a film's premiere, guaranteeing that people would memorize lyrics and download ringtones, and increasing the chances they would buy tickets to the screened film. On this commercial point, Rachel felt confused. Did the music sell the films, or were films made to sell music? No matter. There was, indeed, something for everyone.

On the floor, Melina strung a necklace. "My resolution for this year," she said, "is more beading and poetry."

"Together?" asked Rachel, amused.

"Before I start high school and have to worry about my transcript."

"Simple," Rachel said, and nudged her with an elbow, "work hard and don't worry. Everything will be all right."

Floats had driven past without incident, football players had run or thrown or hurled themselves into each other without substantial damage, and Rachel had put a major dent in the pages awaiting her. Now to further chip at them. She maneuvered to the center of her bed. The comforter stretched before her like Siberian plains, flat and winter-white.

"Nisha's sending me another poster."

"Don't tell me, it's Hrithik Roshan again!"

Melina nodded. "Her cousins mail them from India. Her mum's still into Amitabh, Parvati's a big Shah Rukh fan, so Nisha's got Hrithik all to herself."

"Not a bad choice, he's talented and hard-working and handsome. And he sounds like a decent guy in real life, seems to love his wife and children," Rachel mused. "You could do worse."

"When the poster comes, I'll use the tube to send her this necklace. Maybe some earrings, too. Can I get some of those Indian earrings, the really long ones that fasten over the ear? I could figure out how they're made."

"Sure." Rachel tucked her pen into her hair. "Listen, I just had this vision: all over the world, girls are sending each other posters, they're gossiping, e-mailing, texting, about their favorite Bollywood actors, who are virtually unknown here in the US, except for NRIs."

"I know. It's like a secret club!" exclaimed Melina.

"There's something oddly reassuring about that, hon. It means there still are differences, we haven't yet come under one corporate American umbrella. Forget McDonald's and Burger King. People still speak distinct languages even if they've learned marketplace English, they still eat *parathas* and *idlis*, they either adore Kareena Kapoor or can't stand her. There's richness in that."

Melina grimaced. "Ugghh. Sounds like one of your lectures."

"Forget richness, then. Call it cool."

She was in the midst of e-mails on the third floor, in the tiny room that functioned as both office and guestroom, when Melina appeared with the phone. "It's Jenny from work, but I'm talking to Sarah –"

"Give!" Rachel extended her hand.

"Later," Melina told Sarah regretfully, pressed flash, and landed on the sofa.

"Hi, Jen. What? Um, I don't think so . . . really? . . . well, I don't . . . okay . . . okay. No, it's okay. You owe me, though! A pound, at least." Rachel laughed. "*Next* Monday? Put me down as a show, then. No problem. Good night." She handed Melina the phone and turned back to the computer screen.

"What's next Monday?"

"Departmental meeting," said Rachel, "a week in advance. So Harris will get only half of us. Which means he'll have to call another meeting a week later."

"What does Jenny owe you a pound for?"

Rachel flushed. "Nothing. No big deal. Call your friend back, Bini."

Melina dialed. "Sarah? Hi, my mom's done, but she's embarrassed about something she won't tell me, and I'm standing here watching her write my uncle Steve in Denmark and try to ignore me telling you how she's totally embarrassed about –"

"Ohmigod!" Rachel protested. "Jen asked me to go out with some relative, just as a favor, I'm the only single woman his age she knows. In this whole city, how is that possible?"

"Did you hear that?" Melina paused. "Sarah says better luck with *this* one," she told Rachel, and bounced out.

CHAPTER 9

F riday afternoon, and Rachel had essentially mopped up her get-up-to-speed reading, inking notes in the books' margins. Only a few pages remained. She had – again! – scrubbed and straightened, so the house was radiant, a good omen for the coming year.

It was her Bollywood book that seduced Rachel's attention. Chapter 4, The Hero. Naturally. A hero's quest centered the story, though the Bard wrote within the Western tradition well-described by Joseph Campbell and others. She should throw that in, Campbell was useful shorthand. In the Indian tradition, however, and – she scribbled – within the modern film tradition, the hero's quest was sometimes related to the family quest. *Where the hero stumbles*, she wrote, *what picks him up?* Then there was the hero as classical striver, as warrior, as lover – aha! – as dutiful son, dutiful subject in Shakespeare's day . . . her list lengthened. This would be a fruitful chapter.

Cold, sunny weather held, which meant tomorrow's encounter would be a pleasant stroll around Greenwich Village with Jenny's husband's cousin, beginning to date after a painful divorce. "It was last year, totally Stalingrad," Jenny had confided, "and by the end –"

"He was boiling leather?"

"Just about. Had a lawyer with bipolar. He sounds like a nice guy, Rachel! Been out on Long Island for years, but he'd like to come into the city. I can give him your e-mail? Don't back out on me! Chocolate!"

"Oh, twist my arm. The darker the better."

"Noted." Jenny smiled.

The resultant exchange of e-mails revealed a man who sounded amiable, interested, and knew how to use spellcheck.

"And you give extra points for spelling," noted Melina, a bowl of gorp in her hands. Her scarlet nails selected a dried cranberry, which she regarded with distaste. "I don't like craisins."

"I know, but they're packed full of good stuff and antioxidants and miracle drugs and the Holy Grail," Rachel replied. "By the way, your uncle Steve will be here for two days in February."

"Good! So what are you and," Melina peered at the screen, "Michael, going to do?"

"One of those self-directed walking tours through the Village. His suggestion."

"Aren't those kind of long?"

"It depends how fast you go. There's lots to see, and people around, and you can skip over a house, or cross the street," explained Rachel. "Then there's food, and things to talk about, it's not like being stuck in a dark theater."

"Oh," Melina said, her voice full of doubt. She picked up an almond.

"Steph thought it was a great idea."

"Fine."

"What?"

"Nothing!"

"I'll be back by three, do homework first, then you can use the phone, and there *will* be a quiz."

"My jailer," Melina complained. "Do I get time off for good behavior?"

"Does 'good' mean finishing homework?

"Go, go!"

The day held chill radiance. In a few hours, downtown would warm. Rachel strode west, avoiding a dog on a long leash, its owner engaged in conversation on his phone. Her mind ran again to her book. Chapter 4, The Hero. Chapter 5. The Heroine? As few as there were in Shakespeare's work, and of less importance in Indian film than the hero, still, they deserved their own chapter, if only for parity. And just because male filmmakers might consider them of less consequence didn't mean their audiences felt the same.

Memory carried Rachel back several months to a dinner with the Patel family. The table was animated, since Pinky and Sanjay's older daughter, Parvati, had brought her fiancé, Arjun.

"I like movies as much as the next NRI," Arjun said, passing Rachel the eggplant *raita*, "it's just what in the world do most Indian movies have to do with real life?"

A torrent of protest arose.

"I'm serious! I'm in business, I see clients all day long, solve this problem, Arjun, what do you have for me today, Arjun? So when I have to watch all that singing and dancing, when Shah Rukh Khan teases a woman or shakes his finger or runs his hand through his hair one more time. . .."

"He doesn't do that anymore!"

" . . . what does that have to do with my life? And Karan Johar, so sentimental, tug at my heart!" He played an imaginary violin. "So excessive!"

"How about entertainment value? Keeping your fiancée happy, yeh? Oh, and the latest James Bond?" Parvati asked, nudging him. "You're going to fire guns, run round rooftops, do parkour?"

"Granted, that's escapism of another kind, but at least –"

"You liked 'Lakshya'," Sanjay pointed out from the head of the table.

"'Lakshya' was different."

"It had Hrithik in it," observed Nisha, "and he's brilliant."

"And Farhan Akhtar directing," Parvati added.

"What about that first song, the hero dancing in front of black mirrors?" Pinky teased Arjun. "That, you like, *javai.*"

"All right, *saas-ji*, that was good," Arjun responded, smiling. "But the story's of a boy becoming a man, not the usual Bollywood nonsense."

"They're not nonsense!" Nisha protested.

"How about 'Rang de Basanti'? You liked that, and 'Don', the remake. *So* ordinary life, gangsters!" Parvati pointed out, ironic. "You said 'Om Shanti Om' showed how much Farah Khan loves Bollywood, to take the mickey that way! What about –?"

"'Eklavya'!" her father interrupted.

Movie titles shot at Arjun from the table.

"'Omkara'!"

"'Dor'!"

"'Swades'!"

"'Krrish'!"

"'Chak De India', you liked it more than 'Bend It Like Beckham'!" shouted Nisha.

"I'll give you lot another title, all right?" said Arjun. "'Welcome'." Around him, the Patels groaned. "See? Ridiculous film, but Indians ate it up! Entirely proves my point!"

The air filled with protest and more titles.

Arjun's hands came up in surrender. "Stop! Let's give Rachel Aunty a chance to talk."

"Thank you. Look, each year, eight hundred movies are made in India –"

Arjun rolled his eyes. "Most of those within a few weeks, Aunty, the mythologicals, little dialogue and traditional plot."

" – they can't all be nonsense," Rachel continued. "And when you remember they have to be made with so many considerations, that children will watch, and people in very rural, conservative areas, and –"

"That's what's holding back Indian film!" Arjun slapped the table. "It's the rare movie that shows India for what it is."

"Oh, and American and British films aren't fictionalized?" Sanjay put in. "Rose-colored glasses, *beta*."

"Maybe that's a strength, too?" Rachel asked. She took the bowl of chutney from Arjun. "Because Hindi movies, the ones rated U, anyway, don't dive into Hollywood lowest-common-denominator trash . . . let me put it this way, it's nice to know there are movies my daughter can see without my worrying *what* she'll see. And the tenderness of the couples, the sweetness and playfulness, that's something almost entirely lost in American film. Tenderness, commitment, what's wrong with those? Better than cynicism and emotional darkness and sex, sex, sex. Better than focusing on entertaining a demographic of adolescent boys. From where I stand, the best of Indian film grows better each year."

"I heard you say you didn't like 'Kabhi Alvida Na Kehna'," Arjun objected.

"Because it didn't even suggest the possibility of marriage counseling for the two couples! They're in New York, therapists are thick on the ground!" said Rachel, exasperated. "My best friend is one, in fact. But no, Shah Rukh and Rani have to fumble around and lie to their spouses, cause them intense pain, and eventually leave. No mediation, even! But that's a good example," she leaned forward, "of an Indian movie that's different from the standard. And really, Arjun, doesn't the standard change every few years? It's a lot like fashion, I've borrowed enough movies now to know that Indian cinema re-creates itself perhaps more than any other. Right?"

"Eh, Arjun!" Sanjay tapped his almost-son-in-law. "Listen to the Shakespeare don!"

"Because if you think –"

"But that's it, innit?" Arjun protested. "We don't like to think!"

Catching her husband's eye, Pinky attempted to broker some peace. "Arjun, *beta*, please."

"I don't mean . . . look, Indians, at least the ones still in India, they go to the cinema for what? Intellectual challenge? It's not France!" exclaimed Arjun, leaning forward. "They go for entertainment, yes, forget all about how their life is one bloody thing after another – sorry, *saas-ji* – but mostly they go to feel. Right? Am I wrong, here? Eh? Parvati? Your *naani*, didn't she love to cry at films?"

Parvati nodded.

"It's all about emotion! The way the film makes you feel inside, if it turns you inside out, you're laughing, you're crying, you're scared, elated . . . all of it, Rachel Aunty!" Arjun leaned back in his chair. "If you get tears in your eyes, good. Tears running down your cheeks, even better. Bawling like a baby, hey, the director really knows his stuff! And that . . . that's Indian movies in a nutshell." Arjun's breath came in a whoosh. "Pass the *dal*?"

Remembering the discussion – which ended only when Pinky Patel brought out dessert, a creamy *kesari rabdi* ("I make it in the microwave, you'd like the recipe?") – Rachel pondered. What would Shakespeare say, aside from a well-turned witticism? The man loved to play with words. But darkness . . . Shakespeare had nearly invented comic relief, after all. Classic drama allowed for either tragedy or comedy. Shakespeare mixed them up. And – well, this was the thing, wasn't it? – he was whole-hearted about his tales. Darkness, where it existed, was horrifying. The Macbeths, for example, were a grim, appalling couple. No effort was made to excuse them or coddle their sensibilities.

The same recognition kept Bollywood busy. Rachel dug into her purse for a scrap of paper to jot down this bit of clarity.

Speaking of clarity . . . Rachel realized she had no detailed description of the physical Michael. Jenny hadn't mentioned hair, eyes, build, height. Neither had he, and for some reason Rachel had forgotten to ask. "Blue shirt", the man's only identifier, might mean anything from pale buttondown to navy Izod to a turquoise T. She might have to ask dozens of blue-clad strangers if they were named Michael. Fortunately, she did have the number of his cell.

Ninety minutes later, Rachel wished she had called that number and faked a cough, persistent fainting spells, anything for avoidance.

Running late, Michael agreed to meet her on a street corner. He showed up out of breath, with one gold earring, a soul patch beneath his lower lip, and a thoroughly shaved head. No wonder Jenny had omitted physical details. She had also failed to mention Michael's enthusiasm for Islanders hockey, his first – and nearly sole – talking point.

"You like hockey? No? Man, what are we gonna talk about? I go to every home match," he told her, "no way was my stinkin' ex-wife gonna get those season tickets! Sometimes me and my buddies, we paint our chests with 'Islanders' and line up together."

"Really?" said Rachel, bemused.

"I'm an S! The first S, that is, the last S is a guy named Conor, he just joined. But what I really wanna do," he leaned close, "is move out to LA. Man, the weather, their market's gonna shift, and then there's the Ducks!"

Baffled, Rachel shook her head.

"The Ducks, the Ducks, the Anaheim Ducks! You don't know the Ducks? The Stanley Cup? Man!" He regarded Rachel with disbelief. "Plus, like I said, the market's gotta shift someday."

"The stock market?"

Michael's expression displayed pity. "Real estate."

Comprehension dawned. "You sell houses?"

"I sure do!" He fished out a business card. It displayed the uppercase R. He pointed to it. "See? With the S, that makes me a capital guy! Get it?" He roared with laughter.

Rachel felt a surge of empathy for his stinkin' ex-wife.

"Pass the mint chutney. Okay, imagine you and I are walking along, I say, 'hey, Melina, look at that roof detail up there, looks like waves, maybe the original owner was a sea captain', and you say –?"

"Maybe he built ships?" With a torn-off bit of whole wheat tortilla masquerading as *roti*, Melina scooped up a bite of *kadhai paneer*. "Or he was once shipwrecked?"

"Ah, but if you're Michael, it's 'oh, yeah, let me tell you about the house I sold last week', and you think maybe the house was on the water, or it's owned by a boatbuilder, or at some point we're actually going to link to the wave motif. But we never do. It's about sales, it's all about sales. Or ice hockey. Or sales of hockey equipment." Rachel shivered.

Melina popped a piece of green pepper in her mouth. "So how long were you with him?"

"I'm not sure. Once the space-time continuum imploded, I kind of lost track."

"What happened to the new yardstick?"

"The new –? Oh, your Bollywood hero one?"

"It would have gotten you out of there a lot sooner," Melina pointed out practically.

"He was a surprise, all right. I don't have time for this," Rachel complained to Steph.

At her office desk, she cradled her phone between chin and shoulder and scanned class lists. Her three sections of comedies contained a fairly even mix of male and female students, which should make for lively discussion, as both were more than willing to initiate comments, even on Shakespeare's double entendres and – to 21st century sensibilities – obscure sexual innuendo.

"You're looking at this backwards," Steph's voice pointed out. "Remember your brother Steve and his baseball analogy about dumb girls?"

"Look at my stupid critical theory class, ten students, nine male? How did that happen?" Rachel stared at the list. "Two Daniels, two Adams, Brett, Takeo . . . one lone Maya."

"Steve was going through first-date hell, remember?"

"Steve? No. Why the hell did so many young men register for this particular course? Wasn't there anything else available? Did they have no seniority at all?"

"Steve kept getting set up with losers, girls who drank too much, were addicted to abusive ex-boyfriends. I felt sorry for him, but he said no, it was three up, three down."

"Talk about imbalance . . .."

"Rachel, there's two minutes before my next client, listen up! Steve pitched baseball! Three up, three down. He was sending them away, but that's success, because those girls couldn't keep up, they didn't have the right stuff!"

"'The right stuff'?" Rachel mocked. "Who died and left you Sports Illustrated?"

"I have a son," said Steph, with a whiff of smug. "Strike-outs, a pitcher wants. You've had two. Fine!"

"Fine, good for me. So why do I feel like I lost an entire morning?"

"You're not thinking baseball. Oops! Bye."

Rachel hung up. Thinking baseball? No, that she wasn't. Definitely not. But maybe . . . an image arose, a rather frivolous scene from a Hindi movie, an arrogant girl looking over a line of eager college guys in her search for an acceptable, good-looking date: "Two . . . three . . . never mind . . . minus!"

Rachel would never do anything so cruelly dismissive, would she? On the other hand, she was no longer willing to ignore her gut instinct. She's done that once before. Twice before, she thought, remembering Ian.

"So how's your book coming?"

Rachel laughed. "Yeah, Steph, you want to hear about the book. Pass me that big knife."

"You're right, I have no desire to hear about the book. Here. What now?"

Rachel opened a cabinet door and brought out a spice grinder. "Crush the *anardana*, the dried pomegranate seeds. This way they don't fly all over the kitchen." She dumped the seeds in, closed the cover and started the machine. A high-pitched whine filled the room.

Over the noise, Steph shouted.

The whine arrested. "Sorry?"

"I said, there's a guy at my temple –"

"*Your* temple?"

"High holy days, I'm there! Anyway, there's this new single man, Chad Weiss, he's getting hits from all over."

Rachel dumped the *anardana* into a bowl of *chakki atta*, India's finely-ground whole-wheat flour. "Forget it. I'm busy, I have no time, and I don't need another stroll around the Village."

"You're so rigid," Steph complained.

"Me? Rigid? Who is it who won't even watch an Indian movie because she's too cinematically pure?"

"You need to eat, right? Drink, maybe?"

Rachel stopped mixing. "What are you saying, three up, three down?"

"There you go!"

"Steph –"

"Rachel. Why don't you tell me all about your book?"

"Why don't you take care of this dough?"

Steph carried the light-brown mass to the table, sprinkled more flour, and began to roll a small ball of dough pancake-flat. "You're not going to shut me up. Think of all the great stories you already have!" She glanced at the open cookbook beside her. "Who would think of adding minced cauliflower and spices to bread dough, then rolling it into circles and frying them?"

"Indians?"

"You can't stop me asking Chad!"

"So ask him. Ask away," said Rachel.

What could she do to make sure her critical theory class discussions weren't flooded by a torrent of male perspective? Rachel rocked in her office chair, gazed out the dusty window at a sky grown increasingly gray, and absentmindedly nibbled her Pilot Extra Fine. She'd never run into this problem before, a class so lopsided as to gender. There were multiple options, of course: talk to Maya Bennett beforehand . . . encourage her comments . . . foster a sense of fairness, and value fairness over justice, for with mere justice Maya would be allowed to speak only ten percent of the time . . . ask for students' birth order and family composition . . ..

Her notes multiplied: ♂ *students – any sisters??* Perhaps there were no sisters, perhaps their own parents had done as so many Indian couples these days, rid themselves of female fetuses so that smaller families contained a greater percentage of boys. The "missing girls phenomenon", it was called. Rachel snorted. Twenty years down the road, what would those young men do? Just as in China, and the stability of every society depended on the balance of –

"Excuse me."

Rachel jumped.

"Sorry, I've been standing here . . . may I?" Marc Harris gestured to the empty chair. He slid into it, leaned his arms on Rachel's desk, and smiled, his eyes very blue. His chin was very firm. His shoulders were very broad.

Rachel gave herself a mental shake. "What?"

"You look puzzled . . . and suspicious," he observed.

"Why call a meeting early in January, when so many of us are on the slopes, soaking up rays, whatever?" Rachel asked.

"Oh, that! Let's see. It could be I need the practice . . . or I'm out to prove what a take-charge guy I am . . . or I welcome the chance to gather with nearly fifty people in a too-small room. Nice and cozy."

"You won't get anywhere near fifty."

"Maybe not. Still, it sets the pace, worth a shot. I'm all for risk, as long as it doesn't involve other people's health or well-being. Going over class lists?" he asked, forestalling her reply. "What's with all the guys signing up for critical theory?"

"I was just wondering the same thing. I thought maybe you paid them," she said with heavy irony.

"Did you? Just make sure they don't barrel over the young woman. Important to encourage honesty, too. It's only that one class that's male-heavy, not the intellectual world."

"Got it, boss."

"Is that your daughter?" He pointed to a photo on the ledge behind her.

Rachel took up the picture. "Melina, yes. She's in eighth grade this year."

"She looks sweet."

"She *is* sweet." She set the photo back with a thump. "Something more?"

"How's your book coming?"

"It's . . . coming."

"Glad to hear it." Marc bit back a grin. "I'd like to hear more. How about lunch? Utterly collegial, we'll talk nothing but your work, honest."

"Lunch? Le Cirque was booked for dinner?"

Startled, the blue eyes met hers. "Well, yeah, it's always booked. But I'll see what they have in the way of a two-top next month."

"No, no . . . it was a joke," she said hastily.

"But I owe you one, and I hate being in debt." He shrugged. "Very Micawberish of me."

"An admirable quality, but still no." Rachel shoved several unnecessary books onto her blotter. She opened the thick one on top. "Too busy, way too busy."

"For Le Cirque? With . . . what is that, *The Odyssey*? A little off-period, wouldn't you say?"

Rachel regarded him coolly. "A good story is a good story."

"Okay, okay!" Marc's hands came up. "You'll let me know, though, when I can discharge my debt?"

"I'll get Jen to page you, right?" she replied, exasperated, and was relieved to see his back.

Problem number one with Marc Harris was his confidence. The man was breathtakingly assured of his own value. Unlike the self-doubting Hamlet, Marc was more on the order – though less bombastic – of the early Benedick from "Much Ado About Nothing", that confident soldier who, while he might feel stung by a well-tossed verbal barb, never doubted himself as a man.

Aha! There was a theme! Rachel scrabbled for a free piece of paper. *Self-confidence as males -- Indians and WS? Ex: Benedick, Amitabh characters. Versus self-doubt/realism, examples?* She paused. Hamlet, naturally. Macbeth, initially swept by ambition. She would take a look at the other tragedies. But in the comedies . . . nearly any lover except Petruchio carried fretful doubts. She added Petruchio's name to the first list. Oh! How about the contrasting young men of "Kaho Naa Pyaar Hai"? The first naïve, innocent, touchingly young, and the other – his visual match, aha, another Shakespearean theme, mistaken identity and twinship! – an Indian raised in New Zealand, thus more Kiwi-assured. And what about – she scribbled – "Jab We Met", where on a train to Delhi the hero Aditya started out suicidal?

There was more, she was sure, a great deal more to be mined for her book.

The book. How would her colleagues in Oxford evaluate her subject? Their imagined disbelief echoed. She could hear Liam's snigger. "Shakespeare and *Bollywood?*" For them, Indian movies were tremendously downmarket, so to compare the Bard's work was the literary equivalent of Mozart versus Dolly Parton, Kensington meets East Ham.

She'd suffer less academic contempt with an absorption in fashion. At least fashion carried names – Dior, Prada, McCartney – with which even scholars were familiar. Yet she was convinced that Shakespeare himself wouldn't have been so arrogant. As she'd pointed out to Marc, there were no new stories, and if

Indian movies cribbed from Western film, so had Shakespeare borrowed from all sorts of authors, and not very subtly, either. Whole lines, even passages, he'd stolen. He'd view Mumbai filmmakers as worthy successors, with a wink-wink and a nod, and contemporary Mumbai – the former Bombay – as a sister to Elizabethan London. Overcrowded and often violent, with an appalling divide between the ultra-rich and those who lived literally on the streets, they were both noisy with persistent traffic and hawkers – in Mumbai's case, electronic music, as well – and smelled strongly of refuse, sewage, manufacturing debris, and heated bodies. While Indians preferred far more frequent baths than Shakespeare's compatriots, getting enough clean water to shower with was a daily challenge for millions.

Yet both cities possessed enormous energy and vitality and hope.

Besides, what was déclassé in the UK was exotic in America. Her Oxford colleagues' derision? Rachel snapped her fingers to it.

She slipped downstairs. Melina had fallen asleep, her head pillowed on a red fleece jacket. It took a steady arm and whispered encouragement to urge her upstairs to her pink blankets.

In Rachel's room, the curtained window let in a dim percentage of city light. The photographs on her walls were a collection of gray petals and sepals and leaves.

She pulled off her turtleneck and tossed it toward the hamper. Overly confident, that was Marc Harris. He might confess to some minor inability – say, with perfume – but really, the man considered himself incredibly competent. Rachel could see it in his very body language. He carried himself with the ease, that basic comfort with his physicality, possessed by athletes. If ever he were to fidget, it would mean it was for effect, or he was truly flummoxed. Rachel could not imagine circumstances that would faze Marc Harris. A recalcitrant administration? Aggressive panhandlers? Charging rhino?

Late in the afternoon, she had stopped by Jenny's desk.

"You're safe," Jenny replied to her unasked question, "he stepped out."

"Not funny, Jen."

"Actually, it is," Jenny said, grinning. She rummaged under her desk and handed Rachel a bar of Lindt bittersweet. "So, I gather the walk with Michael wasn't a ten?"

"No," Rachel admitted, ripping open the chocolate, "not even close. Want some?"

Jenny accepted a square. "Nick doesn't know his cousins that well. Was it the Islanders thing?"

"You *knew* about the S?"

"I'd heard rumors of an S," Jen confessed.

"The S was not good, the references to the stinkin' ex-wife were worse. And cross real estate off your list."

"Well, don't give up hope!" Jenny peered at her, terribly intense.

"In fact, Jen," Rachel now murmured, stretching out in her bed, "I have tons of hope. Mainly, I hope for a life free from bad surprises."

CHAPTER 10

I brought the temple directory!" called Steph. She dodged Melina, who hurtled toward the kitchen, her weighted backpack swaying dangerously from one shoulder. "You okay?"

"Five minutes behind." Melina broke a banana from its bunch and careened to the front door. "Bye, Mom!"

"Wait wait wait wait wait!" and a clatter of descending steps.

"I can't!" Melina wailed, yet paused beside the open door.

Rachel threw her arms about her daughter and immediately released her. "Hug! Kiss! Good luck with French!" she called. She closed the door. "Monsieur LeBlanc from Nantes, with an unfortunate crush on Le Pen," she explained.

"A closet Nazi, that's what her school calls diversity? Look, facebook!" Steph opened the directory on the kitchen table. She pointed at Rachel's legs, encased in black nylon. "You might want to finish getting dressed."

Rachel glanced down. "Oh, no! Well, maybe Hussain Nassir already left for work." She sprang up the steps and returned after a few moments, legs obscured by a wool skirt. "If Noor saw me, I'll never hear the end of it. 'I'm so sorry, Noor, it was a mistake.'" Her voice altered. "'Girls don't need to see that!' Well, yes, Noor, I'm aware."

Steph tapped a directory page. "Chad Weiss. I asked around, like you he's done internet dating, lunches, etcetera, but these days it's personal introductions only. Would it kill you to look?"

"One look." Rachel peered at the photo of challenging eyes, pronounced chin, curly brown hair. "Not bad. But who cares?"

"Divorced, grown children, he and his brother once ran a B & B in Vermont so they could ski. He's a broker. Also a self-taught authority on nineteenth-century British painting."

Rachel closed the directory. "What's in it for me?"

"Rachel! Believe me, half the women in that temple are either rubbing up against him during coffee or setting him up with sisters or grown daughters. The guy's doing family dinners, drinks and chat, lunch meets, these women are like locusts! What does that guy Tannenbaum call people like you, 'psycho-Semitics'? You're sweet, smart, a Jewish shiksa, this man could be your *beshert!* At least you two could hang out in museums. Let me give him your name and number," Steph pleaded.

"You don't care about me or my tender emotions, you just want to beat those women at their own game," said Rachel, amused. "How very Indian of you, Steph! Setting up little *shaadis*, you should print up new business cards."

"Fine, criticize, but can I give Chad your number? I'll throw in a pitcher of sangría!"

"Sangría? Tempting. But not tempting enough."

"Sangría plus tapas, then. No? What? What do you –?" Steph's face fell. "Oh, God, you want me to do something Indian, don't you? Some Indian . . . *movie?*"

"Get a grip, I'm not asking you to dine with Hannibal Lecter."

"Melina said she has a poster on her wall." It was an accusation. "Some Bollywood dude she's got a crush on?"

"She does, yes, beside a poster of whom? Oh, right, a young Robert Redford. Guess who gave her that one, and she was only eight! And if we're roaming into crush-land, there's a director out in Hollywood I know –"

"Don't go there!"

"C'mon, it's three short hours out of your life –"

"Three whole frikkin' hours?" Steph objected.

" – with free popcorn. I'll even toss in Indian snacks."

"In return for which I can give your number to Chad Weiss?"

"If you can hack your way through the slavering wannabe Mrs. Chads." Rachel slipped into her shoes. "I have to get to work. Lock up, okay?"

"Cashews go where?" called Melina.

"Blue bowl."

Rachel surveyed her living room. Was it over the top, this extensive preparation for Steph's visit? Here was a bowl of sweet *gur para*, there a peppery cup of *ratlami sev*, crisp with the bite of green chilis. A plate of *soan papdi* rich with butter and cardamom rested between them, popcorn was in the microwave, and in a minute or so a special order of spinach *pakoras* would be delivered by a skinny teenage boy from Punjab House. Still, nothing pacified Steph so well as food.

Melina set down the cashews. The curved nuts shone pale against the cobalt. "Is the DVD in?"

"It's in, Houston, we have liftoff." Rachel checked her watch. "Almost."

"What if she doesn't like it? You're giving her a glass of wine, right?"

"Of course, not that it'll make much difference, I told you about the time she chugged two beers and still aced the debate team tryouts. Don't worry. If it's thumbs down," Rachel joked, "we just drop her from our lives forever."

"A couple of advisories, Steph."

"It's three hours long, you told me already. These are yummy." Steph crunched another *gur para*. "What else?"

"Men are allowed to cry, it shows they're feeling people, they have heart," Rachel explained.

"Well, I *so* get that. Next?"

"Every Bollywood movie contains songs and dances, and in this one the sets and costuming are very glossy and over-the-top, a lot like opera."

"Rachel, you know me and musicals!"

Rachel handed her the DVD box with actors' photos. "These six are big stars. And big themes," she ticked them off on her fingers, "first, the family separated and then reconnected. That's why this movie's big with NRI families, people who live in LA and London and Dubai. Then there's the father's direction versus the children's desires to choose their own way. And always, maintaining traditional Indian values in the face of Western influences, the balance."

"I'm forewarned. Can we watch, already?"

"Oh, and no sex, and usually no kissing on the lips."

"There was that one in 'Dhoom 2'," Melina reminded her.

"The most incredibly beautiful kiss!" said Rachel. "U-rated Indian films have plenty of sensual posturing, though, and a certain, oh, teasing playfulness."

"Sounds like a return to the Hays Code. I'm psyched," Steph assured them.

"And the heroes are derived from a real hero, Lord Ram. So they're always going to be good men, or see the error of their ways, or be under a sinister influence shaken off in the last five minutes, or –"

"Rachel, will you play the damn movie?"

"There's always an intermission? Why?"

"It gives everyone a chance to buy popcorn." Rachel carried the large bowl back to the kitchen and tossed another packet in the microwave. "But they leave at other times, too," she called. "Melina, tell her what happens."

"Steph, seeing Indian movies at the theater is so different! They're played with the volume way up, so the first time we rolled Kleenex to stuff in our ears. After that, we brought earplugs."

"Why? I mean, why so loud?"

"Because people talk all through! Nisha's mum says movies in India are even noisier, people aren't just chatting, they're reciting lines along with the characters, and babies are crying, and during the songs there's a run for bathrooms and candy, and sometimes the people who stay sing along or get up and dance in the aisles." Melina crunched into a *para*. "Can you imagine the audience throwing coins at the screen just because they see an image of a god?" she asked, her mouth full of crumbs.

"Speaking of gods, Indian megastars are the equivalent of deities. George Clooney, Brad Pitt, they don't get anywhere close to the adulation these guys receive, and on a first-name basis, too," said Rachel. "If Pitt came down with peritonitis, People Magazine would worry, but would the entire nation pray for him? I don't think so."

Scores of attractive twenty-somethings stepped, jumped, ran and writhed on the grounds of a university campus.

"Yeah, your students do that all the time, don't they?" Steph prodded Rachel. "And dress that well? Black leather? Driving red Lamborghinis? Incredibly good-looking?"

"With biceps to die for," observed Melina, her hand full of *sev*.

Onscreen, Anglo extras paused to watch the handsome man. Steph grabbed the remote, pressed pause and turned to Rachel, her eyes wide. "My God, the guy can dance!"

"The triple threat of Indian cinema, looks, dancing, acting. This was an early effort, but Hrithik raised the bar."

"At his first movie, girls passed out in theatres. Mass fainting all over India," said Melina.

"Really? Okay, ladies," Steph wielded the remote with a flourish, "onward!"

"Why is there thunder?"

"He's an icon of Indian film playing the stern unyielding father. It's an auditory cue."

Melina glanced up from the floor. "Now, when it thunders, we say Amitabh's angry."

"But the older son, is he going to –?"

"Wait and see!"

"My butt's asleep."

"But did you like it?" demanded Melina. "Did you? You'd better say yes!"

"No processing, fill out the survey as you leave the theatre." Rachel held the popcorn bowl over Steph's head. "Immediate reaction?"

"It's better than I thought," Steph admitted. "Enormous heart, great acting, a few too many tears, incredible scenery and costumes, plenty of humor. It took me a while to buy into the arranged-marriage conflict, but I get the balance between romance and tradition. Tradition!" Steph sang. "There you go, it's 'Fiddler on the Roof' in Hindi, with lots more money and no pogroms."

Rachel lowered the bowl. "That has to be the most bizarre take on 'Kabhi Khushi Kabhie Gham' *ever*."

If Marc Harris liked his departmental meetings crowded and cozy, he must be feeling let-down. Just as Rachel predicted, only half the department trickled in. The rest were out of town, busy with unbreakable appointments, or voting with their feet.

At least the man's wardrobe was entertaining: NYU T-shirt under tweed jacket, leather belt with large silver buckle, jeans and navy Keds. It drew smiles as he stood behind a lectern after his PowerPoint presentation.

The agenda was long: Marc's welcome; an update on his predecessor, who had unfortunately sunk further; the university's search for six million more square feet by 2030 despite the horror and objections of local residents; a plea for more efficient usage of class space; an overview of the past academic year, and aspirations for the current one. These included more support from various segments of the university, and an increased emphasis on alumni giving.

"Let's be creative about this, let's recognize that students who didn't major in English might have fond feelings for us," said Marc. "Even, dare I say, for the books themselves! If we go back in the database, say, ten, twenty years, we'll find those alums who took any English course above an introductory level. You may ask, why should a student who only read, oh, twentieth-century British novels help us? Well, why not? Those students read Woolf and Snow and, yes, my guy Lawrence," with a grin, "and those works provided them more than relief from number-crunching and abstract reasoning. Everyone in this room knows that literature introduces us to people, to friends and lovers and families . . . to problems and solutions and consequences . . . to joy and, yes, to pain. Literature's about passion and desire, the willingness to part with pieces of the heart. Why shouldn't an alum who majored in finance or philosophy remember *that*?"

Jenny had his number, all right: Marc Harris possessed enormous flair.

"Sounds like a political rally," said Melina. She perched on the sofa's back while whimsically braiding Rachel's hair, each plait snapped off with a butterfly clip. The TV screen pulsed with action, and she nodded toward it. "'Mohabbatein' is sometimes silly. Why wouldn't the headmaster recognize a student he threw out years ago for dating his daughter?"

"Suspend that disbelief, it's the hero returned to straighten things out and transform . . . hold on!" Rachel leaned forward to tear a segment from the day's Times. Her hair fell over her face. "Pen, pen!"

Melina grabbed one from the endtable. "Here."

"More mistaken identity, transformation, okay." Rachel squiggled a final question mark on the impromptu note.

Onscreen, a crowd of teenagers danced in the village square. "So, do people like him? Your boss. Marc." Melina clicked a butterfly.

Rachel felt for her braided hair. "It's hard not to admire the energy, he's obviously bright and hard-working and he can be kind. Helen pants around him –"

"Ewww, the alien!"

" – but Jen says he's determinedly brotherly, though I'm not sure that'll turn Helen off. It helps that he's funny. Today he told a story about getting pooped on by a pigeon. Self-deprecating, everyone laughed. He's disarming, though not in a snarky way. In fact, he's pretty authentic," Rachel reflected. "If he says so, you can count on it."

"Like Krrish," said Melina, dragging a bowl of tandoori-spiced banana chips to her lap.

"Krrish! A superhero? No way. He's not even close to the ordinary Indian hero! Anyway, it doesn't matter who likes Marc and who can't wait to tear him apart, he's got to do the whole shtick again next week. Then we'll see. It won't do him much good to be the darling of administration if his own department wants to toss him to the wolves."

She and Melina shivered on line, the next evening. They were lucky. Counting heads, and allowing for the fact that she'd miss small children hidden by their parents' height, Rachel estimated only thirty people now stood between them and the theater door. Behind her trailed scores more, all apparently South Asian.

"You brought the earplugs, right?"

Rachel stared at her daughter. "Oh, no!"

"You forgot earplugs?"

Pockets were searched. Rachel brandished a fistful of white tissues. "Thank God. I don't think paper towels would work."

"*Suniye?*" The word came from one of the women behind them, by their similar features two daughters with an elderly mother.

"*Haan?*" said Rachel. "Yes?"

All three wore expressions of extreme curiosity. "You speak Hindi?"

"Not really," she confessed. "Just enough to tell when the subtitles are really off. I only speak a tiny bit . . . *mujhko tori hindi ati hai,*" she added, reciting the phrase Pinky had taught her.

The women broke into grins and compliments. "Very good! Good accent! And your daughter?"

"I want to learn more," Melina broke in.

"You do?" asked Rachel, surprised.

"Sure, why not? Maybe I could get a tutor or take a course. It's a great language," she told the women, who beamed at her. "How do you say 'Hrithik rocks'?"

A few minutes later they wove through Coke-buyers and entered the theater, bypassing the rapidly-filling rear in favor of mid-auditorium. They settled into seats on the aisle, and Rachel unzipped her purse, handing over a plastic bag filled with leftover *gur paras* and *soan papdi*.

"You get a lot of mileage out of *tori hindi,*" Melina observed, crunching.

"I didn't know you wanted to learn Hindi! You should tell me these things. Uh-oh, here it comes." The screen grew bright, the sound system cranked into place, and Rachel handed Melina a tissue. "Impromptu earplugs."

"They're worth it," whispered Melina, "to see Hrithik on the big screen."

Three hours later, they headed back up the aisle, stepping around Coke cups and popcorn. Rachel plucked the screwed-up pieces of tissue from her ears and tossed them into a waiting bin.

"Like it?" she asked.

Melina stretched and nodded. "Indian movies are so . . . so . . . warm, you know? I mean, people have real emotions, they're not like robots or –"

"Excuse me, are you . . . is it Rachel? From NYU's English Department?"

Before them stood a small woman in a purple cableknit sweater. Both her dark hair and her white teeth gleamed. She held out one hand. "Chandani Naik, I teach South Asian history, I think we met last year at the Bergers' open house?"

"Of course!" Rachel shook hands, trying to recall the Bergers' traditional party, which last year had been interrupted. "Were you still there when the firefighters –"

"Oh, God, yes!" Chandani laughed. "I was the one who rushed the pan outside."

"Hot chocolate, chai, chai." Rachel lowered the cups to the round table.

" . . . and when you think how far he's come, a man with virtually no connections in the industry, certainly no family, Muslim rather than Hindu, and from Delhi, too . . . oh, thanks, Rachel." Chandani sipped cautiously and set the cup down, splashing a drop over the side. Ripping open two packets at the same time, she let sugar sift down into the dark liquid. "Your daughter and I are discussing Shah Rukh's career. I had no idea you liked Indian film."

"At the Bergers', I didn't. But we landed in Oxford, and . . ." she gave Chandani a brief description of the Patels, "so here we are, the only Anglos in the theater."

"What part of India are you from? Mumbai?" asked Melina.

"No, I grew up in Dehra Dun."

"Indian Military Academy?"

"How did you know that?"

"Movies, of course," Rachel supplied.

"Of course. Well, my parents are in Delhi now. Government work." Her eyes crinkled. "But I do have cousins in

Mumbai, one's a choreographer, another does accounting for Red Chillies."

"Wow, really?" said Melina, fascinated.

"Don't encourage her." Rachel teasingly pulled Melina's braid. "If we lived in Maharashtra, she'd be buying movie magazines."

"I still keep some old issues," Chandani admitted, "the ones with fold-out posters. Twelve years ago, Indian girls were all about Shah Rukh." She gave a fake sigh and glanced at Melina. "No?"

"No," Melina said firmly. "Hrithik. Though Shahid Kapoor and Zayed Khan are cute, too."

Chandani nodded at Rachel. "Excellent taste, your daughter."

Rachel leaned forward to hear in the coffeeshop filled with South Asian families, where children played in the aisles and noise ricocheted off window glass.

" . . . changing so much so fast, the country can barely keep up. In Mumbai, the financial capital as well as films, multimillionaires pop up like mushrooms. But out in the country, farmers commit suicide over debts of six hundred dollars." Chandani shook her head. "There's a generation gap you wouldn't believe. People in their twenties make twice what their fathers did, in jobs that didn't even exist five years ago. Most people are having only two kids, English is the key to rising in any field, and in Bangalore – that's our Silicon Valley – no one has time to cook anymore. India isn't just changing, it's . . ." she searched for the right word, "morphing. You know? Off with the old, keep on but in a new form. That's why there's a widening distinction in films."

"A what?"

"A distinction, would you call it? Between . . . look, there are levels of film in Mumbai." Chandani held up a finger. "The expensive ones with big stars, the ones where the characters use some English. They're designed for NRIs and Indians who're upper-middle-class or higher, those who've traveled and speak English well, who lead more of a Western life. Then," a second finger went up, "movies shot for the rest of us, hundreds of them that you'll never see over here. They're more Indian in flavor, almost entirely in Hindi. No high-end clothes or casual English phrases. Some are made on a shoestring, financially, and forget the really glamorous sets and costumes, they shoot where they can." She frowned. "Those are the ones American film companies want nothing to do with, and banks can still be iffy, so the search for money is endless. And risky, according to my cousin the accountant."

Rachel's forehead wrinkled. "Are you saying those movies are more authentic?"

"No, no! Both are Indian, it's just that the ones you can see here in the US are more, well, sophisticated. In everything, plot, costumes, lighting, even the quality of the film stock used to shoot."

"Americanized?"

Chandani paused. "They're more *global*. Producers who aspire to better quality, but there's nothing specifically American about that, is there? It's comparing . . . look, you teach Shakespeare, right? Okay, Shakespeare in contrast to almost any of his writing contemporaries."

Rachel could not have been more delighted. "Speaking of Shakespeare . . .."

"Did you have to do that, did you have to talk about stupid Shakespeare? For a whole hour?" Melina demanded crossly.

"No, but I did it, and now I have someone to bounce ideas off of." Rachel gave Melina's shoulder a squeeze as they walked to their bus stop. "Plus she knows tons about Bollywood, and who knows, someday we may get to India and look up her relatives. Bini, c'mon, think of this as a gift."

"Yeah, that's what the Trojans said."

The Metropolitan Museum's Cessna-sized announcement banners flapped above Rachel with crisp cold *snaps*. She stood at the top of the building's marble steps, twenty minutes early. On her itinerary today was nineteenth-century British painting, polite-society oils explicated by a self-taught authority.

It was so windy, she really ought to get her blood flowing. She threaded her way down through groups of students and families and artists waiting with their easels.

Steph worked fast. The other night, Melina had silently passed her the phone. Rachel found herself making plans to meet at the Met a man with a deep voice and a professed delight in introducing her to Constable, Turner, et al.

"The last woman I met there was into French Impressionists," he told her with a groan.

Rachel glanced at the framed Renoir print on her living room wall and penciled onto Sunday's square the name Chad Weiss, along with, in parentheses, the word "pretentious".

Now, she pulled back her coatsleeve to take another look at her watch. Still early. Traffic flowed, cabs and buses and cars, and the occasional biker, for pleasure rather than messengering. Perhaps meeting on the steps had been overly optimistic. She cradled her nose and blew to warm it. At least her head was covered.

"You can't wear a hat, Rachel," Steph noted that morning.

"I'm walking into the wind!"

"You'll get hat hair," Melina chimed in. She and Steph had assembled a bowl of *samosa* dough, one that by its size might feed an entire Gujarati village.

"I can't believe I'm cooking Indian," Steph complained. "What happened to homemade fettucine?"

"And then we fill them and fry them." Melina scratched her cheek, leaving a telltale streak of white. "You can borrow my black spandex thingie, Mom."

In the end, Rachel went for the spandex. She stamped her cold feet.

There he was, at the top of the steps, the temple directory's Chad Weiss.

On the steps, they had shaken hands, agreed that it was indeed frigid, and entered the museum's warmth. Rachel reached for a map.

"No need," Chad assured her, "I know this place inside and out." He led her to a large room. "Let's begin . . . oh, over there," he suggested. They stopped a respectful distance away from a large canvas. "He was all about composition," he began, and went on to line and spatial connection. Chad sounded intimately acquainted with the styles and techniques of painters dead for over a century. He was just as well-versed in the painters themselves, murmuring about their lives and loves in salacious detail.

"Then he left *her*, and traveled . . .." The intricacies of the artist's life evidently delighted him. Chad was clearly one of those men convinced they were born in the wrong century, who fancied themselves in Beau Brummel black astride a magnificent and equally sooty stallion, wooing the local heiress and leaving byblows scattered across the countryside. ". . . so he was lost for a time, and retreated . . .."

A quartet of tourists edged closer, and Chad fell silent.

Rachel contemplated the canvas. There was a great deal going on within it. Who was that figure modeled after? She turned to ask. The space beside her was empty. Surprised, she peered around. Chad was not seated on the padded bench, nor surveying canvases on the other side of the room. He had vanished.

Two doorways stood empty. One they had used to enter, the second led to more paintings. If the man had been taken short, or ill, or . . . but why not let her know?

"He went through there, love, next room, like," murmured one of the tourists. Rachel felt the woman's eyes as she passed the uniformed guard.

There was Chad, perusing a work by – she squinted to read the label – Constable.

Chad turned. "Isn't he great?" he enthused, exactly as though Rachel had been beside him all along. "He wouldn't paint landscapes without human associations, you know, houses, mills, he found pure nature depressing." Amusing details and opinions streamed forth. Several minutes later, Chad paused.

"Did he have –?" Rachel began.

Again, empty space. This time she picked a doorway at random, nodded to the guard, and peeked around the corner.

"So, all morning you played hide-and-seek?" asked Steph, hands on hips.

The aroma-filled kitchen embraced Rachel. Flour dusted the floor, and dozens of savory *samosas* stood in ranks on what she devoutly hoped were clean pages of the Times.

"Tell me you didn't find those papers in the basement," she suggested.

"You didn't keep trailing him, did you?" Melina handed her a thumbnail-sized lump of dough.

Rachel popped it in her mouth and accepted a cup of tea. "No, after the second hey-presto, I thought, as entertaining as he is, as informed as he is, it's not connection, and it's certainly not practice in anything except avoidance. And then I thought of you, sweetie. Would the Bollywood men, the Rohans and Rohits, would they behave like that?"

"No way!"

"Definitely no way. But it was cold, and blocks home, and I was already at the Met, so I wandered around the Egyptian temples like Howard Carter."

"Who?"

"The man who dug up King Tut."

Steph turned from the simmering oil in which *samosas* fried. "You abandoned Chad to his own devices?"

Rachel winced. "I know you'll run into him, but –"

"No, I'm proud of you, Rachel!" She pointed the wooden spoon at Melina. "Remember this, in times of avoidance, waltz off. Of course, you realize this means I can't win the matchmaker award."

"Ah, poor you!"

"How were the temples?" asked Melina.

"Fine," Rachel murmured, "they were fine." Shifting uneasily, she discovered two pairs of curious eyes. "They would have been fine," she admitted, "if a certain department chair hadn't been perusing them at the same time."

"*Your* department chair? Marc Harris? At the Met?"

Rachel nodded. "What are the odds?" she muttered.

"Of all the gin joints . . ." Steph quoted. She crossed her arms and regarded Rachel with a strange expression of interest. "Well, well. Marc Harris. Did you say hi?"

"Yes, I said hi," Rachel said crossly. "I said hi, he said hi, we spent five minutes talking ancient Egypt, I said goodbye, he said goodbye, I left."

"Sounds like a blast."

Melina giggled. "Did he break into a dance for you like a real Bollywood character?"

"Very funny. I can't see him dancing at all. He might be an athlete, but –"

"Was he alone?" inquired Steph.

"Apparently."

She nodded, reflective. "Running into your dishy boss at the Met: priceless."

Rachel threw a potholder at her. "Stop!"

"Changing the subject," said Steph, pressing bubbling *samosas* down into hot oil, "Rubén and Franny fly back to the left coast tomorrow, sniff, moan."

"That rolled off your tongue! 'Rubén and Franny', 'Rubén and Franny'. You haven't seen him much during this break, have you?"

"No, and WWRD, what would Rachel do? You'd be happy he's found a young woman so caring, who treats me like I have some intelligence, who's even given me the recipe for her mom's chocolate cake." Steph slapped her thigh. "When you see me shlepping an extra ten pounds, you can blame it on the tall redhead. *Samosa?*"

CHAPTER 11

As her bus rolled south, students occupied Rachel's mind. Some names on her lists were familiar, those of English majors cherished in the departmental nest, fed on choice bits of Brontë, Chaucer, Woolf. Some were regular drop-ins from other departments, the ones Marc Harris wanted to cultivate as donating alums, students who periodically varied their academic diet with nibbles of English-language poetry or prose. Several names were entirely new to Rachel.

Shakespeare's plays generated few real slackers. As long as her students engaged themselves and each other in the work, she'd feel satisfied. They might even manage to have some fun.

Could that be a subset of a chapter? Not "fun", the word wasn't nearly academic enough, but amusement? Slapstick, or the kind of fast wordplay and puns that some of the Bard's characters excelled in. So, for that matter, did Shah Rukh Khan, his Hindi at warp speed.

"Questions, problems, your vindictive ex shredded your book, your roommate hijacked your paper," Rachel waited for laughter to subside, "call, e-mail, my numbers and address are all on the syllabus, office hours, too. Plus, Jenny Sobieski in the department office works magic. We're all human, things happen . . . all I ask is that you tell me the truth." She regarded the twenty-something faces. "Because if you give me 'the dog was hungry', and I find out later you're allergic even to chihuahuas, I will be *most* unhappy."

She sat on the desk placed beside her lectern. Expectant faces regarded her with interest. Over the years, she had taught no boring class. Every one of her classes possessed some humor, a few clowns . . . Shakespeare enjoyed clowns.

"Questions? No? As to me, I was on sabbatical in England last semester. I've adored Shakespeare since I first read him, I want you to love him, too." She slipped from the desk to stroll around the classroom. "A great part of appreciating Shakespeare is understanding his work as it was presented during his life. You didn't go to see a play, you went to hear a play. The crowd was of all levels of society, and Elizabethans were neither mealy-mouthed nor reticent. A bad actor might literally get egg on his face. When you read, imagine the lines said with an all-male cast. In the London of that day, Juliet's dress hid a little something extra."

That gained smiles.

"Molière used actresses – he was France's answer to the comic Shakespeare – and women were onstage in Spain and Italy, too, but because of the law, playwrights in England had to depend on boys and men to play female roles. When you read, picture that. And you aspiring actors, rejoice, we'll do a few line readings ourselves."

Half the class brightened. The others looked as though she'd just wiped their iPods.

"First play, 'Twelfth Night'." She went to the white board. With a bright red marker, in characters two feet high, she printed four letters. "Sophocles said one word frees us of all the weight and pain of life – that word is 'love'. So, what does it evoke for you?"

The ten o'clock class made for a good start, with plenty of volunteerism and wit. Clearly, the optimism and idealism of love had not faded with the 21st century. There was something sweet in that, in the notion that no matter how many times students had been wounded, rejected, even tossed out, most still found love worth another shot, one more risk. Like a Bollywood movie, in fact. Rachel reached for a Post-It, singing softly to herself. *"Dekha tumko jab se, bas dekha tumko yaara . . .."*

"Good lord, I didn't know you could sing! What is that?"

In the doorway stood a woman whose casually touseled, pale-blonde hair framed an angular face. Her extraordinarily slender body was wrapped in an animal-print jersey dress and clinging suede boots.

"One of Melina's favorites. How are you, Helen? Done anything special since I left?"

Helen took a step inside, her eyes covertly on the windows . . . not, Rachel knew, for any view, but to examine her own reflection. "I got a little bit of work done in November. Fine-tuning."

Rachel made a show of peering up. "Blades or Botox?"

"Oh, Botox up above, of course, every few months, I'm on a schedule. The other was a little tuck just to keep firm. He's amazing, you really should start with him, Rachel, if you wait too long the procedures will be more severe."

The word carried unintentional irony. Helen's face, pulled, stretched and altered, presented a collection of geometric planes unsoftened by feminine roundness. Her first surgery had been a self-gifted birthday present, and since then Helen had indulged in repeated facial reorganizations. Rachel recalled Melina's comment on Take Our Daughters To Work Day: "Every year she looks more like an alien, I think she's got antennae."

Minus visible antennae, Helen leaned back against the door. "Of course you've met our new fearless leader?"

"Of course."

"Mmm. What do you make of him?"

"Enthusiastic. Diplomatic. Bright."

"Uh-huh. Anything else?" Helen sauntered forward and sidled into a chair. "Anything personal?"

"Personal? No, not up on gossip, very bad at gossip. Try Jenny," Rachel suggested, "she hears everything."

"Maybe I will. See you."

"Bye." Relieved, Rachel focused on the yellow Post-It in her hand. She'd been about to scribble some idea for her book, an idea that hovered at the edges of memory. What was it? A breath of Chanel No. 5 drew her gaze up.

"Something you forgot?" she asked.

Helen gave a theatrical sigh, followed by an exaggerated shrug. "Marc."

Rachel felt at sea. "Harris?"

"Of course." For some reason, Helen had grown impatient.

"What about him?"

"I'm interested in him."

"Yes, I heard. So?"

"So back off."

Helen had never looked more determined, even at the times she found it necessary to shrilly defend Charles Dickens's extramarital affairs. Perhaps it was the Botox.

"No problem, he's all yours," Rachel assured her.

"No, I'm serious, Rachel."

"So am I! No romantic interest, no jump-his-bones interest, *nada*. I'm totally apathetic. In fact, averse. The field belongs to you."

"Sure?"

"Absolutely, my blessings." For all the good they would do in the face of Marc's brotherly response to Helen. Still, any man might be vulnerable to determined assault.

"Well, all right, then." Helen rose. A turn on four-inch heels and she was gone. Rachel took a long breath. Were shadowy rumors scuttling along the corridors? Was Helen canvassing every female colleague? Were they all as uninterested as Rachel? A movement at the door caught her eye. "I swear to God, Helen!"

"Nope, me."

It was Marc himself. Annoyed, Rachel hurried past him to check the hall. Unfortunately, Helen lurked three doors down, her eyes fixed on Marc's back.

"What do you want?" asked Rachel, abrupt.

"I came to apologize."

Catlike, Helen lurked nearer, her eyes heavy-lidded.

"Come in," Rachel invited, and slammed the door behind him. Better that than enabling Helen to overhear.

"Rachel, do I make you nervous?" he inquired.

"What?"

"Do I make you nervous?" he repeated. "Remind you of some guy in your past? Old boyfriend, ex-husband? Jason, is that right?"

"Right." Rachel regained her chair. As before, Marc drew the second one beside her desk. "You've been listening to gossip?"

"I've been pumping Jenny." He winced. "Sorry! I mean for info."

"For dirt."

"Not at all, everything public access. Who divorced whom, who's been having problems since 9/11, that sort of thing. Where were you, by the way?"

"Sorry?"

"That morning, 9/11, were you here?"

"No, I was home. No class. Watching 'Today', actually, God knows why I turned on the TV, I was supposed to go to D'Agostino for tortillas and cheese for my daughter's class's lunch," she said, recalling. "So I saw it just like the rest of the world. Then ran to snatch Melina out of school, we held hands all the way home. And no, you don't remind me of Jason." Rachel suddenly laughed. "Not at all. Why do you ask?"

"Fleeting resemblance to abusive boyfriend? Nose, eyes, hair . . . what's left of it," he added wryly.

"Nope. Although my brother's an athlete, sometimes the way you hold – " Too late, Rachel recognized how observational that sounded, as though she'd *watched* Marc. She flushed.

"What's he play?" Marc's tone was one of mild curiosity.

Rachel cleared her throat. "Mostly baseball, he pitched in college."

"Amazing! So did I, though I rarely started. What's that saying about coincidence being God's way of working undercover?" His eyes were framed by freckles, the brown hairs on his hands overlay more spots.

"Apology," the word burst from her, "you have an apology?"

"I do," he said, and flushed. "I'm ashamed to admit it never occurred to me that the critical theory class would leave your daughter alone Wednesday evenings. She's in eighth grade? Man, one thing you don't want to do with kids is leave them by themselves in the evening." Marc's right hand nervously tapped his left. "So –"

"Melina's not like that," said Rachel, defensive.

"Of course not, she's your daughter. I'm talking safety. If anything happened, I would feel personally responsible, so here's the offer: I'll reimburse you for anybody you hire to hang out with her those nights. Babysitter, companion, elderly neighbor, whoever keeps her company."

Rachel shook her head. "Thanks, it's a nice offer, a very generous offer, but I don't need it."

Marc frowned. He edged closer. "Look, I've got no kids, so far be it from me to play the heavy dad, but you should take this, Rachel. I'm not joking. Hire someone, bring Melina with you to class, import an aunt . . . just don't leave her alone for over four hours."

He got up. She was being loomed over again.

"Sorry for the hassle. It was my scheduling error, I'll check with you again on Wednesday." He opened the door. "By the way, I enjoyed bumping into you at the Met."

"Wait a minute, you'd use departmental funding for this?" she asked, curious.

"Of course not. My mistake, my pocket."

Her mobile sang with "Swan Lake".

"Hey, Steph!" Rachel shoved folders into her satchel and recounted her conversation with Marc Harris. Ripping a Post-It from the stack, she scribbled MEET ADVISEES! and slapped it on her screen. "What's your take? Savior or buttinsky?" She gathered her coat and locked her door.

"What do *you* think?" Steph sounded tired.

"Six of one, two times three of the other." Rachel leaned against the corridor wall. "Points for good intentions, though. You think?"

"Listen, Melina's got a stake in this, ask her what she wants. Bye."

Rachel pocketed the phone. She had nearly reached the stairs landing when the clacking of four-inch heels reached her. Platinum hair and steely eyes accompanied a cloud of Chanel.

"Are you so sure?" Helen murmured.

"Business, pure business." Rachel darted past.

Helen's sharp words echoed from concrete walls. "Look, if it's not, just tell me!"

CHAPTER 12

"Homework."

"Check."

"Water, food, music?"

"Check, check, check. You're the one dawdling."

"Too true. Books, notes, class list, let's grab a cab."

Rachel and Melina walked west.

"This is sort of cool, you know. I mean, listening in on a college class before I'm even in high school."

"I'm glad you think so, since Steph was booked."

How confident Rachel had been that Melina would feel utterly fearless about remaining at home this Wednesday evening, that she'd laugh off Marc's offer! Instead, at the first mention of options, Melina had visibly relaxed, her shoulders losing tension Rachel had not even observed. She'd readily fallen in with Rachel's suggestion – other solutions failing – that she accompany her mother to class.

Rachel had fumbled the ball, and badly. How had that happened?

College buildings looked remarkably different in the dark. Lighting made them festive, somehow, bright islands of investigation and knowledge in a sea of . . . what? Beyond the whimsicality and dearness of Greenwich Village, what was there? Commercialism, Rachel supposed. All the hundreds of firms, small and large, that made up much of the city, that sold dreams in the form of furniture or lighting or flowers. Or – recalling Foods of India – spices and sweets that carried her back to Oxford, and, in her imagination, east over the Mediterranean to mango groves, where even picnic breads tasted of cilantro and cumin.

She ran her ID through the security box and held the door for her daughter.

Melina was established in one of the room's corners, syllabuses were distributed across the long, seminar-style table, and fifteen minutes remained.

"Good evening."

"What are those," Rachel demanded, annoyed, "suede-bottomed Nikes?"

"Of course! Creep here, pop up there, ultimate spy shoes," said Marc. "This is Melina?"

Rachel introduced them. "Thanks for talking to my mom," she heard Melina say with full-on sincerity.

"My pleasure. Also entirely my fault. Next semester will go better," Marc replied. "What are you reading?"

Melina held up her paperback. "'Antigone'."

Marc grimaced. "Incredibly sad."

"Yeah, but it makes you realize how much things sucked back then, for girls. And she's so brave."

"Good point, she is." He turned to Rachel. "So, you're set?"

She nodded, wary. "Just waiting for my fellow sufferers, I mean my students, to file in."

Marc snorted. "If you give this half the energy you use with Shakespeare, three hours will race by. I got the word on you."

"You really are a gossip! Interesting."

"I don't gossip, I gather information, totally different task. I should be CIA."

"You like cooking?"

He laughed out loud. "I do, in fact. I make a wicked *risotto con peoci*, if you like mussels. You cook?"

Rachel gave a tiny shrug.

"Mom! She's been cooking Indian, working through a book with a thousand recipes," Melina volunteered, "one day it's like we're in Bengal, the next up in the mountains."

"Really? Maybe I can bag a dinner invitation to, oh, Kerala?"

Sorting through books, Rachel could feel Marc's eyes on her. She mumbled polite phrases about schedules.

"And how are you getting home?" he asked. "Bus, cab, horse-drawn carriage?"

She glanced at Melina. "Taxi."

"Come on, let me drive you, instead. I'm here 'til nine, anyway."

"Are you kidding? We're uptown, it's completely off your route."

Marc regarded her. "Is it?"

Two young men appeared at the classroom door. "Critical theory, welcome!" Rachel beckoned. "Thanks," she told Marc, "but we'll be just fine in a nice warm cab."

As predicted, class discussion was all tenors and baritones. The lone female student, Maya, kept her own counsel. Which made perfect sense, but how was Rachel to entice her to speak? Wasn't she frustrated?

Rachel rapped on the table. "Enough, we need a fresh voice! I fully understand how intimidating it is being outnumbered, so for the next five minutes, we'll keep quiet for

Maya to speak. If she chooses to say nothing, we'll imagine we're Quakers and enjoy a refreshing silence. If she speaks, no one, repeat, no one will interrupt for five minutes. Got it? Go."

To Maya's credit, to Rachel's relief, words poured forth.

"That was brilliant!" She and Melina were again alone. Her students, some still arguing, had rushed to greener pastures and bottles of beer. "Dead-on, Mom, dead-on, you were stellar!"

"Thank you, thank you very much," said Rachel, Elvising. "Ready?"

"You know, this critical theory stuff isn't that bad. I know you hate it, but it makes sense, sort of."

Outside, bitter winds clawed through their coats. Rachel stopped. "Hat?"

Melina groaned.

"I know you brought one. Give." She pulled the purple knit cap over her daughter's soft hair, tugging it over her ears. "Your body heat is now preserved for your own use. Let's go."

Was there ever a time when this street did not hold wandering bands of students? Perhaps right before dawn? Rachel was grateful for the comfort of their presence. From behind, though, came the sound of running feet, the heavy *slap-slap* denoting a substantially-built runner, most likely male. Instinctively, Rachel sped up and edged Melina closer to the building on their right.

Slap slap slap slap.

Rachel stiffened. He'd likely pass them by, but how well she recalled a Saturday on London's Cumberland Place, when a runner with a disguising hoodie hurtled into an expensively-dressed couple just a few feet to Melina's right. He'd sent them crashing to the pavement. Thirty seconds later, the two were minus purse, gold chains and a tooth, outraged passersby dialed 999, and the boy had disappeared into the rabbit warren of Marble Arch tube station. Police would never locate him there.

Slap slap slap slap.

"Mom, why are we hurrying?"

"Rachel!" *Slap slap slap.* Marc Harris caught up with them, his breath quick puffy clouds. "Man, you two walk fast!"

"Why didn't you yell?" Rachel trembled with adrenalin and fury. "Instead of letting me imagine some nut?"

"I just wanted to make the offer one more time." Marc gestured to the street. "Car's over there."

"Thank you, but go west, young man," Rachel spit out. "Hit a bridge. Goodbye."

Marc fell into step beside her.

"Don't you have a long drive home? Things to do, friends to call, sports to watch?" Rachel asked, exasperated and fully aware of Melina's burgeoning curiosity. "Baseball stats to research?"

"Nope, off-season 'til spring."

"Basketball, then."

"Hate hoops, full of divas."

"Hockey!"

"Well, the new rules make for lots more speed and higher scores, but I played some as a kid, all I remember is frozen toes and fights. Allow me." At the corner, Marc stepped onto the pavement, extending his left arm. A taxi swept toward him as though pulled.

"Here you go," he said, dragging open the door and tucking a bill into Rachel's mittened hand. "For the fare, I promised reimbursement, remember? See you tomorrow!"

"I've just never seen you like that," Melina persisted.

"Like what?"

"Bothered, you know, sort of nervous."

"I was neither bothered nor nervous," insisted Rachel. "The man's an idiot. Right on 88th, please," she added, to the cabbie. "It's not dumping that class on me, critical theory, he just . . . he just bugs me."

"Like I said."

"Bugged is not bothered, they're totally distinct."

"But it was *nice* of him to offer, Mom. It was! It was like something out of 'Lakshya'. She's sitting there getting cold, waiting for her driver, he offers a ride in his jeep –"

"Hey, look, our lights are on!"

From uncurtained windows, yellow spilled onto Rachel's shoulders as she paid with the cash Marc had pressed on her.

The bolt gave. Rachel tossed her purse at the sofa. "Steph?" she called.

Steph descended the narrow steps with a glass of sloshing liquid. "You're almost out of vodka," she said accusingly.

Rachel ran back down to the living room. She'd bundled Steph onto the sofa, the near-empty bottle of Stolichnaya beside her. Whatever was going on, they'd be two floors and a closed door from Melina's ears, if she stayed in her room as promised.

"Okay." Rachel crossed her legs underneath her and gladly picked up a mug of hot tea. It warmed her chilled fingers. "What's going on?"

Steph's lips curled. "Unlike Garbo, I don't vant to be alone."

"Of course not. Is it Rubén?"

"No, he and Franny, they're both fine."

"And you, you're not so fine?"

"Basically," a vague gesture to the body half-hidden by the plaid throw, "all here in relatively good shape. But I'm so . . . what am I? I'm tired, Rachel. Though that's not actually what I planned to say after I raided your booze."

Rachel patted the shrouded foot. "No problem, it's been in the cabinet forever. You saw another client with an abusive childhood?"

"I should be able to handle it without letting myself into friends' houses and stealing their liquor. I should!"

"Says who, the therapist fairy?" Rachel asked, soothing. "Why should you be a dumping ground without recourse? God knows you're always recoursing me! So, return of favor."

Steph glared. "I should be able to handle this! Or if not," a small hiccup escaped her, "wait until I can talk to a colleague."

"You have a solo practice," Rachel pointed out.

"I mean tomorrow."

"But it's always a day away! Seriously, I'm fine with your shlepping up here. No big deal, okay? Do you want to use the guest room?"

Steph nodded. Rachel wrapped her arms around the thin frame in a fierce hug.

"I should look around for better self-medication than this," Steph told her, eyes wet. She held up the drained glass. "As yum as it is. Maybe, I don't know, massage?"

"Day spa, excellent idea. Get rubbed, polished, defuzzed, re-energized. Tea?" Rachel went to the kitchen. "Herbal?" she called.

"Speaking of yum, how's your commander-in-chief?"

"My what? Oh!" Rachel propped the swinging door open. "Just as towering as ever. Honey? Here you go, careful." She handed off the hot mug. "He offered Melina and me a ride home."

"Did you take it?"

"Of course not, want to see what's available?" Rachel reached for the TV remote.

Steph snatched it up. "Why not?"

"There's bound to be a rerun of 'Law and Order'."

"Why didn't you take the ride?"

"He lives in Jersey," Rachel explained, and grabbed for the remote.

Steph stretched it away from her. "So?"

"So it's entirely off his route."

"Are you saying you didn't want to inconvenience the poor man?"

"Exactly." She wrestled the remote away and clicked. "And I didn't want to owe him."

"He offered to subsidize a babysitter, how is a ride home different?" Steph asked.

"I'd have to sit beside him . . . and know that he was driving north instead of west."

"Mmmm. Doing hard time, all right."

Rachel regarded her. "You want to go out with him? No? Then let me handle this. We're fine as colleagues, let it rest. It's more than enough." She recounted the afternoon's conversation with Helen.

"She wasn't serious?"

"If looks could kill, I'd be sushi."

"Wow, everyone thinks of academics as mild-mannered Clark Kents, but your department just seethes with thinly-veiled passion and unrequited lust. Not to mention back-stabbing ambition," said Steph, impressed.

Rachel nodded. "We might as well be living in the court of Queen Elizabeth. The virgin one."

"No wonder you like the – what do you call it? – the sweetness of Hindi films."

CHAPTER 13

I called her service," Rachel whispered, "so this morning's covered."

"How late were you guys up?" Melina ripped off a banana and tucked it into her lunchbox.

"If Manhattan still had milkmen, we'd have poured ourselves a great bowl of Trix." Rachel grimaced. "She actually begged to watch a 'Bolly molly', as she called it, after another vodka."

"Get out! What'd you pick?"

"'Kaho Naa Pyaar Hai'."

"Did she faint?"

"No, but it tickled her drunken fancy. And the sailing ship! I had to convince her not to drag you out of bed, head down to the docks! Second half monologue was all about moving to New Zealand so she could 'counsel Kiwis'. Every time she said it, she'd giggle. It was like watching with a five-year-old."

"Want me to call, get you excused from class?" Melina teased.

"Just one, I'll be done by eleven-thirty. Oh, damn! Except for advisees, we're all brownbagging. Call it one o'clock." She followed Melina to the front door.

"Mom! Enough hug!" Melina pulled back, straightening her hair. "Were you drinking with her?"

"Only tea. You're good to go?"

"Except for French," Melina said darkly.

The English department office was stacked with boxes. "Color brochure with photos of current faculty, send-money plea, response card to put it on plastic, return envelope, envelope," Jenny, bleary-eyed, identified the stacks. "You look exhausted, too. Sleepless night?"

Rachel nodded, poured hot water and floated a teabag. "Friend in despair. You?"

"Husband with two days off in a row."

"Ah, that explains your cat-in-the-cream expression!"

"Rachel," Jenny hesitated, "the Michael date was a lead balloon, but there's a man from my church . . .."

"Oh!" Rachel stopped in the doorway. "No way, there's not enough chocolate in the world!"

"Indian groceries?"

"I have plenty."

"Movies?"

"Why are you so interested in getting this guy a date, who are you, Rabbi Shmuley?"

"Tell you what, go out with this man once, just once, I'll owe you an overnight with Melina anytime you feel like getting crazy. Street value, a hundred bucks. Nice offer, huh?"

Rachel sat and dropped her head to her knees. She peered up. "Who is he?"

"Is that yes?"

"Yes, okay, fine, yes, who is he?"

"He's English, and I know that's a turn-off for you," Jenny hurried, "but Alan's sincere. Five-ten or so, blond/blue, good dresser, involved in the church, seems like a great guy. Somewhere over forty."

"Who's over forty?"

Rachel hadn't heard Marc Harris's office door – which now bore his nameplate – but there he was with curiosity and raised eyebrows, holding a tennis ball. "No one," she said, irritated.

Marc glanced from her to Jenny. "Jen, you setting her up?"

"No!"

"Yes," replied Jenny, barely hiding a grin.

He leaned against the wall, tossing the ball from hand to hand. "Fascinating. What's he like?"

"Never mind!"

"I'm interested for a reason," he explained. "You won't even have breakfast with me, but I have a writer friend –"

"Oh. My. God."

" – so when Jenny's done with her entry, I'll give you mine."

The phone rang.

"Financial whiz, works investment, let me know when you want that overnight," Jenny blurted. "Good morning, NYU English . . .."

"My turn at bat! Bachelor number two's a writer for a well-known sports magazine, very tall, very thin, once dreamed of playing for the Lakers," Marc noted, following Rachel out to the hall. She brushed at him as at a particularly persistent gnat. "Grew up in LA. Irish-American. Into bikram yoga. Never married, never engaged, though I think he once contemplated getting close to it."

"No, thanks," Rachel said, stern, one hand on the stairwell door.

"Actually, I made up the hot yoga. He's thirty-eight, looking for a woman a few years younger, that's you, isn't it?"

Rachel regarded him with pity. "You know it's not, Mr. Bond, you have my file. CIA, indeed!"

"Well, you *look* ten years younger." Marc ran down the steps at Rachel's heels. "His name's Sean Kennedy, he really wants to meet you."

Rachel paused on a landing. "Why, what the hell did you tell him?"

"I said – is that Tchaikovsky?"

Rachel retrieved her cell from her trouser pocket. "Steph, you woke up! No, your service knows . . . no problem . . . you're welcome. Listen, I've got to go," she glanced at Marc, "call you tonight. Bye."

"I totally talked you up," Marc resumed, "said I had this great new Shakespearean, very pretty, really bright and warm and kind, though you're annoyed at me personally."

"Professionally."

"Professionally, that's what I meant. He's intrigued! The only women he meets want free tickets to the Knicks. Can I give him your number?"

Rachel turned on him. "To a Neanderthal who probably can't even spell Shakespeare?"

"He's a writer, Rachel."

"Of sports!"

"Yeah, but the dude had to take a course on your dude at least once in college, dude," Marc said, gently mocking. "That certifies him as at least Cro-Magnon. Come on, it'll be fun!"

"Fun? It would be ridiculously different."

"Different *is* fun. Or vice versa. So he's not the right guy, what does it matter?"

"What are you offering?"

Puzzled, Marc shook his head.

Rachel snapped her fingers. "Offering. In return. Make it worth my while, Harris. From Jenny, I've gotten chocolate and babysitting."

"I can hardly top those. And the one thing you want from me, I can't give you . . . no subs for the theory class, Rachel, I won't go that far."

"Impasse, then."

They stared at each other.

"Just as a new experience, one thread in the rich tapestry of life?" he suggested. "Plus a pair of tickets, though I can't promise the Knicks."

"Why don't we double?"

"Double?" asked Marc, his voice rising. "So I can watch him come on to you? Besides, who would I ask? I don't run into single women every day, except for students, who are not only off-limits but way too young. Even grad students. In fact, I haven't had a date in . . .." He grimaced. "I can't believe I'm trying to set up another guy!"

"Fine, I'll meet your Laker wannabe!" Rachel gave in, and hurried off. Before her office stood a group of students toting small bags and coolers. Rachel unlocked the door, allowed them to file in, and glanced back. There was Marc, his head quizzically tilted.

Her advisees, an amiable lot, had asked their questions, listened to the answers, debated and argued, all while inhaling lunches that ranged from deli sandwiches to Chinese dumplings to a spicy yogurt curry brought from home. The leftover *sev* she brought disappeared after tentative nibbles.

It was still only 12:45, she could . . . well, she might do anything with an extra quarter-hour, though temptations – she glanced around the office – were few. Her students must think she . . . students, that was it! The idea she'd been mulling when interrupted by the waspish Helen.

Students, sweet/optimistic, young, love, contemp. Bollywood, she scribbled.

On her screen, she opened the outline for her book. Typing it the other night, she'd added notes and insights. The list was now multi-page and headed like a Hydra, carrying tails of quotes and citations and, in one case, a discussion consisting mainly of numerous abbreviations. The long paragraphs looked like Pentagon code.

AMND, for example, was easy to decipher, "A Midsummer Night's Dream". HAM and MAC were not foods, but Hamlet and Macbeth. SRK was self-evidently Shah Rukh Khan, AK another actor Khan, the talented Aamir. HR stood for Melina's favorite Hrithik Roshan. 2GENT had to be "Two Gentlemen of Verona", TAME the easily identifiable "Taming of the Shrew". YCHO was the producer-director Yash Chopra, ACHO and UCHO his sons Aditya and Uday. OSO had to be the film "Om Shanti Om", just as "Kabhi Khushi Kabhie Gham" became K3G, "Rang de Basanti" turned into RdB, and Dh2 represented the immensely popular "Dhoom 2".

But what in the world was TBB? The belle of the ball?

"It'll come," she murmured to herself, and typed new sentences, setting down notions and connections that might never reach a printed page but were useful as mental ballast. Words flowed from her fingers. She began to hum.

"*Agar main kahoon, mujhe tumse mohabbat hai, meri bas yahi chahat hai, toh kya kahogi?*" she sang softly.

"That's pretty."

"Jesus!" Rachel clutched at her chest. "Don't, don't . . . don't *do* that!"

"I'm not that quiet," Marc objected, "I was talking to students out in the hall. What's that song?" He prowled the perimeter of the room, examining the walls and, she noted with annoyance, pausing to straighten picture frames.

"Nothing. From an Indian movie."

"In Hindi? Cool! You've memorized in a language you don't really speak," he explained. "What do the words mean?"

"Nothing. It's . . . it's just a young man wonders why he has to be flowery with the woman he assumes he'll marry. 'If I say I'm in love with you, you're my only desire, what will you say?'" She reddened. "He doesn't want to go through the motions, even."

Marc faced her. "The film's first song?"

"Second."

At her desk, Marc opened *The Odyssey* and flipped through its pages. "And at the end?"

"At the end, he knows why."

"Does he? Good for him." He snapped the book shut. Abrupt, ramrod-straight, he walked out.

" . . . so they echo back and forth, the themes, even – get this – the idea of female desire, how in Shakespeare's time it was constrained and permitted only within the context of male approval, and –"

"Same thing in most Indian films," Chandani finished Rachel's thought. She set down her teacup. "You have something there. And male desire?"

"The classic source of all eroticism. Restrained, though."

"Homosexuality?"

The din surrounding them had eased, and several students glanced over before returning to their own conversations.

"Barely hinted at."

"I agree. And yet . . . remember what I said about morphing." Chandani tapped the table with a manicured fingernail. "To really understand India, you've got to examine its films. Under a microscope, if necessary." She hesitated. "Forgive me, Rachel, but you're not buying into the romanticism, are you? The picturisations, the songs, the yearning?"

"Me? Personally?" Rachel laughed. "Of course not. Colorful, yes, but . . .."

"Do we have any peanuts?" The large bed sagged under Melina as she bounced onto it. "Or almonds?"

"All gone," came Rachel's voice. She backed out of her stuffy closet. "I used to have a fisherman's sweater, what happened to it?"

"Cashews?"

"No. Did I give it to Goodwill?"

"Walnuts?"

"Is this for a science project?"

"I'm hungry. Are you going fishing?"

"No, I just want to be warm at batting practice tomorrow."

Melina's jaw dropped. "Batting practice? You mean, like, with a baseball bat? And a ball? You?"

"Don't laugh, the guy doesn't know I was a total wipe-out at PE. So your mother has the intensely dubious distinction of two first dates on the same Saturday. How this happened, don't ask. Even I don't want to know. Batting cage at one o'clock, Argentine steakhouse at eight. Build an appetite at the former, stuff myself with beef at the carnivores' paradise. Maybe the sweater's in *your* closet?"

Melina dogged Rachel upstairs. "What kind of man takes you to a place where baseballs attack you?"

Rachel ran her fingers along folded garments. "A jock. I suppose I can always sit back and admire *his* form. I don't mean that like it sounds. Aha!" Rachel pulled out a thick ivory-colored sweater. "When did *you* ever go fishing?"

On the bed, Melina tucked her legs beneath her. "Daddy and Ellie want me to visit over winter break weekend in February. That's the third weekend," she added.

"Do you want to? Okay, I'll get online for a flight. Oh, but you'll miss the Tollivers' pig roast!"

"But I can eat a Double-Double at In-N-Out," Melina said smugly, and picked up her phone.

"What do you want for dinner tonight?"

"That Farsi chicken you made last week was good. Plus, it had peanuts."

"And it's thawable in the microwave." Rachel hugged her. "After you finish with your dad, call Punjab House for real *naan*, okay?"

"*Thik hai!*"

"Practicing our Hindi, are we?" teased Rachel. "At least you've learned great nasals from the goose-stepping Monsieur LeBlanc."

In New York, Rachel knew, one could find virtually anything, always assuming a willingness to invest time, energy, and cash in the search. In all her years in the city, though, she'd never chosen to research what the five boroughs offered in the way of sports. Walking, she could stride around Manhattan. For grass, there was Central Park. For water close to home, Schurz Park along the East River, though by now Rachel knew the park so well that in good weather she refused to cross East End and join the throngs of runners, baby-walkers, and knitters in Schurz. Naturally, she'd spotted skaters in Central Park, as well as frisbee tossers, softballers, and footballers of both species, but never joined in. Batting cages were well beyond her ken.

"I feel a wild case of 'When Harry Met Sally' coming on," Rachel told Sean Kennedy as they made their way toward an empty cage. He had called it well, the day was abnormally mild for the end of January. Still, she was glad of the fisherman's sweater. "Except that Sally never made it to the batting cage."

As described, Sean was tall and exceptionally thin. A runner, he assured Rachel he spent at least an hour each morning pounding pavements around SoHo, where years ago he'd bought a loft. Then, he had shared with a roommate-tenant (gender unspecified, Rachel noted), but he now lived alone. He carried a small leather case unbusinesslike enough to compete as a man-purse. For quarters, he explained, since his sweats weren't designed with pockets.

"You like that movie?" Sean asked, frowning. "Why do so many chicks like that movie?"

"It's romantic . . . and funny . . . and Nora Ephron, what's not to like?" replied Rachel. "There's an Indian film, 'Hum Tum', that takes off on it. Same premise, different direction."

"Yeah? Here we go, just step in there, take the bats, will you? I brought the aluminum in case ash was too heavy, Marc said you had small bones. You know, two years ago I dated a woman who could really swing, wham, out to center field! 'Course, she'd played softball in college. Want a glove, batting glove? No? Okay, stand here, you're a rightie, right? Stay there," Sean instructed.

"Wait!"

"What?"

Rachel lowered her bat. "I haven't done this since high school."

"No problem, hon, like riding a bike, it'll come back to you. Just watch the balls," Sean said confidently. "But start with the bat *off* your shoulder, Rachel. It's Rachel, right? But Marc said you're not Jewish? That's why you won't go out with him?"

"What?"

"Widen your stance, hon, feet under shoulders. Okay, bat up. Listen, once you start, you'll love it! Pure power. A woman I went out with once said she never knew anything like it. Here you go!"

From the wall opposite, a tiny white orb shot at Rachel. She ducked. The bat rolled at her feet.

"Pick up the bat! Pick up the bat!" The shout came from behind. Rachel scrabbled in the dirt. "Stay down, stay down!" *Proing!* A second ball hit and bounced on the mesh at the rear. "Get up quick, ready, here you go! Go! Go!"

One, two, three white balls hurtled at her. Clutching the bat in sweaty hands, she swung and missed.

"Next one, get some wood on, Rach! Bend a little, feet apart, that's right, bend your knees! Here it comes!"

The next ball, Rachel grazed. It bounced down in front of her and hurtled up again, chest-high.

"Hold your position! Hold your position!" came the command.

Clunk! Eyes closed, she swung and heard a *thwick.*

"Attagirl! Excellent! Good grounder, decent placement past the pitcher! See, you're getting the hang of it!"

"Fantastic. Wonderful. Your turn," said Rachel, out of breath.

"No, no, get back in there!" Sean shooed her forward. "You've got more!"

"They're yours, really, I insist," she said, firm. "I'll watch and learn."

"Well, and maybe a little rah-rah, too, huh?" Sean regarded her with approval. "My ex-girlfriend wrote a piece on fans' testosterone levels, their team's wins turn them on! I'm serious, women, too. Okay, hon, I'll take over."

Rachel rounded the chainlink fence and sagged against it, relieved to be out of the line of fire. Sean slugged his first three balls high and fast.

"Wow," she called, "I'm thoroughly impressed!"

"Wait 'til I hit a rhythm," Sean replied over his shoulder, "it'll be even smoother, a real smooth ride." *Thwack!* "You know, something I hate about that movie is Billy Crystal" – *thwack!* – "and Bruno Kirby all the time talking when no guys would talk." *Thwack!* "You hit the ball, you do the wave, you don't fucking talk." *Thwack!* "Excuse my French."

"No problem," Rachel said, dry.

Thwack!

"I actually enjoyed that part, it made them look less prehistoric," said a deep voice behind Rachel. "Isn't there some evidence that Neanderthals had only limited speech?"

She turned, astonished. "Where did you pop up from?"

"Jersey. Nice drive," Marc Harris responded, propping a bat against the fence to dig quarters from his jeans. "Have you been up?"

"Yes, and it was total blitzkrieg, I beat a craven and very hasty retreat."

Marc laughed. "Still in one piece?"

"Rach, you still back there?" Sean shouted.

"Uh-huh, you're doing great," she called back. "Hitting his rhythm," she explained to Marc with significant irony.

His mouth twitched. "How're *you* doing?"

"Oh, excellent, really excellent, I'm so glad you asked! I'm with a self-absorbed dodo –"

"Dodo!"

"Didja see that, Rach?" called Sean. "Yo, Marc, when did you get here? Watch this, dude!"

Thwack!

"A dodo who calls me 'Rach' and 'hon' and every few minutes manages to insert references to past women –"

"Oops, forgot to tell you he's a persistent internet dater," said Marc, failing to look at all sorry.

" – and I'm delighted you turned up, you can explain what the hell you saw us having in common! What could you possibly be *thinking*?" hissed Rachel. She trailed Marc to the next cage.

"That you both like words? Hold these."

Her hand automatically lifted. A stream of warm quarters tumbled into her palm.

"All right, a competitor! Get ready to pull it out, man!" Sean jeered.

"Correction, he likes himself," Rachel said.

"He lives in the city."

"So? That far downtown, he's hardly a neighbor."

"He's Christian," noted Marc, picking quarters one by one from Rachel's hand and sliding them into the slot.

"Oh my God, Harris, that's all you have? Where're your big guns? If I met him at a party, I'd move on after two minutes!"

The last quarter fell into the slot. "Has he mentioned Shakespeare?"

"And Kennedy whacks it into the stands!" came a cry beside them. "How 'bout that slugger, sports fans?"

"What with all the self-congratulation," Rachel replied, "he hasn't had time."

Marc tapped his bat in the dirt and eyed her with an odd expression. "Ready?"

"Jesus!" she exploded. "You need rah-rah, too?"

"Nope, I came out here to improve your stats."

Rachel's arms were leaden. Her palms felt suspiciously raw. Muscles she didn't know the names of screamed at her to stop.

Thwack!

"Hey, man, she's a big girl, how long you gonna baby her?"

"A few more, then you'll solo." Marc's voice was practically in her ear, the smooth voice of a flight controller calmly talking her down from the sky. He stood right behind her, his large hands guiding hers. Like a professional dancer, he had led Rachel again and again to swing at the proper height, the correct angle, the most effective speed. At first, tense with nerves, she resented his proximity, his healthy male smell of testosterone and Mennen. Yet she kept at it. Swing and miss, swing and bunt, swing . . . at last Rachel abandoned self-consciousness. Gradually, she got it. Not that high, *this* high. Not that fast, *this* fast.

"Swing and connect, swing and connect. Visualize your bat with the ball," he whispered. "Like E. M. Forster, remember? 'Only connect'."

"Don't listen to the pitcher," Sean mocked. He had retrieved more quarters from his bag, disappointing a pair of tattooed teenagers. They ambled off, grumbling. "Pitchers are lousy bats, they're famous for it. Infamous!"

Swing and connect.

Marc released her and backed to the fence. "You can do it, Rachel."

The ball flew. She swung. *Thwack!*

"Yes! The Babe homes it!" yelled Marc.

Rachel's arms shot up. "I did it! Ohmigod, I did it! I did it!" she screamed. "Can you believe it?"

"Watch out!"

Rachel felt herself tugged forward. *Zip!* A ball sped behind her. Off-balance and joyful, she threw her arms around Marc without thinking.

"You did it!" His arms wrapped about her, for an instant her head was cradled. In the next moment she was released, her cheeks hot.

Marc turned to Sean. "Cash in?" he asked.

"Not yet, man, I've still got a few bucks in there." *Thwack!* "You?"

"Yeah. Mind if I take them?" he asked Rachel.

"Are you kidding?" Avoiding his eyes, she shook out her sore arms. "I couldn't lift a Kit-Kat."

From outside the cage, she watched Marc bend his knees and ready his bat.

"How's the book coming?" he asked.

"Not bad," she said lightly. "I've made a new contact."

Thwack! Thwack! Thwack! Each time, the ball sailed far into the sky, to be lost in the whiteness of pillowlike clouds.

"Wow, Harris!" Rachel's voice was filled with surprise. "What was that trash talk about pitchers?"

"Prejudice. Stereotypes. It's all in the mind."

"And here I thought it was all in the hips," she joked.

"There, too, sure. A good swing depends on excellent lower body strength." Marc tossed the bat up and caught it. "Can I give you a ride home?"

CHAPTER 14

T hen what?" Melina demanded from the floor. Encircled by jewelry findings and assorted vinyl-clad pliers, she arranged a line of tiny orange and green glass beads.

"Then I came home."

"With Marc? With the *other* guy? Why?"

"He was the official date, you know, the one with the Topps bubblegum trading card," Rachel said defensively. "Marc just happened to show up."

"Happened to show up? And he taught you to how to hit! I know you're upset at him, but he's so nice, Mom," protested Melina, "and he doesn't call you 'hon' or 'Rach', either. He's just like a –"

"Etiquette, sweetie, etiquette. You leave with the one you came with, unless doing so would be risky, and trust your gut on that one. Even if the guy has pretty much forgotten your existence as he clobbers the ball. Even if he says . . . Bini, do you think that's what Marc really thinks? That I won't go out with him because of his religion?"

"How would I know?" Melina moved white beads between the orange and green. She placed a single blue sphere in the midst of the white. "Ask him, why don't you? Look at this, look familiar? See, it's the Indian flag! Ten orange, five white, one blue, five white, ten green. I'm doing memory wire bracelets, want one?"

Rachel patted the brown head below her. "Of course. Hey, you could do some for the Fourth of July. Save a few for ten days later, Bastille Day, they're both red, white, blue."

"Speaking of French, do I have to take it?"

"French or Spanish." Rachel held up a black dress. "What about this?"

"Why can't I take Hindi? I already know so many words, from Nisha and the movies, it would be much more fun. Please?"

Surprised, Rachel landed beside Melina on the floor. "Hon, it's *français* or *español*, your school doesn't offer anything else."

"We could get a tutor!"

"For Hindi?" Rachel asked, astounded. "What are you thinking, drop French? No way, missy."

"Then can I do it as a second language? Wednesday evenings, while you're in class! We could post a flyer at NYU: 'Hindi tutor needed for wonderful, hard-working middle school student'. Please?"

Rachel reflected. Melina was a hothouse of notions, some phenomenally impractical, like this one, of course. They had just come to a Wednesday night arrangement.

On the other hand . . . if Rachel could manage to find a competent, Hindi-speaking young woman, and if Melina set her nose to the grindstone, it would resolve the problem of Wednesday nights. Rachel would have a foolproof reason to refuse Marc Harris's offer, and his cab, and his attentions. He would be left with no excuse to even show up at her classroom. In fact, Melina's request might resolve multiple challenges.

"I'll check," she said, relenting. "No promises."

"Great! Now, you do realize you'll be on PETA's hate list for eating a pound of cow tonight?"

"There'll be veggies," Rachel protested. "You know, potatoes. And chimichurri sauce is made with herbs."

Melina hooted.

"Work with me here!" Rachel shook out the black dress. "Like Reagan's ketchup!"

The Argentine steakhouse was indeed a vegan's nightmare. Desk-size platters of steaks – "grain-fed or grass-fed, madam?" – were ferried to tables, a rolling cart conveyed sizzling beef sausages, and lusty red wines poured in streams.

An attractive blue-eyed man, his hair turning silver, summoned a busboy. "More water for the lady," he said, indicating Rachel's glass.

"Yes, sir."

Delicious wine, succulent beef, a physically attractive companion . . . it should have been more than enough for the three hours of her life Rachel allotted to this date. Instead, she yearned to join the table across the aisle, where a party of eight celebrated a birthday with ridiculous jokes and unrestrained laughter.

There were no jokes with Jenny's friend Alan Miller. Rachel had tried. Observations, amusing anecdotes, even an Oxford pub story – an old reliable, too – failed to elicit more than a faint restrained smile.

They had met in the restaurant's bar. This time, Jenny had done an excellent job with Alan's physical description, yet –

"You look different from what I expected," he told her. "I thought somewhat taller."

"Ah," Rachel glanced down, "no heels."

"Women should always wear them, they extend the line of the leg," Alan opined, his eyebrows raised.

According to the Miller rules of order, there were an astonishing number of actions women should take. High heels were only the beginning. They led to the question of décolleté before seven in the evening, and the proper length of earrings. On the way to their table, Rachel's elbow was gripped as if she were incapable of steering herself post-vodka martini.

Once seated, Alan lifted his knife, inspecting it for spots. He smoothed down his thin moustache.

My God, he was using the knife as a mirror! Rachel found herself not just envious of the celebrating group nearby, but positively nostalgic for this afternoon's easy camaraderie. Not that she wanted another date with Sean Kennedy, but even "Rach" now rang endearingly. As to Marc . . ..

"So I told her she needed to think of her child –"

"I'm sorry," Rachel interjected, "it's the noise, I'm not following. Whose child?"

"My former girlfriend, the one with the five-year-old. Who came to me six months ago complaining that the thrill was gone."

"Oh, dear, in those words?"

"No, but definitely her meaning. I told her she had to be sensible, a child, for heaven's sake! The thrill's all very well in your twenties, but for the good of her son, she can't be thinking of her own feelings, her own emotions."

"Of course not," Rachel murmured.

"If she didn't enjoy the relationship as much as before, well, you just put pleasure aside, don't you?"

"Bash on regardless, then?"

"Ah, you understand!" Alan practically chortled. "Of course you do, you have some experience of life! That's what's so wonderful about older women."

"Yes, we older women, we certainly have it together." Rachel sipped her wine. "Take Cher, for example."

Outside, another police siren blared. That was the third in as many minutes. As the sound receded, Rachel counted off the seconds. Ten, eleven, twelve . . ..

Her stomach felt tender.

Rachel's wine-fuzzed brain recalled a spirited discussion of youth versus experience, Alan claiming a devoted interest in the latter despite the fact that his last three relationships had been with women no older than thirty. She had a vague memory of assuring the man that they were just too, too different, and stepping into a cab alone.

"You've wholly misread me!" he said, offended.

"You want this guy should get in the cab?" asked the driver. "Sir, step away from the vehicle!" He jolted into traffic. "Lady, you read him right! Where are we goin'?"

On the way to Steph's, she thought again of Melina's Bollywood comparison. On that scale, Alan had definitely blown it. He'd sounded like the just-wrong guy, the one the heroine rejects as a bully despite strong family ties. What was Alan's insistence that his former girlfriend ignore her own feelings but emotional bullying?

At least Melina enjoyed her own evening, a Meryl Streep retrospective complete with Indian take-out, definitely a nod of acceptance from Steph.

"Melina, did you get the leftover *korma*?" called Steph. "Next time, we watch 'Out of Africa', Streep *and* Redford! It doesn't get any better than that!"

Rachel stroked her belly. The Hindu diet, that's what had eased her past red meat – with both beef and pork forbidden, her cookbook scarcely mentioned them, so she hadn't purchased either in weeks – and her devout digestive system simply rebelled against Argentine steak. As soon as she reached home she dashed for the bathroom and plunged to her knees. Melina hovered.

"Cold water?" she offered.

"Thanks," Rachel murmured. She flushed the toilet. Down swirled an expensive grass-fed meal. With it, she figured, went Alan and his severity. Just put pleasure aside? At his urging? Not bloody likely, even for Rachel. She might have problems with allowing herself pleasure, but there was no way she'd buy into the cold aridity of that man's emotional Gobi Desert.

Now, her daughter asleep, the insecure Alan in the past, Rachel stared at her bedroom's ceiling.

"Marc's so nice," Melina had said, her voice bright. Well, she was thirteen. At thirteen, one is easily impressed by men.

Rachel turned over. Not men. A man. A man who taught Rachel a new skill and rejoiced in her accomplishment. One who apologized for error, and suggested a remedy. One with obvious warmth and intelligence.

Outside, another siren screamed past. Rachel tossed the other way, warming her queasy belly with palms red from this afternoon's tussle with the bat.

It didn't matter, she told herself. Fine, Marc Harris possessed several admirable qualities, but he was still the jerk who'd screwed up every Wednesday night from now until May. Every time she recalled that, fresh irritation swept over her like the horns outside her window.

Hell! Why couldn't she doze off, sirens or no sirens? She'd lived in the city long enough to sleep through a night full of them! Well, she knew why. She grimaced. Today was a first, the first time since Oxford that she'd touched a man's body. How long was that? Nine weeks. Nine weeks since she'd felt that pleasure-soaked mix of muscle and bone and blood. Marc's chest against her back, his arms embracing, his hands over hers . . . the man exuded heat and strength and a sort of happy sensuality that was invitation all by itself.

Two months or so, that was nothing compared to the five years of chastity she'd – enjoyed? experienced? endured? – pre-Ian.

Tough years, those, years of silent anguish for someone who couldn't simply hook up after a movie date, bring a man home and see what transpired. Nor could she fly to Jamaica and play wanton for a fortnight with a local. Rachel was not that woman, would never be her, and forcing her squareness into a round hole others reveled in would only scrape her raw and wounded and self-loathing.

Still, even if Ian had proved a false oasis, at least she'd begun to thaw. She'd discovered enough water to rinse off the dust of celibacy, encourage her to hope for plashing fountains. It renewed the feminine in her. Where she'd erred was in welcoming the masculine in the wrong male.

It was humiliating to make such a mistake. It made her feel stupid. Yet, she reminded herself, she might be a lawyer, physician, research scientist, astronaut, any one of those could choose just as badly. The heart has its reasons, of which reason and academics know absolutely nothing. So, where was the solution? To give up all hope of finding a friend and lover? To divorce herself from the society of men?

Rachel stared at the ceiling. Images of wheat fields appeared there, and a young woman wearing a cotton *kurta* over her jeans. All right, how would a Bollywood screenwriter handle this dilemma? Take the heroine, and for such an important story line she had to be the internationally famous Aishwarya Rai Bachchan, no other Indian actress would do. What would a writer have Aish's character do in these circumstances?

More sirens approached. Rachel flipped again and pulled her pillow over her ears to muffle the blare. In the new quiet, she heard a whispered refrain:

Swing and connect.

CHAPTER 15

". . . hard-working eighth grader –"

"Put ninth, they'll take me more seriously."

"Eighth . . . compensation dependent upon experience . . . respond to . . . okay, done. And print. *Voilà!*"

"Just so you know, just for the record, I hate you."

"What? Steph! What are you talking about?" A warning cough beside her made Rachel lower her voice. The bus was full this morning, and her seatmate had courteously folded his Wall Street Journal into a rectangle the width of two neckties. "What'd I do?" she whispered into her cellphone.

"I am never watching another Indian movie! Ever!"

"Oh, no, what'd you rent? Something awful?"

"It had the handsome dude in it, that was good. It also had a parrot! A cartoon parrot!" Steph screeched. "And a dog whose face went . . . well, I'm never trusting your movie judgment again."

"Oh, Steph, you should have asked! That one will put you off Bollywood for life."

"It sure as hell did. And the misspelled captions, too. Would it be too much to hire a copyeditor?"

"But there –"

"But! No buts! Forget it, Rachel, no frickin' way. Forget the music and the dancing and even the Pyramids, I'm swearing off Bollywood before I swear at *you*."

"Why do they argue? Aside from what we know of the Elizabethan love of wordplay and double entendre, which Shakespeare shows off here not just for his own pleasure but – the audience, always count those heads! – to get respect and laughs, and therefore sell more admissions to future performances . . . why give these two characters so incredibly many words to use as weapons?"

"Tension?"

"Heighten the drama?"

"How?" Rachel demanded. She stood, one finger holding the place in her own well-worn copy of "Much Ado About Nothing".

"It's like swordplay," a student volunteered. "With a foil, you test your opponents' mettle, you try different ways of approaching, see how they respond. Do they back off? Do they meet you? How skilled are they? Do they have the right stuff?"

"Do they, here, do Beatrice and Benedick have the right stuff for each other?" Rachel inquired.

"They're well-matched, yeah."

"How can you tell?" she countered.

"They're always responding to each other. She spins a pun out of what he says, he extends it another way, she carries it somewhere else."

"Responsive," said Rachel, darting to the board to write the word. "He pushes, she pushes back."

"How is that well-matched?" came the question. "He pushes, she should give way!"

"Aha! It's – let's see – Conor, right? Okay, Conor, you like a girl, you approach, what do you want her to do, scamper off like a frightened little bunny? 'Oh, dear me, he's too much, no, no, no!' like some silly nineteenth-century miss?"

The class broke with laughter.

"*We* know the Victorians' love of pretense, but Shakespeare, writing centuries before them, had no idea. Imagine yourself in Elizabethan London. You meet a woman. You advance, you want her to advance. You offer your hand, you want *her* hand. You push, you want her to meet that push." Rachel paused. "Remember that Shakespeare's audience reveled in sexual imagery. 'Much Ado About Nothing', where the word 'nothing' carries a lascivious double meaning? This wordplay, this parrying, is the verbal precursor of a very physical act, the kiss before the kiss. What would Beatrice do if Benedick failed to, er, rise to her verbal challenges?" she pressed.

"Ignore him?"

"Ignore him, yes. Keep her eye out for another man, sure. Flirt! She doesn't have to resort to that, though, because whether she likes it or not, she and Benedick are made for each other, they're meant to be together, and as uncomfortable as that feels to both of them in the first two acts, they keep proving it to one another, don't they?"

Her classes were engaging, at times even playful, and they moved easily from one scene to another. Her students also brought their own experiences to the texts. "He's using his version of a Mohs test" – that from a sunny girl majoring in geology – prompted a fascinating to-and-fro about toughness versus tenderness, and how do we measure that, anyway, as society or as individual?

"Are men allowed to cry?" Rachel asked. "Hands up for yes." A young forest of waving fingers met her. "Guys only: do you let people see you cry?" The space above her students' heads abruptly emptied. "If we don't see you, we'll think you can't," she chided.

"Sort of the point," the young man nearest her muttered.

"I'll have to bring in one of my Bollywood flicks, where men are openly emotional. I'm talking megastars, Hrithik Roshan and Shah Rukh Khan. American actors tend to be analytical about their craft – 'why am I doing this at this particular place in the script?' – but Indian actors use the energy they get from their feelings."

"And the Brits? Shakespeare?" The call came from the back of the room.

"Brits now? Pragmatic. 'Just hit your mark and say your lines, love, all right?' But in Shakespeare's time, there must have been plenty of displayed emotion, otherwise there'd be no struggle between feeling and reason worth writing about. Yes?"

Rachel ate another bite of chocolate doughnut and took stock.

Melina was solidly into school, academically and socially, with friends spending the night and returning invitations.

Concerned about her own emotional turmoil, Steph had scheduled regular pampering at a day spa. Facials and massages apparently worked wonders.

Chandani Naik was developing into a friend with a vast store of knowledge – and gossip – about Indian filmmaking. Just to listen to her opinions of Bollywood producers was an education.

Rachel had had no recent date encounters . . . thank God. Though they got her out ("of my way," Melina observed) and provided fertile ground for recaps and amused discussion, she felt a profound sense of relief when Saturdays rolled around with nothing penciled onto her calendar.

"Men saunter out of their caves pretending they don't belong to a social species, that they don't need love. When what they really think is that they don't deserve it," Steph reminded her. "You know about caves, great stuff back there. But it's only useful when they shlep it down to the shoreline and actually share it with a mermaid. He brings his cave treasure, she's got what she's managed to snatch from under the sea, so together, wow!"

Rachel held her tongue.

"Of course, it's only a metaphor," Steph mused. "I'm not calling you Daryl Hannah. Though Tom Hanks seems like a good guy."

"Film reference, please?"

"'Splash', 1984, Daryl as the mermaid. How come you don't know that?"

Work, daughter, suspended social life, and Rachel's book was progressing, if at a snail's pace. Though generally she wrote at lightning speed, these days, for some reason, she struggled with text. Still, every week she accomplished a few more pages.

Then there was Marc Harris. She had worried that the batting cage lesson might give way to greater familiarity, that she'd have to take measures to avoid further contact. Yet aside from Wednesday nights at nine, accompanying them to a taxi, Marc might have vanished. Rachel made casual inquiries of Jenny, who referred to meetings with administration . . . prospective donors . . . possible new faculty . . . and an obscure conference in Montreal mentioned in passing.

Unfortunately, Jenny spoke very little these days. Perhaps Alan had complained of their date, that Rachel didn't take him seriously, or, heavens, had put her own emotional needs first. "Sorry, Jen, just didn't work!" failed to mollify. Jenny seemed to take the unsuccessful steak dinner very personally.

However, it made Rachel's avoidance of the departmental office a snap.

The doorbell rang.

"He's here, he's here!" shouted Melina. She vaulted down the stairs.

"Look before you open!"

A deep voice from below brought Melina's delighted squeals.

"There you are!" Rachel was enveloped in a bearhug resonant with competing scents of cologne and tobacco. She leaned back.

"Oh, Steve, the nicotine patch didn't work?"

"Nosy! Not yet, I'll try again. How are you?" Her older brother held her at arm's length. "You look good. You look better, actually, than last time. That idiot Ian dragged you down. Things okay at work?"

"Fine. What do you want right now?" Rachel asked, patting his arm. "Beer? Food? Sleep?"

"Yes, yes, and yes. In that order."

It was remarkable how the entrance of one man changed the atmosphere. It was not just Steve's size, or the easy athleticism that showed in the toss of a potholder. It was neither his voice nor the stories he told over a sandwich, stories of family life in Copenhagen with his Danish wife and two potential World Cup players.

"That's how I stay in shape," he smiled, punching his own stomach, "on the pitch with the boys. And biking to work. You should do that, Rachel, what is it to NYU, five miles?"

"Oh, yes," she agreed, "on streets that don't have separate raised bike lanes like yours, so any unregistered Buick can drift over and smash me into a Starbucks."

"Chicken Little!"

"Cluck, already."

It was simply the maleness of him, the different take on life, the refreshing chasm in perceptions between two people brought up by the same parents.

"I like having him here," confided Melina, after Steve, yawning hugely, had closed the guestroom door.

"You're especially into Danish chocolate."

"True, but I also like that he's here." By its gold-colored thread, Melina lifted one of the paper mobiles Mette had sent from the Stroget sales. Cut-out children frolicked before a country schoolhouse. "He's so *him*."

"He is, indeed. Time for bed, Bini."

Gathering her chocolate bars, Melina started up the steps. She stopped and leaned over the rail. "He reminds me of someone," she said.

"Really? Who?"

Melina grinned. "You don't want to know!" she singsonged, and scampered up.

"That takes guts, Rachel," her brother said, sipping his beer. "I can't imagine dating again." Steve shuddered. "Mette better stay healthy! Hey, there's a guy I'm seeing today, I've worked with him online, he seems all right, you know, smart, quick. Maybe you'd want to meet him? Cameron Cho. His kids are grown, he keeps joking about coming over to see our windfarm installations and meet a nice Danish woman. I'll give him your number, Rachel, if that works for you."

"No, thanks. I'm not even Danish," she pointed out.

"You drink Carlsberg, that's halfway. And it would be a favor to me, if he's looking at a transfer. Give me more to go on," Steve said persuasively. He tapped her arm for emphasis. "Please?"

"Oh, that's pretty."

Melina twirled. The silky fabric she held in one hand wrapped about her.

"Beautiful!" That was Chopra Tailors' salesman, preening a carefully-shaped moustache. "We make *salwar kameez* from it, to die for!"

"How long will it take?" asked Rachel

"It's not India, you know," he warned, "not so fast. Maybe two weeks. We deliver!"

"What about saris?"

"Yes, madam, saris straight from India, all places, Varanasi-style to Rajasthan, very elegant. We make you *choli* blouse and petticoat anytime, we have your measurements, just tell us neckline style, sleeve length and all that! We deliver!"

An hour later, not only was Melina satisfied with a saffron *salwar kameez*-to-be ("I'll wear it weekends!" she promised), but even Rachel had succumbed to the lure of black, with a positively luscious rose-hued *dupatta*. She wasn't quite ready for a sari, not yet, but there was something about tunic-and-trousers with a *dupatta* in a good-enough-to-eat color. It drew her like the scent of coriander.

"And we deliver!"

Rachel clutched the sports car's door and slammed her right foot to the floor. Beside her, blatantly ignoring her fear, Cameron Cho leadfooted the gas pedal. The car barreled north.

Why had she given in to Steve's suggestion? What exactly had she welcomed in the chasm of perceptions between her brother and herself? Refreshing, was it? More like suicidal.

It wasn't that Cameron thought she liked speed. At the car's first lurch, the first *zoom* up to an SUV's back bumper, Rachel had protested. "I'm in no hurry," she said lightly. "Back off a bit, okay?"

"Sure," he replied, and eased up on the gas for a good thirty seconds before catching up to draft behind the other vehicle.

It did no good to speak up, she found. Cameron tailgated and wove in and out of traffic. He talked. He gestured. He steered with his knees.

". . . so there we were in Spain, great food, great wine, and all day long she's throwing up!" Cameron chuckled. "Man, she was sick, so I started going out after breakfast, otherwise I'd never have seen anything. I mean, for better or for worse, but pregnancy threw a huge monkey wrench, and we were only twenty-four."

"Look out!"

He hit the brakes just in time to avoid a motorcyclist whose middle finger rocketed up at them.

"Hey, thanks! The biker thanks you, too."

Four appalled faces surrounded her at the dinner table.

Steve cleared his throat and raised his beer. "Here's to getting you back in one piece."

"Hear, hear!" That from Steph, who looked annoyed.

Melina and her friend Talia clinked their water glasses together. "Would an Indian man do that?" Melina demanded. "I mean in a movie."

"Of course not. Which is why, if I were you," Rachel turned to her brother, "I wouldn't bring Cameron out to Denmark. Let him stay here. Or," her eyes twinkled, "maybe there's a windfarm in South Dakota you could post him to?"

Steve shook his head. "After scaring my little sister? Cho's off to Wyoming."

CHAPTER 16

Rachel checked once again: ticket, boarding pass, passport. Chocolate bars, book to read, the ubiquitous cell phone, iPod. And the carry-on bag. "Get your dad to call me as soon as he meets you," she commanded. "You'll be too tired to make any sense, crying babies and all."

"Mommy, I sleep through babies!" protested Melina.

This was true, Melina snoozed through infant colic with enviable ease, something to do with pre-motherhood. "I still wish I could go with you," Rachel said, eyeing the fast-moving security lines. Experienced flyers shucked shoes as though they'd spent childhoods in Bangalore. "Maybe I should have asked for an escort."

"I've done this trip before," Melina reminded her. "I just now saw some of the same flight attendants from when I came back. I know how to attach myself to women with children, honest."

"And if some jerk –?"

"I get up and tell someone in a uniform," Melina recited, "and I keep acting upset until they switch my seat. Don't worry."

"Ha! Like telling me not to breathe."

"I'll be fine! I'll be back on Sunday."

Rachel drew her close. "Hug. Kiss. More kiss. Love you, sweetheart!"

"Me, too. Tell me all about the Tollivers' party!"

"Oh, right, the party. No big deal. But the pig will miss you."

"I don't think so!" Melina joined the line. On the other side of the rope, Rachel kept abreast.

"No, it'll sense you're not there, and be all burned up about it. Everyone will blame Bitsy's uncles, never realizing that the pig refused to cooperate with its own roast."

"*Mom.*" Melina made the U-turn. "I'll be fine. Sunday!"

Rachel blew a kiss. She watched Melina slide off her shoes, place her coat and other items in a gray plastic bin, and sail through the metal detector.

She parked the Tollivers' car, which Dan had insisted she borrow "for flexibility", and reentered her house.

It was quiet. Very quiet. Too awfully quiet. What would she do when this sort of profound silence was commonplace, when Melina left for college? Broken only by traffic sounds from East End, the occasional horn or squeal of brakes, the stillness reminded her of something.

Oh, yes. Rachel frowned. All the house needed was a chorus of "Climb Every Mountain" to make it a perfect, safe little nunnery.

Contemplative, she plunked herself square in the sofa's center. Safe was . . . good, yes, safe was good, in proportion. However, as with chocolate chip cookies, one could add too many sensible walnuts, thereby burying the cookies' raison d'être. Chocolate chip cookies should ooze with semisweet.

The image made her mouth water.

Ransacking cabinets and drawers proved futile. Either Melina had gobbled every morsel of available chocolate – possible – or else Rachel had simply neglected to replenish the supply. Also possible, especially since their tastes had veered toward South Asian. These days, desserts were much more likely to be flavored with cardamom than cocoa, including the creamy *mishti doi* she'd made two nights ago, overnighting it in a cooling oven. It was delicious, and decadent for breakfast. But her body craved cacao.

Going out just for chocolate was ridiculous. Combined with a healthy long walk, however, no longer was it indulgence, it was transformed into virtue, even if she just happened to stop in at the little grocery three blocks away, the one run by the Iranian family. Rachel tossed on a coat.

A hundred steps later, her hair and clothes sparkled with a fine mist of rain. Perhaps even chocolate wasn't worth the wet. She could always improvise. A jar of Bournvita, the cocoa malt powder favored in India, waited on her shelf. There was enough to mix with a glass of milk. It would take the edge off her longing.

On the other hand . . ..

In her pocket, her cell phone rang.

"Hello?"

"Rachel, it's Chandani Naik." Music framed Chandani's soft voice, along with a ragged but enthusiastic chorus: "*Dekho, dekho, hai shaan badi deewani . . .* Hold on!" The phone, half-covered, muffled Chandani's pleas. "*Bas!* Quiet!"

"But *didi . . .*" a girl's voice began.

"I'm searching for somewhere quiet, Rachel. Here, I found a closet. Listen, I'm at my uncle's in the city, if you have time would you like to join us? He's running Yash Raj films in a loop, and we'll be calling my cousin, get the latest word from Mumbai. Will you come?"

Thirty minutes later, a door opened to Rachel and she entered an apartment crowded with merriment. Chandani drew her in.

"*Ao, ao!* Hard to believe, but it's quieter than it was, the neighbors complained. Here's my uncle Rajeev."

Rachel shook hands with a heavily-mustached man who offered her a can of Coke. Smiling, she shook her head, feeling as if she'd stepped into a classic Hindi movie scene.

"Thanks, *chacha*, but . . ." Chandani gestured ahead.

She and Rachel squirmed between joking teenagers speaking New York-accented Hinglish, toward a large plasma TV where the familiar face of the actress Kajol lit up the screen. She must have been barely out of her teens then, thought Rachel.

"There's so much Coca-Cola here, it looks like a Bollywood set," complained Chandani, reading her mind. "What would you like to do, watch? Eat? *Samosas*, snacks, sweets. Talk?"

They had found a corner where the decibel level was subdued enough to hear without shouting. Rachel wished she'd grabbed a pen and notebook, since Chandani provided a running commentary to match the screened movie.

". . . so he's regarded as the original genius of romantic comedy," explained Chandani. "Keeps going in his seventies, and still feuding with Amitabh."

"Aren't they a little old for tiffs?" joked Rachel.

"You'd think so. Then there's Ronnie Screwvala, have you heard of him? Head of UTV? He graduated from Mumbai University, no connections in movies, but went straight into television, and now . . . well, he's shaking up the old guard. Americans love him, and you know why? He makes films on time. You know Indians, everything's IST – Indian Standard Time, meaning *late* – well, Screwvala finishes a movie in three months, and actually on budget. Amazing! Some people hate his guts, because the old ways die hard, but –"

"Chandani, *didi*, come on, sing with us!" The speaker, a ten-year-old in jeans and a Giants T-shirt grabbed Chandani and yanked her up. "You know more than anyone! C'mon!"

Rachel followed them to the round table. People of all ages ringed it. Small children squirmed on grandparents' laps.

"You know this? It's *antakshari*," Chandani explained. "It's a game where we take turns starting Hindi film songs, the first two lines, at least, and the next song has to start with the last consonant of the first song. You'll pick it up!"

"Chandani knows hundreds," boasted a young girl.

Uncle Rajeev waved a hand for silence. In a portentous bass, he recited a verse in Hindi.

"That's always the start," Chandani explained. "Did you hear the last word?"

"Was it name, *naam*?" guessed Rachel.

"*Naam*, right! So the next song has to start with the sound of *ma*." Chandani began to sing in a lovely, melodic contralto, moving her arms as though dancing in place. "*Mera jhumka utha ke laaya re yaar ve, jo gira tha bareli ke bazaar me . . . .*" Around the room, her relatives applauded. Rhythmic hands beat against the table, and Rachel joined in. She'd heard this song before, she was sure of it, she simply couldn't identify it. The others let Chandani sing on. When she reached the chorus, new voices joined in.

" *. . .. aaja nachle nachle mere yaar tu nachle, jhanak jhanak jhankaar . . .*"

"*Ra!* " called a small boy, "next one's *ra!*"

Friday evening stayed brisk. A strong wind smelled of snow. Blizzards in western Pennsylvania might reach the city tomorrow, forecasters cheerfully reported. For now, the stinging wind barely entered Hansen Place, sheltered as it was by high-rises. A six-pack of Kingfisher in each hand, Rachel crossed the pavement to the Tollivers' house. Before it stretched an enormous steel contraption on wheels. Smoke seeped forth, and a man in camouflage cap and denim jacket stood guard as though the gray-stained barbecue grill were a particularly irritable tiger.

Rachel had heard it arrive. With a clanking, metallic grinding accompanied by colorful curses it was installed before Bitsy and Dan's door. She peered out. Two baseball-capped men in their fifties wrestled with the machine, backing and forth-ing to establish it. Under one side they leveled shims.

"Got it?" yelled one.

"Sumbitch still needs a fuckin' quarter-inch, toss me a thin shim, the thinnest y'got!"

A thin shim tossed and placed, the wheeled barbecue was ready. All it lacked was the pig, which Dan proudly delivered in his trunk several hours later. Rachel, whose curiosity salivated, brought out her broom to sweep. Hers was not the only stoop receiving attention. Mrs. Burke brushed dust from her own. She winked at Rachel, and nodded toward the baseball caps.

"Had to go all the way to Queens for this guy!" Dan swaggered. "Look at him!"

"Looks good, Dan," one of the uncles said in a skeptical tone. "Lemme see that purchase order." He examined the yellow slip of paper. "Hundred-thirty. Yeah, right weight, son. Okay, let's get this fucker out!" With grunts, the three men tugged at the plastic-wrapped, roped carcass.

Mrs. Burke scurried inside.

How many months since Rachel last consumed pork? Her body would probably rebel just as thoroughly to barbecue as it had to the steak. Rachel frowned. A tiny portion, then, just a taste, that would be enough.

She fled her frigid stoop, recalling pig roasts from her graduate school years in Virginia, the Blue Ridge rising shadowy in the west. If memory served, the men would stuff the carcass with apples, herbs, and garlic, douse it with beer, and start it on ashy coals tonight. All night long they'd tend the grill, replace fuel, and baste the pig. By tomorrow evening the pig – charred skin or not, Rachel thought, remembering Melina – would be ready to "pick", its meat served on round buns with cole slaw, baked beans, chips, and whatever Big Apple-friendly accoutrements Bitsy invented.

Last night, Melina had persuaded her father to pop her over for dinner-to-go from In-N-Out. Rachel's phone rang at eleven, just a few minutes after she'd gotten home, her ears ringing with Hindi lyrics and in her purse a small plastic bag of round breads, deep-fried *puris* pressed on her by Chandani's *chachi*, her aunt.

". . . double fries," Melina reported. "And we're going to stop by Ellie's office to look at her storyboards."

"Oh, listen to you all producer-y!"

"Hold on, Daddy wants to talk."

"Hey, Rach, how are you? Yeah, she's stuffed, the digestive tract of the adolescent. Listen, I've got business in New York next week, I booked the seat right next to Melina's."

"Oh, Jason, that'd be great. Really." Rachel's shoulders descended from around her ears. "Thank you, I feel so much better."

"No problem. Enjoy your pig!"

How far she had come from those barbecues in Virginia, with their beer-sozzled revelry! The flirtations of unmarried students leavened the constant work and evaluations of graduate programs, but few of those coupled then were partnered now. Rachel counted them on one hand, with fingers left free. Physical attraction alone was a poor foundation for marriage – Rachel's included – compared to friendship and shared values. Without those, a couple was paired in a boat, each rowing toward a separate shore. No wonder if all they achieved were spiraling circles.

Though parent-mandated marriages were on the wane in India, the arranging of marriages was still practiced, in part to avoid those circles. If the couple had similar values and goals, in theory they'd row toward the same green grass, wouldn't they?

Clad in jeans, she nodded to the uncle-in-charge and stepped past the barbecue.

"Rachel! You look great, you sexy thing!" Dan greeted her at his door over a cranked-up rendition of U2. He transferred a glass of bourbon to his left hand in order to wrap his right arm around her waist. "And classy beer, too, look, hon!"

"I see it, sweetheart." Bitsy's voice was high with nerves. A small line curved between her brows. "Thank you, Rachel. Did you meet my uncle, outside? Tom?"

"His divorce isn't final," confided Dan.

"Not *quite*," Bitsy said, pulling on her husband's shirt. "But Bob's in the kitchen, if you don't mind carrying those back? Thanks. Dan, honey –"

Amused, Rachel turned right and peeked into the kitchen. Along the counters stood beer, vodka, tequila, a lonely half-bottle of white wine, more beer. Rachel set her companion six-packs onto the heavy oak table.

"You're Rachel?"

The camouflage cap was the same, but the jacket was brown leather. This must be Bitsy's already-single Uncle Bob. Rachel held out her hand. "Bitsy's thrilled about this weekend, she says you and Tom are pig-pickin' kings," she told him.

"That we are, young lady." Bob removed his cap, revealing a shock of brown hair to match his chin fuzz. Beneath the scuffed jacket he wore a Dave Matthews Band T-shirt. "So, which beer's yours?"

"Actually, I was thinking wine –"

"Nope, gotta be beer," Bob said firmly, "goes better with chips. Bitsy's got some fancy hors d'oeuvres coming out later, save the wine for them. And," he removed the cap from a bottle of Tecate and handed it to Rachel, "let's find us something bigger than a pair of kitchen stools."

Bob Randolph was a born raconteur. A high school coach ("football, hoops, baseball . . . hell, we barely know what a lacrosse stick looks like!"), he told tales of interfering parents and recalcitrant principals. He'd served in the Navy, done a Peace Corps stint, lived in the Philippines with his first wife ("man, were we young and stupid!"), all of which spawned stories delivered in a self-deprecating manner at once humorous and attractive.

He was fit, too. He shed his leather jacket to reveal a pair of extremely muscular forearms. One bore a small anchor.

"Classic sailor tat," he commented, flexing it. "Got some ink on my back, too. You have any? Little butterfly, heart?"

"Me? No!" Rachel laughed. "I pierced my ears, that was enough."

A second Tecate had appeared beside Rachel's empty one. Rachel took a hefty swallow. Bob was right, beer was perfect for tortilla chips and salsa. She wouldn't be driving, Melina was three time zones away, and her own front door only fifty feet off. The time was right for throwing caution to the increasingly Arctic winds. She tipped the new bottle up.

"C'mon, you can tell me," Bob urged her. "It's no big deal, everyone's done something."

"Nope, no enhancements at all, anywhere. Don't plan on any. Ever. Even Botox," she added, remembering Helen. "I'd rather look human."

Bob laughed and patted her knee. "You've made a great start!" He rose to grab a bag of potato chips, using her leg to struggle up from the sofa. He sat back tight against Rachel and tore the bag open. "Bitsy tells me you spent time in the Commonwealth."

"The Comm . . . oh, Virginia. Yes." An arm edged around Rachel's shoulder. She glanced up. Blue eyes, why were there so many pairs of blue eyes?

Bob's lips met hers.

Startled, Rachel reared back. "Wow!" she said. "Didn't see that coming." Suddenly she realized that despite the music of Willie Nelson, she was entirely alone in the living room with Bitsy's Uncle Bob. "Don't you need to tend the pig?" she inquired.

Bob threw back his head and roared. "You're funny, Rachel!" he admitted, wiping his eyes. "A funny woman!"

Too late, she heard her own unintended double-meaning. She, who lectured students on Shakespearean puns! She felt terribly green.

"God, that's what was wrong with my ex-wife. I mean the last one," Bob amended. "No sense of humor at all! Tell her a joke . . . now, I'm a damn good storyteller, aren't I? Tell the truth, now! But do the same routine for Missy, not a smile. Not a twinkle! Nothin'!" Bob shook his head, mournful. "It's a hard thing, Rachel, when a man tries to make his wife laugh and comes up dry."

His arm felt warm and heavy across her shoulders. His fingers stroked her neck. The tiny hairs rose.

"She was fantastic in bed, though. Man! Making love with Missy was –"

"What?"

"Fantastic! In bed, she was the best!"

Rachel inhaled.

Her toothbrush was fraying. She ought to buy a new one. Rachel stretched her wet bath towel along its rail and glanced at the rapidly defogging mirror. Clean teeth, clean skin, clean hair. She'd scrubbed with a loofah, so one shower was probably enough.

She padded to her room and slid between flannel sheets. From outside came men's voices: Bob's voice, Tom's voice, both just this side of nasty drunk. She'd bet Dan would shuttle between the two with peace negotiations.

Fortunately, Melina would never hear *this* story.

And as far as her Bollywood guideline went, Bob was so far off it as to inhabit another universe.

CHAPTER 17

The next morning chimed too bright. Rachel sipped her tea, blinking at the heat. A submerged memory rose: a college party of too many kegs, the walk back to her dorm in sheeting rain, one young man still sober enough to recognize Rachel's tipsy need for cross-campus companionship. Brian? Ryan? By the next day, he had graciously forgotten.

How different last night from the family-centered evening with Chandani's relatives! There, songs and sweets and even amiable disputes welcomed her. She felt a wave of nostalgia for the Patels in Oxford. Even though she and Pinky still kept up via e-mail, electronic communications could never replace warmth and real concern, two more qualities for Melina to add to her hero list. And Shakespeare? How did his heroes demonstrate warmth, beyond scaling orchard walls high and hard to climb?

Rachel watched the second hand of her kitchen clock. Three more circuits, and she might do something more constructive than consume English Breakfast. She was only using caffeine to steel herself, anyway.

The needle began its last circuit. To call or not to call? She had the number, that was no problem. But would it be wrong?

Thirty seconds. She could always leave a message. Ten. She dialed.

"Hi, this is Rachel. Sorry to call so early on a Saturday, but I want to ask a favor . . .."

Plump pillows, wipe dust, rearrange stray books. What was LeGuin doing beside the Hindi dictionary? Really, she ought to vacuum the living room. She glanced into the kitchen. There, too.

Vacuuming led to repositioning counter appliances gave way to cookbook-sorting. Rachel stacked them on the wooden table. There were too many. Did she really need the pizza manual? And two Thai cookbooks?

As it often did these days, her mind veered to her own book. The Heroine, in uppercase. In Indian film as in Shakespeare, whose feminine roles arrived last on the billing, the heroine was far less important than the hero. In a war film or action movie, the heroine might be considered even less vital than weaponry or motorcycles. She would be present, of course, as eye candy. Perhaps she would represent what the soldier was fighting for. To the Indian audience, she was there as the wife-to-be of the hero, even if her sometimes scanty costumes made the conservative among them uneasy.

Clothes told so much. Rachel's own new *salwar kameez*, delivered sooner than expected, fitted perfectly. No wonder, for the two dozen measurements taken. The pants – tight-fitting *churidar* – had even required the tape to slip around knee and ankle.

Back to The Heroine, who might wrap herself in a sari for the last five minutes, when the audience raced for exits, eager to grab taxis and run down tube steps. She had changed substantially, the heroine, even in the short span of Indian film familiar to Rachel. She was less girly, more earnest, and occasionally more focused and down-to-earth than the hero.

"Right there!" Rachel took the stairs by twos, making her Bloomies bracelets jingle. She'd applied lipstick with a nervous hand. God, why? This was not a date, this was a non-date, a marker called in.

At the door, she met a large bouquet. Marc Harris appeared from behind the flowers. "I couldn't resist, call it the floral equivalent of ten percent interest."

She accepted them, cream and pale yellow and periwinkle blue. "Thanks. Pretty, but ten is excessive," she added, frowning.

"I added points for the batting cage blitz." Marc regarded her. "Should I be in costume, too?"

"It's a *salwar kameez*."

"I know, I was kidding. I like the pink scarf thingy. And it covers you nicely against men who brag about their bed partners. But is this –?" He swiped at his jeans and tweed jacket.

"Fine, they're fine, I'll get these in water." Rachel dashed for the kitchen, the flowers at arm's length. Returning, she found Marc perusing her bookshelves, a volume open in his hand.

He held it up. "You really *are* into India."

"Which? Oh, that. Required reading, I heard."

Marc reshelved the book. "Ground rules? Advice? When it comes to non-dates, I'm a novice. But if the object is to keep Uncle What's-his-name at a distance –"

Rachel wrapped her coat about her. "Stick like glue, please. A few proprietarial looks might be useful, he's the kind of guy who understands rejection only if it's accompanied by another man."

"Is he bigger than me?"

"No . . . just older, and more of a jerk."

"*More* of a jerk."

She reddened. "Sorry! Jerk, him. You . . . non-jerk. So non-jerk. It's really, really generous of you to do this, especially on such short notice. I wouldn't have asked, only the Tollivers –"

Marc made her a small bow. "My pleasure. Flexes my acting muscles. Gluestick, a little Petruchio . . . I think I've got it."

Once more in the Tollivers' living room, Rachel was unable to progress. A flushed quartet of men bellowing to "Satisfaction" blocked her way. Beer sloshed from their blue plastic cups.

"Switch with me," came Marc's voice in her ear. Squeezing ahead, he grabbed her hand and muscled forward. Rachel felt his muscled fingers as the men magically gave way like the sea to Moses.

Once in the kitchen, Marc immediately dropped her hand. Bypassing the keg, he examined the bottles. "Beer? Or," he ran his hand over the selection, "beer? We could do a survey, German, Mexican, Indian, Chinese, Spanish . . . that one must be someone's idea of a joke. Oh, a bottle of Riesling!"

Rachel stuck out her tongue.

"*Nein* to the Riesling, then."

"Anything pale, and one only."

Marc picked out three bottles, stuffing one in his pocket. "If we set it outside in the cold," he explained, "we won't have to squeeze back here."

"Ah, brilliant!"

"Follow me, follow." Again the warm fingers wrapped securely around hers as he struggled through the boisterous crowd to the front door. Rachel frowned. Even his hand felt confident. It was warm and . . ..

Ahead, Bob Randolph appeared, baseball cap askew.

"Twelve o'clock, cap, soul patch," Rachel shouted in Marc's ear.

Bob approached slowly. He hadn't yet spotted Rachel. A hand at her waist guided her to one side, on a trajectory apart from the crowd and out of the man's path, searching out an empty spot in the peopled rooms.

He's so nice, Mom! . . . so nice . . . swing and connect . . . swing and . . ..

Rachel's hand crept to Marc's cheek. Startled, he glanced down. She lifted herself on tiptoe and pressed her lips to his. The effect was instantaneous. His mouth responded, warm and tender, pressing hers with a subtle pressure that made her grasp his arm for balance. She felt the tiniest flick of tongue. Just as in Sephora, her head swam.

"Yo, Rachel?"

They parted.

"Bob." The monosyllable was an effort. "Bitsy's uncle," she explained, unable to meet Marc's eye.

"Marc Harris." The voice was calm, the handshake firm.

"You two together?"

At Rachel's waist, Marc's hand tightened. "Yup."

"Oh, c'mon, Rachel, honey! We gotta whole hog here, take lots more!" Dan's Tidewater accent had thickened. He brandished a frighteningly large fork. "Hot sauce down there by the beans. Hi, I'm Dan," he continued, taking Marc's plate and filling it with barbecued pork, "you been with Rachel long?"

"No, thanks, that's great."

"Ah, a new romance!" Dan crowed, stressing the first syllable. "Had no idea! Listen, she's an amazing, amazing lady. Shit, if Bitsy ever left me, I'd plant myself on Rachel's porch the next day, trust me, the very next day! Now, you know she's got a daughter, don't you?"

"Yes, I know," Marc replied.

Gripped by both men, the plate quivered.

"You got kids? No? Why, you don't like kids?"

"Can't make 'em on my own," Marc pointed out. "Plate?"

Dan let go. "I'm gonna have kids, Bitsy and I are gonna have kids. Definitely. And soon, real soon. You got enough meat there, Rachel?" He winked.

Marc joined her in the middle of the macadam. "Back in? Or over to your place? Or," his voice softened, "maybe my part's finished?" He lifted her chin.

"I . . . I . . . ."

"Look, impetuous kisses are one thing. It was nice, it was," he hesitated, "extremely nice." He shrugged. "But if we're done here, we're done."

"I . . .."

"Let's get you out of the cold, anyway," and Marc accompanied her up the steps and watched her fumble with the key. Taking it from her, he inserted it into the lock. Warm air spilled out. He reached in and flipped up the lightswitch, and pressed his plate into her free hand. "Would you toss this? See you Monday." The door closed gently behind him.

After a moment, Rachel carried both plates into the shadowy kitchen. She shoved them into the trashcan and sat at the table, propping her chin in her hands. Staring at the fridge, she worried her lip.

When she was a girl, the house where she now lived had been the prized jewel of her maternal grandmother, what Hindi movies would call her *naani*. On Rachel's trips to the city, landing there after the hour-long train ride had been like reaching a shore full of nooks and crannies into which she burrowed, nose in a book, after a museum or concert or play. The house was refuge for an awkward girl, a geeky loner. She would stay overnight up on the third floor in what was now Melina's room, and dream on the windowseat, nibbling Oreos.

Moving into the house after Gran died, she'd wondered if the sense of safe haven would remain. For the most part, it had, making the house a refuge of calm on a larger island of everyday noise and clamor.

Now, however, peace lay in shards.

CHAPTER 18

T hen he left?"

"He left," Rachel acknowledged, puffing. "Watch out!"

Steph dodged to avoid the stroller in her path. "What is it with this park, baby boom?"

"Citywide."

"But they're all here!" *Puff puff puff.*

Schurz Park *was* unusually stroller-dense this morning. From light folding contraptions to the industrial-strength Hummers of the infant set, babies were on display . . . wailing, sleepy, or round-eyed as puppies.

"Used to nurse Melina here," Rachel panted. "Talk to other mommies. Collegial."

"So how was it?"

"How was what?"

Steph stopped. "The kiss!"

"Steph." Rachel walked in small circles, catching her breath.

"Don't 'Steph' me, he's an attractive guy, can he kiss?"

"I don't want to talk about it."

"Sure you do."

Rachel shook her head. Her jaw felt tight. In her mind, one image of Marc played over and over. "See you Monday." The blue eyes, their question answered unhappily. The door closing. Each time it closed, it shut out noise, the smell of roast meat, and something she could not quite identify, something that niggled.

"C'mon, this is a legitimate academic question!"

"It was a nine, now shut up about it! It was a mistake, we both know that."

"*I* don't know that," said Steph.

"I mean him. God, why did I –? That was stupid, asking him, just to avoid the uncle."

"Nine, huh?"

"Stop. Or I'll start in on your Steven Spielberg crush." Rachel walked on.

They ran south, on their left hand the river. The benches to their right were occupied by women well-wrapped against the cold, who knitted and chatted in Mandarin, Arabic, Spanish, each bench a narrow embassy.

"Too many dogs!" Steph gasped. "Why keep a Lab in the city?"

"Half are borrowed, to meet women. Break?"

Panting, they leaned against the riverside railing. In the soft winter light, its steel had warmed.

"We are so out of shape. Look at these arms! I want Jessica Alba's arms," said Steph.

"How many push-ups would that take?" Rachel gazed east, shading her eyes. "How's Rubén?"

"Slammed with papers and projects. Tell me about your book."

"No way. Ready?" Rachel poked her in the ribs.

"Moment." Steph drew in long breaths, stretching her arms above her. "It may be tough seeing Marc at work."

"I know. C'mon." Without waiting, Rachel sprinted on.

She checked the kitchen clock. Another hour until Melina's plane landed, perhaps as many as two more until Jason deposited her at home. Melina would be tired and over-excited.

The electric kettle clicked off. Rachel pulled a teabag from its canister and filled her mug. To lemon or not to lemon? She examined the produce bin. Not.

She slid a CD into the player, one of Melina's iTunes-produced ones replete with Indian movie songs. The air filled with soaring melody. Steaming mug beside her, Rachel bent to Shakespeare. Tomorrow her three classes would begin "A Midsummer Night's Dream", one of Rachel's favorite plays. "Dream" was popular, both romantic and erotic, amusing in its confusion of the lovers, and with the added fillip of the rustics' play-within-a-play to elicit raucous laughter.

At any rate, it would provide for plenty of discussion. Perhaps Rachel ought to press more on the Act Two conflict between fairy king and queen? In contrast to Beatrice and Benedict of "Much Ado", who reveled in quarrels as part of their initial relationship, Oberon and Titania sounded seriously at odds. She glanced at the clock. Forty-five minutes 'til ETA.

The doorbell rang.

Rachel peeked out. She pulled the door open. "Noor, come in! Are the girls okay?"

The woman stepped inside. She wore expensive wool trousers and three-inch heels Alan Miller would have approved.

"Would you like some tea? The water's hot."

"No, no time," said Noor. She hesitated. "Girls are fine. Melina?"

"She's been with her dad, she'll be home soon," replied Rachel, puzzled.

Noor's expression relaxed. "Good. She won't hear."

"Hear what? Would you like to sit down?"

"No, thank you. My girls saw you last night. On doorstep with man. Then man inside with you."

"Oh!" Rachel shook her head. "He stayed only a moment, Noor. That's all. Although," she added gently, "even if he had, it would have been okay, right?"

"How okay? Girls see!"

"Well – wouldn't you like to sit down? – they only see if they're watching out their window." An image rose to Rachel: the two Nassir girls, starved for a break in the routine of schoolwork and music, peeping over their windowsill. "They've got enough to worry about without stressing about their neighbors' dates! This wasn't even one, really, he's just a friend. A colleague." Recalling their kiss, Rachel unaccountably flushed.

"I understand Quentin not right." Noor examined her. "But don't want girls see man stay."

"Noor." Rachel's fingers wound together. "I'm sorry to offend you, truly, but my life is not really intended for your daughters' consumption. I'd never do anything vulgar in front of them, I promise."

"And Melina, then what?"

"You're right," Rachel agreed, "I haven't quite figured that one out yet. No plan. Yet. Working on it!"

Noor sniffed. "You *make* plan."

"Yes," Rachel said, drawing the door open, "good idea, I'll do that."

Noor *clack-clacked* back across the street, where her daughters likely waited to hear how Rachel weathered the challenge. She sagged against the door and looked down at her notebook plans for "Dream". So Titania was at odds with Oberon, was she? Rachel felt her pain.

Rachel scrolled down. She had stopped . . . here it was. She put her fingers to the keys.

    . . . *three pillars of Hindi-language films: emotion, drama and romance. Thus in the 2008 opulent historical epic "Jodhaa Akbar", based on the 16th century Moghul emperor Akbar's relationship with his Hindu wife . . ..*

A film starring two of India's most bankable stars, she thought, and the male one of the three Indian actors who could make a film profitable on his name alone, even with only a tiny cameo role. Rachel grinned. Perhaps those actors were the real pillars. Shah Rukh Khan, Hrithik Roshan, Aamir Khan, the three pillars of Bollywood, supporting its ornate carved roof by the force of their own work and celebrity.

Not a bad image. She scrolled further, quickly typed her thoughts under The Hero, and returned to her original paragraph.

. . . *Shakespeare, as well, in "Henry V". In the oddly poignant scene between the gruff, victorious soldier and his francophone wife-to-be, romance is a trait Henry confesses he . . ..*

". . . it was way into the hills, Daddy says coyote country. Their daughter was thirteen, we played pool."

"Ah, that sounds fun!"

Rachel hugged Melina, who in just four SoCal days had somehow acquired a tan. Across from them sat Melina's dad, Jason, whose former what-me-worry clothing style had morphed into an Italian élan that looked at once hip and expensive. His hair was lighter, too, perhaps he was listening to a stylist. Los Angeles was a world unto itself.

"But tomorrow's school, hon, that means bed, which means get books and stuff ready so you can shoot out in the morning."

"But –"

Rachel tugged her daughter up. "Come on!"

Melina threw a pleading look to her father. Jason shrugged. "Mom's house, Mom's rules," he said.

Melina flung an arm around him. "Good night!"

"Good night, Mel! Sweet dreams!"

Her footsteps dragged up the stairs.

"She clearly had a good time," said Rachel. "Thanks. And for bringing her back."

"No problem. As I said, I have a week here." Jason sat back with his half-finished glass of wine.

"A week! You didn't say. What kind of work?"

"Scouting locations, I'm onboard with Ellie's production," he explained. "Thanks for letting her come to us, Rach. It means a lot. Ellie tells all her friends about Melina, she just loves being a stepmom."

Rachel carried glasses to the kitchen.

Jason followed. "So how's it going? Work. Life."

"Work is one unexpected class, the rest delightful. The rest . . . well, February in New York, what can you say?"

He cleared his throat. "Melina said there was a man."

Rachel looked up. "She what?"

"No man?"

"No," Rachel said, firm. "No man."

"So my daughter's wrong?"

"Your daughter's *young*."

"A very observant and insightful young," noted Jason, leaning against the counter.

"Nonetheless, wrong. There was a maybe-man in England. She barely knew him. Totally over, non-issue."

Outside, two sirens screamed along East End Avenue.

"I'm not trying to hammer you, Rach. If there's a special guy . . . I mean, you're entitled to a life. You'd make sure Melina was safe. It's just I'm . . .."

"Curious? Wondering? Hopeful? I'm very busy, Jason. I go out on rare occasions. So tell Ellie her cards are way off-base."

"What does Ellie have to do with it?"

Rachel recounted the tale of the tarot. "No more, okay?"

"No problem." Jason's laugh held an underlay of nerves.

"Early day tomorrow," she reminded him, "want to call a cab from here?"

"I can't wheedle the guestroom? Just for the night?"

"You booked a whole week, I'm sure, and hotels are valid business expenses. Wheedle away, but no."

Jason thumped the door he leaned upon, a rhythmic *rum-pum-pum*. "Worth a shot."

"Was it? Next time, soften me up with lunch or a gift bottle of chardonnay." She handed him the phone. "Speed dial five."

"Lunch would work?"

Rachel smiled. "Probably not."

Jason punched in the number. "Probably not," he agreed.

CHAPTER 19

The next morning, Rachel locked the door behind her. Across the way, Mrs. Burke retrieved her newspaper from her steps. Rachel waved. The woman fluttered her fingers.

Beside Mrs. Burke, the Nassirs' door opened, revealing Noor. Rachel waved again. No reply.

Noor must still be feeling offended by Marc's visit the other night. Damn.

It was more than a little ridiculous to be watched by teenagers, and totally absurd to believe, as Noor evidently did, that just because a man entered Rachel's house for two seconds meant she was wanton. More than absurd, it was ill-informed, prejudiced . . . was any woman Rachel's age less wanton than she? Without a wimple and habit?

"He's *what?*"

For some reason, the sidewalk was crowded this morning. A group of foreign tourists, a school field trip, assorted bridge-and-tunnel twos and threes. Rachel felt hemmed-in.

"He's *here?*" Steph's voice came loud and appalled from the tiny phone. "What for?"

"For work. See him in the evening, maybe. It's only a week."

"How do you know? Maybe Ellie's tossed him out, maybe he's staking turf, a drop here, a drop there."

"I don't think so." Rachel dodged the man ahead, who had bent to tie his shoelace. Just as she reached the corner, the light turned red. Next to her, an impatient jogger shadow-boxed.

"Oh. My. God." A heavy sigh came from the phone. "I get a bad feeling from this. Like it's thundering."

"Drama queen!" Rachel crossed the street, dropping the phone to hip level. Reaching the curb, she brought it back to her ear.

" – it doesn't do her any good, either! Are you still there?" Steph asked, suspicious.

"Yes."

"I'm coming to dinner tonight."

Rachel bit her lip. "It's curry."

"I'll bring Chinese."

"Steph –"

"I'm coming to dinner and I'm finding out what exactly is on Jason Spinos's mind. Bastard! It'll be a memorable experience for him."

"I'm sure he'll wave his lighter and sway."

"Of course, it's really *your* ass I should be doing a Gordon Ramsay on."

"Didn't you call to complain about Rubén? How'd we get on *my* back?" asked Rachel. She frowned. "What am I supposed to do, ban him from the Big Apple? Stop worrying."

"I'm not worrying, I'm frantic."

"What are you, three years old? I need to go, my fifty minutes are up."

"See you at dinner." The line went dead.

"Morning! Tea?"

Rachel turned. His breath in clouds, Marc stood behind her with a pair of carry-out cups. "Earl Grey or . . . Earl Grey?"

Rachel hesitated, then chose the closest cup. "Did you . . . were you . . . how did you know I'd be here?"

"Here, here?" Marc led her back into the pedestrian flow. "I didn't expect you at all. The guy at Starbucks thought I said two, so . . . consider it an apology."

"What on earth for?"

"Blanket apology." He pawed at his pocket and pulled out a phone. "Excuse me. Hello? . . . hello!" His spine straightened. "That would be very enjoyable. Give me ten, twenty minutes? Thanks." He closed the phone. "Well, that changes my morning! Have a good day, Rachel." He stepped to the street, arm out for a taxi. In his other hand, tea sloshed over his fingers.

On the way to her classroom, lost in thought, Rachel let her own cup of Earl Grey grow cold.

"Because in a forest, in the woods, anything can happen," explained one student.

"*Into the woods, into the woods,*" sang another.

"Wonderful! Sondheim, confusion, death, disaster, toppling giants! Why does this happen in woods, what's special about woods? To the Elizabethan mind?" Rachel queried.

Her students met her with blank faces and frantic scrabbling for the text.

"Difference between a sonnet and free verse?" she demanded. "A sonnet has –?"

Answers shot at her from different parts of the room. "Rhyme . . . a given length . . . prescribed structure . . .."

"A sonnet has structure and order, good. So does the civilized world, farmland, a vegetable garden. But in the woods, there's random growth, unregulated by plow or harrow or spade, and it's that very lack of order that attracts people who reject structure. Robin Hood . . . prison escapees . . . lovers who flout their fathers, as here in 'Dream'." Rachel paused. "There's something reassuring about imposed order, isn't there? Fundamentalism, for example. You know where you are, what the rules are, and that was attractive in Shakespeare's time, when so much of the world was wild and unknown. The word 'hag' originally referred to a hedge-woman, a woman who lived in or near woods, maybe with a foot in both worlds." Rachel shivered. "Both worlds! Uncontrollable! Wild!"

Marc's door was ajar. Rachel peeked in. He had removed his tweed jacket – it slumped in a chair – revealing a pair of suspenders over his white buttondown.

"Hey," he said, surprised. "Come on in."

Rachel chose a chair. She sat very straight. "I'm the one who owes an apology."

"No, you don't." Marc leaned back. "Absolutely not."

"Just let me do this, okay?" For a moment she pressed her lips together, the better to ignore the memory of Marc's, their taste, their warmth. "I just . . . I don't know what made me ask you to that party, or why I kissed you, and I have no idea what prompted me to stand there and say nothing when you left."

"That's a remarkable amount of ignorance."

"It is! It is!" The words burst from her. "It's ridiculous! Wildly ridiculous. Anyway, I'm sorry. When I figure things out, I'll . . . ." She fingered the edge of her jacket. "But there it is. Apology. With a compliment tossed in: you're a very good kisser."

Marc blinked. "Thanks."

"Welcome. Thought you should know." His hands, she noticed, were active in small ways, their thumbs nervously fidgeting. "Okay, that's it." She pulled her purse and satchel from the floor. The satchel strap was entangled in the chair leg, and by the time she twisted it loose, Marc was waiting beside his closed door. She met him there, avoiding his eyes. And stopped short.

"What the hell is that?"

He followed her stare to the part of the wall obscured by the door when open. "That? You know Bollywood, you must recognize him."

"He's younger there than I've seen." The photographed man gazed out with soulful brown eyes. "What's Shah Rukh doing in your office?"

"A friend from Oxford gave it to me years ago. I promised to install 'King Khan' wherever I taught, since his father had gotten it autographed. He's now quite a big noise in Mumbai . . . the father, I mean," Marc amplified.

"You know who he is, then?"

"Shah Rukh? Of course. I haven't watched much recently, but I used to see Indian movies in their London releases."

"So you know –?"

"Something about your topic?" He nodded. "Yeah, I can tell one Khan from another. Shah Rukh, Aamir, Salman, and so on. Perhaps, sometime, you'd lend me one of your newer DVDs?"

She shrugged. "Sure."

"For purely educational reasons." Marc opened the door.

The kitchen table held white boxes bearing red ideograms, packets of hot mustard, and printed fortunes:

You are on the verge of something big.

Nothing in the world is accomplished without passion.

If you want to win anything, you have to go a little berserk!

"Good dinner, Steph, the eggplant was inspired."

"Thank you, Jason," Steph purred. Rolled in her red-tipped fingers, her own fortune was a tight cylinder.

"I've got homework," Melina announced.

Rachel gave her daughter's hand a squeeze. "Go, go."

"Another beer?" Steph wrenched the cap from a bottle of Tsingtao and placed it before Jason. "Rachel said you're here for locations?"

"Yeah, had a good day. Stuff that's still there, stuff that's changed. Found a terrific new Italian grill. The whole security thing's a challenge, though, I can't stare at a building too long, someone will report me . . . dark-haired man in shades acting suspicious, digital camera, shots from all angles. I'll get online later, download today's pictures."

Rachel telegraphed Steph with her eyebrows. *See?*

"I thought filming in New York was too expensive," Steph commented.

Jason stretched and yawned. "The city gives us a financial break. Used judiciously, you get a sense of authenticity."

"Judiciously means a quickie? So this is just popping over?" Steph probed.

"Yeah, sure, what else would it be?"

Two pairs of eyes studied him.

"Hey, I learned my lesson! Plus, it's good to see Melina. Here, I mean."

"You're brighter than that, Jason. I *think* you're brighter than that, though the waxed eyebrows tend to point the other way," said Steph.

Rachel cleared her throat.

"No harm, no foul," Jason countered. "So you hate me, you hate men, who gives a shit?"

"I don't hate men!" Steph sputtered.

"You don't like them! You're a relationship-avoidant man-hater, the only male you can tolerate is twenty years younger, and where did Rubén choose to go to school? Three thousand miles away! Coincidence? You don't prefer women, I know, but a man your age, any age, forget it!"

"Stop it, you guys!" Rachel rapped on the table to hammer it home. "House rules, right?"

Jason yawned again, an artificial break in the acrimony. "I always enjoy Brady Bunch-ing with you, Steph. But I need to get those pictures off to my wife." He let the door swing behind him.

Rachel swept empty boxes into the trash. "Gee, Steph, that was fun."

"Ooh! That *man!* I'd like to kick Peter Pan's ass!"

"Go ahead, I won't disapprove. But since when did you fight with forces of nature? Four wise words: Time wounds all heels. What he did was a while ago, and he's moved on. In his road, it's a dead horse."

Steph sniffed. "Dead something."

"Think of it this way, if we were in India I'd have been under a lot more pressure to stay with him. And dating, or remarriage, my God, Steph, it's still so unusual over there! We did counseling, we did separation, boom, that was it. Let go."

"Have you?"

"Haven't I?" Rachel asked, surprised. "Yeah, I think so. I mean, he's so definitely not a Bollywood movie dude. If I met him now . . .?"

"What?"

"If I met him now," said Rachel, with a growing twinkle, "I'd shove him toward Ellie."

CHAPTER 20

But, like a sickness, did I loathe this food;
But, as in health, come to my natural taste,
Now I do wish it, love it, long for it,
And will forevermore be true to it."

T he reading student ended with a flourish.
        "Excellent!" Rachel resumed center stage, perched on the
desk. "But what does it mean?"

        "Demetrius comes to his senses," suggested a second
student.

        "How?"

        "From unnatural taste to natural?" came the hazarded
guess.

        "Nature, yes, absolutely. It's in Demetrius's *nature* to
love and desire Helena. Lusting after Hermia was a sickness,
because he's not designed for her, he's designed by nature, or
God, or fate, for Helena . . . and she for him." Rachel tossed her
red marker from one hand to the other. "Made for each other.
Like Rome, all roads lead there. Even where you have a father-
arranged marriage with someone else."

Her thoughts swam with the father-arranged marriages of classic Hindi cinema, and how daughters and sons managed to thwart them. There was a certain heroism in simply trying.

"As you'll see over and over, if love is in the stars, it cannot be denied."

This third Comedies class had been slowest to congeal, to develop a personality, but by now – last meeting of the week, too, they'd begin another play on Tuesday – they left ennui outside.

She closed her books, dumped pens in her purse, glanced around the room for items forgotten.

Steph was right, Jason had insinuated himself into Rachel's life . . . and she let him. Balancing that was Melina's delight in knowing that her dad would for a few days pop in and out, available for a chat, a cookie, a hand with algebra. He'd always been good at math.

"What does it matter, a few days?" Rachel mumbled to herself. She shouldered her purse and satchel. Once outside, she flinched at a brisk wind that swirled, scattering gum wrappers. A man was seated on the concrete steps in a place that usually held a group of female students comparing notes. They had presumably sought warmth elsewhere. She passed him with a cursory glance.

"Good lord, don't you have work to do?" she demanded. Stopping a careful distance away, she leaned against the cold steel railing.

"I was in the neighborhood, so to speak," explained Marc, with a wave at surrounding buildings. "I wanted to give you something." He stood, reached into his coat pocket and handed her a photocopied sheet of paper.

"What's this?"

"Read it, see if it's useful for your book."

The suspension of disbelief in India is prompt and generous, she read, *beginning before the audience enters the theater itself. Disbelief is easy to suspend in a land where belief is so rampant and vigorous.*

"Wow. Where's this from?"

"A book called *Maximum City*. It's about Bombay. Mumbai, I mean, and a Pulitzer finalist. Suketu Mehta's the author, born in India, but he's been here for some time here. Here at NYU, even, he teaches journalism. He's got a long chapter on Indian film, I started it last night."

"Would you lend it?" she asked.

"Of course. Give me three days."

They fell silent. Bits of paper flew past, twists escaped from a shredder.

"A cautionary note," he began.

"About the book?"

"No, about diving headfirst into a culture. You're doing an Indian film project –"

"Shakespeare and Indian film," she reminded him.

"– you wore a *salwar kameez*, your house smells of ginger and turmeric . . .."

"So?"

"So, it's fun, I know that, but all I'm saying is every culture has an underbelly. Things that skitter on multiple legs. Not everything Indian is happy and good, okay?"

About to launch into sarcasm, Rachel hesitated. Marc's facial muscles were tense. In another minute, his voice would break. What he had against . . . what did he have? History, perhaps, an Indian friend's sister, a Hindu girl who'd given him the push? Rachel peered at him with new interest. "Point noted. So, how's Lawrence?"

"Lawrence who? Oh, my Lawrence. Right now there's a certain amount of canoodling I have to do with prospective donors, I have no space in my life for David Herbert. I'll get back to him, it's just, right now, screw *Lady Chatterley*. Sorry, that came out badly! Poor man had tuberculosis when he wrote that book. Nothing like chronic illness to make one reflect. Have you read it?"

Rachel shook her head. "I watched the mini-series."

"That!" Marc's laughter rang against the stone. "Appetite in the woods, Mellors perpetually out of breath!"

"I read they made the actor run laps before shooting," she told him.

"That explains a lot. But the book itself is really more about breaking through artificial class barriers to find tenderness. It's not sex. All right, it *is* sex, but a lot more. It's always a lot more."

On the bus, its windows spattered with rain, Rachel leaned her head against the cold glass. The woman beside her overflowed into her space. A purse escaped and landed on Rachel's knee. She barely flinched. Marc's unnecessary admonition – "not everything Indian is happy and good" – held tones of the personal. Could his ex-wife have been an NRI?

She felt again Marc's hands on hers, shaping them round the bat. The warmth of his fingers as he pulled her through the crowd at Bitsy and Dean's. His lips, even warmer, when . . ..

On her lap, her own fingers clenched.

Six Granny Smiths, one for *raita*, the rest for muffins and afterschool nibbles. The apples gleamed green, their color more bright between McIntoshes and the ubiquitous Red Delicious. One by one, Rachel dropped them into her basket.

Tonight was chicken grilled with *garam masala*. Rachel called up a mental picture of her fridge's interior. White boxes, a couple of yogurts, an expanding array of condiments . . . yes, there were onions and the jar of intense green chilli paste.

Chicken, rice, *raita*, and some leftover mung bean *dal*. That was tonight. Now, tomorrow . . . with a pleasurable start, Rachel remembered that Jason was in town. He would handle dinner with Melina, and she and Steph could do something together, hit a movie, grab sushi, perhaps.

"Excuse me."

Her eyes on a pineapple, Rachel made room in the narrow aisle for the woman who'd spoken. She looked around to see Noor Nassir, dressed as usual with effortless chic.

"Noor, how are you? The family?"

"All fine, thanks." The brown eyes focused on apples.

She might as well take the bull by the horns, Rachel thought grimly. "Noor, I know you don't like my dating –"

Noor stiffened. "Don't not like. Feel angry. For girls," she amplified. "They should not approve. Melina should not."

"But," Rachel grew earnest, "it's part of growing up, isn't it, making decisions? And just because a man is there wouldn't mean there's anything, well, wicked happening. It could all be perfectly innocent, a card game!"

"You play cards?"

"Uh, no."

"You kiss this man?"

Rachel flushed. "Once."

"Ah. And more than kiss?"

"No, definitely not."

"You think about do something?"

"Not with this man, no."

"He married?"

"He's divorced," said Rachel. An interior voice begged to know why she was justifying herself to a mere neighbor. "He's my department chairman. But you haven't said anything yet about the other man who visited me, did you know about him?" Rachel asked.

"Of course, your brother."

"No, no, the other one, the dark-haired one with Italian clothes."

"Of course," Noor repeated. "Melina's father. Girls tell me." Noor rolled her cart toward the melons.

"Ah, but do you know what we're doing?" Rachel probed.

"He visit Melina." Noor selected a large spotted specimen.

Undaunted, Rachel placed herself before the small cart, blocking its progress. "But you don't know what we're doing! Maybe we're doing something, maybe we're having superlative sex in every room of the house! Even the kitchen, with the fruit and veg!"

A bag of onions landed in Noor's cart. "Do something, I see in face. Not in your face," Noor observed. She dodged around Rachel, avoided a man weighing garlic, and pushed on to the meat counter.

Rachel followed, her basket swinging. "Noor, you can't tell just by looking! And even if it were there –"

"Five pound chicken thigh, skin off," Noor told the butcher. "Not *there*."

"But say it were. Would you disapprove of that, too?" Rachel persisted.

"Of course! Not your husband anymore."

"So I need to be married to have fun, is that it?" Rachel's free hand flew into the air in frustration.

Noor gripped the package of chicken thighs. Her eyes met Rachel's squarely. "Was fun? Other man, in England? Was fun?"

Memories of Ian flooded Rachel. Their initial meeting, increasing intimacies, the wine and food that lubricated their time together . . . then growing unease and discontent, a vague dissatisfaction, and the final betrayal with its gut-wrenching pain, feeling fragile and at odds with herself even weeks later.

"No," she admitted, "not fun at all."

Noor laid her hand on Rachel's arm. "Don't want girls to see that. You, too, don't want that. Not again."

Melina and Jason hunched over cards on the coffee table.

". . . so in Polish poker, you want the lowest hand," he was explaining. "Aces one, kings zero, queens are the highest. Start with four cards face down . . . .."

"That sounds awfully pejorative, 'Polish poker'," Rachel observed. "Like 'blonde day', 'senior moment'. Cruel, even."

"Cruel?" Jason objected. "How, cruel?"

"You could change the name."

"Mom changed Hangman to 'Tiger'." Melina placed the remaining cards face-down. "She doesn't like drawing a hanged person, so we draw a tiger instead. Body, head, legs, tail . . . though they don't look much like Hobbes. It would be cooler if we could draw Hobbes."

"'Tiger', huh?" Jason smiled.

"Why not opposite poker, lowball poker? Ozzie poker?" Rachel offered.

"Ozzie who?"

"Australia. Upside-down."

"In Hindi, *ulta-pulta*. I love that word. *Ulta-pulta!*" Melina exclaimed, tossing cards into the air.

Three of them fluttered into Rachel's lap. She turned them over. A four, a seven, and the king of hearts.

Jason would fly away early Sunday morning, and that was only three days, thought Rachel. Two, if you didn't count the rest of this evening. She ought to focus on something quite different . . . like what to do tomorrow evening? That was different. She dialed Steph's number.

"It's Rachel, you're free tomorrow night, aren't you? Let's do something fun! Gallery, pretend we're zillionaires? An Indian movie? Stuff ourselves with *jalebis*? Give me a call, I want to do something totally atypical! I mean, you know . . . ring me, okay?"

She clicked the phone off and laid it on the kitchen table. It was time to embrace the computer screen again, work on her overview of Indian film, incorporating the quote Marc had given her and several of Chandani's insights. Before Rachel, the screen turned blue. Idly, she wondered if Marc would remember to lend her the book he was reading. Perhaps she'd have to zip him a reminder. If necessary, she could request the book through the university's library system. But it was kind of him to even think of her own work while reading at home, to scribble the passage, to lie in wait –

He hadn't lain in wait, of course, he was just passing by.

Had it been Rachel whose heartbreak carried an Indian twist, she'd choose to avoid reading about the subcontinent. It would feel too much like picking a scab. Ian, for example, had tainted some of her Oxford memories. *This* they had done together, *there* they had joked or shared a bottle of beaujolais, therefore those places were placed off-limits to her memory. It was irrational, of course . . . and quite human. Maybe it wouldn't always be so. Someday they might carry a soft glow in her imagination, Ian's influence cleansed.

Emotion, drama, romance . . . her life in Oxford had unexpectedly held all three. That wasn't the plan. Flying over, all that was on her mind was work and a chance to travel the UK with Melina. A basic, no-frills plan. But drama and romance, and then scuttling emotion, had crept in. In those months Rachel had lived out a good portion of an Indian movie – the lighthearted first half, and a large slice of the more-serious second half, complete with anguish and betrayal. Nothing could turn on the tears like those two. They were exhausting.

It was time for a bit of resolution, the film wasn't close to its end, a song ought to wind through it, with perhaps a picturisation set in, oh, the Pyrenees. The heroine rededicating herself to work and her daughter. Something snappy with a bright flute overlay.

The plot, however, was still stuck.

As was Rachel. She shook out her hands to loosen them, blew on them to warm, and applied her fingers to the keys.

. . . *Western ironies do not hold for Indian film, and it is hardly surprising that American and British movies are rarely screened outside major Indian cities with large educated populations, for irony requires the abandonment of . . ..*

Barely aware of her own rising dissatisfaction, Rachel typed on.

CHAPTER 21

"T his is the only place I've found with more than four kinds of *parathas*," Chandani told Rachel. Flatbreads were heaped high on her side of the table, dipping yogurt at the ready. A mango *lassi*, pale orange and luscious, waited beside them. She ripped a hot *paratha* in four, dunked a steaming quarter in cool yogurt, and popped it into her mouth. "Bliss!"

Rachel dug into her creamy lentil *dal*, and followed it with a forkful of spicy cabbage salad, warily avoiding its slim, intense green peppers. "You said your cousins, sorry, nieces, do the same as Melina?"

"Oh, God, yes, their walls are plastered. Hrithik here, Hrithik there, even baby pictures they found on the internet. Occasional breaks in the scenery for Saif –"

"Saif Ali Khan?"

Chandani swallowed. "There's only one Saif," she said, amused. "Or a small picture of Arjun Rampal – Esha says he's almost *too* handsome – or Shahid Kapoor or Zayed Khan . . . though since Z is Hrithik's brother-in-law, it's all in the family, isn't that the expression?"

"And the music, they're into that as much as –?"

Chandani's fingers arrested in mid-rip. "That's what I meant to tell you! When I go home to Delhi, that's what hits me most. Not the smells, not the crowding, not even naked children. It's the noise, the film music blaring from all sides. Remember when you came to my uncle's, we played *antakshari*? Tip of the iceberg! Walk down a street, an alley, you're surrounded, followed! After a week," she dipped the bread in clinging yogurt, "I'm re-addicted." The bite disappeared in a single gulp. "Which movie's coming out, who did the music? If it's someone like, oh," she paused, "well, definitely A. R. Rahman, I have to hear it *now*. Or Shankar Ehsaan Loy – they're a triumvirate – I'm very fond of their work. Music propels India, Rachel, it really does. New York is so quiet, in comparison." Chandani paused again, reflective. "Now that I think about it, maybe Indian films are as much about selling music as they are about selling stories and images?"

"And ads? Commercials?"

"Well!" Chandani leaned back. "You make more money doing those than acting in movies. Every actor who can, does commercials and ads for magazines, billboards, all that. Shah Rukh is the most famous, of course, he's represented everything from cookies to cars to Pepsi. Remember in 'Om Shanti Om', the Heuer watch billboard? That was his, the real thing! You'd see that along Marine Drive in Mumbai! When it comes to India, Rachel, film and music and ads, they're like spaghetti, so tangled you can't separate them."

"Why does Steph want me to bring the bangles?"

"She didn't say. But that outfit would look better with stupid shoes," Melina offered.

"The kind with red sequins?" Rachel sat on her bed beside her daughter, inserting her foot into a flat shoe of soft pliable leather. "Well, tough. These jeans are almost new, the top is only a year old, I'm nearly off the runway! Besides, I couldn't walk more than a block in stilettoes even if I had them."

Melina turned an interesting shade of pink. Her eyes shone. "I've got shoes."

Rachel laughed, ruffling her daughter's hair. "Runners? Clogs? Only with Saxon braids and a dirndl."

Melina slid from the bed, beckoning.

Once in her own room, she dove under the twin bed. Scrabbling sounds ensued. Melina emerged with five glossy shoeboxes Rachel had never seen before.

"Where did those drop from?" she asked, astonished.

"Los Angeles. Ellie." Melina opened one box, revealing a pair of silver sandals. A second lid flew off, showing pink mules. "Daddy checked them in his luggage, that's why he had so many bags." A third box contained black suede pumps. "Aren't they pretty?"

"Melina, honey." Rachel held her daughter's cheeks. "Ellie bought you designer shoes last week? All at the same time? Were you by any chance at the register when she paid for them? I mean, when her assistant paid?"

"It was Ellie. She asked me to wait by the door."

"I bet she did," Rachel said, thoughtful. "Sweetheart, please understand, I'm so happy your stepmother's nice to you, but, and this is an elephant-sized objection, these shoes are not a fly in the ointment, they are the Concorde. They're trouble with a capital T. Take a guess, how much did these five pairs cost?"

Melina opened the last two boxes – blue satin sandals, kitten heels in white with a striped bow. "Five hundred dollars?"

"Honey, Ellie paid a lot more for this." Rachel balanced the mule on her palm. "Seriously, large crates of money went for things that would barely protect your feet from city sidewalks."

"She meant to be nice!"

"I'm sure she did. She wins Miss Congeniality hands-down. But these shoes are the definition of beyond the pale."

Melina bit her lip. "Are you saying I have to return them? Ellie will feel bad."

"She might. Is that it?" Rachel dangled the pink mule. "Or were you going to slip these into your backpack and Cinderella yourself at school?"

Melina flushed and hugged a shoe to her chest. "Why do I have to return them? They were a gift! I can't return a gift!"

"A gift, no, I wouldn't ask you to. This is five gifts at once, though, and shoes so ridiculously expensive that if you put them on eBay, you'd make a stash."

"Well," Melina scooted onto her bed, "why don't we do that instead?"

"What?"

"Put four of them on eBay, get money and give it away. To, like, that program – or, no, I know!" She sat up, her eyes shining. "Send it to India! There's got to be an orphanage in Mumbai that could use it! Can't we do that?"

"Four pairs?"

"You said I could keep one!"

"You can. Pick your favorite, missy." Rachel brought the silver sandals up to eye level. "Unless you think maybe, just maybe, an orphanage in India could use a teensy bit more cash, hmm?"

"Well, that's so duh." Regretful, Melina stuffed the pink mule back in its box. "What is it you say, cotton candy is fun, but you can't live on it, it's not whole wheat bread?" The last lid fit over the last box. "These are cotton candy, right?"

"Afraid so."

Melina placed shoeboxes one atop another in a colorful tower that reached her elbows. "Daddy won't like it, either."

"No, your dad's never been fond of whole wheat. Leave him to me."

Rachel met Steph at a coffeeshop that had become a useful launchpad for evenings when plans were vague and almost anything might suit. By now they knew the waitresses by name. Susanna, originally from Bosnia, slipped a packet of melba toast underneath the tea saucer.

"You look hungry," she told Rachel before moving off to a young couple who held hands and whispered in accents of South Asia.

Rachel tore the cellophane packet and pulled out a wafer, half-listening to the lovers.

" . . . couldn't get out before, my sister's covering for me . . .."

Another mixed-faith couple trying to overcome the expectations and prejudices of parents? Rachel sneaked a peek. How pretty she was, her hair parted in the middle, her greenish eyes rimmed with dark liner. How pretty . . . and how young. They were too young, that was part of the problem. Give it a few years, stay unmarried, and parents would be overjoyed at the thought of any grandchildren at all.

Yet staying single might be fatal for Indian and Pakistani girls, who could suffer under enormous pressure to marry the particular man the family wanted, and to hell with love.

To hell with love. What was the opposite of that phrase? Love made in heaven? That would be a decent-size subchapter for her book, the discussion of Bollywood's treatment of destiny. Made for each other . . . Rachel pulled out her checkbook and jotted key phrases: *destiny/fate/kismet, Demetrius/Helena, use of astrologers.* Hindi movies occasionally referred to astrologers, essential for determining the best dates for formal engagement, and, of course, the wedding, the *shaadi.* Not-so-coincidentally, that word also meant marriage, matrimony . . . and delight.

"Where are you, I've been waving!" Steph slid into the chair opposite, sliding a bulky plastic bag onto the small table. "Did you bring the bracelets?"

Rachel shook the bag beside her. It jingled.

"Great! Because while I seriously doubt that movies can explain a nation of a billion people to me, I come prepared with my own brilliant idea. And skirt." Steph drew a bit of red fabric from the bag. "Skirts, I brought two. There's a studio six blocks from here with walk-in lessons, they start in fifteen minutes, come on!"

"Lessons for what?"

"*Bhangra*, babe! Come on!"

The dance studio, located steps above a Starbucks, held two dozen very fit people and a petite instructor whose orange camisole was already drenched with sweat. Strands of hair clung wetly to her temples.

"Walk-ins here!" she called. "I prefer cash, people!"

Rachel joined the line of those digging into their pockets. From their conversation, it was clear she and Steph would be the only *bhangra* novices. "Two," she said, forking over the bills, "she's in the bathroom."

The instructor wiped her neck. "First time? No problem, it's a traditional harvest dance, no complex moves, just a lot of energy." With a broad grin, she mimed wringing out her soaked cami.

Steph appeared wearing a long red pencil-pleated skirt. She pushed a mass of turquoise into Rachel's arms.

"You know we're the only ones here without experience, don't you?"

"It's dance-by-numbers, you won't have to follow." Steph's tone coaxed.

In the tiny bathroom, Rachel shed her jeans and pulled the bright skirt up past her hips. The interwoven fabric shimmered. She tied the drawstring at her waist. If only she'd known she was in for a two-hour dancefest . . . she could have worn her new *salwar kameez*, with the pink-decorated black tunic hitting the knee. She tied her hair back and glanced in the mirror. Her pale self stared back.

She had modeled the outfit for Melina.

"It's kind of dark."

"Sophisticated," Rachel corrected.

"Dark." Melina had a critical eye. She flipped her own new yellow *dupatta* over its embroidered saffron *kameez*. "Can I wear mine to school?"

"Uniform, remember?"

"I hate the uniform. I do! And I hate French, my teacher gets worse every day. Isn't there anybody who wants to teach me Hindi?"

"Oh, I forgot!" Rachel folded her *dupatta* onto a hanger. "Three anybodies, so I set up interviews Monday evening here at home. They're from different parts of India. Delhi, Mumbai, and somewhere on the west coast just southeast of Pakistan."

Melina peeked out from her draped *dupatta*. "Girls?"

"Young women."

"I want the one from Mumbai."

"You haven't even met them. Hand that over."

"It's where all the movie stars live, maybe she knows some." Melina folded the long rectangle and gave it to her mother.

"You'd think hanging out with Ellie would teach you, hon, it's just a business. Creative, yes, but plenty of hard work and long hours and monotony. Have you ever asked Ellie who she knows in LA?"

"Of course not, I don't care about them. They're not Indian."

Rachel laughed. "Taking this a little far, aren't you? If you know nothing about American movies or TV, what do you talk about at school?"

"Boys." Melina regarded her mother with pity. "Weren't you ever thirteen?"

"Hands up, up, up! Stomp and back! Stomp! Back!" The pulsing beat of a *dhol* drum nearly drowned the words. Her long braid shaking in rhythm, the orange-clad instructor clapped her hands to the beat. "Fun, you're having fun, and stomp! Back!"

Rachel stomped. She stepped back. Her bracelets rang. She stomped again, and again moved back, her arms in the air, keeping her knees bent and shrugging her shoulders – a combination she would have sworn, thirty minutes ago, was much too complex for her to synchronize.

"Isn't this great?" screamed Steph. Her skirt shook and twirled.

"Great!" Her arms describing small circles, so the bracelets gave off a happy noise, Rachel shrugged her shoulders and stomped. Sweat dripped down her chest. By now, her new *salwar kameez* would have been just as soaked as if caught in a monsoon.

Stomp!

"Five minutes, people!" The crowd groaned. "Bottled water for sale in that corner, there's a fountain over there, somebody open that window!" The instructor jumped down from the chair she'd climbed to make herself tall.

Her back against the mirrored wall, Rachel sat on the floor and fanned herself with her hands. She gazed longingly at the dark window.

"Outside, instant pneumonia. You looked good, Rachel, no one would suspect you can't really dance!" Steph praised her. "Another thirty minutes, we'll be pros, drop us anywhere in your beloved India."

"Rachel?"

She scrambled to her feet and brushed back her sweat-soaked hair. "Marc! I didn't know you were into . . . this is my friend Steph, Steph Zimmer," she said.

"I remember, we met outside Bloomingdale's," said Marc, shaking hands. He brought forward a pretty woman with freckles and auburn curls. "Camille . . . Steph . . . Rachel, one of my colleagues."

"Oh, good, I finally meet one of Marc's NYU crowd," Camille told Rachel in a girlish voice. She, too, wore bangles, and her yellow *lehnga* skirt was covered with sequins and minute mirrors. The tiny mirrors caught the light and spangled it. Camille fingered them as she spoke. "Have you been there long?"

"A few years," Rachel said.

"I teach, too, second grade in our old school." Camille patted Marc's arm.

"You teach in the same school you went to as a child?"

"Yes, I love it! Have you taken this class before? The instructor, Sonali? – she's the little sister of one of our friends. Marc's and mine." Camille held onto Marc's shoulder. In response, he flung that arm around her, drawing her close.

He turned to Rachel. "Like it?"

She wrenched her eyes from the hand at Camille's waist. "It gets under my skin. The music. And then, everyone else . . .." She indicated the room. "You can't help joining in."

"I know, it's like watching the Tour de France, then dragging out the old bike you haven't ridden in a year . . . since the last Tour, in fact."

The joke drew a thin smile from Rachel.

"Marc, it's starting!" Camille pulled at him.

"Okay, people, up, up, raise your arms, here we go!" shouted Sonali. The furious beat of the *dhol* filled the room. "The harvest is in, come on, stomp!"

Rachel found a place and adjusted herself to the music. Her shoulders shrugged, she stomped and turned and . . . there was Marc, one row away. His body moved with frenetic energy (*stomp!*), but considerably more style. His shoulders, now, shook in perfect echoes of the passionate drums, and that tap of his foot, with the slight torso turn . . .

Her eyes caught his. Marc gave her a nod. Briefly, Rachel returned it, and edged closer to Steph, who was thankfully dancing with eyes closed. She should have forced her way to a spot near the open window, thought Rachel, the room was still hot, much too hot, no wonder she flushed.

"Half-ginger, half-mango," she requested. The man behind the counter loaded two orange-colored lumps of gelato into a cup, scraping and piling it high.

Steph defended a small table against a noisy trio. "Here she is," she told them, and scooped up her own gelato with a tiny blue spoon. She pointed to Rachel's cup. "I'm surprised you didn't ask them to sprinkle it with spices."

"Not a bad idea," mused Rachel. "Not *garam masala*, but what Indians call dessert spices. Cinnamon, coriander, cardamom? Yum!"

"So, Marc Harris on a date?" Steph eyed her spoon. "If I had to teach at *my* old school, I'd scream."

"Your old school wouldn't want you."

Steph let out a riotous laugh. "Isn't that the truth?"

Rachel shook her head. "It can keep you too young. Teaching, I mean. My students are seventeen to twenty-six, that's young enough. Camille . . . how old is second grade, eight? Gel pens and Hello Kitty."

"Think he was interested?"

Rachel swirled her two gelato flavors together. Like life: sweet, sour, tingling. "Was who interested in what?"

"Marc. Camille." Steph's tone was extra-dry. "What are you biting your lip for? You won't even go out with him for practice!"

"He's not exactly a Bollywood hero, so if he likes redheads in sequined skirts . . .."

Steph regarded her with new interest. "Oh, meow!"

"Not at all." Rachel's cheeks grew warm. "They're perfect for each other, he can admire himself in the mirrors."

"Rachel, Rachel! Can you blame the man? It's flattering, such an obvious crush."

"Speaking of crushes, how's your beloved Steven Spielberg, hmmm?"

Steph sniffed and took a large bite of pannacotta.

The group of three left, two of their chairs immediately taken by a 30-ish couple evidently new to each other. Their overheard conversation ranged round people in common, his passion for the Mets, and work. Not eavesdropping proved impossible.

". . . and one of the best parts is, I get to do it at night, like Batman . . .."

Steph choked and wheezed.

"Okay?" Rachel leaned forward.

"Yes," muttered Steph, "I just can't listen and swallow gelato at the same time."

" . . . I refuse to go to street fairs, nothing of substance ever happened at a street fair . . .."

Rachel bit back a grin. "Pretend it's a Monty Python audition," she encouraged.

"I'm so sorry, I take it back, I take it all back," Steph whispered, "*don't* practice-date, it must be horrible, how do you keep a straight face?" She lifted a spoonful of cream-colored gelato.

" . . . is that your own haircolor, or do you have something done to it?"

Explosive drops of pannacotta spattered Rachel's arm.

"Next week?" Steph made her bangles ring before sliding them off and handing them to Rachel. "More *bhangra*, babe?"

"Maybe. It was okay, but . . . what if Marc's there again?" Rachel made her voice deliberately casual. "Maybe he'd feel, you know, stalked."

Steph shrugged. "What do you care? Listen, what's Melina doing for spring break? Is she off to LA? So, we'll go wild that week, too! Come on, let's escape somewhere, I'll hit the internet, see what's cheap."

"Out of town?" asked Rachel.

"At least! Seven continents, six of them warm, let's spin the globe and see where it stops!"

CHAPTER 22

M ore emotion, please!" Rachel pleaded. "He's the cute guy you just met at your parents' party, aside from cousins he's practically the only marriageable boy you've ever seen, you're head over heels! Imagine you're making a Mumbai movie, honey. Feeling!"

Melina flapped her copy of "Romeo and Juliet". "Why do English teachers make us act? Okay, okay! 'O gentle Romeo, if thou dost love, pronounce it faithfully, or if thou thinkest I am too quickly won, I'll frown, and be perverse, and say thee nay, so thou wilt' – I can't do this!"

"Once more, then an Indian movie, I promise."

"Can I choose? 'Veer-Zaara'?"

"With King Khan stuck in jail flashbacking to his younger days?"

"And Preity! And Rani!"

Today's office hours were unexpectedly, deliciously free, Rachel discovered. No one waited outside her office door with barely-restrained impatience, not a single student suffered enough curiosity or panic to seek wisdom or, in a pinch, an extension.

With a sense of liberation, Rachel tackled her inbox's e-mails, including "Dear Professor" queries, many of which contained typos. Did no one write in Word and then paste into e-mail? Some typos were understandable (*form* for *from*), some amusing (*bridle* for *bridal*), others perplexing. Where did Apurna K get the word "gorgromary"? What could she possibly mean?

"*. . . broke r wrist, typing w l only, wd like ext on paper, cn cm ur ofc, sho u cast, u sign! Sara Geller.*"

A mildly tempting offer, that. Melina had never broken a bone – Rachel's knuckles knocked on her wooden desk – so the last cast carrying Rachel's initials had surrounded the arm of a college friend. She tapped a reply inviting Sara to swing by the office. "*Extension will be predicated on the existence of a cast and whether you bring a red marker. In all seriousness, sorry to hear about the break, hope it's not horribly painful.*"

"Swan Lake" sounded from her purse. She cracked open her mobile. "Steph, hi, what's up?"

"Why aren't you in class?"

"Office hours, but all my students are happy. Or playing hoops. Why?"

"Spring break, great news, my high-flyer aunt in New Orleans just sent me an enormous birthday check!"

"As I recall," Rachel said, extra-dry, "your birthday was last November, and she sent a check then, too."

"I know, I know. I'm splurging, and I want you to come along. You deserve a good splurge! So where do we go?"

"Steph, she meant it for *you*. Go hit LA, sniff out the elusive Spielberg!"

"Funny, very funny. You know me, I hate traveling by myself. So, again, where to? You choose!"

"Okay, okay, Goa."

"Where?"

"Goa. Goa, the place, Goa. On India's west coast. Miles of beaches, paradise on earth. Steph? Steph?"

"I'm sorry, did I forget to say 'anywhere but bloody India'?"

In the end they compromised on Paris, which was sufficiently foreign to satisfy both of them, and reassuringly European for Steph, plus cold enough this early in the year to be a bargain despite its muscle-bound, kick-sand-in-your-face euro. They were both familiar with the city. But this time, they promised, this time would be different. They'd avoid tourist sites, even the Louvre, and with luck they'd find a tiny apartment to rent for the week, forcing them out to markets and shops like real Frenchwomen.

"You can sample Goa another time," Steph said airily, "with Melina."

Rachel pocketed her phone. Steph bore an odd collection of neuroses. At times daring, she could dig in her heels for inexplicable reasons. India, now, was not only "bloody" but out – perhaps because it featured so largely in Rachel's life? She nibbled at a sweet, crunchy *gur para*, reflecting that the tie between Steph's reason and her dislikes was sometimes shaky, as liable to snap as an oak branch in a hurricane.

That was not a bad sentence.

. . . hurricane, she typed, in the initial seesaw of courtship. Just as Beatrice and Benedick joust with each other . .
.

A lyrical phrase kept running through her head, an earworm, as the Germans put it. She could almost hear words sung by soft feminine voices.

"*... bumbro, bumbro, shyaam rang bumbro, aa'e ho kis bagiya se tum?. . .*" Bumblebee, bumblebee, dark-hued bumblebee, what garden do you come from?. . ..

. . . so the initial not him *or* not her *may begin in Indian film with a difference of caste, class, religion, education or background (e.g., rural versus urban). Religion is fruitful as a divisive device in films, and was used as a verbal pillory by the comic Shakespeare. During the reign of Elizabeth I, of course, Roman Catholics were persecuted, stripped of property, tortured and killed, just as had occurred to Protestants during the reign of her half-sister, Mary.*

Yet Jews in England were few, Muslims fewer, and by the beginning of the 17th century other religions were still barely known north of the English Channel.

Contrast this relative homogeneity of belief with the profusion of faiths in contemporary India, whose film directors and producers must weigh with caution the assigned religions of every major character so that perceived offense – and its possible consequences, public protest or violence – is kept to a minimum .
. ..

Rachel paused. In India, public protests about religion were not only volatile and dangerous, they often resulted in changes in perceptions of a movie, even one approved by governmental censors, and those changes might hurt ticket sales. Producers were between a rock and a hard place. No wonder they weighed characters, dialogue, even shooting locations, so carefully. With even the best intentions, Indian filmmakers faced boycott of their movies because of purely imagined slights. Religious, after all, hardly meant spiritually mature. It was a miracle – in any faith – that Mumbai movies ever made it to the screen.

Rachel frowned at the screen. She needed a good quote. Where was that book Marc promised to lend?

. . . bumbro, bumbro, shyaam rang bumbro, aa'e ho kis bagiya se tum?. . ..

Why pick Paris? Rachel mused on her way to the English departmental office. Steph's offer – even minus Goa – was generous, but why had she capitulated to Paris? After all, she and Melina had spent a weekend there just last October, two days of brilliant sun and cool winds, so that pretending to be Petit Trianon milkmaids was replete with visions of frothy petticoats and flying ribbons. They had walked for miles in the City of Light itself, exploring, and in one memorable afternoon tasted hot chocolate at three different cafés. Their dinner that night was very late. "Oh, you are the Spaniards!" the waiter teased.

Why choose Paris when thousands of acceptably non-Indian locations beckoned?

In the department office, Jenny stared at her screen, her brow permanently furrowed.

"Hey, how are you, in *bhangra*-recovery?" Marc breezed in from the hall carrying a briefcase. He set it on one of the chairs and, for one brief moment, shook his shoulders in classic *bhangra* fashion. "Whew! Long walk. Brisk. You been outside?" He glanced from one silent woman to the other. "Okaaayyy . . . something I can help with?"

"No, thanks." The responses flew in stereo.

"Fine, I'll be in my . . . actually, no, I won't. Rachel, do you have a minute?"

She joined him in the hall, ten yards from where Helen leaned against the wall in conversation with a student and regarded Rachel with the kind of unnerving focus usually reserved for celebrities. "What's up?" she asked.

Marc held the stairway door open for her.

"Thanks,"she murmured, passing him. The door closed behind him.

"That's charming, you know."

"What is?"

"A lot of women don't thank me."

"Well," she said, awkward, "I'm matching your courtesy in holding open the door."

"So we're both being terminally polite?"

"Exactly. Did you have something important to say?"

"Are you and Jen at odds?" queried Marc.

"No, not really, just bad-date fallout. She takes other people's rejections very personally."

"Ah." On the landing, Marc's body language spelled relaxation. He seemed to have no worries and an excess of time. "Funny how we keep running into each other . . . good to see you dancing, the other night."

Rachel hesitated. "You, too. And, um," she fumbled for the name, "Camille?"

"Camille. She's much more into it than I could ever be. Wants nothing to do with India otherwise. As opposed to you, you embrace it all."

"She a significant other?" Rachel asked lightly.

"Not really. Occasional dinners, movies. Why?" Marc's eyes bore into hers.

Rachel shook her head to telegraph lack of interest, feeling that she'd overdone it. She should have stayed silent. Damn.

"So, what are you doing over the break?"

"Paris," she said, perversely pleased at his surprise.

"Really? I have an old friend in Paris."

"Covered with vines? With twelve little girls in two straight lines? Sorry, send me her name, I'll give her a call, is she Indian?"

"*He* is, how did you know?"

"Didn't. So," Rachel glanced at her watch, "you said a minute five minutes ago, what's so important?"

Marc shook his head. "Nothing, really. Just felt like being out here on the landing."

The man was weird, he was bizarre, he was . . . Rachel stopped at the intersection. Beside her was a bouncing trio of male adolescents wearing kneepads.

"Man, it's all around us, just use your eyes and your muscles will follow, man! That's what PK is!" The speaker, British, pierced and lithe, caught Rachel's eye and nodded. "That's right, eh?"

"Parkour?" she asked.

"Ah, you've heard of it! Real thrills, a challenge, yeh?"

The boys ran across the intersection. Rachel leaned against the lightpost. Real thrills? She worried her lip. Mild-manneredly delightful events, such simple pleasures as a ripe apple, a sun-filled day, yes, she got those. But thrills? Those implied the acceptance of a dare. A taunt to launch herself into the unusual, the unexpected, the –

Heavens, was Marc Harris right after all? Was different really fun?

In an act of voicemail overload, the same purring, ridiculous message had been left on Rachel's cell, at home, and on the office line. "Rachel, this is Helen. You must not have taken me seriously with regard to Marc. Listen, hon, this is way more than you want to mess with. Okay?"

About to erase, her hand hovered. Helen was an absolute fool if she thought Marc Harris held any interest for Rachel. Still, in case of further misunderstandings, she'd keep all the messages, everything. As Hindi movies had it, *sab kuch*.

Set an hour apart, the interviews she and Melina conducted – together, despite Melina's protests of piles of homework and "can't you just pick the one from Mumbai?" – sped by.

Perhaps there existed young Indian women who were rude or arrogant or simply clueless, but the trio of Sunaina, Anjali and Priyanka shared a competent, charming sweetness along with dark hair. They all had younger siblings, as well, and immediately regarded Melina as a prospective substitute. Though the length of their time in the US varied – Priyanka had arrived only a few months ago – their English was well beyond basic, and their enthusiasm for tutoring Hindi to one eager student took even Rachel aback.

"Why?" she asked.

Their faces displayed astonishment. Why not?

"You understand," the last one, Anjali, told her with graceful gestures and an impressive American accent, "hardly anyone here wants to learn Hindi, even though millions speak it and India's growth is booming. I love my language, I'd enjoy teaching your daughter. She looks eager, she gets good marks in school," she gave a tiny shrug, "and it would make my parents happy."

"Why?" repeated Rachel.

Anjali adjusted her red *dupatta*, worn over jeans and a knit top apparently more for warmth and fashion than tradition. "My mother's PhD is in literature. There's so much great writing in my country, our shelves at home in Mumbai are heavy with books. With Melina, I've got the chance to start one more person on the path to reading them."

Minutes later, having found Anjali a southbound cab, Rachel stepped back inside, rubbing her cold arms.

Melina waited on the stairs with doe-eyes. "Anjali?" she asked.

"After that speech? She should run for office. Yes."

Ecstatic, Melina flung her arms around her mother. "You won't be sorry, you'll see!"

CHAPTER 23

W hat happened to the *parathas*?" asked Rachel, rummaging through the fridge. "There were five left, weren't there?"

"Um . . .."

She straightened. "You packed all five for lunch?"

"To share," Melina said, popping an apple into her lunchbox. "I've been talking about them at school, my friends want to try them. I packed yogurt, too, to dip. Bye!"

A hug later, Rachel stared again into the fridge. No *parathas*. In that case . . .

"Now look at 'Shrew' from Kate's perspective," she told her class.

"Totally sucks." A young woman with an interesting, scrubbed-skin face spoke. "Her dad's essentially going to auction her off to a prospective groom, it's all money, money, money. It's disgusting. Especially since Kate's not the pretty package her little sister is, and there's something wrong. She's wounded."

"She *is* wounded. Somewhere, sometime, and she's floundering, she doesn't think she can take much more. But up pops Petruchio, and –?" Rachel prompted.

"This dude isn't scared of her, and right away, wow! That's different. In fact, that's wonderful. No one's ever attempted to take her on, one-on-one, with her wit and her . . . physicality." The student paused, grinning. "From the start, she wants to *do* him."

"But listen to the man:

"I will be master of what is mine own.
She is my goods, my chattels; she is my house,
My household staff, my field, my barn,
My horse, my ox, my ass, my anything;
And here she stands, touch her whoever dare.
I'll bring an action on the proudest he
That stops my way in Padua."

Rachel stopped. For a moment, the only sounds came from beyond the classroom's closed windows.

"Pretentious jerk!"

"Controlling asshole!"

"For a man who's supposed to be Christian, he's not."

"Yet when this was written," Rachel observed, "plenty of Christians owned slaves. So, Petruchio's a jerk?"

"Not always."

"He meets her," another student stepped in, "and something . . . I dunno, something clicks. Something chemical. Pheromones."

The classroom rang with laughter.

"Yes, people, there were pheromones back then. I think it was Maimonides who prohibited men from even breathing in a woman's scent, for fear of emotional entanglement," Rachel noted. "So, inside Petruchio, something shouts yes. Yes! Go for it! She's the one!"

"Professor —"

"I'm serious! Whatever it is, and it could be anything at all, maybe she reminds him of his mother, or a horse he gentled, or a wild bird, but Kate, for all her anger, has that resonance for

Petruchio. And by the time he says these lines, they're wed, so she's not only legally his, in terms of control and responsibility, but she is also his –"

"Emotionally?" A doubt-filled voice.

"Oh, ye of little faith! What's the man describing with this list of field, barn, house?" Rachel rapped on the desk. "To the audience in the theatre pit, cheap admission because they had to stand throughout the play, to them, Petruchio's describing wealth! More property and riches than they expect to earn in a lifetime! To him, Kate means –"

"Everything?" The voice held less doubt.

"Everything! He'll protect Kate, he'll sue anyone who prevents him from reaching her, and he'll guide her to become a happier person . . . even though we in the twenty-first century frown on his technique."

Her one o'clock Wednesday class knew not to expect Rachel to delay afterward to answer questions and meet requests for extra office hours. She'd pared it to a swift routine. End class, make the #1 bus north, meet Melina from school, a quick snack and caffeine and catch a cab for two – no, one, because Anjali started tutoring today, so this evening the house would ring with Hindi! – back down Fifth to arrive at Critical Theory by six without too much huff and puff.

So she abandoned her students and dashed east.

"Rachel!"

Not "Professor Hill!" Reluctant, she turned. Oh . . . Helen. Oh, Helen.

"Can't stay," called Rachel, "bus!"

"Wait!"

"Can't! Bus!"

"Wait, dammit!"

"Bus!"

With a clatter, Helen reached her, her forehead wishing it could knot.

"How do you run in those things?" Rachel asked. "Keep up, I must make this bus."

"What . . . the hell . . .."

Rachel threw words over her shoulder. "I got your message times three, and if you think I have any interest in continuing this ridiculous dialogue – watch out!"

Amazingly agile, Helen twisted on her spike heels to avoid a rough patch in the sidewalk.

"Marc is my colleague, that's all. Got it?"

Helen pulled at her arm. "I'm so glad you see it that way," she purred.

Rachel tore her sleeve from Helen's long fingernails and ran, waving her MetroCard so the bus driver would, if well-intentioned, keep the door open.

Rachel slid into the just-vacated seat, out of the standing crush she'd been part of for the past twenty blocks. Her seatmate stared out the window. Telltale white wires peeked from his dreadlocks. He hummed and half-sang.

A buzz at her hip sent Rachel into a cascade of motion. She dug her phone out and checked the number. Oh. My. God. Helen's call went to voicemail without a quibble.

". . . *ab to mera dil* . . ." sang her oblivious seatmate. A smile played at his lips. ". . .*jaage na sota hai, kya karuun haa'e, kuch kuch hota hai* . . .."

Rachel listened, amazed.

Kuch kuch hota hai . . . something's happening . . ..

Was there a more famous Hindi lyric?

"Are you, like, insane?"

Rachel considered. "I don't think so."

Melina's head bobbed up and down. "Oh, yes, you are! You're . . . Mom, how could you agree to a dinner with an alien's friend? I know men are from Mars, but at least that's in our own solar system!"

Rachel shrugged. She stuck a fork into Melina's reheated Parsi chicken, and tossed a *roti* on top.

"I said it was practice, didn't I? Take singing, you try different techniques, all sorts of notes. Dancing . . . like that *bhangra* class, different styles."

"Any friend of Helen's will be different, all right," Melina predicted darkly.

"He *is* different. He's Indian."

Her class broke just after nine. Here two students made plans for a late movie, there a quartet headed for the gym.

" . . . I can recommend others, just e-mail to remind me, okay?" said Rachel. She glanced over. At the door, unexpectedly, stood Marc with a satchel and a puzzled air. What was he doing – oh! She must have forgotten to tell him about hiring Anjali. "It's due in ten days," she reminded her student, "don't go overboard with research."

"Thanks," said the young woman. "Hi, Mr. Harris!" She received a courteous nod from Marc, and paused as if to pursue conversation. Then she slipped off, her backpack hung over one arm.

"You're daughterless?" Marc asked. "She okay?"

"She's probably learning how to ask, 'where is the movie theater?'" Rachel gave him a soundbite version of the hunt for a tutor. "Wednesday seemed like a good night."

"It's a very good night. The offer still holds, though, my car's two blocks away. *Aap chahati hain?*"

Rachel nearly stumbled. "Where in the world did you pick up Hindi?" she asked, amazed.

"Oxford, surrounded by some of the Indian millions, fellow students, shopkeepers. A few phrases, just a few. The most useful things, obviously, were dirty lyrics and curses."

"Obviously. And your Paris friend?"

"Oh!" He dove into the satchel. "Here's that book. Fascinating stuff, Mehta has an eye for darkness, and very enlightening on Bollywood. And this," he flourished a card, "is the Paris friend."

Rachel accepted both book and card. "Sandeep Malhotra," she read. The man's name was followed by e-mail and phones and an address that set him in a very posh *arrondissement* of the French capital. "I take it he doesn't teach?"

Sandeep, it appeared, was a banker. Located in Paris for six years, he had connections to Swiss institutions and Indian princelings, a potent combination. Never married ("his parents keep searching for a wife, but he likes Italian women, so it's still a stand-off"), his first love was cooking, and last year he had remodeled his apartment kitchen by demolishing walls. He and Marc had journeyed together on a weeklong road trip eighteen months ago.

"North Africa, Morocco to Cairo. The whole way, no alcohol."

"By choice?"

"We figured it'd be safer. The flight back to France is still hazy."

That made Rachel laugh.

In the dark cab, Rachel found herself humming. What was that evocative tune? Where had she heard it? It took ten blocks to prod her memory.

". . . *kuch kuch hota hai* . . .."

From the sofa, two heads turned as one.

"*Namaste*, Mom! *Aap kuch khanna* . . . um . . . *chahati hain? Main bhi!* Me, too! You won't believe how much I can say!"

"Melina's made an incredible start," Anjali added, "she's quick, she's got a good ear, and watching all those movies has helped."

"Movies certainly are a classic way to learn a foreign language," Rachel agreed.

"Can Anjali stay? We just started 'Koi Mil Gaya', she's never seen it!"

Rachel dropped her purse and satchel by the door, her keys into the bowl on the table. "The first Indian sci-fi movie?" she asked, dropping a kiss onto Melina's upturned nose. "But I'm sure Anjali has other things to do, Bini, and you need sleep."

"I'll get out of your way," and the young woman moved to go. Her hand was caught. "Melina!"

"She doesn't have class until eleven tomorrow morning, can she stay in the guestroom? She can borrow one of my nightgowns! Please?"

Rachel hesitated. To see Melina enthusiastic about a language tutor was a welcome change from the persistent complaints against Monsieur LeBlanc, and it looked like Anjali wanted only a little persuasion to stay. Perhaps she was homesick, or missed the little sister. In any case, they wouldn't watch the whole movie, for even if Anjali wasn't due at her first class until almost lunchtime, Melina would have to wipe sleep from her eyes, drag on her uniform and run to school early tomorrow morning. Another half-hour of "Koi Mil Gaya" wouldn't hurt anyone. And it *was* in Hindi.

The sun rose too early. Rachel shook Melina awake and pointed to the clock. Groans met her.

They had all three watched the entire film, Rachel soothing her conscience by taking desultory notes for her book. Anjali, it developed, knew quite a bit about behind-the-scenes Bollywood: her uncle both directed and produced movies, and, with no children, had favored Anjali with visits to the set and movie premieres. A store of anecdotes emerged as she realized Melina was all ears. The end of the movie arrived, they stumbled upstairs, and now, as predicted, Melina scrubbed sand from her brown eyes and pulled on her uniform blouse and skirt, quietly sullen.

"No complaints!" Rachel warned. "Nap when you get home."

"Meh," was the only response.

"I feel terrible," Anjali confessed after Melina scrambled out the door.

"My fault," Rachel assured her. "I should have pressed stop after thirty minutes. Got the extra MetroCard? And maybe it's always safer to spend the night here on Wednesdays, what do you think?"

"If you don't mind . . . ."

"Of course not, look how much Melina heard just this morning. Not that she paid much attention, but the next time she hears *kela* maybe she'll think banana."

" . . . so then Jason yelled, I yelled, he stopped because he never hears me yell, God, conflict resolution, it wasn't!" Rachel admitted. "Except that it was, in a strange way. He finally agreed that moneybags shoes at age thirteen were just inappropriate."

"So, consignment?" Steph reached for another apple slice. Her legs curled under her, and a Cheshire cat grin fixed itself on her face.

"No, eBay, the cash to be sent to an Indian orphanage of Melina's choice. But yelling? Not cool, even over the phone," said Rachel, embarrassed.

"Maybe yelling is what you need to do now. Go ahead, scream! At work, even. At Helen, isn't that the alien's name? Sounds like she deserves a good tirade!"

Rachel dissolved in laughter. "But it's not funny," she said, wiping her eyes. "I mean, she's got a huge streak of strange. Even though the field's open."

"And Marc?"

"I'm giving him a wide berth. Double-wide."

CHAPTER 24

"M elina!" Rachel shouted from the bottom of the stairs. Impatience edged her voice.

"Coming!"

"Just get your butt down here, we're late!" A softsided suitcase landed at Rachel's feet. "And quit throwing luggage, where are you, Madrid?"

Her arms stretched behind her, twisting her hair into a bun, Melina clattered down. "Wow, Mom, you look nice!"

Rachel twirled. Her skirt flared out and swished back against her knees. "You packed something pretty for brunch tomorrow?"

Melina nodded. "Sarah's mom was *bahut* disappointed I couldn't wear the shoes."

"The shoes? She knows about them?"

"Sure, from her I got lots of poor-you." Melina examined her reflection in the long mirror. "And tonight, you're getting rid of me to Sarah's just to go out with some stupid man who will probably be like the others and say something completely rude. And stupid. I don't know why you bother."

"Perhaps he won't. He's Indian."

"That's right!" Melina was suddenly energized. "What's-her-name's friend! Maybe he's got that hero thing down, Mom."

Helen's friend was an alien in the most ordinary and earthbound way, reflected Rachel. Krishna Shetty proved to be an ophthalmologist born in Delhi, now doing a stint of teaching in New York. Tall, with the hazel eyes of northern India and long, graceful fingers, he held the restaurant door for Rachel.

"Thanks," she said. Just then a heavy blonde jostled her, sending her caroming into Krishna.

"Whoa! You all right?" he asked, steadying her. His English was excellent, the product, he had told her in the cab, of five years' residence in Dallas before his move to New York. The hands gripping her arms were warm and assured.

"Fine."

"Sure? Five minutes' wait, then, want to spend them in the bar?"

Ten minutes with a bottle of bordeaux led to a tiny table with privacy afforded by the column beside it. Krishna opened his menu. "You know, it's refreshing to be with a woman who actually thanks me for holding open a door."

Rachel glanced up, startled.

"Sometimes I wonder, should I even try? But for better or for worse, my parents drummed manners into me." He knocked his fist against his head. "Now, veg or non-veg?"

For a man with the name of a god ("Oh, but Krishna is fairly common in India!"), Dr. Shetty was remarkably light and engaging. He was also courteous, a good listener with a ready smile and stories about cultural quirks between the two countries he called home. After a half-hour, Rachel realized her shoulders were where they should be, instead of elevated around her ears. She was enjoying simply being with this man. She'd given him extra points from the start, just for hailing from India, but he deserved them. She hadn't felt this relaxed on a date since . . . well, when? Learning to bat with Marc, but that wasn't official.

In fact, that might be called an anti-date, since Sean Kennedy hadn't called again.

"Do you eat Indian food here in the U.S.? Or only when you go back to visit?"

"Everywhere!" he said. "I love Italian food, for example, but I miss the flavors of home, especially when I speak English all day. Are you familiar with our cuisine?"

"A little. The other day I made my own *paneer*."

Krishna's mouth fell open. He stared. "You're joking! No one makes . . . how do you do it?"

Rachel embarked on a brief description of cheese-making, the magical curdling, the heat of the mass as it dropped into a cloth-lined stainless steel bowl. "Then you twist it in the cheesecloth and tie it to the kitchen faucet to drain as it hangs. Later, press it with a weight."

"A brick?"

"I just set a bowl of cold water on top. Then the fridge."

"Unbelievable. Only *daadi aur naani* make *paneer* at home. Grandmothers," he supplied.

"Yours?"

He burst out laughing. "Mine were far too elegant! They sat in their air-conditioning and bemoaned the lost Bombay of their youth."

"Ah, that's good, hold on." In her purse, Rachel found a scrap of paper and scribbled his words. "I'm writing a book on Shakespeare and Indian movies," she explained. She tucked the scrap away and looked up.

To her surprise, Krishna wore an expression of horror. "You're writing about *Bollywood?*" he asked.

"Relating it to Shakespeare, yes. You know, one of those academic treatises no one reads, but if I'm lucky it might get a mention in the Times of India."

"Bollywood? The scourge of Hindustan? And the rest of the world, too, those movies go everywhere, the Middle East, Balkans Europe," he threw up his hands, "even the Philippines!"

"I take it you don't care for even the best Hindi-language films?"

"My God, they're so artificial!" He set down his wineglass. "All that singing, dancing, yearning! And three hours long? The same plot points, the hero, the . . . frankly, I can't stand them."

"Even 'Dhoom 2', with the anti-hero transformed at the end?"

"What's that?"

"'Dhoom 2'," Rachel repeated. "The sequel to 'Dhoom'? Hunting down the master thief, car chases, Mumbai, Rio?"

Krishna shook his head.

"You never saw 'Dhoom 2'?"

"Should I have?"

"Yes!" she sputtered. "You're Indian, this is your cinema!"

He tipped his glass to her. "Are you calling me unpatriotic?"

"Un . . . aware. What was the last Hindi movie you saw, then?"

"First-run? Let's see, a few years . . . oh, my mother dragged me to one about villagers who outplay the British at cricket, and . . .."

"That was 'Lagaan' in 2002, you've missed so much!" exclaimed Rachel.

"Have I? I don't think so. The majority of Indian films are ridiculous. You're an educated woman, how can you watch such tripe? Thank you, I'll take care of it," he told the waiter, and grabbed the new bottle to pour Rachel a generous measure. "Cheers!"

"Cheers." She sipped. The wine slipped across her tongue like a warm blanket, making her bold. "Admittedly, what I see is geared to the overseas market. But they're better than you think, Krishna. They've got themes and treatments Shakespeare would recognize and appreciate, and he'd be green with envy over their financial success, too. Reaching hundreds of millions? Not too shabby."

"At a price. I have a cousin who does computer music for film. It can be, er, precarious. Organized crime still likes to finance."

"But American studios are pitching in with investment money," Rachel noted, "about time, too, as long as they're hands-off with regard to values and plot, which many of us appreciate."

"See, that's where American studios *should* move in! The provincial melodrama!"

"Provincial?" She sipped again. "In Mumbai, *über*-metropolis? I think you might want to get caught up with the current crop of movies. Besides," Rachel added, "there's so much that's valuable about –"

"About?" Krishna paused, ready to pounce.

Ah, well, she might as well go for broke. "About love and longing and the kind of playful sensuality of picturisations. Romanticism, which the West doesn't have much time for anymore. *Ke dona, ke dona,* you are my *soniya,*" she sang.

"At the time, the most downloaded ringtone in the world," he said, dismissive. "Even I know that."

"Of course! Everyone wants to be called 'darling', even if it's only by their phone. Like Shakespeare, Bollywood taps into the most universal themes. That's part of its success."

"I can't believe I'm hearing this from a woman who lectures on the most revered writer in the English language!"

"He's revered now. In his own time, he was merely popular. There's nothing wrong with popular, that's what Bollywood is!"

Krishna cocked an eyebrow.

"It was the same with Shakespeare, his audience was largely illiterate. The plays are packed with all sorts of draws. Take 'Hamlet'." Rachel leaned forward, eyes alight. "Yes, it's deep, it's extraordinary, but then there's the gravedigger, the visiting players. Those characters are amusing, or touching, or intriguing. And the comedies, they're full of silliness, rubes, clowns, mixed-up identities, because Shakespeare wrote for anyone who'd pay up. You like laughter? Here you go! Want a swordfight? We have those, too!"

"Yes, but –"

"Vulgar double entendres, yearning, pining, the classic theme of falling for someone your parents won't approve of. Bollywood paints with the same strokes, and you know what? A good story is a good story. Besides, in most Indian schools, students read Shakespeare as a matter of course. Didn't you? See, he's bound to affect your literature, and that includes screenwriting. Look at 'Omkara', Othello written for rural India, and just as intense as the original."

"'Omkara'?"

"Write it down. Rent it. You'll be amazed . . . it's got the usual Hindi songs and dances, but so amazingly dark and brooding, and the Iago –" She shivered.

Krishna, whose eyes had fixed on her throughout this outburst, now stretched out his hand. His fingers grazed Rachel's, their nails narrowly scraping. "You're passionate about this, aren't you?"

"Passionate?" She took up her fork. "To me, it just makes sense."

A smile played on his lips. "And the rest of your department, your colleagues, how do they see this book?"

"My colleagues?" Rachel thought a moment. "I've really only talked to my department chair about it, and he . . . well, he seems enthusiastic."

"Lucky you!"

An hour later, she felt light with wine and the knowledge that across from her sat a man who made her feel desirable. Their verbal conflict seemed to inspire Krishna, and his interest could not be more clear. A touch of the hand became two, then three, then a light grasp. Much ado about nothing, indeed. No wonder Rachel's smile blossomed. It was more than "Hum Tum", there was genuine liking here.

"I'm really glad Helen called me," said Krishna. He lifted a strawberry to his mouth. "She's rather a strange woman, so I was skeptical, I thought how could she possibly be acquainted with anyone I might be taken with, but . . .."

"Me, too! How would Helen know anyone who might be interested in more than chemical peels and Charles Dickens?"

He laughed and chose another strawberry. "That's actually how we met," he said. "My father used to quote to me, *David Copperfield* to *Bleak House* to . . . well, I met Helen at a Dickens conference, in fact." Once more his hand brushed hers. His hazel eyes were deliberate, their pupils enlarged and black.

"What if . . ." Krishna glanced about. "What if we go on? Somewhere quiet?"

The night air, crisp and still, swept the wine from Rachel's brain as she walked beside Krishna. Their breath floated in silver clouds that clung before vanishing. Spilled light from stores and restaurants set their skins aglow.

"So, next Saturday! I'll introduce you to the best Indian restaurant in the city, bar none!" Krishna beamed. He stopped and took her hand, stroking its palm with his thumb, making her knees tremble. She wet her lips.

"Cards on the table, Rachel, I like you. I like you a lot. What I don't understand is how is it possible a woman like you has never been married?"

Rachel glanced up. "Years ago, I was."

"But Helen told me you were unmarried!"

"I am. Well, divorced. I haven't been married for some time," Rachel explained.

"But . . .." He searched her eyes. "You're not *single*? As in, never married?"

"No." Rachel paused. "Does that make a difference?"

"Yes, of course! I'm looking for someone who hasn't been a wife, my parents are very traditional . . . why on earth would Helen say you were unmarried?" On Rachel's palm, his thumb rested.

"To us, unmarried or single means, well, you aren't currently hitched. You've never been married?"

"Yes . . . yes, I have, but –"

"But?"

"But it's different," he said, rather lame, and dropped her hand.

She stood in the cold, debating, her finger poised on the button labeled "Zimmer". Part of her said she should be able to handle romantic ups and downs by herself. Yet the other part, the emotionally-intelligent half, asked an essential question: What would an Indian woman do in the same circumstances? Easy. She'd search out a sister, mother, or friend, and pour out her heart. Rachel had no sister, her parents had died years before . . . so here she was, ready to summon Steph.

"Excuse me." A bulky figure joined her on the step. The man glared at her over his shoulder, ready to defend the door should she try to shove her way in. "Wait a minute . . . you're Steph's friend, aren't you? Begins with an R? Raquel?"

"Rachel."

"Rachel, right!" He stuck out his hand. "Luca Doherty, we met after the St. Patrick's Day parade a couple years ago."

"Luca, I remember." What she remembered most, besides the painful pressure of his hand, was that Luca, who worked for the mayor's office, had hit on her with what-the-hell post-parade enthusiasm. There was a particularly ugly memory of beer-soaked breath.

"You wanna see Steph?"

"Yes, thanks."

"Sure thing, just pay the toll!" Luca grinned and patted his cheek. "Lay one right on me, baby, right here!"

Shivering in the wind, Steph held the street door open. "Next time I see that Luca, I'll knee him one. Idiot!" She pulled the door to and followed Rachel through the second door to the stairs. "Where does he get off?"

"He was probably lit." Rachel stepped aside so Steph could lead the way. "It's just this time, the beer wasn't green."

Steph had left her door ajar, a rare thing. "You want something to drink?"

Rachel tossed her coat over a chair, slipped out of her heels, and mutely held out her arms.

"Oh, sure!" Steph's embrace was warm. "Are you okay? What happened?"

"Life happened. *Zindagi* happened. Great word. *Zin-da-gi.* No, I don't need any," said Rachel, waving away the wine bottle Steph pulled out of the fridge.

"Did the alien turn out to be creepy, the kind with tentacles?"

Rachel laughed. "He was alien only in the Homeland Security sense. Krishna was, oh," she curled into the sofa and gathered her memory, "he was good-looking, bright, funny, courteous. He listened, he gave me his opinions, he did everything well."

"Except?"

"Except he needs a woman who hasn't ever married. Someone me-ish, only, you know, not-me. The Bollywood hero gauge doesn't have any clues about once-married women. Okay, I take that back, in 'Kuch Naa Kaho' he ends up marrying her. The exception that proves the rule. But it was Aishwarya Rai, who wouldn't marry the most beautiful woman in the world?" she asked, querulous, and held her hand out for the glass.

Steph gave it to her and went into the kitchen to pour more. "Tonight was half-good, then," she called.

"Until the end. I was feeling comfortable, I was letting my guard down, I was even telling him about my book!"

Steph reappeared with a bag of pretzels. She ripped it open and placed it on the coffee table. "Why?"

"He was derisive about Bollywood, I was its impassioned defender. To an Indian who hasn't watched a Hindi-language movie for years! Incredible. But it doesn't matter," said Rachel, firmly setting her glass down, "he said the thing about never being married, I said fine, we shook hands, I hailed a cab. End of story, thank you, and exit."

"Listen, you've gotten that off your chest, glass of wine, now for a little planning . . .." From her bookcase Steph retrieved a handful of printed brochures, two maps, and a Paris guidebook. "From the ridiculous to the sublime."

Rachel unfolded one of the maps, stretching it out on the floor. Kneeling, she traced the Seine with one finger. "Where's our hotel?"

"There, that blue circle."

Rachel squinted. "In the shadow of the Eiffel Tower?"

Steph knelt beside her. "It throws a hell of a long shadow, my friend."

"Bye!" Rachel closed the door as Melina's friend Sarah walked off the next morning. She turned around and leaned back against it. "So how'd it go?"

"How'd yours go?" Melina countered, dropping her bedpillow on the steps and plunking herself bleary-eyed beside it.

"God, did you get any sleep at all?" Rachel demanded, examining Melina's bloodshot eyes.

"Two hours." She yawned. "All the regular stuff, ate chocolate, drank green tea, her mom won't buy soda anymore, watched Brad Pitt movies," Melina grimaced, "she's in some sort of phase, so I brought my Indian DVDs back. Went to brunch. I had French toast. Happy?"

Rachel squeezed onto the same narrow step. "My date was handsome, educated, polite, intelligent, had dinner, went for walk, he wasn't interested in anyone who'd been married before, I zipped down to Steph's and fantasized about Paris. Happy?"

Melina's yawn threatened to swallow her whole. "Delirious."

CHAPTER 25

First tests were always a trial.

Not just for students, either. A blizzard of pages had engulfed Rachel's coffee table, drifting into stacks sorted by class. Three separate Comedies classes, a total of over sixty students, multiplied by a test incorporating ten short answers, two small explications, and a single long essay, made for –

"Too much." Melina appeared over her shoulder. "Skip the two little ones."

"I gave them a choice, six quotes," Rachel replied, defensive, "you can tell with six. Something for everyone to rant on. How's homework?"

"No homework," Melina reminded her, clambering over the back of the sofa to join her mother, "tomorrow's that all-day mediation workshop."

"Oh, right. I'm filled with envy," Rachel sighed. "I'm chained to paper, submerged by paper, and in a moment you'll be sitting down to a movie shot somewhere exotic, Kashmir, Delhi, Singapore –"

"New York City, 'Kal Ho Naa Ho'. Want some help? I'll do the short answers," Melina offered, "your red pen, check, X, they'll never know."

"Tempting, but no thanks. Best thing right now is order dinner."

"Punjab House?"

"Goat curry?"

"Mom, no! They probably use baby goats!"

"You mean kids."

"See, that's just gross."

"Fine, no kids, no lambs, how about chickpeas and *paneer*?"

Where Shakespeare wrote prose instead of verse, what were his objectives?

Why are Theseus/Hippolyta and Oberon/Titania often played by the same paired actors?

How does Beatrice's spinsterhood affect her choice of language?

Spinsterhood. A barely-used word, these days. Perhaps, on future tests, Rachel should re-name it. "Singleness", "single state". Something.

From above, playback singers belted out in Hindi, the soprano a thin wail. She glanced out the window. Dark, cold, damp. She shivered and drew her sweater closer. In Southern California it was only six o'clock with darkening skies, dry and perhaps sixty degrees. Angelenos were grilling outside, they were setting marinated eggplant over the coals, turning salmon . . ..

Her mouth watered.

Rachel scrambled from the sofa in search. Aha, one *gulab jamun* left from dinner, one lonely little ball of fried dough drenched in sugar syrup. Nibbling, she flicked on the kettle just as the phone rang. She answered, cradling the receiver under her chin while she climbed the steps.

"Hi, Jason, I was just thinking of you guys grilling fish. Hey, honey, your dad!" she called through Melina's door.

Back down the steps into the kitchen, pour water, choose teabag, dunk.

First tests were always a trial. Transported twenty-some years, Rachel saw herself as an undergraduate at a long oval table in a room crowded with dusty shelves. The window, too, was yellow-brown with dirt, adding to the atmosphere of neglect.

He would enter late, Professor . . . Professor . . . anyway, he was invariably late and distracted, with the air of a scholar torn from hand-copied vellum texts, manuscripts complete with marginal comments scratched by bored or irritable monks. His hair was greasy, complexion pale, fingernails shudderingly long. A running debate divided his students: did he clip his toenails?

With one foot in the period, the man knew his subject, but his personal appearance was bizarre enough to distract. Perhaps that was why Rachel avoided excess before her own students. Not for her Helen-like cosmetic enhancements, nor Helen's wrapped von Furstenburgs that would sometimes, distressingly, part.

Melina appeared in the doorway, her hair plaited into slender dark braids twisted and pinned to her head.

"*Et tu*, Bini?"

Her daughter handed over the phone and disappeared.

"Hey, Rach! You must be psychic, we've got tilapia and shrimp to toss on the grill." Jason's voice carried a plaintive note, a tone that over years she had learned to recognize preceded bad news.

"Yum." Rachel stirred her tea, waiting.

"Listen, I know you like to be asked, so I'm asking: could I stay with you guys next week? I need to come back, do some more looking, and I'll take you out to lunch!"

Rachel silently beseeched the ceiling.

"Rach? You still there?"

"You know, Jason, lunch is supposed to precede the ask."

"So that's a no?"

"That's no. Melina will love seeing you in the evenings, though. Maybe this time Ellie can come with you? Or is she swamped?"

"Yeah, she takes care of things here."

"Great, enjoy your fish and shrimp and palm trees."

Rachel clicked the phone off and skidded it across the table. She drank a sip of tea, a gulp of tea, the whole hot mug.

Paris.

Dozens of tests later, her work e-mail inbox carried a message from Marc, the subject line consisting of the single word: Paris. Rachel clicked on his name. Click, a name, click, a communication, click, delete. How much more disposable current communications seemed than in the time of Lady Macbeth, who – if she were even literate – might have destroyed an incriminating missive in the nearest flame.

Repeating info, just in case, he'll expect your call. With Sandeep Malhotra's telephone numbers, address and e-mail. An old friend of Marc's, and Indian, who inhabited a leafy stretch of the City of Light? There was promise there. Really, she ought to write the old friend, and the earlier the better.

"What would Shakespeare do, then?"

"In that situation?" Rachel frowned and stirred batter in a stainless steel bowl. "Well, instead of banishing the eldest son who married the wrong girl, I suppose he'd disinherit him. Although primogeniture meant the first son got the lot, regardless of his father's feelings. Maybe he couldn't disinherit. Maybe," her eyes narrowed, "if he were really evil – but we're talking tragedy here – he'd hire thugs to kidnap the son and at least imprison him long enough to be legally declared dead, so the second son would get the gold."

Chandani gave her a long look. "Now, that's evil. Here, the oil's hot. Hand me that metal thing, please. Okay . . . narrow hole at the bottom, so in goes the *jalebi* batter, hold it over and . . .."

From the aperture a thin stream of batter fell sputtering into the oil. In Chandani's hands, the container danced in small circles. Rings of *jalebis* blossomed and bubbled in the heat.

"Pick them out . . . drain on newspaper . . . bang into the sugar syrup. Here come more!"

"Do Indian fathers do that? Disinherit?" Rachel looked up from the frying *jalebis*. "I take it the answer is no."

"It would take something awful for a father to do that to a firstborn son. Awful? Unheard of. Beyond murder, even, plenty of convicted murderers inherit."

"The family bond is that strong?" asked Rachel, impressed.

"Stronger. It'd take more than a crime. Extreme moral turpitude – watch out, it's splashing! – or the rest of the family taking a stand against him."

"For?"

"There, that's all of them, they'll cool in the syrup. Considering the headlines, some men get away with a great deal. And if they're still at home, do their parents rise in court and ask for forgiveness from the victim? No, they're too busy protecting their little *rajkumar*, their prince!" Chandani's voice rose. "Indian men talk about respect for women, but rapes keep climbing, even in Mumbai, which used to be much, much safer than Delhi. And do you know where the highest rate of abortions of healthy female fetuses occurs, just because the parents don't want a daughter? Delhi, the capital, and Chandigarh, in the Punjab! Northern cities, both of them, the better-educated, richer north! God!" She thumped down the funnel. "Sometimes, being Indian . . . I just want my country to get *better*."

"Do you see a . . . aha!" Marc grabbed a pile of envelopes from his desk, revealing a slim red-bound folder. He opened it, paging through documents. "Sorry, I'm getting ready to roll out of here on a dangerous mission." He glanced up, his blue eyes alight. "Always risky business, asking for money."

"At least you're dressed for it," Rachel joked, "not doing the Tom Cruise thing."

"Yeah? Tie straight, all that? It's raining, I need my umbrella, umbrella, umbrella – there!" He snatched it from the corner. "Sandeep's a good guy, let him know what you'd like him to whip up. Haute cuisine without the high prices. What *do* you like to eat?"

She shrugged. "I'm pretty easy."

His head snapped up, his smile wry. "Easy? That you're not. But if you promise to eat it, he'll cook it."

Stung, Rachel sought some way to catch him off-guard. "So . . . how's Camille?"

"Fine, I think. She's looked for you at *bhangra*."

"Accha?"

At her own desk, thoroughly irritated, Rachel tapped computer keys. Pretty easy, low maintenance, a wonderful woman. She was all that. Certainly she was all that.

No, you're not, she heard in her head, adding a nyaah-nyaah note to match her mood.

Yes, she was, perfectly easy, a delightful companion, good listener, capable of taking pleasure in the myriad of possibilities within the tri-state . . ..

That was a dating profile.

She *was* easy. It's just that Marc did not recognize it in her, the amiability and congeniality that marked her as distinct from the majority of women who . . ..

Now she sprang from the pages of *Pride & Prejudice*.

Well, what would Marc know? He'd never spent quality time with her.

Her fingers played a useless tattoo. With a burgeoning sense of unease, she acknowledged that the one person who'd placed her in a position to be described as difficult was, in fact, hers truly. She knew as well as Marc that his remark referred not to Rachel the colleague, Rachel the teacher or *bhangra* dancer.

The Rachel he meant was the woman who refused to go out with him. The one who ignored his interest.

She didn't ignore it. She simply refused to cooperate.

From memory rose the taste and feel of his mouth, their kiss, that night of the pig roast. Rachel shoved the image back down. It made bad sense, no sense, in fact, to date people at work. The inevitable falling-out would make the university a field of landmines and daily explosions. She'd seen it happen to friends, to couples.

Then there was the parceling-out of shared acquaintances. So-and-so was my friend first! But we play racquetball together every Saturday! But our friendship preceded your racquetball!

It was wrenching. Better to avoid the whole mess. Marc was welcome to turn his interest elsewhere. Toward Camille, for example, with her mirror-spangled skirt and come-hither *bhangra* jerk of her shoulders.

"Busy?"

Rachel jumped. Wooden floors and a rhythmic, sweat-soaked male body gave way to Helen's sinuous approach.

"I hope you're not here to interview me about that dinner," Rachel said, as dry as slate, "because as far as Krishna's concerned, he wants someone nuptially untried."

"He told me, I'm very upset with him!" Helen maneuvered herself into a chair. "What the hell is he thinking? Shit! He never said he needed a *single* single woman! He's divorced, I thought . . . and where the hell is he going to find someone educated, amusing, and – you won't mind my saying this – dependable, who's always been single?" Her fingers drummed on Rachel's desk. "Where?"

Rachel tapped keys. "Calcutta?"

"He's so stupid! I had no idea!"

"I'm fine. A little chopped liver-ish, but everyone's got their deal-breakers. It would have been far worse if we'd gone on to a drink, nuzzled each other's ears, etcetera. Especially etcetera." She rose. "I've got to go, Helen."

"If anyone else comes to mind –"

"Absolutely, let me know." The chances that Helen might know another man as presentable as Krishna Shetty were anorexic. She appeared to be on intimate terms with her dermatologist, perhaps there was an anesthesiologist or two whose numbers were stored in her phone, but otherwise? Not unless Rachel wanted to inject a variety of cosmetic substances. "Enjoy the evening."

"Wait." Helen sidled closer. The wrap dress parted. "Now that Krishna's out of the picture, you're still steering clear of Marc, aren't you?"

"Cross my heart and hope to die, Helen, Marc Harris is safe from my depredations." A sudden urge to mischief overtook Rachel. "But . . . well, no, you don't want –"

"What?"

"It's nothing." She brushed it away. "Just . . . I overheard him talking about a woman named Camille . . . an old friend . . . something about mangoes." She directed a glance at Helen's chest, whose extreme dieting had left her with nubbins of breasts. "Just good friends."

CHAPTER 26

S o I followed him, dear, all the way downtown, on that hot evening, end of July, you can imagine! And do you know where he went?" The white curls nodded. "A hotel, and not a very nice one, either, and when I saw that, well, it was all over, I tell you!"

With an internal sigh, Rachel remembered from last year, and the year before, and the year before that: Mrs. Burke, observant as ever – and clearly possessed of as much energy as when shadowing an errant husband – had watched the two of them leave for the airport this morning. She had later observed Rachel return sans Melina. Thirty minutes after that, Mrs. Burke gained Rachel's door bearing a tin of homemade cookies ("real butter!"), and launched her assault on the living room.

"So, spring recess, you're off to Paris, and Melina is –?"

"California."

"You know you can always leave her with me, darling, don't you?" The woman selected another of her cookies. "I might be a little bit older, but I still know how to look after a young girl!"

Rachel nodded, in her memory Melina's words of warning several years past, something about calling child protective services if Rachel ever again left her with "anyone who wants to load me up with mascara and shadow and pink gunk!"

"Whoa, whoa! Mrs. Burke used to be a makeup artist, she probably just saw you as a fresh canvas."

"Weirdo!"

Perched on the sofa across from Rachel, the weirdo nibbled a cookie. "It's a shame her dad's so far away."

"Yes, it is," Rachel agreed, and glanced at her watch. "This has been lovely, Mrs. Burke, but I need to finish packing."

The bell sounded. Rachel opened the door, resigned to revealing her visitor, how else to usher Mrs. Burke out? On the stoop was Steph with the kind of oversize suitcase useful for stashing a body.

"Hey, am I –?"

Rachel dragged her in. "You're fine, Mrs. Burke was just leaving."

Cookie in hand, the older woman edged past Steph. "Have a good time, Rachel!" The door closed.

"I'm obviously an untouchable," Steph complained. "Are you packed?"

"With a smaller one, you won't have to risk checking it. Or paying for it."

"We can't all be minimalists," Steph grumbled, kicking at Rachel's single, overhead-binnable case. "So we spend a few minutes at the baggage carousel, so what?"

"Yours may not even make it to the carousel. It may go to Caracas. *Olé!*"

"Fine! You have another?"

"No, but I'll borrow one from Noor."

Rachel skipped down the front steps and ran across. The day held the kind of pre-spring glow that filled her with childlike energy. It brought unusual words to mind: caper . . . gambol . . . cavort.

Noor brought forth a black suitcase the twin of Rachel's. "You go alone?" she inquired.

Rachel bumped the boxy thing across the threshold. "No, my friend Steph, too. That's her." She pointed. Across the macadam, Steph waggled her fingers.

"Ah, good." The bright eyes examined Rachel. "Hard to be alone."

Lambswool clouds frolicked above. The grass was lush, the sky azure. Snow-dusted mountains thrust up against the blue. Below lay small wooden houses scattered like toys, their fields fenced by branches shorn of twigs and thrust into the earth. Amid tumbled boulders shrugged off by the hills, goats grazed.

Marc Harris appeared. He was dressed as a peasant, dirt-colored *salwar* pants topped with a homespun vest wrapped about his chest. His smile shone.

"Where does your heart wander, will it wander with me?" he sang, dancing toward her. *"Will your bracelets chime for me?"*

Rachel edged toward him, her glance flirtatious. A chiffon sari floated about her like crimson cirrus.

"Will your earrings dance for –"

She woke with a start.

The jet's drone was loud, yet not quite loud enough to drown the couple behind her arguing in Caribbean-accented Spanish. The darkened cabin held several pools of light, those of inveterate readers or card-players. She stretched her legs and shoved her feet against the cabin floor, twisting her spine to ease it. In the seat beside her, Steph grunted in her sleep.

A red sari! Of all things to wear! She shook her head, bemused. In the Bollywood vernacular, there was nothing more meaningful. Red saris were the costume equivalent of a silk-and-satin wedding gown.

And Marc in the simple dress of her dream?

Such a traitor, her unconscious mind! It snatched up pleasant, romance-laden scenes, mixed in personnel from her own life, and presented the result with giggles and a knowing nudge. Take that, Rachel! As if she would ever, awake and aware, associate her department chairman with the emotion-laden music and passion of such a film. Ha!

She gave a weak laugh. You had to hand it to the unconscious, it was inventive as hell. The idea of Marc Harris, last seen dressed for success in a gray chalkstripe, wearing designer-adapted clothing of northern India . . . well, if it weren't so ridiculous, she'd share the image with Steph for a good chuckle. And singing? To her knowledge, the man could not sing. Dance, yes, she had seen him on that second-story wooden floor, pounding his feet and jerking his shoulders with the rest. He could dance. So?

Bas. Enough.

The man to her left read a sports magazine, something about the upcoming baseball season. Rachel saw again the batting cage, heard once more the whack of the ball, Sean Kennedy's "pick up the bat, pick up the bat!" and his ridiculous question about Rachel's refusal to date Marc. Because of his religion? Please. She chuckled. Clearly Marc hadn't let Sean in on the dispute over Rachel's seminar and the critical theory class, the dark cloud that . . . that . . ..

She twisted uneasily.

In her continual irritation at Marc, wasn't she just as prejudiced as if she held his religion against him? And, more uncomfortably, just as stubborn? Though he'd screwed up once (every Wednesday! her churlish memory insisted), was he then, well, a screw-up? After apologies, attention, offers of rides home? One error, months of bad feeling? Her cheeks felt hot.

. . . *kuch kuch hota hai* . . . something's happening . . ..

Perhaps she'd been misusing Melina's hero yardstick after all.

Rachel pulled her water bottle from the seat pocket at her knees. She uncapped it and gulped. Flying was thirsty work, and dreams such as hers . . . she checked her watch. She had set it ahead right after boarding, it was already timed *à la française*. Another sixty-five minutes would land them at Charles de Gaulle, by which time the sun might be up. They would herd through security and immigration, and up escalators to a cab.

Perhaps there were other passengers willing to share a taxi. These days, the dollar was a weakling against the mighty euro. It made no financial sense for Rachel and Steph to visit Paris at all. Yet the heart has its reasons . . ..

The stomach, however, is intensely rational, and Rachel's clamored to be filled. She searched her roomy purse, pulled out a small Winesap she'd tucked in for this very moment, and bit. Her mouth welled with apple juice so tart, her eyes watered.

Steph stirred, mumbled, stirred again. Rachel prodded her.

"We're close. Less than an hour."

Rachel shoved the taxi door to and waved to the three Houstonians she and Steph had met in the non-EU line, who'd responded with dollar-wise fervor when she proposed sharing a cab.

A Paris apartment, they'd found, needed to be booked weeks and weeks ago. Back to the Internet they went, and found a small, undistinguished room within minutes. The Hôtel Cézanne would be pleased to house them.

The hotel did indeed have a room, located one floor above the reception desk. It contained little more than twin beds, an armoire, and – "didn't we ask for a loo?"

"I thought we did."

A few minutes downstairs produced not an ensuite bathroom, but voiced regrets, Madame, several guests had overstayed, the shared bathroom is only two doors down the hall, the room is less expensive than the one originally chosen!

"Twenty euros less, then," Rachel told the wary manager. "*Vingt euros de moins*."

"*Ah, non, madame, je regrette, on ne peut pas . . ..*" Fifteen euros, however, he would slash the rate by fifteen. They parted with mutual respect.

"In any case, we'll hardly be here at all," Rachel commented.

"Middle of the night," Steph predicted with gloom, "emergency fumblings into the hall to pee without even remembering why I'm headed out."

"We'll meet interesting people," said Rachel. "You meet fascinating people in hallways."

"Who'll be racing us to the shower."

"I'm calling Melina."

"Who has her very own bathroom!" called Steph.

"What do you mean, weird?"

"Weird weird." Melina's voice sounded as clear as next door. "It's not the words. Something's wrong, but I don't know what, and Daddy laughed at me and said I was crazy when I asked him."

"You're not crazy," Rachel told her daughter. "How are he and Ellie together?"

"Fine," Melina insisted. "It's me she's weird around. Maybe I did something –"

"I'm sure you didn't."

Melina hesitated. "She still took me shopping, she wanted to get more shoes and keep them a secret."

"Did she, now?" Rachel gave a rueful laugh. "I think I prefer tarot cards."

"I said no, my closet was too full."

"Liar. What do you want to do?"

"Well . . . it's really pretty here, and there's a new neighbor with a daughter in eighth grade, she's coming over after school."

"If you change your mind," said Rachel, "we can figure something out."

"I don't want you to lose your trip," said Melina.

"Me, neither, but you count more than it does. If weird turns to strange or bizarre, or especially if it becomes uncanny, call me!"

"Uncanny," Melina repeated. "How would I know?"

CHAPTER 27

First thing every morning, croissants, butter and apricot jam at bedside evoked Paris for Rachel. A simple call downstairs, and ten minutes later, with a knock on the door, the laden tray was presented every delicious day, along with two cups of tea. She slathered jam over pastry, spilling crisp flakes.

"It's the first smell of Paris, apricots and butter," she explained to Steph, who yawned and rubbed her wet hair. "How was the shower?"

"The last guy left his Swedish shampoo. Sniff." She ducked her head.

"We've got Marc's friend Sandeep tonight."

"Sure," said Steph equably, "unless you want to go alone?"

"Alone?" asked Rachel, taken aback.

"Marc's friend?" Steph's eyebrows rose. "A little connection?"

"Cut it out! That's ridiculous!"

Steph watched with narrowed eyes as Rachel pulled out the Paris map and lifted the phone. "Marc said he was a good cook? Excellent sign."

"Of what?"

"A memorable meal." Steph bit into breakfast.

" . . . you'll reach my flat, on the right, just buzz."

"Got it." Rachel scribbled. "Can we bring wine, dessert?"

"No, no." Sandeep Malhotra's voice carried a London accent and a full smile. "Come at seven, I'll still be cooking. And don't worry about the Métro, I'll drive you back. Any friend of Marc's is a friend of mine."

"*Are* you a friend?"

Steph posed the question as they stood outside a charcuterie in whose windows gleamed an assortment of hams and sausages and delicacies presented in pots. Rachel held a *bâtard* bought from the bakery next door. A casual picnic was the idea, the map showed a small park four blocks away which was bound to be scattered with the steel benches common to Paris greenspaces, in which grass was to be admired but never walked upon.

"Ham?" asked Rachel. "Or some of those preserved thingies? They're almost too pretty."

"Friend?" Steph pressed.

Rachel sighed. "God knows what Marc told him."

"We can guess what Marc told him," Steph pointed out. "That if he could ever get to know you one-on-one, you might mean something to him beyond faculty meetings and undergrad lectures." She nodded at the window. "Those?"

Rachel shrugged, putting a Gallic flavor into her shoulders.

They ate on a bench, spreading out an abandoned copy of Le Monde as a tablecloth. A paper bag held a pair of hand-dipped and very expensive chocolates. Faced with luxury foods, the dollar did not go far. Yet French chocolates eaten from a copy of Le Monde that emanated from a newsstand only a block away was chocolate well worth its cost.

Across the park, small children with their mothers or nannies played with a large red ball on the gravel path, keeping well off the grass.

"Where to next? Oh, this was the point we were going to split up. I want to go to Pompidou, you said no," complained Steph.

"Melina and I were there last fall."

"That's too much Pompidou?"

"It is for me. Why don't we meet back at the hotel at, oh . . ." Rachel glanced at her watch, "five-thirty? That'll give us time to change."

"You'll miss the Kandinskys inside. What are you planning? Are you blushing? Oh, my God, you met a man! You didn't! On the way to the bathroom?"

"I met a fifteen-year-old boy in rugby uniform," said Rachel, irritated. "No, I just want to do a bit of academic exploration."

"Shakespeare was never in Paris, was he?" Steph opened the bag of chocolates.

"I want to see the Grand Rex. It's the largest auditorium in Paris, opened in 1932. Shah Rukh Khan and Rani Mukherjee were there a few years ago for a premiere."

"You're off to a movie theater," Steph said, incredulous, "in Paris, the city of light?"

"Also the birth of film," Rachel reminded her. "The brothers Lumière started here, they even carted their cinématographe to Mumbai in 1896, which is why Indian film predates Hollywood. There are ties, Steph!"

"Ties?" Unconvinced, Steph bit into her chocolate. "You just hate Kandinsky."

With a sense of sneaking off, Rachel headed to an internet café she'd spotted several blocks away. She invested several minutes looking up Indian grocers in Paris. Her search was rewarded. There were three streets to try, and one review also noted a nearby Indian tailor. Melina had been making sari noises ("Anjali can show me how to wrap it"), though buying Indian fabric in Paris would be a huge financial error. Better to save the exchange rate difference for a week in India itself.

She stopped. India was too big, too complicated, too rich in history and energy for just a week. A week's stay there was the merest nibble of a ripe fruit, while all about them in the grove hung mangoes of equal ripeness and perfume.

That was the trouble with Paris, it made her poetic. Still . . . she scrawled the words in the margin of her guidebook, underscoring the word *perfume*.

She was right. Buying fabric in Paris would be fiscal madness. They were beautiful, certainly, georgettes and crepes in reds and pinks and Caribbean turquoise. In this upscale shop, the cloth was embellished with embroidery and sequins, even semi-precious stones. Such a sari would be worn at only the most festive occasions. To which Melina was unlikely to be invited in the next ten years, and while a sari itself could be wrapped around a woman of any size, if Melina had the *choli* made now, she'd outgrow it by the end of high school.

Rachel pored over the silky fabrics. They *were* beautiful. It was a shame she had no festive occasion to justify purchasing a sari of her own.

There was the grocery with a printed window: *Alimentation Indienne*. There could hardly be a more welcome sign. Rachel's mouth watered. There might be few Indians in Paris, but they knew their way around cardamom and ginger. She crossed the narrow street midway, drawing the horn of an angry motorist.

What was it about India that drew her? It was more than the movies, more than the food, clothes, language. Some aspects of the nation – harassment of women and the lack of clean water, for instance – she doubted she could live with. Always, there was extreme poverty. And organized crime could make urban life like 1920s Chicago. Yet there was extraordinary persistence and energy in India, as well, and the country was still politically young, only sixty years since independence. Though it was difficult to layer new ways of seeing, new perceptions, onto millennia of history, culture and art, still . . . India possessed so much hope!

Perhaps, in rooting for the underdog, Rachel was being quintessentially American.

All I'm saying is every culture has an underbelly . . . not everything Indian is happy and good, that's all. Marc's words filtered up from where she'd stowed them. He meant his ex, of course. Unless . . . was he referring to Sandeep? Rachel frowned. Surely not. He wouldn't have given Rachel the phone number of a man he considered risky. Not Marc.

She opened the shop door.

An hour later, the Grand Rex was disappointingly closed. That is, the theatre itself was *fermé*, though the box office contained a cashier whose afternoon was threatened by questions. In vain Rachel pleaded in French for just a glimpse inside.

"But your theatre is a monument! Since before the war!"

"Evidently."

"Largest screen in Paris!"

"Yes, madame, but closed. *Au revoir.*"

"Oh, *pute!*"

She turned away, then back as an idea struck her. But in the window the cashier was engaged in situating a placard just so, a placard which bore a familiar name, the familiar face of Steph's favorite American film director, the one for whom she maintained that persistent, ridiculous crush.

"Oh my God! *Madame, qu'est-ce que c'est que ça?*"

The woman's sarcasm scaled new heights. "He is a world-famous American director and producer who will speak tomorrow night to a select group of extremely important guests." The prices the select group was paying to attend were splayed across the placard.

"Any tickets left? Please check."

The woman made a token show of glancing into a drawer. The infamous shrug.

"Returned tickets, perhaps, just two, for my friend and me, visitors to Paris," Rachel explained.

"No."

"None?"

"None at all, madame."

"But –"

"Sorry, madame." She showed no sign of regret.

Frustrated, Rachel paused. What next? "If –"

"No, madame." The tones were steel.

"Standing room, I'll take standing room!"

"It's not a rock concert!" said the woman, outraged. "There are only seats!"

"Two, just two!"

"If you wish to come tomorrow evening and beg for a lap, madame, you are welcome to try. But there are no seats."

Rachel stepped back a pace and examined the intelligent, still-handsome face on the placard. Behind, the purr of an expensive car turned her around. A Mercedes sedan pulled into the drive beside the Grand Rex and drew up twenty yards ahead, past the cashier's line of sight. All four doors opened, and the same number of black-clad men emerged. Two had dark hair and matching moustaches, the third a tousle of styled blond locks, and the fourth . . . Rachel stared. The fourth man's graying hair framed a face of warmth and humor.

The blond's words floated to her. "*Par ici, s'il vous plaît, Monsieur Spielberg?*"

The fourth man nodded and disappeared through the door courteously held open for him.

That did it. Determined, Rachel approached the cashier once more, ignoring the woman's ill-will. She nodded toward the placard. "You know his work, of course," she said wistfully.

"Everyone does."

"Of course."

Rachel sighed. "To my friend, Stephanie," she gave the name its French pronunciation, "Mr. Spielberg is like a god. Even in his lesser-known works. 'Empire of the Sun', for example."

"Oh, yes?"

"But you must know 'Empire of the Sun'? No? Well, 'Saving Private Ryan'?"

"Of course, fantastic film."

"'Schindler's List'?"

"Wonderful! *J'adore* Liam Neeson."

"So do I! Oh, and 'Indiana Jones'? Incredible."

"I agree." The woman's cheeks grew pink. "I find Harrison Ford amazing," she confessed.

Rachel nodded, reflective. "Me, too. And Steph, well . . .." She shrugged.

After a moment the woman drew open a smaller drawer to her right. "You said two tickets?"

Rachel slid her credit card across. "My friend will be thrilled! It's so kind of you, madame!"

"*Bof*, for such a fan of Monsieur Spielberg . . .."

Rachel's plastic returned accompanied by two cream-colored tickets for tomorrow night. She happily fingered their sharp edges. Steph would be beside herself!

Around them the *Métro* train clacked and hissed, the colorful robes of West African women shouted. Between the two women, however, was only silence.

Rachel couldn't understand it. With the tickets, she'd anticipated Steph's delight, effusive thanks, a swift embrace. Instead, her friend turned away with a brief "no, thank you", in her eyes finality and a warning not to persist.

What the hell was wrong?

Worried, Rachel had asked. Steph was apparently neither ill nor injured nor even eager to skip dinner with Sandeep Malhotra. Everything was fine, just fine, she insisted, she simply did not care to hear Steven Spielberg, film director-producer extraordinaire, speak tomorrow night. Or, in fact, any night. Ever. Okay?

"Not okay! What are you talking about? He hardly ever does this, he's too busy, he must be in Paris and someone twisted his arm, this could be your one chance to see him in person!" Rachel grabbed at Steph's wrist. "Come on!"

Steph shook her off. "No. Period."

She carried a haunting look of . . . reluctance? Confusion? She was dressed in black this evening, a real *parisienne*, pearl earrings dangling beside her set jaw. Steph looked both intelligent and fashionista. She also resembled a wall of somber marble.

Swaying in the west-dashing subway, Rachel clutched the overhead bar. Two more stops and they would climb into early evening, reach a warm, aroma-filled apartment and a glass of wine. Marc's friend sounded welcoming as well as rich, and eager to meet them. He was Indian, of course, not French. That would account for it. By adulthood, the French often considered they already had enough friends, *merci*, from schooling and neighborhood and military service, why extend oneself for more?

The doors opened. They shut. One more stop. Would the two of them be as silent *chez* Sandeep?

"Is he a sports guy?" Steph asked as though reading her mind. "Maybe he's into cricket, Indian men love cricket. You okay?"

"Fine." Fine, if fine meant thoroughly confused. It was as if Melina had suddenly spouted perfect Punjabi. Things were topsy-turvy, *ulta-pulta*, because since when did Steph, obsessive American movie fan, not admire Steven Spielberg? When had her romantic crush evaporated? Why not listen to her hero speak in person?

Her hero. Frustrated, Rachel realized she was thinking in Indian terms, *filmi* terms. The director's role might be played by the towering Amitabh Bachchan, with the lovely Rani Mukherjee cast as Steph. Transformed by Bollywood, the story of anonymous passion for a man decades older would be transmuted to a tale of paternalism pro and con, and the changing landscape of fatherhood as the West exported its views into traditional India. Shakespeare would have thrown in references to divine rights, from monarchs through nobles and finally to fathers, who even during the Renaissance exercised life-and-death control over their daughters.

Bollywood . . . Shakespeare . . . but she was here in the Paris *Métro*, and the train was slowing. Rachel stepped out behind Steph. The two flowed with the peopled current to the right and up the grubby stairs, avoiding chic briefcases swinging from tired shoulders.

Above, the sky muffled them in light-spangled flannel. Cafés lined this street, their cigarette-bearing – now that restaurants had gone smoke-free inside – outdoor patrons warmed by metal heaters. The smell of *steak-frites* filled the air. Rachel's stomach rumbled.

"You hungry?"

"Why not? Why the hell not?"

Steph's eyes were perfect round saucers. "Why not what?"

"The tickets!"

"Drop it, Rachel."

"Drop it? What's going on, since when –"

Steph stopped dead on the sidewalk, so livid that passersby edged around her, their faces averted. "What is wrong with you, Rachel? What is it with you, that you don't get it? I *like* to live in my dreams! In my dreams, Rachel, he's perfect! No challenges at all! None! No marriage! No kids! No potential strokes or heart attacks, no bad habits, no friends to think he's completely insane being with a woman as young as me! He's smart and funny and impassioned, fantastic in bed, he'll even waltz me around, anything that here," she tapped her temple, "I can make up!"

"Steph . . .."

"That's what imaginations are for, Rachel, to make life more pleasant! If I go to that stupid talk, what happens to my dreams? Voosh! They vanish! Gone!"

"You can't mean it, not really," Rachel coaxed. "Your professional life, it's all about getting people to cope with reality!"

"I know. Nice work, isn't it? Look, babe, leave it, let's just go."

Rachel grabbed her arm. "You're kidding, right? This is a joke? Come on." She stared down the eyes measuring her. "We can trade for seats in the last row, you won't have to see much of him, he'll be smaller than on the screen. Come on! It'll be fun!"

"Jesus, Rachel! Stop being so goddamn stubborn! I said no! No! And since when –" Steph paused. Across the street, restaurant patrons' voices erupted in laughter. "God, Rachel, how are you different from me, huh? Don't kid yourself, you're in the exact same place, babe, you're doing the exact same thing!"

"What are you talking about, I don't have a crush on anyone," said Rachel, bemused.

"Anyone, no. The dream, though, the portrayal . . . look, most of the men you've gone out with weren't winners at anything besides putz-of-the-month, but there's a perfectly decent guy hanging around you at work, and why do you ignore him? You know why?" Steph's voice rose. "Screw that change he made in your schedule! You know why? Because you're so frikkin' stubborn, and you don't trust your gut, and you have this ridiculous Indian movie idea of the hero, and you think any guy's got to fit that, he's got to match that ideal! Fairytales! He can't be some nice American man who's smart and hard-working and cares about you! You're so caught up in the stupid Bollywood fantasy that a real man can never be good enough!"

The cold slap of her words made Rachel gasp.

"So don't tell *me* to hang with real life!" Steph spat.

"But –"

"You're just as messed-up as I am, Rachel! You teach your stupid Shakespeare, you watch your cute little Indian movies, you write about Indian movies *and* stupid Shakespeare, sure, you go out from time to time, but . . . Jesus, Rachel, guys can smell your negativity! Why Marc Harris is still interested is beyond me!" Her hands flew up.

Rachel dropped her own hand. "Steph!"

"It's frikkin' true! Take a good look in the mirror, babe!"

"How can you be such a . . . such a . . . 'guys can smell my negativity', where the hell does *that* come from? What does that even mean? How you can . . . it's just like Jason . . . ohmigod, Jason has your number, doesn't he?" said Rachel, aghast. "He really does! For all his flaws . . . living in dreams, you *never* wanted a relationship, not with a man! Did you? A boy was all you could handle! And now you're criticizing *me?*" Sarcasm curled her mouth. "So what happens when Rubén finishes college and goes off with Franny, huh? What next, another little orphan boy you can save from foster care? A replacement, to obey you and keep you company on cold nights? Is that it, is that your plan?"

Under the streetlamp, Steph's face was flushed, and her lower lip quivered. "Screw dinner, screw this! I'm outta here, I'll see you back at the hotel! Or not," she added, and set a furious pace into the night. "*Bon appétit!*"

The hurled phrase hit Rachel like a chunk of ice.

White wine flowed into a slender piece of Swedish crystal.

"Do you think your friend might need a doctor? I can give you names."

"No, she's basically okay. Something she ate, I think," Rachel replied shakily, "what do the French call it, liver problems?"

Sandeep Malhotra nodded. "Nothing liver-ish at all, of course. Here you go." He handed her the glass and pushed back his thick wavy hair. "Like to see the place?"

"Yes . . . yes . . . Marc said you'd done heavy demolition?"

"Get the right bloke with the right machine, *voilà*, instant light and air. I followed the Parisian route of paying off my neighbors beforehand in cash or favors, so no complaints."

The apartment was gorgeous, exposed stone and rough beams contrasting with polished surfaces of white and steel and marble. The kitchen was twice as big as the average French *cuisine*. Sandeep patted the gas range. "Six burners, I can cook for dozens." It was no idle boast. Though only a two-bedroom, the flat apparently hosted a constant flow of visitors, Sandeep's extended family who at night filled its beds and spilled onto the lounge floor on makeshift pallets.

"It's the Indian way. Relatives, always 'who are you related to?'. So they visit, they bring me ingredients I can't easily find here, spices, *mishti doi* from Calcutta . . . I work, I come home, I chase my mother out of my kitchen and cook. She despairs of me. Hold on!"

He clicked off a buzzing timer and opened the oven. Aromatic smoke whooshed out. Rachel caught a glimpse of *ghee* brushed onto reddish lumps, then the rack slid back and the oven door banged shut.

"You said Indian, so, an approximation of *tandoori* chicken," he lifted pot lids, "*dal*, some *gobi*, a chopped salad, and," he displayed a foil-wrapped package, "these *naan* I got from a restaurant, but I'll heat them and dribble butter on top!" He beamed.

Dinner was a harmony of tastes and textures that provided excellent distraction from Rachel's churning emotions. Sandeep was both inspired cook and attentive host. He told stories of his Indian princelings, laughed at her account of the ticket purchase ("Oh, you discovered how to get the French to cooperate!"), and described his father's work in Mumbai. Getting a movie financed there involved more than applying to people with money, "though more people have money, these days. Who could imagine a time when the most expensive Mumbai flats would cost millions? Not rupees, dollars!" Sandeep moved on to the intricate bribe mechanisms essential to remodeling his own flat, a project unhappy neighbors could have stalled for months. It drew her weak smile.

"Marc says you're writing a book about Bollywood?" he asked.

. . . you watch your sweet little Indian movies . . . you're just as messed-up as I am . . ..

Rachel sipped her wine and nodded. "Shakespeare, as well. How the two share themes, how he would love it, if he were alive."

"Really?" Sandeep's eyes were very dark. "A Mumbai lad at heart? What a fascinating spin!"

"Of course, he'd be overwhelmingly envious of the numbers. Of moviegoers, I mean, and the profits."

"It's true," Sandeep agreed, "Hindi film is phenomenal in the Middle East, eastern Europe, as well as all over Asia. And then there are NRIs in the US, Australia, Europe . . . not me, of course," his eyes twinkled, "but plenty of them queue up every week to see first-runs."

"See, Will would give his eyeteeth for that kind of response!" She laid a hand on Sandeep's muscular forearm. "Can't you see him in Mumbai, in Film City, taking meetings, talking over his ideas with producers, actors? 'Then the ghost tells Hamlet who murdered him,' he tells Amitabh, 'and we'd like you to consider both roles, father *and* uncle!'"

She was drinking too much, she really ought to stop. On the other hand, the wine revealed how very attractive Sandeep was. Drinking also clouded Steph's words, her anger, her attack. It threw a mist over them, blunted the edges of that bitter "*bon appétit*" and the thought of what Rachel might find when she returned to the hotel tonight. Which would be worse, friend gone or friend present?

Wine softened everything, even the chill marble floor. She drew her feet underneath, having followed the Indian custom of leaving her shoes at the door beside Sandeep's. His own pair, custom-made leather, were Italian. How different the footwear of

Mumbai's heat, where a pair of sandals would do for nearly anyplace.

. . . you're so caught up in the fantasy that a real man can never be good enough!

Sandeep, now, was an incredibly handsome man, with his long lashes, thick wavy hair, skin the shade of *crème* after a generous splash of *café*. Rachel felt washed-out and oatmeal-y in contrast. Her own arm, now, displayed every freckle and vein, her skin lacked the . . . *finish* was the word that came to mind, as though she needed more color to come truly alive.

Slender fingers tapped the table.

"Sorry, lost in thought," Rachel apologized.

"No problem. Coffee?"

She followed him with plates.

"Right there, please." He filled a kettle and set it on the flame. "I hope you won't mind me saying you're quite different from Lora."

"Lora who?"

"Harris. Marc's ex-wife."

A bowl of cucumber *raita* clunked onto the counter. "I thought his ex was Indian," said Rachel, confused.

"Indian? No, no, not at all."

They'd known each other for years, from school, from temple, from her brother's participation on the same baseball teams. It was an oddly South Asian courtship, according to Sandeep, both sets of parents pushing them together as a way to cement the families.

Though the dénouement took place years later, it was a bad match from the start. Lora spent more time with friends and co-workers than with her new husband. She was amiable, lively, pretty – Sandeep's description gave Rachel's insides an odd twist – but empty, at least where Marc's heart was concerned. They looked like any other young American couple, but instead of solid wood, there was only veneer.

"No tenderness," said Sandeep, carrying out a plate of mango slices and *patisas*. "No pats on the arse, kisses across the room. I got the sense she wasn't too fond of bed, it would interfere with her schedule."

While Marc's work life soared, as a husband his existence was one from which he saw no honorable exit. Finally, though, possibility flew at him with outstretched claws.

"What was it?"

"Another man." Sandeep shook his head, remembering phone calls that ignored the six-hour time difference between Virginia and Paris. "He found the bloke's backpack. Hard to miss, propped against the wall that way."

Marc divorced a woman whose protests rang hollow. After signing the final papers, he ran. Miles of road were pounded into submission. It was a way to forget, and he avoided others, as well. No membership in a runners' club, no 5Ks, no marathons. Marc ran to escape.

Rachel swallowed the last drops of her wine. Sandeep's hand lay beside her on the blue leather sofa. Small spots dotted it. The creases of his knuckles were dark, the skin rimming his fingernails was the same lovely shade, a border of evening surrounding the pink and white. She took a breath.

Suddenly the hand was on Rachel's cheek, and Sandeep's lips followed. His kisses grazed her cheek, her chin, and caught at her lower lip, gently pulling. Rachel gasped. He felt so familiar, he tasted so familiar, so much like . . . Marc? Her wine-inspired body turned to him, her mouth opened. Agile fingers were at her breast now, cupping and stroking, and Rachel's head swam. Sandeep's hand became Marc's hand became . . . a note of reluctant protest caught in her throat, unspoken.

Sandeep, however, heard it. His mouth pulled from hers, and liquid dark eyes weighed her. Slowly, she shook her head.

He kissed her cheek, a quick catch and release.

"Marc's a good mate," he said, his smile wry.

Rachel cleared her throat. "I'm sure he is."

CHAPTER 28

Ten minutes later, Sandeep slid a CD into his car's player. "Film tunes," he explained. Music filled the silent sedan, familiar words entered the awkward space between the two of them.

"Turn it up?"

He flicked at the control.

" . . . *mehendi laga ke rakhana, dolii saja ke rakhana . . .*" Rachel sang with the CD, rolling her R's tight to give herself focus. Sandeep's voice rose with hers. ". . . *lene tujhe o gorii, aaenge tera saajna . . ..*" The words ended, a frenetic beat began. If they'd been on a dance floor, shoulders would have shaken, bracelets rung.

Another song, another soaring soprano. Rachel shook her head. This one, she didn't know. Sandeep turned it down.

"Has Marc talked to you about Sarah? No?" he asked in a surprisingly level tone. He took a left turn very wide. "I'm sure if you ask him –"

"Who's Sarah, his daughter?" she joked.

Sandeep recovered from the turn, avoiding a motorcycle with a leather-jacketed driver and a helmetless girl hanging on. Her blonde hair streamed back.

"His older sister. She was killed when her boyfriend drove into a tree. Marc was thirteen or so." Sandeep glanced over. "It's no secret, probably he thought it wouldn't interest you."

Rachel kept her eyes on the passing lights of Paris. Acknowledgment of one's ignorance was sometimes close to humiliating.

A nod to Sandeep, a *bonsoir* to the hotel's reception clerk, and Rachel trudged up the stairs, key at the ready. Outside the room, she listened ear to the door, shy of being caught. It was late, though, perhaps no one would pass by on their way to the shared toilet, wondering what she was doing.

She listened hard. Steph must be asleep.

Rachel turned the key in the lock, making it squeak, and pushed the door ajar. All was dark. She slipped in, closed the door and rested silent, willing her eyes to readjust. From outside came the *aa-oo-aa-oo* of French sirens. Was that steady breathing she heard in the corner?

She felt her way to her bed and sat, shifting the pillow aside. Perhaps she imagined the breathing. She reached over to the bed opposite, sliding her fingers across its nubbly blanket, which she knew to be forest green. The blanket felt flat and uninhabited. Her hand traveled to the bolster and headboard and over. She felt nothing beyond linens.

So. Steph was gone. If it was for good, perhaps she'd left a note. Rachel switched on the light. Yes, right beside the lamp. She took up the thin white sheet embellished with a blue intertwined H and C.

Headed home. S.

Why was Rachel surprised? She knew it for a possibility, and that the nerve ending she'd exposed with those tickets was frantic to cover itself. Like Marc years ago, Steph ran. It was more about reaching the safety of her burrow – apartment, that is – than it was leaving Rachel and the week in Paris. It was always more.

That night, restless, Rachel awoke in the dark and twisted to read the time. Three o'clock. No wonder little traffic rolled below, self-respecting truckers were deep in dreams in their cabs, huddled against the cold night. She turned over.

Images of Marc Harris – lecturing, meeting her outside, greeting Melina – popped and fizzed in her drowsy brain. She summoned other, different images, nothing to do with him, a *shikara* that floated on a mirror-like Kashmiri lake, the rower's heart-shaped paddle dipping and lifting. Tumbling waterdrops held shattered tiny mountains. On and on and on, from one shore to another the boat was rowed, the only sound the dip-splash of the oar and the *slursh* of water flowing past. An evocative image, an image of peace.

"Perhaps, sometime, you'd lend me one of your DVDs, one of the newer ones?"

Marc again! As Rachel recalled, she'd responded with little grace. She was now feeling unanticipated empathy for a man who, according to Sandeep, had apparently taken a number of blows from life. When she returned, she could do better. Invite Marc to watch a DVD with her, maybe. In the dark, she blinked.

She'd never fall asleep this way. Switching on the light, she picked up the book she'd tucked into her suitcase at the last minute, the one Marc had lent her, *Maximum City*. She flipped it open and settled herself against the hard pillow. Yes, here was the page.

. . . Hindi film music is like Hinduism. All who come to invade it are themselves absorbed, digested, and regurgitated . . ..

The next morning passed in a blur. The open air *marché* at Rue Poncelet was as beguiling as described, and the street itself a hothouse of food shops, from bakeries to *charcuteries*. A jar of honey weighted her large purse, along with two apples and several breadsticks. The pastry shop relieved Rachel of more euros, and she munched one of the rectangular almond cakes called *financiers* as she walked.

She missed Steph.

It was only with lunch of breadsticks and apples that her heart firmed. A glance up at the slate-tiled rooftops was proof-positive she was no longer in New York, and she meant to appreciate the fact, with or without her best friend . . . the woman who might still be her best friend. The two cream-colored tickets remained. She had no desire to attend tonight's talk herself, but she could offer the tickets to Sandeep to thank him for dinner. Perhaps, since his father was in films, Sandeep might enjoy listening to an American director who was – what were Steph's words? – smart and funny and impassioned. Rachel went in search of a public phone.

Sandeep had another suggestion.

"It starts at eight? Get there at seven-thirty and flog them to someone else. I'll meet you there, we'll hit an Indian movie, if you like, and follow up with dessert, I know a place with fantastic hazelnut soufflé."

Rachel rang off, relieved at his tone, the confident air of a man who knew he could have pursued her wine-induced interest but declined, and was perfectly comfortable with that course.

It was very Shakespearean of him to esteem Marc's friendship – her students' voices echoed in memory – and eminently Indian, as well. Friendship, *dosti*, was highly valued in Bollywood movies. As one character summed it up, "every relationship begins with friendship".

Truer words, etcetera. Without friendship, love was incomplete . . . and passion curiously sterile.

"Two tickets!" Rachel called. "*J'en ai deux!*"

"*Ah, deux!*" and the transaction was quickly completed, to the French couple's delight, for Rachel asked only the tickets' face value. They beamed as though they'd won the national lottery.

"That looked easy," came a second male voice. Sandeep leaned over and briskly kissed her cheek. He might be Indian, but his friendly *bisou* was authentically French, and thankfully had little to do with last night's seductive embraces. "All done? Good price?"

"All done, same price."

"Ah, so American!" From his pocket he brought out a list, two Indian movies within the same *arrondissement*, the one she'd visited. "Choose."

She examined the titles. "Paris must be Khan-crazy. Shah Rukh, Salman, Aamir . . . I'm not that fond of Aamir," she confessed, "I know I should be, he's a fantastic actor, but there you go. So, Shah Rukh or Salman?"

"New release? Or a well-known singsong with the rest of the theatre? You do know how Indian audiences behave, don't you?" He grimaced.

"That does it," said Rachel, "let's go for the nostalgia of 'Dilwale Dulhania Le Jayenge' and sing along with the audience. *Mehendi laga ke rakhana, dolii saja ke rakhana . . ..*"

She'd seen the movie before, of course, the Yash Chopra-directed romantic comedy that gave birth to a new era in Bollywood. A perennial favorite shot partly in Switzerland, it had played on one theatre screen in Mumbai every single day since its 1995 release. "Fall in love all over again" was its tagline, and with the initial bars of the first song, the theater filled with voices, giving new meaning to the phrase "audience participation". Sandeep buried his head in his hands.

"No big deal," whispered Rachel.

Embarrassed, he sank further in his seat.

At least, she thought, it was unlikely anyone in this audience would pull out a gun and fire at the screen, as sometimes happened in Latin America. Singing, dancing, parroting dialogue, and chatting throughout a film were, in comparison, trivial offenses.

Rachel spooned up another delicious mouthful of hazelnut soufflé, conscious that she sat across the tiny table from a man determined to ignore the events of last night. "So, Marc's sister? Did he have just the one?"

"Yes." Sandeep's hands fidgeted with his coffee cup and the edge of the table, as though their owner was not quite sure where disclosure would lead.

"Sarah?"

"Yes." The hands clasped each other. One thumb drummed the other. "It's a common story, really. Out on a date, too much celebration – it was her eighteenth birthday – too much speed, too much tree. Both died before reaching hospital." A nod of regret. "A waste."

The words were so stark, so clear. She saw it. A dark night, a pair of teenagers, laughter and bravado and loud music. The curve taken fast, the tree racing to meet them. Sandeep had it, the story was all too common.

"My God. And Marc?"

Sandeep gave a short laugh. "He became the perfect son. She was about to go to university, a very good one, as I recall. As he got older, his awards filled a shelf in his parents' home. School, sports," he shrugged, "he made it up to them. He tried to make it up to them."

"Where was he when it happened?"

He scratched his chin. "Home, I suppose. Reading, homework. Why?"

"Nothing." Except that the image of a lonely boy haunted her. Her perception of Marc – talented scholar and athlete – was intensely altered.

There were those who would call it loss when a sister was killed, but good fortune when a wife left. Especially an unfaithful wife. Yet to the man Marc became, the two departures might be heads-and-tails of the same coin. A sister leaves with her boyfriend and never returns. A wife leaves in spirit. Then she leaves, period. Not that Marc would want her back. Would he?

"If she begged? No. No, of course not. He knew what Lora was."

Alone again . . . unnaturally.

Rachel laid down her spoon. "Thanks for telling me. *Shukriya*, Sandeep."

On a Paris night, eleven o'clock minus six was early evening in New York. Subtract another three to get to LA, where it would be two in the afternoon. Melina was bound to be awake. Rachel dialed her cell number.

"Hi, Mom! I mean *bonjour* . . . ."

There was little to report from California. Life on the left coast was pleasant. Melina was swimming a great deal. Ellie was calmer than usual, for no apparent reason, and she and Jason bent over storyboards or listened to music samples. The day before, Ellie had asked Melina to come into the office and scream.

"Into a tape," Melina amplified, "she heard me with a spider, called it 'bloodcurdling'."

"I agree, you and arachnids don't mix well."

"Oh! I forgot to tell you the biggest news!"

Rachel braced herself. Biggest news of . . . what? For a moment, she imagined a baby. A baby! But . . . no. Not when Ellie didn't want children and Jason's vasectomy was presumably still functional. What other big news could there be?

"Nisha says part of an Indian movie is going to be shot in Oxford this coming summer, all sorts of stars will be there, and she and Parvati are going to audition to be extras! Isn't that cool? I wish I lived in Oxford, can't we go back?" Melina pleaded.

"I'm sorry, you're speaking from where? The 310 area code? Isn't that near a little place called Hollywood?" A large sigh blew into Rachel's ear. "Somewhere in Britain are girls who want to live in New York or LA. Somewhere in India, too," she reminded her daughter. "In fact, all over both places."

Melina understood, or claimed to. Yet Oxford grass was very green, and she was filled with envy over Nisha's chances to breathe the same air as people she adored from the screen. "What if Aish is there, or Preity, or Rani, or Deepika? I'd give my arm to be in a scene with any one of them!"

"They wouldn't want you to, honey, I'm sure."

Melina was unpersuadable. Nisha was too lucky for words, and the SoCal sun was wonderful, yes, but she was stuck in the house, and the only way she would ever see Rani or Preity or Aish or Priyanka was on DVDs, whereas Nisha . . ..

This time Rachel sighed. Might there be some way Melina could help with the current Ellie-project? No? Would Melina ask, anyway, just to make sure? There was no better way to avoid envy over Nisha's very speculative shot at the big screen than to work on the preparation of another film, even if it would eventually employ actors Melina had never heard of.

"Before 'Thelma & Louise', nobody'd heard of Brad Pitt, either," Rachel pointed out.

Melina laughed. "Who's Brad Pitt?"

Rachel propped herself against her twin bed's headboard, wedging the classic French bolster behind her vertebrae. She needed just a few pages, nothing too enticing, nothing that would keep her alert far into the night. Exercising a little self-restraint, she'd likely doze off after a few paragraphs. She rubbed her eyes, and opened the book borrowed from Marc.

"*. . . The funds required for a production are huge, and a family in the industry may be working on several projects at once. The time between investment and return can be years if the film doesn't do well. Who would have that amount of cash lying around? Only the underworld . . ..*"

CHAPTER 29

The sun rose warmer on Rachel's last full morning in Paris. She returned from the shower – the Swedish shampoo had disappeared, its owner perhaps returned to Stockholm – semi-dry and open to suggestion. It was time to play catch-up. Where to go, what to do with her last hours? She slathered raspberry jam on a croissant, and paged through the guidebook. She and Steph had vowed to avoid the touristic, but Steph was an entire ocean west, and Rachel felt free to be as first-time-in-Paris as she desired.

The Eiffel Tower? The Louvre? A *bateau-mouche* to float down the Seine, gazing up at Notre Dame? Now, there was a possibility she hadn't entertained before . . . *rrring!*

"*Allo?*"

"*Allo, bonjour!* It's your last day, where can I take you?"

"Sandeep? Sorry, I just didn't expect to hear from you," Rachel fumbled. "Are you free?"

"As a bird. An unexpected lull in work. So, what delights of Paris can I reveal to you? Or outside . . . ever been to Versailles?"

After checking to make sure Sandeep was sincere, that he was truly at liberty, and measuring her desire to trek a solitary path versus the pleasure of being with an intelligent, Paris-resident man, Rachel confessed to the *bateau-mouche*. "It's cheesy, I know. But other places, the tourist schedule, nothing holds the same appeal as the river."

"I agree. It's always fun to mess about on the water. But instead of a giant boat carrying dozens of naive tourists, what about one kayak with a friend?"

Astonished, she listened to Sandeep's description of the picnic lunch he or she, or both, could assemble. A friend's kayak was available to borrow for casting off and spending the entire day on the water. The weather was cool but clear, the sky an enviable blue. As to larger boats, oof! Rachel could practically feel Sandeep's dismissive shrug. Boats were easy to spot and just as easy to avoid. At any time, the two of them could paddle the kayak to the riverbank and rest. And then there were the Ile de la Cité and Ile Saint-Louis themselves, smack in the middle of the Seine, the site of the original tiny Paris, and did she know it wasn't just shops with postcards, people still lived there?

The plan sounded too, too good. Rachel considered. The Seine's *bateaux-mouches* would forever roam the river, but when would she get this chance again? Never. She made up her mind. In return for meeting Sandeep, she would bring food, and how would she reach this fabulous craft?

The friend whose kayak it was lived on the Ile Saint-Louis himself. Sandeep recited directions. Across the bridge, turn right, look for this sign . . . she jotted it all down. Would Rachel meet him in two hours? That would be delightful. *Au revoir*, then.

Rachel crammed the rest of her croissant into her mouth, fitted her feet into comfortable shoes, grabbed her purse and left.

What to choose for lunch? She examined the sparkling window of a *charcuterie*, then realized she was weighing the prices of pork products. No, definitely not for a Hindu, and no beef, either, obviously. Next door, however, was a fishmonger's. She dove in and discovered lovely smoked salmon and whitefish.

"*Trois cent grammes de chacun, s'il vous plaît.*" That would give them over a pound of fish, plenty even for famished kayakers.

Down the street, they told her, was a cheese shop, and of course the *boulanger* around the corner was renowned throughout France, if not the world, for his authentic loaves . . . she thanked them and held the door open for a woman with a minuscule poodle dressed in pink, its tongue out, delighted by the prospect of being cooed over and fed fish-bits.

Down the street she headed. If the baker was as authentic as advertised, his bread deserved good cheese, and she ought to pick up a small gift for Sandeep's friend, though if he lived on some of Paris's priciest real estate, he might be more client than friend. No matter. Camembert was beloved by all.

Two rounds of cheese and a tiny jar of olives later, Rachel emerged to tackle the *boulanger*. Around the corner she found the bakery, its line extending into the street. She glanced at her watch.

Yet the line moved rapidly, and Rachel obtained two loaves within minutes.

"Ahoy!" Sandeep waved an oar. He wore a lightweight jacket stuffed with expensive microfibers, and on his head – Rachel stifled a giggle – a beret. This time a light kiss hit both of Rachel's cheeks.

She handed over a bag. "For the boat's owner," she told him, "if he's home?"

"I'll slide it into the postbox, it should keep cool enough there, and the postman can lay his letters on top." He disappeared for a moment, then returned. "Luc grew up in Bayeux, so he'll appreciate the camembert. Ready? Have you ever kayaked? Well, it's not hard, and this one's from Revolt Boats, brilliant idea, really, build a retractable electric motor into the rear. Paddle alone, paddle with its help, or just lie back and let it zip you along. Silent, too, not that it matters on this stretch of the Seine."

He offered a hand to help her down steps reinforced with stone. There was the kayak drawn up to the embankment, which looked steeper from this vantage than it had from above. They collected the foodstuffs in one bag, pushed it as far forward as possible, donned lifevests, and, as Sandeep held the boat in place, Rachel entered, praying not to fall. She felt Sandeep take his place, then with a tremble, a shudder, and a push, they were free and floating tiny in the narrow width of the Seine as it flowed past the two islands.

"Paddle." Sandeep handed it forward to her. "Let me know when you get tired, we can put the motor down. Look at that!" He pointed up. There at two o'clock was the height of Notre Dame, its towers jutting above the water's surface. "This is how some Frogs must have seen them when they were first constructed, people who weren't walking over land but drifting past in their boats and rafts. Fishing, conveying trade goods . . . think how immense the towers were then!"

"When even a two-story building was unusual. Is the motor strong enough to bring us back against the current?"

"Oh, yes."

Rachel turned around. The kayak shivered.

"Don't shift! We've got plenty of power, so look up at the city, have a good time."

The light played upon the river, making it glint and sparkle. The current here was strong enough that Rachel needn't paddle hard, just enough to show she was making an effort. Ahead, the Ile de la Cité was about to end, giving rise to the full width of the Seine. She spotted a *bateau-mouche* afloat and full of passengers.

"Better than that, eh?" Sandeep called.

"Much better!"

There was, in fact, absolutely nothing like messing about on the water.

They had covered perhaps two miles of river, drawing stares and waves from pedestrians on bridges, and warning *toots* from bigger – much bigger – boats, whose wash they paddled into as though it were whitewater. Sandeep called out descriptions of overhead bridges and surrounding buildings. He knew a great deal about the building of Paris.

"I've always been interested in construction, urban planning. If my parents had been poorer, I'd probably have become an engineer," he amplified.

"But your dad's in film, why aren't you, too?"

"Good question. It's like that in India, fathers and sons . . . and daughters now, too. Look at the Kapoors, four generations of actors! And lots of families have had three. I suppose I don't have the director's eye, for one thing, and I wasn't keen on marshaling my forces like a general. Then, production," he gave a short laugh, "let's just say I'd rather handle other people's money than go begging for it, especially in India."

"Why?" Rachel almost shifted around, remembering just in time. She waved toward a little boy dressed in a sailor outfit who peeped down at them through a bridge railing. "Is it hard to get Indian banks to agree?"

"Banks? Even five years ago, banks kept themselves apart from film financing. Now it's different, they're interested, certainly, but only for the right names. If you're a Chopra or Roshan or Akhtar or the right kind of Khan, no problem. Anyone starting out, though, forget it. That's why there's so much product placement. If Coca-Cola will pay, producers will insert Coke cans into multiple scenes, or the name in lights. The West makes fun of us, but nothing shameful about it, really, even Hollywood does it, just less obviously. Watch out!"

Rachel shoved her paddle hard through the water on her right, in order to avoid a bobbing branch that rode the current.

"There are other, riskier options, too," said Sandeep. "My dad, for example, in order to get his early films made, like many men in the business he went to . . . let's say, unusual sources. What you would call organized crime," he added.

"Funny, I just read something about that in a book Marc lent me. I thought the author might be exaggerating."

Another laugh sounded behind her. "No exaggeration, it's one of the ways it's done. Business as usual. Not amusing at all, and it can be dangerous. It certainly was in the nineties. Even in 2000, someone placed a contract on a director who was approached but refused to play along. Rakesh Roshan recovered from the bullets, thank God, but it scared the piss out of everyone. Those stakes are much too high."

"I heard American studios are investing, though."

"They are, and American money is welcome. Where does it go, though? To big projects! Disney-supported animations, and movies like 'Saawariya', with Bhansali directing, then it was released the same weekend as 'Om Shanti Om' with Shah Rukh Khan. Big mistake, King Khan ran right over 'Saawariya'. But of the hundreds of movies made in India each year, how many will have American studios' backing? No," and he must be vigorously shaking his head, Rachel could feel the kayak's vibrations, "for financing a picture, sometimes you go to men you want miles away from your family."

Over several kilometers of river, the kayak drew catcalls and what even Rachel could identify as crude remarks from men on board other boats, remarks Sandeep returned with a cheerful array of invective.

"Hungry?" he asked, when the sun was high. "See the quay over to the right? Pull that way!"

Avoiding a plastic bottle ("the river's actually much cleaner than in the 1980s, if you dipped a hand in you'd get a rash from all the chemicals dumped in upstream"), they paddled the kayak to a small quay where three teenage boys held fishing rods and a net. Sandeep called to them, and the one with the net dropped it to catch the kayak's line and pull them in. Sandeep scrambled onto the quay and made the rope fast. He offered a hand to Rachel.

A moment later, she stood beside him with the bag of food from the kayak's bow. Sandeep chatted with the boys, gave them something, and shooed them up the steps to the street above. They called down, laughing, then ambled off.

"What did you give them?"

"Money. Told them I needed to be alone with you, they understood that." He stuck his hand out. "Don't worry, it's just to buy a little peace. What else do we have besides cheese?"

Cheese and bread, smoked fish, olives, all were gone a half-hour later, and the sun had begun its westward decline. Rachel lay on her back. The quay beneath was chilly, but sun played on her cheeks. The drone of city traffic above them was soothing, the anonymous sound of a huge beehive. Her stomach was full, her muscles wanted a break, and she found it difficult to attend to Sandeep's occasional comments.

Yet 'don't kid yourself, you're in the exact same place, babe!' ran through her memory on a continuous loop. She felt her cheeks flush.

Finally, Rachel gave up on rest and propped herself on her elbows.

Sandeep tossed a bit of leftover bread into the water. Something large rose to the surface to nab it, flicked its tail and disappeared to the river bottom.

"What was that?"

"Looked like a carp, though they prefer backwaters. If the boys had left their rods, we could catch dinner." He glanced down at her. His eyes were warm. "Or stop by the fishmonger's on the way back to my place, if you like. I'll cook you a real Bengali *macher jhol*. Mustard oil, that's the secret."

Struggling upriver against the current, the paddle was heavy, the water more resistant. Rachel wondered when Sandeep would start up the fabled motor. It was all very well paddling downstream, but with the current against them, plus river traffic menacing in the faded afternoon light, the trip back would take longer and be much tougher than Rachel had foreseen.

"Sandeep, the motor?" she flung back.

"Ah, motor! I forgot!"

Rachel heard a metallic snap. A shudder traveled through the kayak. Experimenting, she lifted her paddle from the river to find the kayak miraculously progressing at a silent, steady speed, as if scenting Ile Saint-Louis upstream.

"Works!" Sandeep called.

Rachel's shoulders relaxed, she could once again gaze up at Paris. This bridge, now, fainter against the darkening eastern sky than when they had passed beneath it earlier, still held amused pedestrians who waved at the small craft.

"*Attention!*" one called, and pointed upstream. *Watch out!* – watch out for what?

"Oh my God! Sandeep!"

"What . . . *behnchod!*" A jerk, and the kayak pointed to the south bank. "Bloody hell! *Jao! Jao!*"

With a series of terrifying honks like an enraged goose, a huge pleasure craft bore down on them. On its deck, children called and ran to the prow to peer ahead at the kayak.

Rachel and Sandeep swept the water in a frantic effort to reach shore. Rachel pulled at her paddle, throwing her shoulder and back into every stroke. Behind her, Sandeep's Hindi came fast and furious. Their motor was still running, she could feel it, but would they make it out of the larger boat's path in time?

Her shoulders burned, the paddle weighed a ton, one more stroke, one more! "*Jao, jao!*" panted Sandeep. *Go, go!*

One more stroke! Another! Another!

"*Thik hai*, but we'll still end up in the water, get ready!"

Up rose the boat's wash! It shoved against the kayak, pushed it over like a child's bathtub toy, and hurled them into the cold river. It closed over Rachel's head. She kicked, broke through the surface, and spluttered. She threw an arm over the upside-down kayak. On the other side floated Sandeep, his dark hair plastered in dripping strings across his forehead.

"Okay?" he called.

"Freezing!" Her voice chattered with cold.

"I'd say," and he paused, "let's get over to those steps, we'll tie up, climb to the street, and get a taxi to Luc's place. If I still have my wallet." He began an awkward sidestroke, towing the kayak like a recalcitrant walrus. "Luc will be glad to hear the motor worked."

"*Bonne chance!*" called a man on the bridge, and followed the two words with a stream of untranslatable French, shaking his fist at the terrorist boat vanished into the west.

An hour later, after the hottest shower of her life, Rachel swathed herself in a giant sweater belonging to Sandeep's friend Luc, who was built like a triceratops. Limp with relief, she smoothed back her damp hair and regarded herself in the bathroom mirror.

"*Bonne chance!*" *Good luck* . . . they had been very, very lucky, indeed.

Luc had constructed a blaze in his fieldstone fireplace. He placed a glass of amber liquid in her hand. "Cognac," he said, and returned to poking the logs.

Rachel swallowed. The liquid swirled hot into her throat and stomach, and spread warmth through her limbs. Immediately giddy, she lowered herself into a chair and felt alcohol ooze through every vein.

"One moment," said Luc, his accent thick, "and I make *omelette espagnole*. Sandeep!"

Sandeep stuck his head around a door. "*Ouah?*"

There followed a muted conversation which Rachel caught none of. She examined her hands. Two blisters were already filled with fluid, and her reddened palms recoiled at touch. Gingerly, she explored her head. It felt bruised. In tumbling, her temple must have struck the kayak. Still, what she bore were the minor wounds of a skirmish, not the tragedy that might have unfolded.

She thought of Melina for the thousandth time. Melina would have been frightened to watch the kayak upended. No matter. Rachel was still alive, was about to be fed, and with this much cognac in her bloodstream – Luc had poured a healthy inch – felt extremely content.

Narrowly avoid messy death, soak in frigid water, feel happy? That *was* different.

Different is fun. Or vice versa.

Before her hotel, a kiss on one cheek, the other, and a *"bonne nuit"*.

"Good luck with your book," Sandeep added. "Let me know when it comes out, I'll want copies for my family in the business. They'll love being compared to Shakespeare! And, Rachel," he hesitated, "about Marc . . . no, never mind."

She nodded and watched him walk the long pavement, his slender figure growing shorter. At the light, he turned and waved. Her own hand came up, and Sandeep disappeared around the corner.

Rachel trudged up to her room. It was no use packing tonight, she'd stuff clothes and trinkets into her suitcase early tomorrow morning. She'd set the alarm, dial the desk for a wake-up call, then fling herself into bed, enormous borrowed sweater and all, for some glorious sleep in the city of light. Light, as in movies, as in Bollywood, she mused. As in, opposite of darkness. Darkness in many pockets. Abruptly, Sandeep's words resounded: "sometimes you go to men you don't want anywhere near your family".

If even Sandeep's father had used criminal connections to finance his films, what might others have to agree to in order to see their own visions meet the screen?

In her pre-sleep haze, a man dressed in white danced before surrounding mirrors, though his face was obscured and she couldn't tell who he was . . . *ab mujhko yeh hai karna ab mujhe woh karna hai* . . . now I feel like doing this, but then again, it's that . . ..

Rachel drifted off.

The New York cabbie, marveling in a Russian accent at her suitcase's small size ("but . . . Paris!"), dropped her on 88th and sped off in search of the next fare. Rachel fitted her keys to their locks. The red-painted door swung open. She entered, bumping her bag up over the threshold.

After the seven-hour flight's constant engine noise, nearby passengers' chat, and the wailing toddler two rows behind, the house seemed to exist in a vacuum. She needed to adjust her ears to relative quiet, her emotions to . . . Rachel was not sure, but she would sort through them to reach some kind of balance. Between Sandeep and Marc and Steph, her life held enough twists to land her on "Oprah".

She had half-hoped that Steph had used her own key to let herself in and deposit some token. Flowers. One flower. A note. Something to acknowledge friendship of many years, the undulation of longterm. Something that said "sorry". But nothing carried that message.

Perhaps a note was taped to the bathroom mirror or placed on Rachel's pillow? She had her doubts. Still, the suitcase belonged upstairs. She slipped out of her shoes and counted the treads.

No note.

She ran back down to unwrap her scarf and doff her coat. Flipping the kitchen light on, she filled the electric kettle. First, she'd drink some tea, then, after the liquid warmed her core – still a bit chilled after yesterday's dunking in the Seine – only then would she brace herself to check phone messages.

Weeks ago, when she gave up on Goa and fell in with Steph's Paris, Rachel had thought of nothing beyond a week in a city known for brilliant architecture, seductive food, and access to centuries of art. That was a fairly accurate description of the vacation's first days. After that . . . after that, a crevasse opened, and Paris-that-was disappeared, leaving Paris-that-is.

Her almost-collision on the river didn't exactly qualify as a near-death experience, but it had brought clarity. Ever since, image upon image crowded Rachel's mind. Things she hadn't accomplished, things she'd done badly, people who deserved apologies, who deserved hugs under the heading of "there's never a wrong time to do the right thing". Melina was top of the list in that last category, and though fatigue haunted Rachel, she could hardly wait to ride the bus to LaGuardia tonight to meet her daughter. And if Melina brought stepmom bribes in the shape of expensive shoes, well . . . Rachel shrugged.

People who deserved apologies. Who was on *that* list? First off, Steph. On a whim, she reached over and opened the fridge. No note there, either, and the only bottle of wine was the pinot grigio she'd left half-drunk.

Then there was Marc. He, too, deserved an apology. Rachel had treated him rudely, she saw that now, even if blowing him off had been in her own best interests. Best? She was of two minds about that. Cold water, enough to drown in, was very conducive to reflection. Like a slap, it woke her up. She'd been using the Hindi movie hero gauge wrongly, hadn't she? Because while, yes, he'd screwed up with the theory class, Marc had done a lot of things right. Right enough, anyway. He deserved more than an apology.

Three new voicemail messages, the first from Melina. "Hi, Mom, when you get this you'll be about to meet me! See you at the airport!"

The second was from Mrs. Burke, but so garbled that Rachel could make no sense of it.

The third was not from Steph. She must still be angry, then. The last sip of tea drained from the mug, and Rachel considered whether to call or not. Not, in fact. Let the mountain come to Muhammad. She glanced out the small window toward the Nassirs' house, which looked forlorn despite its pale blue curtains, and pressed play for the third message yet again.

She knew it by heart now, knew just where Marc had taken breath, where his voice grew high with worry.

"Rachel! Marc. I heard from Sandeep, and, uh . . . well, I'm glad you decided not to take on that boat. Good thinking.

Especially in the cold. Listen, um . . . I'd appreciate a call, okay? Just to say, you know, '*bonsoir*, I'm back'. I'd be grateful. Bye."

Her new regime called for courtesy, didn't it? Rachel dialed.

CHAPTER 30

Y ou're awfully quiet." She nudged Melina and picked up her left wrist to admire the new watch.

"So are you."

"Tired."

"*Main bhi.* Me, too."

They rode in silence behind the cabbie, whose family was prominently displayed in overlapped photos taped to the dashboard. The children's names, typed on thin slips of white paper, overlay their chests. María Fulgencia, Joaquín, María Ofelia, and the baby María Violeta. Their mother's picture was centered among them, they surrounded her like petals.

"There really is something weird out there."

Rachel followed Melina's line of sight to the East River. Boat ablaze? Candlelight protest in the park?

"I mean out in LA."

"Oh! Words? Signs? Vibes?"

"Yeah, man, vibes," Melina repeated, with a 1960s intonation.

"Seriously?"

Melina had sensed it immediately upon pick-up from LAX, where Ellie's PA chattered too brightly and had completely obliterated all memories of Melina's fondness for Double-Doubles and chocolate shakes. If In-N-Out came as a surprise to Molly, her reaction to Melina's suggestion that perhaps Melina might contribute to Ellie's current project in some small teenager way was a shock to teenage altruism.

"She got white."

"She *is* white."

Melina punched Rachel's arm. "She blanched. Is that how you pronounce it? When your skin gets all pale and the freckles show?"

It could be coincidence, Rachel noted. Or a sudden drop in blood sugar.

"It could be," Melina said darkly, "she knows something."

Ellie, too, was bright-bright, as though shaking the invisible pompoms of the cheerleader she used to be. She seemed determined to show Melina the best possible week. Jason, absorbed but friendly, would break off intense phone conversations punctuated with casual profanity to pull Melina over for a hug. The couple scheduled dinner around Melina's desires, spent an extra half-hour at the table, made sure she saw enough sun and sand, and offered to invite the neighbors' friendly daughter. Ellie even detailed her office peon – a boy who'd dropped out of junior college to explore the 9-to-9 – to escort Melina on a tour of the Warner Brothers lots, courtesy of a producing pal.

It was all lovely and enviable. As Melina described it, weird. "I asked Daddy what was wrong, he looked at me like I said one and one makes three."

Rachel paid the cabbie. "Maybe in this case, it does." She caught the suitcase. "Let's get you into the shower."

On the stairs, Melina turned. "What do you mean?"

"Maybe what they're really producing is a little Ellie."

It took a moment to sink in. "Get out!"

"Up, up." Rachel pushed. "Maybe not. But since when does your stepmother eat a half-hour longer?"

Behind the closed door, water fizzed. Rachel paused, a clean blue towel on her arm. Could a baby Ellie be about to make an appearance? A continent apart, Melina would be able to measure her half-sister's growth season by season. Melina's own heart would grow to encompass a small sweetpea who'd likely call her "Ina".

Sometimes life was kind.

The bathroom door opened. A hand blindly groped. Rachel inserted the towel. The blue disappeared into steam.

"Sleep tight."

"Mmrgh." Melina was already semi-conscious. Rachel pulled the coverlet past her thin shoulders, and kissed her soft cheek.

Now, yawning, back to the manuscript she'd neglected for eight days, Shakespeare and his imagined delight in and envy of Hindi-language cinema, with which he had much in common. What if he were a 21st century contemporary? My God, the man would spend half his life in Mumbai! It was a delicious thought, Will S. flirting with Bollywood hopefuls while dressed in stonewashed jeans and a leather jacket, his moustache morphed to a Zapata. No, not a jacket, not in Mumbai's heat and humidity. Yet . . . yes, leather, to combat the arctic air-conditioning of Indian soundstages, places where, without layers, it was possible to court a fine young influenza.

Rachel had made notes, of course, and collected them in her pockets as ideas shifted over the French week, as she came up with new and different ways to illustrate her thesis. Yet now, doubt assailed her. Her hands refused to type. Perhaps it was ridiculous, comparing the work product of a Renaissance playwright to the last few years' crop of Indian films. What in the world was she thinking?

No, wait . . . wait. She was merely exhausted past affection for her work. She shouldn't even be sitting at her computer. In this mood, sleep would be far more useful to the book than ineffective paragraphs she was sure to groan over tomorrow. Her thoughts flitted to Steph, to their sidewalk confrontation, accusations spoken in anger, regrets and reflection. That wouldn't help her book, either. Finally, she picked up the phone.

"Hello?"

"I hate my thesis," Rachel announced. "Don't you use caller ID?"

"My glasses are in the kitchen. You have a great thesis."

"It sucks."

"No, no, it's –"

"Stupid."

"It's not stupid, it's just dry as the Mojave. You have miles of passion for Indian film, but I bet that's not coming through your prose. Am I right?" asked Marc.

"Passion doesn't exactly fit with academic arguments."

"It could. However, as your department chair, I don't give a damn what you write as long as it's engaging. So be bold! Lose the academic stuffiness, forget about university presses, go mass-market. Be amusing, be appealing. Write for moviegoers, people who love film but don't know anything yet about Hindi-language ones. What's your title again?"

"West Meets East: Shakespearean Themes in Indian Cinema," she recited.

"That's like putting Coke-bottle specs on a beautiful woman. Call it," he hesitated, "okay, here you go, cheesy but catchy: 'Shakespeare Loves Bollywood', we could silkscreen T-shirts! First line in black, his signature . . . or an approximation, as I recall the guy wasn't big on penmanship. 'Loves' in lower case. Third line, big font, the top half in orange, the bottom half green, like the Indian flag. For the book jacket, too."

"You think?" Rachel asked, dubious. Rewriting her book into a commercial work sounded like an agonizing, daunting prospect. She'd have to delete whole pages, alter the entire tone, and –

"I do. Start tomorrow morning, I'll call my guy in Ts."

"But how can I –"

"You can do it! Different, yeah, tough, certainly. A hell of a lot more marketable, though, and I bet a hell of a lot more fun. Who wants to wade through a book you don't believe in? Change it, you'll feel better."

"Shakespeare loves Bollywood?"

"Tomorrow. Good night, Rachel."

"G'night." She stood, and caught a glimpse of her startled expression in the dark window. Reworking the entire book, weaving humor into it? Was he crazy? Was she? Was it possible?

Even the scratchiest woolen blanket warms.

Steph's finger-pointing filtered into Rachel's conscience, and after initial denials – what? who? me? – ran their course, she acknowledged that her friend was right. In a mood of gratitude the next morning, she dialed Steph's number after sending Melina off to school counting in Hindi, *ek, do, teen, char*, all the way to *bis* and backwards. Melina had e-mailed back and forth with Anjali over spring recess, so if she trilled her Rs instead of keeping them in her throat, Monsieur LeBlanc would just have to understand.

Steph's number rang only twice before an authoritative voice interrupted to declare it no longer in service. Astonished, Rachel clicked the phone off. Then on again. Two rings later she received the same anonymous message. The service component of Steph's phone was on strike. Worse, it had folded its tents and stolen away.

She hung the phone in its vertical cradle and propped her chin in her hands, confused. What was the right thing to do in such circumstances? On the one hand was the desire to contact an old friend and find out what exactly she felt, versus honoring her apparent warnings, do not trespass, do not disturb.

In an Indian film, the heroine would rush round to her friend's house to talk it over, work toward reconciliation, put the relationship first. Yet in the US, there were competing concerns. Respect for another's space, for example. Steph had always insisted on going her own way. Was it right to intervene? On the theory that it's always more about others' hang-ups than your own, perhaps Steph felt the time was right for a break. Maybe friend-divorce had been on her mind for months.

Rachel locked the bolt and pocketed her key under empathetically gray skies.

The bus held the reminiscent smell of city newspapers and somber suits. Its familiar stops and starts punctuated the ride.

Rachel knew her book's table of contents by heart. She saw it now as dull, as plain as the Amish. She might not be savvy about commercial publishing, but she'd read enough to recognize it ran by a four-letter word: sexy. Both her chapters and their headings needed a smashing, crashing makeover before she even thought about dealing with text.

Chapter 1. This time, why Shakespeare? Why Bollywood? Marc's suggestion had reinvigorated her passion. How to transmit her own pleasure so the average reader with a penchant for movies would take the plunge? She glanced at her seatmate's Wall Street Journal. No help there. She turned to gaze out at the street. Shops and pedestrians ambled past as the bus trundled south, and a toddler waved from the security of her mother's baby sling.

"Phool, titli aur kaliyaan, ho gaye tumse khafa, chhen li joh tumne inse, pyaar ki har ek ada" . . . flowers, butterflies and buds, they're all sulking, you've stolen their ability to evoke love
. . ..

The words and lilting music trickled through her mind. *Phool, titli aur kaliyaan* . . . the words were from . . . ah, the Hindi film song "Koi Tumsa Nahin", There's No One Like You. Having identified it, Rachel relaxed and brushed it aside, shoo, go away –

She straightened, impelled by an idea both frivolous and downright commercial. Why not head her chapters with song titles? It was a hopelessly non-academic notion, and therein lay its charm. Music propelled Indian films in advance of their release, and at four to eight songs per movie, there were more than enough in simply the ones she and Melina knew. She could use more titles as sub-heads, section separators, in all three forms: English translations, Romanized Hindi, and Nagari, the Hindi script, where the symbols representing phonetic sounds were suspended from their long bar.

Rachel pummeled her memory for titles to scribble. This one for Heroes, that one for Family, was there one for Bad Dudes? – now there was a title for the chapter on villains! *Ask Anjali*, she wrote, and followed it with *her cousins?*

Her office voicemail held no messages, none from worried students returned from spring recess to their postponed work, none from friends. So Rachel's internal debate, confront Steph versus let it be, persisted. So did her song list, which in the blocks since its birth had grown three inches on the back of a battered Thai take-out menu she'd scrounged from her purse. Small red peppers punctuated her scrawls. "Chayya Chayya" was decorated with heat.

All her worries about the book, her concerns, fatigue and occasional dislike – books were like babies, and although she enjoyed writing them, there were times Rachel felt as resentful of sections and citations as she sometimes had with dirty diapers – all that had vanished. It was as if the book had magically sorted itself. Things fell into place. She saw each chapter whole, what needed to be said, even humorous asides, from one page to the next, section by section. Gone was the slogging, academic stuffiness. "Shakespeare Loves Bollywood" would be so . . . so . . . different!

"Good break?" Helen slithered through the open office door. Wide bone bracelets embraced her sticklike arms.

Rachel nodded and scribbled "Salaam-e-Ishq". "You?"

"Incredibly relaxing. I stayed in town. I heard you traveled."

"Dil Chahta Hai" made for another peppery title. "Mm-hmmm. So you worked?"

"From time to time."

A twist to the words brought Rachel's eyes up. Helen's expression was that of a schoolgirl who'd snitched the last piece of fudge. Rachel's pen stopped. "Consider me a subtlety-free zone."

"Marc and I had dinner." Helen nodded, affirming the incredible news. "Wonderful date."

"I'm . . . happy for you," Rachel got out. Which, though untrue, was an acceptable substitute for *what the hell was that man thinking?*

"So am I." The fragile hand fluttered. "So am I."

Rushing into the classroom, Rachel clumped her bags down. She was late, more than five minutes late, which hadn't happened in years.

"Good break?" she called. A sea of nodding heads broke around her. At the white board she scribbled the initials WS. "No more Sea Breezes, it's the Bard from here on!"

Rachel had forgotten how exhausting teaching could be when she truly gave herself to a class. It was like wading into a sea of peckish vampires.

Yet today she'd broken through professorial reserve to describe her book, naming it with the new title, and while the eyes of three Indo-Americans grew large with doubt, the class as a whole showed enough interest to make her think she might sell more than a dozen copies.

Most surprising was a request from a young man with a Texas twang. "You know 'em so well, Professor, the movies, I mean, how 'bout screenin' one for us?"

Simultaneous groans rose from the three with the Ganges in their history. "Trust me, you don't want that," commented one.

"Okay, y'all are tired of home product," he said, turning to face them, "but the rest of us don't know nothin' 'bout them."

"Anything," murmured Rachel. "Are you serious? It'd have to be outside of class, and I'm not requiring this," she assured them. "Next Tuesday night? Not tomorrow, next Tuesday. Seven to ten? Here? How many of you –?" It was gratifying to see the hands. Even the three who initially objected changed their minds when they saw so many others' arms go up.

Rachel returned to her office on automatic pilot, considering film after film. Their first taste of Bollywood should contain nothing too serious. That knocked out excellent movies like "Swades" and "Rang de Basanti". Nothing too escapist, either, so forget the gangster movie "Don" – both the 1970s original and the excellent remake – and the con artists of "Bunty aur Babli". She reached her door in a state of debate.

"Take a look at this!" By the voice it had to be Marc, though the man's face was obscured by a sheet of paper containing three large lines of print. "Not the real thing, I found a fake signature online." He handed it to her with a proud grin. "Good, huh?"

"He had six, you know. Six known signatures."

"You're joking. What, to evade creditors?"

The third word was divided between saffron sky and green sea, the middle word was tinted the color of blood. "Is 'loves' too much, in red?"

"Is it?" Marc crowded beside her. "More surprise if the bottom line is the only color? Okay," he plucked it from her, "redo."

"And that book you lent me, *Maximum City*? A little dark." Rachel shivered.

"Maybe it's not so much the author as the material." Marc leaned against the doorframe. "Ever think of that? Films are one thing, especially Bollywood romanticism, but real life's another. There's plenty of darkness there, you just haven't wanted to see it. Maybe there are places you haven't wanted to see light, either. Hmm?"

Flustered, Rachel flapped her song title list at him. "Thanks for the new take, it makes so much sense. I'm fired up again."

"Enough renewed passion to invite me to your place to watch a movie with you? Oldie-goldie, new release, anything. Toss in Melina and the Hindi tutor for safety, if you like." Marc's eyes dared her.

"Sure. How's next Thursday at six? Dinner first." She was pleased to see him look not merely gratified, but stunned.

He found his voice. "Absolutely. Fantastic. I'll bring Indian, spicy?"

Rachel nodded. "See you then." She waited until he was nearly out the door. "Oh, and Marc?"

"Yo?"

She mustered a candid expression. "What was dinner with Helen?"

"That?" He paused. "That was good manners, entertaining a lonely colleague over the break. In fact she talked about you, what a good mom you seem to be, the rest of the conversation was work-related. If she implied anything more . . . there was nothing more. Absolutely nothing. How do you say that in Hindi?" he asked.

"Kuch nahin."

"Are you committed to rewriting this book? It won't add much to your list of publications, not as far as your CV's concerned. Of course, it's your chair's suggestion," added Chandani, her eyes crinkled. She sipped a mango *lassi*.

Rachel leaned back against the elephant-bedecked yellow cushion. Rebelling against the sameness of local coffeeshops, Chandani had suggested they meet at an Indian restaurant called Pani Pani. Small and cozy and painted an evocative turquoise, its walls held framed posters of rippling mountain streams and waterfalls. The room was empty at this hour, except for the two of them and the restaurant's young owner, who moved quietly to and fro.

"It's different," admitted Rachel. "It's like nothing I've ever tried before. No footnotes, no cites. But I wasn't getting anywhere, and this . . . anyway, I'm in, no turning back, so let me show you."

She spread out her organizational pages, arranging the sheets on the table beside them. Chandani leaned over to read.

"What is . . . oh, I see . . . uh-huh . . . uh-huh . . . *accha!*" She glanced up. "I never thought of that connection!"

Pleased, Rachel nodded.

"You know what's missing?" Chandani's arms flew out to embrace the restaurant space. "Water. That's what *pani* means, and when this owner named it 'Pani Pani', it's like, in English, putting extra stress on the word. *Water*. It's crucially important in India, can you think of a single movie that doesn't contain rain or pools or scenes beside a river? Clean water's at a premium everywhere, even more so now. No technology, no cell phone or cheap Tata car replaces the basic need for water. The monsoon season can tip the balance between life and –" Chandani's slender hand fell. "But Shakespeare lived in a wet land."

"Yes. Yes," said Rachel. Reflective, she bit her lip. "And yet, it's not just water, it's nature. Water in India, definitely. In the England of Elizabeth and James . . . .." Her eyes searched a photograph of a river swollen and quick with melted snow from mountains hazy in the distance. "Light and heat. Would the summer be warm enough to produce a good harvest? And they had their own droughts, too. Shakespeare referred to all of those."

"It needn't be a long chapter. But it won't change, ever. Unlike this." Chandani tapped a chapter heading. "Love? *Pyaar?* In India, the rules on romantic relationships keep shifting. Every few years, small tremors. *Jaise ma vaise beti,* like mother like daughter? Not anymore. Among the middle class, there are still arranged marriages, sure, but everyone's clued in . . . it's not just parents maneuvering to gain a perfect daughter-in-law." She grinned. "And how's your own love life, Rachel?"

CHAPTER 31

I ce cream and milk weighed heavy. Rachel adjusted her plastic grocery bags, two in each hand, redistributing their weight. Only two more blocks home. At least it was still cool. It would be hot in summer, time for sleeveless dresses and camisoles, sandals and flipflops. She'd leave windows open at night, the city's smells and sounds unwelcome until familiarity made them barely-sensed reminders. Leaves would be full, flowers grown beyond their first tentative buds, and everywhere insects. She could hardly wait.

"Want some? Mint chocolate chip," Melina offered. She plopped onto the sofa, a large glass in one hand, the blender jar full of milkshake in the other.

"No, thanks," said Rachel. "It's getting late, are you hungry for dinner?"

"Pizza?"

"No, we've got that Kashmiri dish in the fridge . . . carrots . . . *parathas* . . .."

"Are you ever going to stop making notes for that book?"

Rachel shook a sheaf of small pieces of paper. "Never!"

She clutched a bouquet of mixed cut blooms whose freesias brushed her cheek, leaving a trail of scent as she pressed "Zimmer". Mondays were often slow days for Steph, she might be here. If she weren't . . . Rachel pressed again. She stepped back onto the sidewalk to look up. The two therapists whose windows overlooked the street appeared to be home, shadows passed from one side to the other behind gauze curtains. She remounted the granite steps and pressed their button.

"Yes?"

Quickly she identified herself and her errand, waving the bouquet as her bona fides. The answering *bzzzz* was loud.

There were twenty treads to the first flight of stairs. Above, a face peered down. Rachel displayed the flowers. "Thanks."

"Birthday?" the man asked.

"Apology." She reached Steph's door and laid the stems before it, turning them so the roses faced up. From her pocket she took an envelope and laid it on top. The neighbor watched her with curiosity. "A falling-out," she amplified.

"We haven't heard much from her."

"No?"

He shook his head. "The phone rings. My partner saw her last . . . Friday, I think. She's been quieter than usual." He nodded to the flowers. "Will they stay fresh without water?"

Rachel certainly hoped so. A wilted peace offering would be less than consoling.

Back on the street, she turned left, then right at the corner, zigzagging her way north. She had always rather envied Steph's choice of neighborhood. It was lively and flowed with energy each year as residents shifted. Odd, that Steph rarely talked about it. It struck Rachel now that she hardly ever heard Steph refer to local concerns, while Rachel regaled her with the gossip of Hansen Place, though "gossip" was a relative term, since Mrs. Burke and the neighbor next door, Dr. Fiedler, lived on memories, and Bitsy and Dean were too caught up in billing lawyer's hours to get into much beyond work.

Up ahead, a bright red awning beckoned. Chinese restaurant? Japanese emporium? As she walked beneath it, Rachel glanced at the door.

Prem's Spices, another Indian shop, a small tendril of the diaspora. Despite her fondness for Sinha Trading and its catchy "We Stock Everything Indian You Can Think Of", Rachel turned to enter. The door refused to budge. She looked for a buzzer, found it, and pressed.

The door gave with a click. She entered to the familiar scents of coriander, turmeric, cumin. Something indefinably smoky wisped its way through the sweeter aromas. Behind the counter, near racks and racks of DVDs, a dark-haired man – Prem himself? – looked surprised.

"*Namaste,*" she greeted him.

"*Namaste.*" He broke into a question.

"Sorry, I really don't speak Hindi. I'm looking for one of those things to roll *chapattis* on?" With her fingers she described a seven-inch circle.

"*Ah, ji, ji!*" and he led her toward the rear, where merchandise was stacked twelve feet high. The small candle lamps used in Hindu devotions competed for space with bowls, hanging strips of colorful *bindis*, and jars of garlic-ginger paste and lime relish. The owner pointed to a shelf. A half-dozen wooden circles sat there, their round surfaces ready for smooth *chapattis* or *puris* and, with an extra shove, Melina's favorite *parathas* stuffed with finely chopped cauliflower and spices.

"Flour, *chapatti*, roll," he said, demonstrating. A small bag of stick cinnamon served as a stand-in. "Flat!"

"*Parathas?*" she asked.

"*Ji, bilkul,*" though he looked less than absolutely certain.

Never mind, she would buy the round platform and lug it up to the East Side. Melina could take over the task of rolling bread. She nodded to Prem and trailed him back to the counter. While he rang up the purchase, Rachel skimmed the DVD racks.

Prem owned quite a collection of 1970s films, the ones with angry young men like the flowing-haired Amitabh Bachchan. Eighties, nineties, turn into the new century . . ..

"Ah! Would you –? That one." She pointed.

He handed the case to her. "Good movie, funny!"

"Aunty? Is that you?"

A hand on her arm brought her round to find Anjali, her long hair braided, regarding her with astonishment.

"This is amazing!" The young woman embraced her. "I was just thinking of Melina and here you are, Aunty! Excuse me," and she broke off to speak with Prem, whose greeting contained what sounded to Rachel a great deal of respect. Accepting Anjali's written shopping list, he snatched up a basket and left the counter.

"Aunty?" asked Rachel, amused. Nisha's explanation back in Oxford rang in memory.

"You don't mind? It's just he," her head indicated the shelves, "will understand that, too complicated to explain."

"You know this place, then?"

"Oh yes, he's related to my family's cook in Mumbai. But why are you . . . oh, of course!" Anjali exclaimed, spotting the wooden rolling circle. "Melina's *parathas*! No wonder. Listen, Aunty," for Prem had returned, his basket filled with bags of spices and, balanced precariously on top, a box of *patisa*, "will you wait while I pay for this, and walk with me?"

Anjali was a pleasant companion, chatting about life in college, the struggles she had overcome to be allowed to come to New York alone, even though a cousin – there was always a cousin, Rachel reflected – was already established here with his family, and of course her parents insisted she live with them. How much fun it was to tutor Melina! From her words, Rachel gathered that tutoring gave Anjali a sense of home.

"You're kidding. Just the two of us? In New York?" Rachel asked.

"My own family's not large, just me and my sister, and Mumbai's very New York-ish in some respects. Not the weather, of course, no palm trees here. You and Melina, though, you're a bit like me and my mum, you'd fit right in in Mumbai, to my family, I mean. You should come sometime." Her hand stopped Rachel's progress, her dark eyes glowed. "Yes, come visit, there's always room!"

Rachel envisioned Sandeep's extended family asleep in his lounge. There *was* always room. "We'd love to," she replied, "anytime you're there, and if it's convenient for your parents."

Anjali's hand dismissed bother. "Whenever you like. My mother will call her sisters, they'll take you shopping."

Rachel was delighted. Hitting sari shops with Hindustani women might justifiably be called collateral research. "That would be wonderful, if she could find time in her teaching schedule. What does your father do, again?"

"Like my uncle, films. Uncle produces, Dad oversees the budget. You know, it's fantastic how much Indian cinema Melina's seen, and her memory! She remembers scenes and dialogue I've totally forgotten. When you come to India, a party, my parents will invite their film friends." This was said with an air of pleased assurance.

Rachel agreed to a prospective party at Anjali's insistence that it would be no trouble at all, there were so many people to make it easy. Hesitant, she related Sandeep's description of the challenges of film financing. "Does that really . . . is that often the case?"

"Often? I don't know. Uncle does it, makes deals with those men. It's money-laundering for them, a way to finance for us. They didn't mean for me to know, I just overheard Dad's end of the conversation one day and put two and two together." Her tone was matter-of-fact. "You do what you have to do to get the movie made, see your vision achieved. There are recognized partners, of course. Media partners like Zoom and Times Now, then there are product partners."

"Coke?"

Anjali laughed. "Coke's a big one," she admitted. "But sometimes you need more. Sometimes there's pressure to accept more. So when Uncle's film is finished – it's taking longer than they like, they're getting impatient – he'll look around for financing for the next. It's good the Americans have brought investment, though, because sometimes the other way is risky. But at least it's not like here."

"More financing options, you mean?"

"Well, yes, that, too. But in India it's all between men, the families aren't involved. Oh, look!" Anjali pointed ahead, where a rolling cart displayed a "Jewelry" sign. "She's back! I've bought from her before, let's see if they have something for Melina." Her finger drew a line down the central parting of her smooth hair, and tapped her forehead. "Clear nail polish on the back of the pendant, it'll stay there all through dancing. Even the *garba!*" Taking Rachel's hand, she pulled her ahead.

Rachel gave the pendant to Melina the instant she returned home. The dangling, bead-bedecked ornament elicited a "wow!", then Melina rocketed upstairs to try it on with a *salwar kameez*. Although, she informed her mother, such a piece of jewelry was really more appropriate with a *lehnga*, the full-length gored skirt suitable for dancing. Melina admired herself in the long mirror, turning her head this way and that so the pendant caught the light, swishing her imaginary long skirts.

After dinner, Rachel began once more on her book. It was amazingly easier to write, especially after the hours spent with Chandani. Some paragraphs she lifted entirely from the first, dry draft, dressed them in colloquial phrases, and pasted in. Others were newborn. She'd typed her list of songs into another document, so it was a snap to insert them as melodic, evocative headings.

Her chapter on heroes, though painfully reminiscent of Steph's tirade, was essentially finished. She'd completed notes on the next two chapters, and it ought to take her just a few days to zip out the text for those. "Zip out" was the essence of this book.

So non-academic a phrase, no one zipped out a scholarly volume. This was Shakespeare in a T-shirt, an iPod tucked into his jeans.

Rachel giggled.

. . . even the internationally-flavored, bare-chested hipness of "Dhoom 2" (2006) can give way before the strong masala *of traditional Indian values,* she typed. *When master-thief Aryan asks his new apprentice Sunehri if she isn't afraid to be alone with him, she replies, "There's something about you that tells me you'll never harm me" – reassuring the audience that even the bad dude respects classic Indian ethics. Shakespeare's heroes are cut from the same hand-loomed* khadee *cloth . . ..*

Eyes on the screen, she picked up the ringing phone. "Hello?"

"Nice flowers, thanks."

"Steph?" Rachel's astonishment set her chair twirling.

"Yeah." A pause. "Sorry, Rachel."

"No, you were right. *Mea culpa.* Can't see the forest, can't see the trees . . . you weren't the only one living in fantasyland." In the silence, her own breath was loud. "In fact, I've turned over a new leaf and talked to Marc."

"And?"

"And . . .." The words, *something about you that tells me you'll never harm me,* burned the screen. "He'll be over next Thursday for movie night. Want to join us?"

Steph's tiny laugh was a welcome note. "What are you showing?"

"Well, Bollywood."

"Obviously! Does Shakespeare know?"

"Will S. knows and thoroughly approves, he can't wait to plop his skinny ass down and grab the popcorn."

. . . evolution of the heroine from the buxom girls of U-rated movies as late as the 1990s, whose characters might be filled with simple virtues but were also much too smart to be taken in by the wiles of Westernized men. In "Pardes" (1996), for example, when a man attempts to bed his fiancée, she's outraged

enough to lecture him that Indians' code of ethics is a barrier to premarital intimacy for both sexes. In 2002, that kind of in-your-face speech was left on the floor, along with the heroine's simplicity – virtue suddenly had a college degree. And by 2007's "Chak De India", starring the inimitable Shah Rukh Khan, an engaged couple is portrayed actually in bed, their argument not about sex, but whether her career in field hockey is as important as his in cricket.

Enough. *Bas*. Rachel's hands hurt, and Melina had gone to bed hours before. She yawned, clicked and saved. Shakespeare and his penchant for Indian film would just have to wait until tomorrow.

She glanced in at Melina, whose covers were pulled over her head, and trudged down to her own room. She shucked off her clothes, slipped a long-sleeved T-shirt over her head, and slid into the large bed, twisting to ease her back from the seated hours. If only there were someone with large hands . . . she pushed the thought away. Not the right time, not the right time. If it were, then the way would be easy, things would fall into place, and difficulties overcome without too much struggle. Wouldn't they? *Hai na?*

A male voice flooded her sleepy head with Hindi, singing of struggle and achievement. *"Roke tujhko aandhiyan ya zameen aur aasman, payega jo lakshya hai tera"* . . . and with the words receding into the distance, images of a training camp and a young man being all he could be. *Nothing can hinder or stop you . . ..*

She smelled the distinctive perfume before she saw the knee part its wrap dress. "Hey, Helen. How're you?"

"No chitchat, I have to get uptown to give a talk, but I was wondering," the coral-colored nails flicked, "if Marc really likes Indian movies?"

"Well, I think he . . . how did you know about that?"

Helen gave her a thin smile.

"It's not a date, Helen," said Rachel, choosing simple words. "It's a movie at home with my daughter. Possibly a friend. End of story."

"Oh, Rachel! Come on, it doesn't matter!" Helen laughed. "I mean, I have much better things to do. You couldn't possibly take my little message seriously!"

"Well . . . " she began, taken aback.

"Rachel, get real." Helen turned on her stylish heels. At the door, she paused. The dress again parted. "And for God's sake buy some lipcolor, you look like a ghost." She slipped out.

From her bag Rachel hauled a small mirror. Was she really so very pale? She snapped the mirror shut, and for a delicious moment entertained fantasies of harm inflicted on a colleague who was absolutely, definitely, finally getting on her nerves.

CHAPTER 32

"A nyone else coming, anyone know?"
An astounding twenty-five students lounged in their seats at an hour when they could be anywhere. One of them had even brought an immense bag of fragrant popcorn, distributed to the rest in red-and-white striped bags.

"Okay, this movie is called 'Hum Tum', meaning 'Me and You', and it was inspired by 'When Harry Met Sally', which was itself at least reminiscent of –?"

"'Much Ado'," came the hoped-for response.

"Exactly. So we have a new Beatrice, a new Benedick, meeting at odd times, always the wrong times. Yet somehow," Rachel pressed play, "they end up together, and pay attention to anything you see as Shakespearean!" On the screen, a giant pencil sketched.

Rachel bolted the front door behind her. Upstairs, music played, by its rhythm some tune from yet another Hindi movie soundtrack. The high soprano confirmed it. She set her purse and satchel down and removed her jacket. Evenings were no longer so frigid. The coldest weather had receded north, and New

York's natural moderation – between Long Island Sound and the warming effects of skyscrapers, the city retained heat – made it recover sooner from winter than its suburbs. The difference between Manhattan and upstate, still buried in snow, made tonight's milder air especially welcome.

"I'm home!" she called.

No answer. Rachel shrugged. No matter. Flicking at the kitchen light switch, she clicked the kettle on and rummaged for a teabag. She leaned over the mug and dreamily dunked the tea, up, down, remembering the evening's movie and her class's enthusiastic response. They'd grown absorbed in "Hum Tum", even the skeptical ones with Indian parents, and there was no higher praise than a rapt audience.

Her eyes wandered with her thoughts. On the table rested Anjali's purse and backpack. Had she and Melina finished the tutoring portion of this evening, then? The backpack held children's books in Hindi, books Anjali used to teach Melina. Perhaps they *had* finished, and were painting nails or braiding hair in Melina's room, watching a movie.

She went to the foot of the stairs. "Melina! Anjali! I'm home!"

No answer.

Rachel took the steps slowly. Maybe they watched TV in her own room. But that room was dark, the door open to shadow. Upward, then, to Melina's. Its light was on, the door must be ajar.

"Hey, guys!" No happy answering voices. She stepped in. No Melina, no Anjali. The soprano wailed from a DVD stuck on its main menu. Rachel pressed a button to silence her.

This was very strange, especially after ten o'clock on a school night, but maybe they'd run out for a candy fix? Three blocks up was the Iranians' tiny market, they might be chatting their way there for emergency chocolate. It was unlike Anjali not to leave a note, though. It seemed unlike her, Rachel corrected herself, Anjali appeared so responsible. Even Melina was used to letting her mother know of changes. They could at least have called, Rachel thought, irritated. Her cell phone was attached to

Melina, after all, she could . . . no, it wasn't, there it was on her twin bed, the black case shiny on the rumpled coverlet.

A fresh wave of annoyance swept Rachel. Why the hell had Melina left her phone? Now there was no way for Rachel to contact her.

Back in her own room, she opened the phone. One missed call, evidently from Jason. He must have tried during the Hindi lesson. Rachel snapped the phone closed and placed it on her dresser. When Melina got home, she'd –

The truth hit Rachel like a truck. Melina would never leave her phone. Taking her cellphone was an integral part of Melina's routine. Her daughter would *never* leave the house without her mobile, not unless she were forced out with no chance to grab it.

Hurtling down the stairs, Rachel grabbed for the railing and stumbled into the kitchen. She ripped open Anjali's purse. Flinging pens, combs, a French canal-boat brochure onto the table, she found what she sought: Anjali's phone. Oh, no. No. There was no way on earth that two girls headed out for candy, pizza, even beer, would both leave their phones behind. They might not need a wallet, their pockets might be stuffed with cash, but phones weren't about need alone.

Rachel stared at the table, her heart pounding, her breath shallow. Now she remembered. When she unlocked the door a few minutes ago, the bolt was already clear. She hadn't needed to use her key on that one, and why not? Melina knew to always lock the bolt. So did Anjali. If it were unlocked, then . . ..

Rachel pulled open the door to the basement and flicked on the light. Quickly taking the narrow winding stairs, she found the bottom with a sense of embarrassment and dread. "Melina? Melina, are you here? Anjali?" The stone walls echoed. She crept forward. Nothing was there, nothing but old boxes and the clutter every basement owned. "Melina?"

Nothing.

Back in the kitchen, she reviewed her options. First, search the house, make a thorough job, every floor, every closet. Then . . . then she'd start calling. She bit her lip, and tasted blood.

Each level, each nook, under the beds, behind the shower curtains, and as she searched, Rachel's mind raced with phrases read, cautions heard.

. . . *a family in the industry may be working on several projects at once. The time between investment and return can be years if the film doesn't do well. Who would have that amount of cash lying around? Only the underworld . . ..*

Melina's room, the guestroom Steve had used, check the closets.

" . . . *for financing a picture, sometimes you go to men you don't want anywhere near your family . . ..*"

Downstairs yet again, to search spots she knew she'd already examined.

" . . . *it's good the Americans have brought investment, though, because sometimes the other way is risky . . ..*"

Melina and Anjali weren't in the house. They weren't anywhere. The girls were gone, truly gone.

" . . . *men you don't want anywhere near your family . . ..*"

. . . *only the underworld . . . only the underworld . . ..*

Rachel knew now what had happened. Melina and Anjali must have been taken as a way to ensure that Anjali's family's film was finished, so those who'd financed it could see a return on their investment.

They had warned her, hadn't they? Marc and Sandeep and that Suketu Mehta book, and even Anjali, with their casual discussions of organized crime, of shadowy figures who directed illicit actions by cellphone. *Every culture has an underbelly*, that was Marc, and hints of a dark side, of those who got things done their own way. Hidden men always on the move, their mobiles used to issue orders to other men in, say, New York, to take action. Preemptive action. Retributive action.

Two girls snatched, and Anjali's blithe assurance that the Mumbai underworld didn't involve families? Naïve. She was young, she was naïve, though not, Rachel realized, more so than Rachel herself. Through no fault of Anjali's, Melina was caught up in a scheme originating a world away, dragged along with her tutor to –?

By an act of will, Rachel made her shallow lungs expand. She pulled the kitchen phone off its hook and dialed.

"Something horrible's happened." Pacing the living room, she explained in rapid sentences, filling Marc in on what she'd learned about Anjali's family's connections to the Mumbai underworld.

"Call 911," said Marc. "Use this phone, I'll call you back on your cell."

"My –? Wait." Scrounging in her own purse, Rachel came up with her cellphone. "Okay."

"Dial 911. When I reach your cell, just answer, you don't have to say anything."

The line went dead. She pressed buttons. Almost immediately the 911 operator asked her to define her emergency.

Outside, a car stopped. Rachel flung the door wide. Marc ran up the steps, dropped his briefcase and held her a moment, then pushed her to arm's length.

"NYPD?"

"They don't think it's that serious! They think they ran away! But these are girls who don't run, and it's ninety minutes since I got here, even if they went for a whole pizza they'd be back by now, Marc!"

"Did you tell the dispatcher about Anjali's background?"

She shook her head. "I thought it'd confuse them. Should I?"

"Not yet." Marc shoved the door closed. "Look, chances are that if they were taken it's someone American, not associated in any way with Anjali's family, or with movie-making at all. Maybe even Jason?"

"Jason? No, no way. Jason's a lot of things, but he wouldn't do this."

"Okay, not Jason. One of the neighbors? Someone who couldn't stand you in college? Someone who hated that you married Jason, but hated you more once you divorced? Look, just in case, I don't know where the hell Sandeep is, but I left a message, it's early morning in Paris." He glanced at his watch. "Six-thirty, if he turned his phone off he should check soon."

Rachel felt dizzy. "Sandeep, why Sandeep?"

"Connections. He knows people who can ask the right guys in India, the message will get through to the higher-ups. I mean, just in case your wild idea has some . . . come on, I'll make you some tea." He guided her to a kitchen chair. "Hot water?"

Rachel pointed to the electric kettle. Her throat felt dry and raspy.

As if he read her mind, Marc asked, "Have you cried yet?"

"I'm too worried to cry."

"Let go, then. It's okay."

Leaving the tea, he came round behind Rachel. His hands rested light and warm on her tense, tight shoulders. Her eyes welled at this tenderness, and as if by magic, tears flowed oily and soundless, dripping onto her jeans. Each plash was round, a dark-blue button.

"I can't, I'm drowning, I'm —" A metallic buzzing brought her head up. Drops ran down to her chin.

Marc fumbled for his cellphone. "Hey! Thanks for calling back . . . I know, I know. Here's the deal . . .." He left the kitchen, Rachel heard the front door open and close. He must be standing underneath the streetlamp's glare, describing the situation to Sandeep, asking for . . . what? Connections, what connections? Rachel stared dully at the empty mug. She wanted to be alone, happily puttering in the kitchen, the girls upstairs. Mixing spices and yogurt, blending chopped cilantro with *chakki atta* flour, anything, anything, as long as Melina was safe upstairs. As long as she was safe with Anjali, whose mother would be equally worried once she learned . . . oh, God, what was the cousin's name, the one Anjali lived with? Rachel had never heard it, had she? She searched her memory, what if she couldn't think of it, what if –

"Listen, Rachel." Marc was beside her. "Are you listening? Sandeep thinks no way it was those guys, any of them, but he'll check. He's on the phone to India now, people who know people. You understand? He's asking questions, Rachel." Marc took her by the shoulders. His nose met hers. "Understand?"

"Yes."

"I'll call 911 again, put their feet to the fire, but one thing they'll ask, Rachel, is enemies – does Melina have any?" He flipped his phone open. "Do you?"

"Good God, no! Me? Melina?" She stopped. "Anjali?"

"Crazed boyfriend?" His eyes were sharp. "Was her family planning to marry her off to some old guy from the home village?"

"She's not that kind of Indian. Wait, that sounds . . . I mean, they sound much more sophisticated than that. Graduate degrees, plenty of money. But I have no idea where she lives, Marc, the cousin's name, all I have is her cell number!"

"Check her purse," he said, and dialed.

Once more Rachel dove into the large purse, the kind many college students were toting these days in addition to their backpacks. She added to the small pile of belongings already decanted. More pens, a tin of Altoids, tampons, a photo book. She skimmed through it. Without labels, she was forced to guess. Mom, Dad, little sister, those first three were gathered with Anjali in a fourth photo. The remaining images were of elderly people. Grandparents, likely. Lifting the purse, she upended it, dislodging bits of paper. Within the zippered pockets was nothing of substance. She replaced the contents one by one, an uneasy voyeur.

The wallet rested in her hand. Of course, the wallet! Rachel cursed herself for a fool and unsnapped the clasp. There, an Indian driver's license with a New York address taped to it, Anjali with her hair swept back, and oh, where was a current photo of Melina? The police would want one. Rachel started up the stairs, then turned back to write down the cousin's address. She grabbed a pen and peered at the numbers, the street. Her mouth fell open.

Anjali's cousin evidently lived in an extremely posh section of Manhattan, much more upscale than Hansen Place. The deference shown by Prem in the Indian grocery suddenly made sense. Not only was he vaguely connected to Anjali's family. More importantly, he knew who they were in New York as in Mumbai, and he knew them to be extraordinarily wealthy, the kind of people who could afford a kidnapper's ransom.

"Marc?" She placed the driver's license before him.

"We have an address for the other girl's family," he told the phone, and read it to them. "That's right . . . no, we don't have a name. You are? Terrific. Are we done? Thanks." He turned. "They're sending a car."

The too-quiet house was now filled with clamor and confusion, feet clumping up and down. From above, lightning erupted. No, not lightning. Flash photography. They were capturing images of Melina's room. "Just routine," a deep voice told Rachel.

"In case of?"

"In case." The man's chest held a name. LAR . . . LARKIN. He hooked a thumb toward Marc. "Boyfriend?"

"Boy –? No, no," she said too hastily. Larkin's eyes grew interested. "He's a colleague, my department chair, I called him when I realized the girls weren't here, I was so afraid."

"Friend?" It was less a question than a test.

"Yes. He came when I called, he knows Melina, he knows my daughter."

"Does he?"

"Are you a detective?" asked Rachel.

"No, ma'am. They'll be here in a minute." He took out a walkie-talkie and ambled off.

Near the front door, Marc watched police search for prints. They lifted strips and stowing them neatly in plastic bags. Shifting, he caught sight of her and left the fingerprint detail.

"How're you doing?"

She shivered. "They think you might be involved."

"They have to," he said easily, "there are too many jerks out there. I've already given them my movements. Went home, gobbled dinner standing by the sink, and worked. My car was visible to my own neighbors, one of whom called to see if I'd sit on the watch area board. I declined. She was memorably irritated. I mean, she'd remember being annoyed at me."

"Marc, you don't have to tell me all that."

"You don't need more to worry about. Ah!" He plucked his buzzing cell from his pocket. "Great, it's him. Yo, Sandeep, what'd you find out?"

He wandered into the kitchen. Rachel sank to the shelter of the sofa, grateful for Marc's calm.

"Ms. Hill?"

She looked up. A woman leaned over her, a thirty-something with a badge and auburn hair pulled back in a ponytail, her face powdered with freckles.

"I'm Detective Lasorda. I need to ask you some questions."

Detective Lasorda was scarcely more enlightened later than when she'd begun asking the questions she called "routine".

"I'm sorry," Rachel told her, "there's just nothing I can think of other than the . . . well, the Indian thing."

The detective nodded, though clearly skeptical. "How about internet? MySpace? Facebook? Online chats, online friends?"

Rachel shook her head.

"C'mon, Ms. Hill, she's a teenager."

"No, seriously! Melina's . . . she e-mails friends, does research, that's it. Phone calls, yeah, she talks to friends, but she doesn't even have her own computer."

"Ms. Hill, virtually a hundred percent of the kids in your daughter's class must have their own computers."

"She's the 'virtually'."

"Mind if I look in her room?"

"Go ahead. Third floor."

"Thanks." Lasorda beckoned to her partner and began climbing the stairs.

"Hey." Marc landed beside her. "Okay?"

"She doesn't believe me," said Rachel, bewildered. "Why won't she believe me? What did Sandeep say?"

"He says *nada*. No one's heard anything about this, everything's disavowed. There are guys on their mobiles talking to the UK, Switzerland, Italy, and they're pissed his original contacts would even ask. They're also explosive that it's an Indian girl. Upset about Melina, yeah, but furious about Anjali. They're saying, to quote Sandeep's translation, this is not their style, they're not the fucking Russians. I have to say, he and I agree. These guys are no saints, far from it, but they don't do shit like this." Marc nodded toward the ceiling. "Detectives ask the usual routine questions?"

Rachel nodded. Her eyes welled. "Melina knew not to open the door. They both knew. Why would they open the door?"

"The police haven't found any forced entry, then?"

"No." She brushed at her eyes. "God, how useless. What time is it?"

His displayed his watch. Its golden second hand swept up. "Two."

The other detective wandered over. "You check your messages, home, work, cell, Ms. Hill?"

Rachel lifted her hands and let them fall back to her lap.

"Try not to worry, ma'am. We're doing everything we can."

Try not to worry. It was like asking her not to breathe.

"Mr. Harris says the tea will be ready in a moment."

Tea. What tea?

Her fingers ached from hours spent clenched. Rachel splayed them. That, too, hurt.

"I found some chocolate stuff." Two steaming mugs and the orange container of Bournvita were placed on the table in front of her. Marc handed her one of the mugs. "Drink?"

She wrapped her hands around the comforting hot stoneware and shook her head.

"I'll rephrase that. Drink! Look, it has," he read from the container, "malt extract, vitamins C, B6, B1, B12 . . . iron, zinc, manganese, this stuff practically stands up on its own! Drink, already."

Rachel's tight hands welcomed the heat. "Time?"

"Drink, and I'll tell you. Three forty-two." Marc slipped his sleeve back over the watch. "Feel sleepy?"

"No way." The strangers must have collected themselves in the kitchen, she and Marc were alone in this room. "Any news? Non-news?"

"Nothing yet, sorry."

She sipped. He sipped. They regarded the curtains.

"It seems like such a long time ago, the pig roast," she murmured.

"Ah, the pig roast! Whatever happened to Uncle . . . what was his name?"

Rachel's mind swirled, just like the time in twelfth grade when, hot and hungry, she had managed to faint in the parking lot of an A&P. "Uncle . . . .."

"Make one up," Marc suggested. "Thaddeus, Brutus, Augustus . . . why do so many men's names end that way?"

"It's all Latin. Marcus, that's what Steph and I thought your name might be. Before we met you, I mean."

"Marcus, huh?" He stretched. One arm came to rest on the sofa back, beside her shoulders. "'Marcus Harris' would be way too sibilant. Ssss!"

Rachel attempted a brief smile. "You can go, you know, you don't have to be here."

He transferred his mug to the table. "I'll listen if you want to talk, talk if you want to listen. Question the cops. Or be a pillow. Your choice." His eyes met hers. "What I won't do is budge."

A granola bar swam into Rachel's vision.

"Keep up your strength," Marc suggested. He edged onto the coffee table, knee to knee with her, and broke off a corner of the bar. He held it to her lips. "Eat, just this bit. C'mon, Rachel, you can do it."

She glared at him.

"C'mon, it's like batting, you can do it. Atta girl," he said as she took it from his hands and popped it onto her tongue, "see? One more, c'mon."

"I can't eat that whole thing."

"I'm not asking you to. One more bite." He broke off another. Their eyes met. "I'm subdividing, so sue me! Number three . . . there you go."

Rachel chewed and swallowed past the lump in her throat. "You're being very kind to me."

"I threw that Wednesday night class at you, I'm not particularly kind." His expression was gently self-mocking. "I can be as self-serving as the next guy."

"Oh, right."

"It just happens that my self-servingness makes me want to help you. Last bite . . . after they find Melina, and you get a chance to think about it, you might consider how much fun it would be to hang out with a helpfully self-serving guy."

"*After* they find Melina?"

"Of course." He brushed crumbs from his hands. "Another?"

Rachel's eyelids opened stickily. Her head was supported by something with knobs. She looked down and discovered Marc's shoulder beneath her cheek. He'd drawn his jacket over her, and Rachel's nose was suddenly tickled by the collar.

"Time-zit?" she asked, alarmed.

"Five o'clock." Marc patted his shoulder. "Nothing's happened, get some more rest."

"No!" The strangers' voices, both upstairs and in the kitchen, must have woken her after a smidgen of sleep. "God, I can't!"

"Sure you can. Come on, Rachel, not much else you can do at this point." Again he tapped his shoulder. Past it, an inquisitive face was framed by the kitchen doorway. It wavered and disappeared.

"Sandeep?" she queried, giddy with fear and fatigue.

"He called again. Absolutely dead end. It's midafternoon in India, I got the impression some wiseguys have had a rough time explaining their movements, the bosses are making sure no one's gone outside his brief and taken the girls, thinking somehow they'd score points. I told *them*," Marc's chin jerked toward the police, "not that they want to suspect an Indian perp at all. Fair warning though, Rachel, this will be top news once the sun comes up."

"Reporters, you mean?" A series of unwilling yawns interrupted her. "Maybe they'll help. Maybe . . . Marc, I can't come up with anyone who'd have even a mild grudge against Melina. It's not like she stole a boyfriend or was elected prom queen."

"Someone envious, maybe? She gets good grades, she –"

"Kids don't hurt each other over good grades. Not these days."

"Well . . . start thinking outside the box. Outside your New York life. There's Melina's dad, her stepmother."

Rachel sat up. "What do you mean?"

Marc shrugged. "Does Jason have enemies? His wife? Somebody who'd want their current project delayed?"

"But that's so . . . that's so distant!"

"It's a hell of a lot closer than Mumbai. Think about it. The detectives came back, I'll go talk to the one with the red hair, what's her name?"

"Lasorda." Rachel caught at his hand. "But I don't know anything about their life in California, whether Ellie even has enemies!"

"Don't worry, Los Angeles police will find out." He squeezed her hand.

"Don't go!" She held on. "I mean . . . I mean . . .."

"Don't worry," he repeated. "I'm here for the duration. Yo, Detective!"

"This doesn't happen in Indian movies. The ones I watch, anyway." Rachel rubbed her red eyes, which were again wet. She swiped at them and at her nose. "There's a macabre energy here. Cynicism. Lies. Short and bitter. Even the words they use. 'Perps'."

"C'mon," Marc said, gentle.

"No, it's dark," she said bitterly, "it's like Stephen King, or Rome in ancient times. Ancient anywhere, I suppose. Doesn't need to be ancient. Shakespeare's London was dark, Dickens's London, too, Victorian – ohmigod, ohmigod, ohmigod! Where is it, where is it," her fingers scrabbled over the coffee table, "where's my cell?"

"What's wrong?"

"Dickens's London! Dickens, Dickens! Helen, how could I have forgotten Helen? She's the perfect – where is it, God, where is it? And I never told Melina! No, wait, I don't need my cell, I can use –"

"Here it is. What are you talking about, Helen from work?" Marc handed her the small black phone.

"Yes!" Rachel snatched it and tapped on the keys. "They wanted to know about enemies, it should still be there, the saved message, where's that detective?"

"What saved message? What are you talking about, what about Helen?" Marc asked, baffled. He gestured to Detective Lasorda.

"This one!" Rachel held the phone up so all could hear. "*Rachel, this is Helen. You must not have taken me seriously with regard to Marc. Listen, hon, this is way more than you want to mess with. Okay?"*

"Well, it's a lead," said the detective, bringing out a notebook and pen. "She's a colleague, is that it? Let's start with where she lives, got an address?"

Marc led the woman back to the kitchen. To a phone book. And, of course, to the laptop he'd brought with him. It would contain faculty addresses, in case Helen's number was unlisted. It would be so unlike Helen, however, to choose anonymity.

"They want us – you – to remain here."

"No!" Rachel half-rose.

Marc caught her hands. "Rachel, listen to me! Listen! Helen may not be involved! She might not! Even if she is, the girls might not be there at her place, she might have taken them elsewhere. They might not be in New York."

A wave of fresh horror swept Rachel. "They might not . . . that means they might not be in the country! What if she, if they . . . oh my God, what if they've been injected with drugs, sold off? How can we –"

"Shhh." Marc pulled her back to the sofa, back to earth. "It hasn't been much time, less than twelve hours, probably, and –"

"How long does it take?" Her tone was as bitter as unripe persimmon.

". . . and while I think Helen is past due for intensive psychotherapy, I can't see her being that –"

"Cruel?"

"Rachel, Rachel!" He gripped her shoulders. "Hope for the best! That they're at Helen's, that they're just scared. And stay."

"Easy for you to say!"

"Not easy at all when I feel responsible for this mess, Helen's on my staff. Why didn't you tell me about that message?"

Rachel blew her nose. "I didn't think she was serious! The last time we talked, she sounded carefree, sort of casual. Not like a woman who'd blitz over you."

"Me?" he asked, astonished.

"She didn't see herself as just a colleague."

"Yeah, well . . . in times of trouble, silence is an enemy," Marc said. His eyebrows knit together. "You should have told me."

The phone rang. Rachel regarded it with a mixture of anticipation and dread, then handed it to Marc.

"Hill residence . . . she's right here . . . sorry, she asks that I . . . oh, good . . . thank God . . . fantastic, both, fantastic . . .."

Rachel's hands reached blindly for the phone.

"Bini?" she began.

CHAPTER 33

Little by little the story emerged from Melina and the police, whose detectives were modestly amazed by their luck.

"What if you hadn't kept that message?" asked Lasorda. "Or just forgot about it? God knows what the professor might have done. She didn't really plan for success."

"What did she do?"

"More what she didn't. Like she went out thinking steak but got cheap and bought a Big Mac instead."

Spotting out-of-work young men in her neighborhood, Helen persuaded them with a C-note apiece – scarcely the price of one wrinkle, thought Rachel – to help her. She'd stashed the men beside Rachel's front door where they could not be seen in the dark, and pressed the bell.

"So when your daughter ran down, she didn't look –"

"Yes, I did! But I recognized her. I'm so sorry, Mommy!"

Melina had flung the door wide. A hand scented with machine oil covered her mouth, her legs were lifted, and she was toted like a kicking four-year-old to Helen's car, where a rough cloth pressed over her nose until she lost consciousness.

"Then apparently the young woman, Anjali, came looking for her. Same thing. It wasn't hard, they're small enough. Those guys drove them downtown, unloaded them at the professor's building."

Melina had vague memories of stumbling, half-dragged, into Helen's flat, of her hands and feet being bound. The young men had disappeared. Perhaps they grew frightened of Helen herself. All through the night the woman ranted at Anjali and Melina, words that made little sense to them, until, tiring, she ripped the tape from their lips. No screaming, she warned, or . . . the butcher's knife she waved was incentive enough.

"It wasn't like yours, it was bigger. Way bigger. Like for chopping up rabbits." Melina shivered.

"That's when they got their spirits up, though," a police officer told Rachel. "They promised they wouldn't scream, and they didn't. But the other girl thought it might bother the neighbors if they sang songs, especially in a foreign language, so they started off soft and got progressively louder."

"In Hindi, too," said Melina. "Anything we could think of, and we got pretty loud." She rested sleepily on Rachel's chest. "The songs from the medley, 'Chayya, Chayya', all the 'Bunty aur Babli' ones. Anjali knows a lot of songs, she taught me the national anthem . . . *jana gana mana adhinayaka jaya* . . .."

"Where was Helen?" asked Rachel, perplexed.

"In her bedroom, on the phone."

"Calling friends and relatives, leaving voicemails," the officer told her. He glanced at Melina, and his eyebrows rose in warning.

Yet no one complained of the singing. Helen's building was apparently occupied by tenants who were either tolerant or gone. Or perhaps – visuals of the butcher's knife tormented Rachel – they were themselves already too leery of Helen to confront her over noise.

"It didn't take long once we got there." The officer tapped Melina's shoulder. "We found the girls under a spindly-legged table."

"We rolled under," Melina explained.

"What happened to the knife?" Rachel asked.

"She dropped it behind the curtain, but we told them while they untied us." This was said with a matter-of-fact air. "Can we go visit Anjali later?"

"Of course." Rachel caught sight of the open front door. Marc was slipping out. "Hold on!"

He stopped. "You need rest, I'll catch you later. Hey, hey!" for Rachel flung her arms around him. He patted her back. "No big deal, I'm glad it wasn't Sandeep's friends' guys, that would have been," he grimaced, "well, it could have been long and confusing and very bad."

"Thank you so much." Rachel's words tumbled over themselves. "For calling Sandeep, talking me through it, being here, staying, everything, I couldn't have made it through, really."

"Yeah, you could," he said gently. "And you're welcome. I'll check in tonight, okay?"

She nodded, one hand tight around his. "I wish you would."

As Marc predicted, the story led the local news, though not until the noon edition and in a far happier mood than seven hours earlier. Reporters and photographers carpeted the narrow terrain of Hansen Place until a breaking story downtown called them away.

A knock on the front door was followed by a recognizable female voice. "Rachel? Rachel, are you home?"

"I'm asleep," whispered Melina, and dashed up the stairs. Rachel opened the door to Mrs. Burke, virtually hidden behind an enormous plate of cookies.

"These are cinnamon walnut, sweetheart, real butter," and the woman was inside and halfway to the kitchen. "I'll set these on the table, and oh," Rachel was enveloped by two soft arms and a cloud of Elizabeth Arden, "I talked to those reporters, you must have been scared to death!"

"I was."

"Awful! Awful! I hope they lock her up, that woman, and to think she worked with you! Melina resting?" Mrs. Burke glanced at the ceiling. "I brought a movie for her, get her mind off what happened. I know she likes classics, and this is not, but it's light, it's romantic." Mrs. Burke's hand dove into her coat pocket and brought out a DVD.

"Oh, thanks, that's –" Rachel turned it over to read the title: "Kaho Naa Pyaar Hai". In her amazement, she nearly dropped the plastic case. "Mrs. Burke, you like Indian movies, too?" she asked.

"You've seen this?" Mrs. Burke sounded just as surprised. "Oh, yes, my heart's divided, half to Amitabh," she admitted with a satisfied sigh, "but half to Shah Rukh, too, and this young fellow," she tapped the DVD, "if I had my twenties back again! Such a handsome man! Which reminds me," and she led the way to the front door, "then I'll go, I can see you need some rest, but Rachel, I talked to your friend who was here, Marc –?"

"Harris, yes?" asked Rachel.

"I grabbed him before he reached his car, and I want to tell you, sweetheart, he's a keeper! Reminded me of him." Again she tapped the DVD. "Raj, I mean, in the second half, the smart one." The bright eyes looked up. "Too good to waste, Rachel, I'm telling you! Give Melina my love . . . and a cookie, tell her real butter!"

Like a small dolphin, Melina kept to Rachel's side, following her every move.

That afternoon, she asked again to visit Anjali. "I really want to see her," she told Rachel, "and her cousins expect us."

The dark hair slipped under Rachel's fingers. "Of course. She sounds very brave, and what if she hadn't been here?"

If Rachel hadn't been acquainted with the Indian notion of hospitality, she might have felt at sea while visiting Anjali's cousins. They welcomed her with alacrity and embraces, calling toward the wide hallway, "Rachel Aunty's here!", and made an enormous fuss over Melina and what they were pleased to call her fluency in Hindi. Rohan, his wife Kamini, and Anjali herself could not have acted more delighted. No recriminations, no whys, only relief and joy.

An invitation to tea followed, sweets were brought out, and the two families beamed at each other.

Rachel cleared her throat. "Still, I'm just so sorry –"

Rohan made a silencing sound. "*Bas*," he cautioned, "enough, it was bad, they're safe, that's all. Evil things happen, we're grateful you and the police acted so quickly. That woman," he tapped the side of his head, "you know. My uncle's family ask me to convey their gratitude. Things don't always end so happily."

That night, Melina appeared at Rachel's door, her face a question. Wordlessly, Rachel patted the mattress. Melina scrambled in. "Just for tonight," she confided.

"For as many tonights as you need."

"I had a good time at Anjali's this afternoon."

"They were amazingly gracious. They could have said . . . well, never mind."

"Good *laddoos*, too." Melina yawned. "Marc helped you a lot, didn't he?"

"So much, I can never pay him back." Rachel kissed her daughter's forehead and held her close. "It just occurred to me, Bini, he'll either have to find a replacement for Helen, or teach those classes himself."

Melina twisted a strand of her hair. "She won't be there anymore?"

"We can't allow her back."

"Cool."

The very word spoke of health. What if Melina hadn't had Anjali with her? What if . . . ? *Bas*. Enough ifs.

"Can you put on a movie?"

"Sure. Which?"

"Something big," Melina's arms stretched to encompass the room, "bigger than everything that happened."

"We've got just the thing." Rachel inserted a DVD. "Sixteenth-century love story, an elephant-taming emperor, and I'll even throw in a few camels."

The sweet haunting music of "Jodhaa Akbar" filled the air. Melina settled back against the pillows.

"I like the sixteenth century," she murmured.

Rachel turned off the light. Melina curled against her as she had when small. Her breath was shallow and even. Rachel could picture her singing, though, she and Anjali recalling lyrics . . . she, too, was slipping into sleep, into song . . . *le jayenge, le jayenge, dilwale dulhaniya le jayenge . . . the brave heart will take the bride . . .*.

A number of people had been very brave. The girls, of course, and NYPD. Rachel herself, she deserved a pat on the back. And Marc, summoning Sandeep, exhorting confidence, staying with her . . . *dilwale dulhaniya le jayenge . . .*.

With a start, Rachel realized that during the confusion and chaos of the past thirty-six hours, she had never even once thought of calling Steph. She stared at the ceiling, now thoroughly alert.

CHAPTER 34

Wearing dark glasses and a head scarf, Rachel scurried around a knot of reporters. She made it into the departmental office, queried Jen with a look, knocked on Marc's door, and rushed inside before his "come in!" had finished echoing.

The door slammed behind her. "Send them away!" she pleaded.

"I just called campus security," Marc told her. "If they can't chase them off, I'll get NYPD. Were they at your house this morning? Rachel, that's why I suggested you stay home! God, woman, write your book, bake some brownies, you shouldn't be here!"

"Here feels normal. Normal's good," she said, taking a seat. "I feel more than usually inarticulate today, I thought maybe here would help. Being here. Oof! I can't even talk, there's been too much stress, too much everything."

"And Melina's at school? Of course she is. Hold on ten minutes, and I'll peek out in the hall."

Rachel sank back and watched him scribble notes in the margins of letters. "Will you cover Helen's classes?"

"Nope, I found someone to fill in." Marc glanced up. "By the way, Helen's listed me as a supportive face."

"Oh, no!"

"Oh, yes, I need to call her lawyer. Excuse me." He bent once more to his work.

Watching him, Rachel grew pensive. Unrequited desire in the hands of the wrong person was such a dirty bomb, scattering destruction along far-reaching planes. Never for Helen the "I love him, but I'll give him up to you" generosity seen in Shakespeare. Reflexively, Rachel reached for one of Marc's Post-Its to note the thought. His fingers came down on hers.

"You okay?" he asked.

She nodded. "Pretty much."

"This time next month it'll seem like a bad dream."

"This time next month can't get here fast enough." She drew the paper from its holder and wrote a cryptic scrawl. *Generous friend, S: 2 GENTS = NTJNH.*

"Oh!" The word burst from her.

Marc's eyebrows rose.

"Weeks ago, I made a note, TBB," Rachel explained. "Shorthand, but I couldn't remember what for until now."

"The big Bachchan? Amitabh Bachchan? Yes? Didn't know I was a trivia king, did you? Wind me up and send me to Alex Trebek, I'll take ancient civilizations for six hundred," Marc joked. "Who were the Assyrians? What is cuneiform? Where is Cuzco? Aha, there's that smile! All right, finished. I'll scan the halls, report back."

He closed the door, allowing the soulful-eyed poster of Shah Rukh Khan to pop into view.

"You'd probably adore all this attention from the media," Rachel told the photo. "I wish I could just beam them to you."

"The law hath not been dead, though it hath slept.
Those many had not dared to do that evil
If the first that did th'edict infringe
Had answered for his deed. Now 'tis awake,
Takes note of what is done, and like a prophet
Looks in a glass –

"The law, which has been dozing, has awoken, looked around, and is now saying, no more acceptance, no more excuses, no more, 'oh, it was just an immature mistake'," continued Rachel.

"Angelo's going tough-love," a student commented.

"Tough, certainly. But he's a hypocrite, right?" She walked back between the desks, pausing beside a young man with an ill-disguised BlackBerry. "Tell us about Angelo's personal corruption, how does that occur?"

Two weeks of sailing toward normalcy – police interviews and repeated no's to the "Today Show" slowed them only slightly, a few barnacles on a ship's keel – and Rachel, reflecting, concluded that they'd been incredibly fortunate. Both Melina and Anjali treated what happened like a terrifying rollercoaster, frightening while onboard, yet survivable. After such an intense shared experience, their relationship had leapt from student/tutor to that of sisters. They spoke frequently by phone, Melina calling Anjali "*didi*", and their happiness on Wednesday nights would be hard to fake, even by experienced Bollywood actresses.

"She looks good," Melina's school counselor told Rachel with quiet enthusiasm, "she's got perspective. Classes help, you help, but for her the most help is Anjali. From what I gather, it's a two-way street. You're lucky."

They were all very, very lucky.

Rachel purposely avoided newspapers. Marc, she knew, was aware of the status of Helen's defense, but he kept those developments to himself. Rachel was grateful – yet again! – and didn't care if she never heard what Helen's lawyer planned. The times she ran into Marc were still too full of appreciation and new energy to waste on Helen.

To think she'd nearly shelved the Bollywood yardstick as too idealistic, too unsustainable! In light of the recent storm, Rachel was ready to re-evaluate. Such a standard made for tough calls, certainly, and Steph hated it. Too, it was like shooting for the stars. Why not, though? Rachel might reach something different, anyway, vastly different from Jason or the nearly-forgotten Ian.

Different is fun . . . or vice versa. Against Hindi-speaking protagonists, Marc stacked up well in multiple departments. Intelligence, courtesy, ethics, self-restraint . . . Rachel chuckled. The man could even dance *bhangra*, and what more could a self-respecting Indian movie heroine ask?

CHAPTER 35

I want to ban electronics," Rachel fumed. "Cell phones, BlackBerries, iPods, just dump them in the bin when you enter my class, collect them at the end. Do I sound bitter?"

"Not excessively," replied Jenny, "considering what you've been through."

"How's Nick doing?" Rachel ventured.

"He got a yes from Long Beach Memorial."

"Oh, congratulations! I didn't even realize you guys were looking west. I'll give you Melina's dad's number." She printed the name and ten digits.

Marc's office door opened. A trio of conservatively-suited men emerged, followed by Marc himself, the four immersed in discussion.

" . . . the loss of English literature . . .."

" . . . humanities funding . . .."

" . . . even electronic books have . . .."

Marc winked at Rachel and ushered the strangers to the hall. Their voices faded.

"What are those? Potential donors?"

Jenny nodded. "Deep pockets. Marc's been grooming them for weeks, this was their first up-close and personal. PowerPoint, tour, lunch."

Rachel felt for a chair and sat, stunned. She'd had no idea that Marc faced such pressure. Yet he seemed perfectly comfortable answering her frantic call for help. There was a great deal of quiet courage in that, the kind that Bollywood heroes exhibited. Perhaps Steph was entirely wrong about the effect Indian movies had on Rachel. Maybe, taking the long view, she'd been preparing herself for –

"Round three, he's still on his feet. Barely." Marc stood in the doorway, his expression as exuberant as his crimson tie. "You okay?"

"Fine," she said, "and how are those deep pocketses, Bilbo?"

"Those guys? They're impressed, enthusiastic, lots of give-and-take. Whether they give and give is another question. They survived the Wall Street bear, but they'll want more facetime before cutting a check. Are you here for tea?" he asked.

"For postponement. Can we do the movie tomorrow night? The one you were coming over for," she reminded him.

"Tomorrow, sure. Give me a time and I'll bring food."

"Lamb for me, if you would. Melina doesn't like me to cook things that go *baa*."

In her hurry, Steph slopped a drop of espresso over the side of her cup. She slid a paper napkin between cup and saucer, and noisily dragged her wooden chair across the coffeeshop's tiled floor. "Here's an idea," she said, "really flat cookies you place under cups, they'd absorb spills, then at the end, you eat them! Brilliant, huh?"

Rachel's lips pursed in thought. "It'd have to be a very stiff dough, like a fortune cookie before it's folded."

"Absolutely. We'll sub it out to the fortune cookie guys, get them to color the dough brown, call them 'Tough Cookies'!"

Steph tapped the table, sending more espresso overboard. "We'll rake it in, Rachel!"

"A penny a cookie?"

"A nickel!"

"You talk to the cookie boys, I'm in," Rachel assured her. "How are Rubén and Franny? Is there still a Rubén-and-Franny?"

"Uh-huh, they sound better than ever. I might even have to hunt for a mother-of-the-groom dress. Who knew, weeks ago?" Steph tapped Rachel's hand that lay on the table. "Listen, babe . . . hard stuff, you and me."

"Very hard stuff," Rachel agreed. Tougher, perhaps, than Steph realized. Yet all relationships were subject to growth.

"Relationship survival, though, a hundred percent." Steph leaned forward. "I like settling dust."

"Of course you do." Rachel grinned. "You get to sweep."

"Tomorrow night, though, I can't make it, but it's not because . . . it's not! It's that I've been hanging out at *bhangra*. Camille's asked how you are, by the way. I claim ignorance."

"*Accha?*" said Rachel, interested.

"You were right about her from the first meow. Too juvenile. Still, dance is dance! When it comes to subtitled movies, though, I'm definitely a made-in-the-US girl, but –"

"Made by anyone, not just the brilliant Steven?"

Steph shifted. "Okay, fine, it's a crush, all right? If I examined mine the way I would a client's, sure, I'd find issues. Father issues, escapism, rejection. But you know what? I don't care." The brown eyes locked with Rachel's. "I don't. So don't you, either."

"Deal! No problem, crush away. No more comments," Rachel promised.

"Thanks. So, how's the book? You're not the only one who's turned over new leaves! Besides," Steph's cheeks grew rosy, "I have this new client who's originally from Madras, and she –"

"Is into Bollywood?"

"Honest to God, Rachel, she said the exact same thing you did, about how you can't understand Indians until you watch their films!" She pulled out a cloth-covered notebook. "She gave me a list."

"Let's see." Rachel skimmed the titles. "Well, she hit the goodies. Any chance you'll rent one or two?"

"Excuse me, Stephanie? Is that little Stephanie Zimmer?" The inquiry came from one of the older women at the table beside them. Behind bifocals, her eyes gleamed.

"That's right," Steph answered, doubtful. "I'm sorry, I don't –"

"I knew I recognized that voice! Such a small world! Judith Brody, dear, you were on the swim team with my daughter Shari, dark hair, freckles, butterfly?" The woman's hands moved in imitation.

"Oh, wow," Steph hesitated, "oh, God, seventh grade! How *is* Shari?"

Rachel carried her cup to the counter and slid it across. It might not be the kindest act to leave Steph alone with a woman bent on reminiscing, but having made up the quarrel, Rachel wanted only to meet Melina. With her fingers, she mimed walking out the door, ignored Steph's silent protest, and departed.

Outside the school, Rachel watched young mothers, the ones who waited with small children in slings or strollers, pacifying them with organic designer snacks and the ubiquitous Cheerios. She was well aware that younger women envied her freedom from diapers and toddler TV.

Yet they knew where their kids were.

Although Melina was perfectly capable of walking home accompanied by friends for all but the last two blocks, and she might resent the maternal presence, Rachel couldn't help it. Her own mothering traits peeked menacingly through the painted-on veneer of civilization, and if her daughter had problems with that, well, tough.

Melina finally appeared, attached to a quartet of classmates. "What are you doing here?" she asked Rachel, impatient.

"I have this distressingly-close, overly-dependent relationship with my adolescent daughter, I'm checking up on her because I have no life." Rachel kissed the rosy cheek. "I came because that's what moms who've been frightened out of their wits do. They show up. They hug, they kiss. How are you?" They fell into step.

"Good."

"How was your day?"

"Fine."

Rachel stopped. "Could you be less articulate, sweetie?"

"It was fine. People have stopped asking questions. Do you have chocolate?"

"Not until we reach Mahmoud's in the next block."

Rachel paid the cashier – Mahmoud's middle son in his afterschool gig – and handed Melina the three packets. "M&Ms original, peanut, Snickers."

"Thanks."

They paused outside the store so Melina could rip into the first candy. Across the street, workmen dragged a raking board across a sidewalk's fresh concrete, sliding the wet gray smooth and pristine.

"So what's with the emergency ration of cocoa bean?" asked Rachel.

Melina crumpled the Snickers wrapper and stuffed it in her jacket pocket. "Nothing."

"Yeah, there's nothing like nothing to make people self-medicate. Bartenders everywhere need to learn that. It's what happened, isn't it? You've been thinking about it, you haven't been able to concentrate?"

"Dad called again today."

"What?" Astonished, Rachel ignored the glances two passing women gave her. "Since when does he phone you at school?"

Melina ripped open the peanut M&Ms. "Since it happened. He calls during lunch. I'm fine until I talk to him, then after he hangs up I'm all scared again." Melina held out her palm. Misshapen lumps glistened on the smooth skin.

Rachel chose one. "I'll get him to stop. If it happens more, though, just don't answer, okay? Promise?" She sighed. "And I thought my latent mama bear instincts had all they could handle."

"Is Marc coming over tonight?"

"Tomorrow, I postponed. So let's do something nurturing."

"Can we go downtown and get pounds of *jalebis*?"

"Definitely. *Gulab jamuns*, too?"

"Yes!" Melina's expression was alight. "And *laddoos*, and those pretty diamond-shaped things, the pink-and-green ones, what are they called, oh, and . . .."

They walked on. Behind them, the workmen encircled the wet sidewalk with orange cones and yellow caution tape.

CHAPTER 36

H ell, I wouldn't do it!" the young man objected, with unusual indignation for a Friday.

"So, unlike these two gentlemen of Verona, you'd embrace love rather than friendship?" Rachel prodded.

"Duh!"

Through the laughter that followed this monosyllable, Rachel pointed to a second student.

"It doesn't occur to either Valentine or Proteus that the girl might have her own opinion?" The sarcasm elicited an approving chorus of *yes.* "It's all, like, hey, I love her, but you love her, too? . . . okay, dude, I give her up, she's yours."

"Disinterested love," supplied a young woman in blond dreadlocks. "Very Renaissance."

Rachel sat up. "Actually, several Bollywood movies contain that as a theme, as well. Friendship over love, particularly where there's already been an engagement ceremony."

"If I give her up, hey, aren't I a generous guy?" More sarcasm, accompanied by a seated prancing, and the student turned to high-five the one beside him. "But," his voice now earnest, "what if she prefers *me*?"

Derisive hoots met this.

"Seriously, what if she thinks my friend here is fine, sure, he's okay, but he just isn't what she wants? No chemistry, no passion! I hand her over to him, in this play I look like a hero, when what I really did was condemn her to a sterile marriage. On her part, anyway."

"Yet the Elizabethans –" Rachel began.

"No, no, no! Sorry to interrupt, but all along we've been talking about that concept of nature, designed for each other? What's natural about this? If she and I love each other, but I let the other guy have her, then both of us are in the wrong place, she's unhappy, and I'm a dick!"

"A frustrated one," another student offered, to more laughter.

"Both guys are world-class idiots," he finished. "Elizabethan or Bollywood or whatever, who the hell does that to a woman he loves, who loves him back . . . sends her off to another man?"

. . . different rationales. At the start of "Swades", Mohan is certain that bringing an elderly woman back to the US is the right thing to do. By the end, his opinions have been challenged, shaken out and remolded. His sense of himself as a savior – in terms of just one woman – grows big enough to encompass an entire village. Yet rescue is a two-way street. He can't aid the village without seeing his own transformation sneak up on him . . .

Rachel's fingers pressed laptop keys as she saw a dry land with tentative power supply and a village school ready for more students, no matter their caste.

What she felt for her book was a mounting sense of joy. The word was an odd one to apply to any book, especially one that dealt with Shakespeare on nearly every page, and yet . . . and yet, there was a certain joy in his work, echoed in the best of Indian film. In her many motives for this project, one that stood out was her pleasure in celebrating Bollywood – and introducing it to the American audience to whom the words "Indian movie" meant only "The Last of the Mohicans" – while revealing how appealing it would be to the Bard himself.

She shoved the coffee table's magazines into a semblance of order. How long ago it seemed, that night of the pig roast, when she'd dithered over dusting! She was back to basics. Alive and well, check . . . Melina, too, check, and Anjali . . . there, that was it, three objectives covered. Housekeeping could take a seat way in back.

The doorbell rang.

"Melina! Dinner!" she called up the stairs.

"Things that go *baa*," said Marc, handing her a heavy paper bag from Punjab House. "And this." From inside his leather jacket he pulled a white bundle and shook it out. A plain white T-shirt cascaded open. "Oops, wrong way." He reversed the T back to front. Words and colors leapt out at her.

"Oh, fantastic!" she exclaimed, delighted. "What is this, a prototype?"

"Exactly. Like it?"

He held the shirt at arm's length. There was Shakespeare's name, printed bold above a saffron-and-green "Bollywood", just as Marc had proposed weeks ago. "It's fabulous, I love it!"

"Great, it's yours." He draped it over her shoulder.

"Mine?" Rachel set down the bag and pulled the T over her own shirt. She stepped to the mirror. The letters were backwards, of course, but the colors snapped at her. "I love it! Book jacket, too?"

"Cool, can I borrow it?" Melina spoke from the steps. "Hi, Marc."

"How are you?" He wrapped the ordinary words in kindness.

"Good, thanks." She skipped down the rest of the stairs and headed for the kitchen. At the door, Melina stopped. "Thanks, really. Mom told me about your calls and . . .."

"You're totally welcome."

With a shy nod, Melina disappeared.

"Another surprise." Marc handed Rachel an envelope and mimed opening it.

Rachel lifted the unsealed flap and peered in. There lay a pale-blue check, the large sort favored by corporations. This one was written to the English department. It contained an impressive number of zeroes. She gaped.

"Never seen one that big, huh?"

"Scary, actually. What happened? How did you do this?"

"You did it."

"Me?"

"In a roundabout way. The guy who authorized it told me your ordeal prompted him to add a zero. There's no accounting for donor rationale." Marc took the envelope from her and folded it into his jacket pocket. "I wrote one hell of a thank you letter."

"That check puts you in stellar territory," Rachel pointed out. "Major gifts. The development office will want you on their junkets."

"Junkets, does anyone do those these days? Isn't it all by e-mail? No, the English Department's stuck with me. So, there's your spicy lamb, something for Melina?"

Rachel nodded toward the kitchen. "Chicken *korma*, nice and mild. By the way, we're going easy on you, 'Dhoom 2' is definitely a guy movie. Car chases, special effects, pyrotechnics, the beaches of Rio de Janeiro. Oh, and a scantily-clad former Miss World."

"This movie was made in India?" Marc asked, doubtful.

"Mm-hmm. It's a sequel, everything that the original 'Dhoom' was and much, much more."

The TV screen pulsed with dancing figures.

"Pause?" The figures stopped mid-jump. Marc's mouth hung slack with disbelief. He shook his head. "What's his name, Hrithik? No wonder you like his movies. Forget *bhangra*, man, this guy can dance!"

"Word for word, that was Steph. She was also impressed with his looks," Rachel recalled.

"He's got looks," admitted Marc. "In a purely aesthetic sense I get that. And you," he shook a finger at Melina in mock-admonition, "with his poster on your wall, a man three times your age?"

"Mom says he seems like a very decent guy. Who should I put up next to Robert Redford, celebrities who live on the covers of 'Star'?" Melina bit into a sweet *gulab jamun*.

Marc shook his head. "Play on."

"*. . . koi ye maane naa, koi ye jaane naa . . ..*"

"So that's contemporary Bollywood! I had no idea. It's changed a lot since the nineties. What happened to all those cute, zaftig young women?" asked Marc.

"The heroines? They slimmed down, got some education, and moved into the city. Where it's harder to retain traditional Indian values, so actually the stories got more interesting, don't you think? Before, the heroine saved the confused young man from falling into the trap of Westernization, and in return he rescued her from a forced marriage. Now, they both have to balance. And for the ones shot in other countries . . . well, they've demonstrated that Indians function perfectly well away from the *desh*, the homeland, that they're not polluted. One can live outside India and still cherish some traditional values. And then, India itself is changing so fast it's practically a different country from the 1990s. *Gulab jamun?*"

Marc took hold of Rachel's hand and brought the *gulab jamun* to his mouth. His teeth caught at it. "Mmm! Tastes even better. Rachel, come on, let's connect, let's go out, let's date! I promise not to make rude comments about your so-called boring life, or talk only about myself, or drive like the Indy 500. Yeah, Jen told me. Idiots, those guys were idiots."

"Will you avoid comments on my haircolor?" Rachel asked, amused.

Marc's arm eased behind her shoulders. It reminded her of that terrible night . . . and of his persistent kindness.

"They were jerks. You know that, right? On their best day, they didn't deserve you. Not that you're completely perfect. There's a chicken pox scar on your temple, and a funny freckle on your wrist." His eyes widened. "What's the matter?"

"I'm waiting for more."

"Wait away." His fingers clasped hers. "If we were in a Bollywood flick, or a Will S. play, would I focus on your flaws?"

"Benedick would."

"At the start of 'Much Ado', but not later. This," he tapped her knuckle, "this isn't the beginning for you and me. Not after all these months, not after all that's happened. And no Bollywood hero worth his salt would think about *pyaar* with anything but a ready heart, right? What are the words to this?" He hummed.

"*Dekha tumko jab se, bas dekha tumko yaara.* When did you watch 'Kabhi Khushi Kabhie Gham'?" Rachel asked, astonished.

"Rented it after I heard you mention the title. What does it mean?"

"'Ever since I saw you, I've seen only you' . . . something like that," she fumbled.

"That's true, that's so true. There you were, in Sephora. And then you left, and I wanted to see you again . . . and then I did, and again . . . and again. Like ocean waves. Listen, it's time we actually joined forces." Marc squeezed her hand. "Come on, it'll be fun!"

Rachel squeezed back. "It *would* be fun. And very different. But you know, I think I deserve your kind of different! I finally . . . I don't know, I was so reluctant. And then, there was the Bollywood hero, using him as a yardstick. Chandani asked me once whether I'd bought into the romanticism of Indian movies, and I said no, but really," she blushed, "I could have been any fourteen-year-old. Then later I was discouraged and thought, screw it, no way. No way would I ever find that, that kind of . . .."

"*Pyaar?*"

Rachel nodded.

"Oh, yeah?" Marc's grin teased.

"Yes! But these days, I'm happy to be wrong." She leaned over and kissed him. Marc's lips tasted of the *gulab jamun*, of sweetness and warmth and cardamom.

Rachel's head swam.

CHAPTER 37

H ere."
"What's this for?" Perplexed, Rachel took the bill Steph handed her.

"It's the five I owe you. Remember? 'I'll give you five bucks for every ethical man you unearth by June.' This is payoff time, and I'm happy for you, Rachel, honest."

"Unearthed?"

"Found, then. Take it, buy some of your Indian desserts. Now, you'll appreciate this, babe . . . I'm starting on that movie list my client gave me. The Indian one."

"Get out!"

"Nope, I am." Steph leaned back in her chair. "Not without profound doubts, I'm not forgetting that damn parrot, but she has a favorite, 'Dor' or something, she said I'd understand her better."

"Maybe so. It's about two very different women who become friends. Remind you of anyone?" Rachel sipped her chai.

"Maybe so! Hey, listen, I talked to the cookie guys, you know," Steph prodded, "the cookies you slide under coffee? They say we should mold them with a center circle so the cup doesn't slide."

Rachel set down her mug. "How do we do that?" she demanded. "They're different diameters, aren't they?" From a cabinet she pulled a half-dozen cups and mugs, turning them upside-down. "That drawer, hand me the ruler?"

Steph rummaged and passed it over.

"Two-and-three-quarters, two-and-a-half, this one's three, another two-and-three-quarters. Ask the cookie guys how they'd handle that!"

"Okay, okay! I will! Maybe there's a universal . . . anyway, before I got here, let me guess, you were working on your book, right? How's it coming?"

"Good, actually. Plus, there's a publishing spark of interest. Remember that man I met at the India Association meeting, Purandar Dutta? I found his card, called him, he's excited, wants to see it," Rachel told her.

"Excellent!"

"Then there's the last chapter, the wrap-up –" A muffled tune played. "Hold on."

"Wait a minute, I recognize that! It's from that movie you made me watch, they're in a club, sequins, how does it go?"

"*Ke do na, ke do na*, you are my *soniya*," sang Rachel. "One of the most downloaded ringtones in the world. Everyone wants to be called darling!" Smiling, she flipped open her phone.

From the sequel, Shakespeare Adores Bollywood

My editors do want another book from me," Rachel admitted.

"Another Shakespeare and film book?" Marc joined her at the windows. "This time, Danish? Shakespeare loves Dogme, handheld cameras, natural light, on location?" He stroked her cheek. "No, I can tell from your guilty expression there's no Copenhagen in your future."

"Actually . . . it's more India, my publisher wants a tie-in, a related book on Bollywood ins and outs," the words rushed. "Sort of condensed Mumbai movie biz for Mr. and Ms. Totally Uninformed American, major players, some history, only with a personal touch."

"A personal touch. I take it that means yours?"

Rachel nodded.

"But you don't live there, you don't know anyone . . . ah, they want you to go? They'll pay you to go?" Marc took her by both hands. "On their dime?"

"Yeah."

"Well, fantastic!" He pulled her close for a hug. "Excellent! What's wrong with that?" he murmured into her hair.

"Well, see, they want it to come out soon after the first one, so that means –"

She felt herself being examined by a pair of uncomfortably piercing blue eyes. Her teeth caught at her lower lip.

"Please, sir," Rachel adopted the dulcet tones of Oliver Twist requesting more gruel, "two months off this fall?"